The Shy Guy

The Shy Guy

John Allen III

MOUNTAIN ARBOR PRESS

Mountain Arbor
Press
Alpharetta, GA

ISBN: 978-1-6653-0301-9 - Paperback
eISBN: 978-1-6653-0302-6 - eBook

Printed in the United States of America   0 1 0 7 2 2

∞This paper meets the requirements of ANSI/NISO Z39.48-1992 (Permanence of Paper)

Cover created by Christopher Williams, AKA, C. Will

Photo captions
About the Author photo taken by Latron Nelson of Uncaged Photos

This novel is dedicated to anyone and everyone with a vision that's hesitant, or even scared, to pursue it. Whether it's doubt, fear of failure, whatever, stopping you from pursuing your goals or passion, my advice to you is to JUST JUMP. Jump on out there and do it. It's not going to be perfect the first time you do it, or any time you do it, and that's okay. Use me and this novel as an example. I wasn't an English major in college, nor do I have any experience writing a novel, BUT, I wrote one anyway. I had a vision I wanted to share, so I jumped to it and did it. It wasn't easy, but nothing worth having or doing ever is.

———

The toughest part about writing this novel was realizing it was never going to be perfect. It took me months on top of months to realize that and accept it. I wrote every word from the heart during one of the darkest times of my life. No one knew the battles I was fighting. It was just me and God. I started praying more, and it led to this. The light that was birthed out of my dark abyss. And that is why I can happily accept my finished product and live at peace with the results.

———

Now to wrap it up, whatever your dreams/goals may be, don't be afraid to chase them. With God, hard work, resilience, perseverance, and faith, ALL THINGS ARE POSSIBLE.

"She's been on my mind since the first time I saw her...I don't know anything about her except that she's God's greatest creation. But at the same time, it's like I don't need to know her to know that she's the one for me. I know it's cliché, but I think it really is love at first sight."

I

―――――

M Y ALARM BEGINS TO GO OFF. IT'S 7AM.
          "Uuugh!", I exclaim.

Exhausted from my antics the night before, I roll over and hit snooze. Fifteen minutes later, my alarm rings again. Still tired, I hit snooze for a second time.

I'll just get up on the next one.

Normally, you'll find me enthused and ecstatic on a Monday morning. I like the excitement that comes with starting a new week full of the unexpected. Not knowing what the future holds keeps me anxious. It keeps me on my toes.

Usually, I'm showered and dressed by 7:30, but not today. Why, you ask? What makes this Monday different? Well, this isn't just any Monday, it's the Monday after the Football Championship. Even though basketball is the main sport here in Ricoville, a tailgating party is still a tailgating party at the end of the day. You know, a long night full of drinking, yelling, and loud music.

After I hit snooze for the second time, I close my eyes and drift off back to sleep. What I expected to be a fifteen minute cat nap turned out to be an hour and a half long slumber. When I do finally wake up, it's not to the sound of my alarm that I had anticipated, but to the sounds of dogs barking and cars honking that filled the street outside. As I slowly begin to wake up, I roll over and look at my phone. The time is now 8:47, I have to be at work by nine. It's a thirty minute, sometimes forty-five minute, drive there depending on the traffic. I'm stuck.

Astonished, I quickly sit up in my bed. *I'm late for work! What am I going to do?! Even though I'm one of the best there, I'm still relatively new. I'm approaching the end of my ninety day probation period, so showing up over an hour late definitely won't bode well for me. Mr. Jacobs is already a hard ass as it is, I can't give him another reason to be on my case.* I move to the edge of my bed, bow my head, and sigh. *Man, I just know I'm about to get fired, there's no way around it. Mr. Langston is going to kill me when he finds out.* I sigh again in frustration. *Then, my mom is going to revive me just to kill me herself.*

I sit and mope for a moment before I suddenly get an idea. I take a deep breath, grab my phone, and send a text. Now, all I can do is hope for the best. I then get up and continue with my day as I normally would. I begin to get ready for the job I hope to still have when the day is over. I take a shower, brush my teeth, then go to my closet to find something to wear.

Twenty-five minutes passes by, my phone buzzes. I check my phone and the message reads, "I got you but you owe me." I breathe a sigh of relief and a smile consumes my face as I finish getting ready. A couple seconds later, my phone buzzes again, "And bring me some breakfast too. The usual with extra cheese."

I wasn't initially going to go today because I was running late for work, but now I have to. The Spot, it was an old rundown building that my good friend Chino bought, renovated, and transformed into one of the best breakfast/lunch spots in the city. The food is exquisite and rejuvenating, and Chino will always have you laughing. Over time, eating there has become a part of my everyday routine, like brushing my teeth and taking a shower. The Spot is about twenty minutes from my apartment, and fifteen from my job.

After I get ready, I walk out into the sunny, brisk day. I find my car, then drive to The Spot wearing a black blazer and matching pants with a sky blue shirt and black tie.

I get there and see Chino as soon as I walk through the door. He's wearing a white T-shirt that has *The Spot* on it in big, bold, black letters like he always does. "Wassup, Chino?! I'm surprised you made it in today after last night.", I say as I walk towards my seat.

My short, dark skinned, bald, and bearded friend is like the cool and funny uncle that every family has. He's the first to clown you, but also the first to help you if you're in need. He jokes a lot, but in the end, he will always have your best interest at heart. We've been cool since the first time I ate there almost two years ago. Long story short, after I graduated college, I moved to Ricoville in search of a job opportunity. Things didn't go as planned, and I ended up working at a retail store. One morning before work, I decided to try The Spot for breakfast and ordered a bacon and cheese omelet. I told Chino he made the best omelet I'd ever eaten, and we've been friends ever since.

"Me?! I'm a professional, my brotha. Once you get my age, you become immune to it. You're the one that's late for work." He begins to shake his head. "I tried to tell you that wasn't regular punch."

I laugh and respond, "I'm good man. I'm certified over here.", as I take my seat at the counter.

Chino sarcastically says, "Yeah, okay. Well your nondrinking ass can be my new certified dishwasher after you get fired. How about that?" We both laugh. "But look, you remember that girl I was telling you about at the party last night? She usually comes in around this time. You might have a chance to finally see her."

Mockingly, "Oh yeah, the girl you claim is straight from heaven. I'm dying to see what the hype is about. She probably looks like one of those old rag dolls up close. You know your vision is bad."

He smirks and nods his head, "Alright, you gon' see."

"Yeah, see you need better glasses. But anyway, I gotta use the bathroom. We'll finish this conversation when I get back. While I'm gone, can you put in two Rico Specials to go for me please?"

"Roger that. And make sure you wash that crust from around your eyes while you're in there. You look a mess." I get up and go to the bathroom as Chino laughs and walks back to the kitchen to place my order.

When I finish in the bathroom, I do a quick check in the mirror. I see that Chino was lying, and begin to head back to my seat. I open the door and BOOM, there she is. A stallion. I knew this just had to be who Chino was talking about. *He definitely wasn't lying or exaggerating with this one.* This woman was the most beautiful being I'd ever seen. She looks like she walked straight out of a magazine. Her eyes are light brown, hair is naturally long, black, and curly, and her body is on MHMM MHMM MHMM. I didn't know if it was the glow of her golden, melanin skin, or the mesmerizing and radiant smile she had, but one thing I did know, was that it was love at first sight. She's sitting in my seat wearing a red dress that fits her perfectly. It's hugging and complimenting every single one of her elegant curves, from her breasts to her hips. Her long legs, glistening, as they sit in the chair. Her dress was sexy, but professional enough for work.

What do I do? What should I say? She's absolutely gorgeous, I can't afford to mess this up. I only have one chance to make a first impression.

As I begin to walk her way, I start to think of a plan. So many options, so many thoughts, too little time. I'm getting closer and closer and I still don't have the slightest idea of what I'm going to say. I get about ten feet away from her and it hits me.

I got it! The perfect plan. Step one, give her the good old wink and smile to get her attention. Step two, say a corny, yet smooth joke to get her laughing. If you can make a woman laugh, you're already halfway in the door. Step three, get her number because I'm still running late for work. Step four, pray that steps one through three were successful. Step 5, make her fall in love.

As I'm getting closer, I start cheesin', licking my lips, and rubbing my hands together. I'm 100% sure this plan is going to work.

It's showtime!

Just as I begin to open my mouth to speak, a customer walks in.

This causes her to look up from her phone and give a quick glance my way. My walk comes to an abrupt halt. My heart, and mind, melt as I look at her. My five-step plan takes one giant step out of the window. Now, I'm just standing there. I'm about five feet away from her and there's not a word, nor sound, coming from me. And to make things worse, I'm almost sure I have a little bit of drool creeping out the corner of my mouth playing peekaboo.

II

I'M NOW STANDING FIVE FEET AWAY FROM HER, MY melanin angel, and I still haven't said a word. I can't move, I can't talk, I'm just standing there, frozen. Luckily, she's back on her phone so she doesn't notice how pathetic I'm looking. It's only been ten seconds that's passed by, but it feels like ten hours.

"Call-in, number 27!", Chino yells.

"That's me.", she says as she gets up and grabs her food. "Can I get some blueberry syrup please?"

I love blueberry syrup, this must be a sign.

"I got you sugarfoot. Just let me go back and get it for you."

As he walks back into the kitchen, she turns my way and we lock eyes. Being the shy guy that I am, all I could do was give a nervous wave.

She waves back and says, "Good morning."

I finally come to my senses and reply, "Morning."

I begin to get excited thinking we're about to start an actual conversation, but before I could say anything else, her phone starts to ring. "Is it her boyfriend? Or is it just work?", I asked myself.

She answers it and aggressively says, "What do you want?......I don't have time for this right now!" She then hangs up, grabs her food then proceeds to leave. "Don't worry about the syrup Unc, I gotta go! Y'all have a good day!", she says as she storms out the door.

I just shake my head and take my seat as I admire her elegant physique as she walks away in her nude heels. I sigh. *A guy like me barely had a chance to begin with, and now I probably just blew my one and only opportunity to talk to her.*

Chino finally walks back out and says, "Winston you have that takeoff game, huh playa?"

Puzzled, I reply, "What's that?"

Chino starts to smile, then says, "All you have to do is start talking to a woman and she's just gonna takeoff." I can't do anything besides smirk and shake my head as he laughs. "Don't worry about it son, not everybody is as gifted as the great Otis Chinord Jenkins."

Embarrassed and ashamed, I just ignore him. "Is the food ready yet?"

"It's on the grill cooking, along with your manhood and dignity." He laughs then continues to talk as he walks over to tend to my food. "Aye! Tell me I was right about her though. She's the real deal, right? She definitely had you like a deer in headlights just now. Give me my credit."

Smiling, I say, "Yeah, yeah you were right. She's a melanin angel." I pause for a second. "I need her. I think, wait, I know she's my future wife and mother of my kids."

Chino sucks his teeth and says, "Maaaaan you can't handle her. She's what we like to call above your paygrade, my good sir. Strictly eye candy. You might be able to be her food guy or maybe Mr. Manipedi though."

"Stop trying me, Chino. I'ma get her, just watch."

Sarcastically he says, "Yeah and I'ma be the next king of Africa."

"I'm serious."

"Yeeeah anyway man, like I was telling you at the party, she just started coming to The Spot last Thursday. She just moved to the city from North Carolina not too long ago, so there's still a chance she's single. I'm not sure how long that'll last though. She's definitely a dimepiece if I've ever seen one. She's a stallion, has a beautiful personality, and her mind is on another level. She's a different breed."

Playfully, "If you think she's so different, why didn't you get her for yourself Chino?"

"Shooot! Man you don't think I tried? I gave up once she said I reminded her of her daddy and started calling me 'Unc'. Also, Shareeda stopped by and surprised me the other day while baby girl was here. Shareeda said if she ever catches me looking at her, or another woman, like that again she was going to put both of us six feet under."

I start to laugh. "Yeah, the warden gon' kill y'all with a headshot as soon as you cross that gunline again my guy."

He stares at me with a straight face and his left eyebrow raised. "Now Winston, you know who wears the pants in this relationship. I'm the king of my castle!"

"Is that Shareeda I see coming around the back?!"

Frantically, "Where?!"

I laugh again. "Yeah, that's what I thought."

He sucks his teeth. "I was just going along with your little corny joke Mr. Cornyman."

"Sure you were Chino, sure you were."

"Anyway, back to what I was saying. That's gonna be a tough fish to catch man, I'm tryna tell ya. All that shy guy stuff you got going on ain't gonna cut it. She's only going to go for someone that's assertive. I'm still pulling for you though."

"Chino, be cool. Like I said before, I'm going to get her. She just caught me off guard today that's all. If I get another chance with her, I'll have her wanting to get married in a week. Maybe even after the first date."

Chino looks at me and laughs. "I have an idea. You should buy matching running shoes, because from what I just saw, you gon' need them trying to chase after her."

"Haha, whatever. Just hand me my food so I can leave, I'm already running late."

"Hey, you know Valentine's Day is next Friday. You might be able to get some on sale."

"It is?"

Chino shakes his head. "Tsk, tsk. See, you already messing up *Mr. She's going to want to get married.* You're not in touch with your romantic side. Now listen here youngblood, Championship Sunday is the highlight of February for men. But for women, Valentine's Day is like the Football Championship times infinity. If you don't bring it, you might as well call the coroner. Don't worry too much though, you got about two weeks before you can officially run her off."

He chuckles and I just look at him. "My food Chino."

He tells his cook to bring me my food and he bags it. "Here you go, it's on me. Can't have you heartbroken, jobless, AND hungry out here. And watch one of those lovey dovey movies that the women like when you get home, you might learn a thing or two."

I laugh and get my food. "Don't quit your day job. I definitely don't see comedy in your future." I get up from my seat and begin to walk towards the door.

"At least I *have* a job to quit! I see multiple unemployment checks in your future."

I continue to walk out the door as I laugh. I enter my car and begin to be on my way to work.

III

———

I 'M OVER AN HOUR AND A HALF LATE WHEN I FINALLY arrive at work. I'm a financial advisor at an up and coming firm. I graduated from college two years ago at the top of my class. Offers didn't come knocking on my door, so I started working at a retail store for a while. One day while I was working, I ran into a man named Robert Langston. He's a prominent businessman that's well known throughout the state and even the southeast region of the country. He came in searching for an "I'm sorry" gift for his wife, and he just so happened to ask me for help. While looking for the perfect gift, we talked about everything, from life to a couple of the business ideas I had in mind. He loved my ideas and thought I had potential. One thing led to another and he got me this job at the firm. We've been close ever since. It's not the most exciting job, but it pays well.

I walk in the building and make my way to my office. I place my things on my desk and take my seat. As I dabble through my briefcase, I can't help but think about HER. Her smile, her voice, her hair, her beauty, just everything about her. That's when it started, my obsession. That was the moment I stopped being so focused on work and began to focus on HER. Maybe the most beautiful creation I've ever seen in my entire life. As I sat at my desk, all I did was daydream. I sat there thinking about her, about us, about our future. The different scenarios that could've happened. What if I did this? What if that would've happened? Constant questions flowing in and out of my head with the biggest question being, "Who was she?". I've started to fall in love with a woman whom I haven't said five words to. The longer I sit, the deeper my fantasies roam. I'm stuck in a trance for about fifteen minutes before...

KNOCK, KNOCK, KNOCK, KNOCK.

"Winston, you got my food?!"

I look, and it's Sharon wearing a black skirt and her pink sweater that she never forgets. She got tired of dressing up to sit at a desk all day, so she usually always wears a black skirt, she just switches up her blouses. Sharon's the office secretary. She's smart, beautiful, and my ex-lover. We dated for a while when I first started working here, but it didn't work out. We just wanted two different things and thought it was just best to be friends.

"Winston! I know you hear me talking to you.", she sassily yells.

"Well good morning to you too Sharon. Who me? I'm doing great, thanks for asking. Oh, and your breakfast, it's right here.", I say with a sarcastic smile on my face as she grabs her food. "Thanks, again. What did Mr. Jacobs say?"

"I told him you had a last-minute breakfast meeting with an important client, so he didn't say anything. Did you get extra cheese?"

"You're the best, and nah. It slipped my mind when I was ordering. I'm sorry."

"Yeah, yeah, I guess it'll just slip my mind to cover for you the next time you're running late.", Sharon says as she's leaving my office.

"C'mon! Don't be like that!", I tell her as she ignores me.

With not much work to do, I spend the rest of my time responding to emails, checking voicemails, and thinking about HER. My melanin angel.

I can't believe I didn't even think to ask Chino for her name. I'll just have to ask her for myself tomorrow morning. If I want any chance with her, I'll have to throw that shy guy stuff out of the window and just go for it.

Monday's are usually the slowest days, so from that moment at work until the time I went to sleep, all I did was try to think of a perfect plan to get my melanin angel. I constantly asked myself, what will I wear, how will I approach her, what will I say?

It wasn't until around midnight that I came up with it. I was so excited. I spent hours laying down fantasizing about how it would go. I didn't go to sleep until around 3am because I was so anxious for it to transpire.

IV

———

M Y ALARM SOUNDS. AS I WAKE UP TO A NEW DAY and stare at my ceiling, there's only one thing on my mind. *HER, My Melanin Angel, My Valentine, My Future Wife. There are so many things that I don't know, but want to. Like, where is she from? Where does she work? Is she single? Does she have kids? How many kids will we have? How will she want our wedding? What's her name? The anticipation is killing me.* I sit up and swing my feet off the side of my bed. *Today's the day I officially meet my wife, and I'm ready. I've planned out every possible scenario, from it raining today to her spilling coffee on herself. I'm not going to be caught off guard this time.*

It's now 7:30. Before I do anything else, I text Sharon to let her know I'll be late again. I told her I have an actual breakfast meeting with a potential client. She replies, "Ok." With that taken care of, I start getting ready. I shower longer than usual, brush my teeth longer than usual, and take a little longer getting dressed. "This moment has to be perfect.", I tell myself as I give my suit one last press before I put it on. I then check myself one last time in the mirror. I brush off my black fitted, purple striped blazer and matching slacks. I straighten my purple tie along my black shirt, brush my hair, spray on cologne, then leave out the door. I walk to my car then head towards The Spot.

As I walk into The Spot, the first thing I hear is Chino's voice.

"Booooyyy you casket sharp ain't it! Lemme find out you all dapper and what not because you're trying to impress Natalie. You would've been better off wearing gym shorts and running shoes. You can't be having any restrictions when you chasing after her. You need all the flexibility you can get. The full range of motion."

I just laugh and blush, "Nah man, I have a big meeting today. I'm just trying to make a good first impression that's all." *It's not like I was lying. I did in fact have a meeting today, but it wasn't at work. I had an appointment with the love of my life, Natalie.*

"Well, do you want me to get you something while you wait for your *meeting* sir? If not food, maybe something to drink? Cause you look thirsty, son."

"Haha I see you got jokes today."

Grinning, "I just call it like I see it my brotha. Do you want something or not man? I'm about to step out for a second."

"I'm all business Chino. And yeah, let me just get a lemonade before you go."

Chino hands me my lemonade then walks outside. As he leaves, I begin to look around for her. *Natalie, a beautiful name to match an even more beautiful woman. Natalie, the name of my angel, the name of my soon to be bride.* I look around, but I don't see her. *Natalie, where are you?!*

Every time the door opens, I turn and look with glee. *Where could she be? She's probably just running late today, that's all. I'll give her some more time.* An hour and a half passes by, and she's still a no show. My mood is killed, appetite's gone, and I wasted a good suit just to sit in a diner. I check my phone and the time is now 10:17.

Dejected and heartbroken, I throw in the towel and face the fact that she's not coming. "Hey Chino, I gotta get to my meeting. I'll catch you later." I get up and walk towards the door with a dispirited look on my face.

As I'm about to leave, Chino stops me and says, "Hey man,

you still got tomorrow. Maybe she wasn't hungry today. Something could've came up too, you know how it is." I just wave my hand and walk out in disappointment.

I get to work and go straight to my office. I close my door, then the blinds, and then I plop down at my desk. Sharon calls, but I don't feel like talking so I send it to voicemail.

I can't remember a time I've been so sad, so disheartened, and so distraught. The fact that she didn't even show galvanized me into a gloomy state. I lean back in my chair as I try to relax for a few minutes.

My phone goes off. It's Sharon, "Meeting didn't go well huh?"

I sigh, *Knowing Sharon, she's not going to leave me alone until I say something.*

I hesitate, then reply, "They didn't even show. Could you forward my calls straight to voicemail please? Also, can you let anyone who comes in for me know that I'm unavailable? I'm really not in the mood to converse with anyone right now."

She replies, "I got you, keep your head up. It'll be ok :)"

I put my phone down and continue to lean back in my chair.

Why am I feeling like this? I'm sprung over a woman I've barely met. This is crazy. I've only seen her once, yet Natalie is the only thing I can see.

Two hours pass by, and nothing's changed. I'm still in my office, alone, with nothing but Natalie on my mind. I said I didn't want to be bothered at all, but maybe a distraction is what I need to remain sane. I open my office back up, and walk outside to go to the bathroom. I then take about a fifteen/twenty minute break to see what's going on throughout the office. While I was searching for a distraction, all I seemed to get was an abundant amount of redundant compliments. I get back to my desk after hearing "You look good" and "Somebody must have a date tonight" about a million times and see I have a text from Sharon. "So you in the mood to talk now?"

She must've seen me out talking while she was coming back from her lunch.

I reply, "Wassup?"

Seconds later, Sharon knocks on my door. "Come in.", I exclaim.

She enters my office. "You have 8 messages, you missed a meeting, and Mr. Langston dropped something off for you."

"I'll take care of the other stuff tomorrow. What did Mr. Langston leave?"

"He dropped this envelope off. He came by wanting to see you, but I told him you were swamped and wasn't seeing anybody today. He said 'Okay', and told me to give this to you and for you to enjoy."

"Okay thanks, I appreciate it."

"You're welcome.", she starts to exit my office then suddenly stops and says, "And in case nobody has said it yet, you look nice today. You know, purple has always been your color Winston. It looks good on you. You look handsome."

I blush and say, "Thanks, Sharon."

She proceeds to leave out and closes my door. I hold the slightly heavy, manilla envelope in my hand and shake it around. *What could possibly be in here?* I don't waste any time and open it. I empty it out onto my desk and see it's Wardog tickets to tomorrow's game. I'm ecstatic! The Wardogs have been my favorite basketball team since I was a little kid. I admire the tickets for a moment, then I put them in my briefcase.

It's only one, but I've been clocked out mentally since yesterday morning. I try to focus and check my emails, but I only last about fifteen minutes before I decide to pack it up and go home.

As I'm walking out towards the parking lot, I run into Sharon.

Shocked to see her, "Aren't you supposed to be answering calls and what not?"

"Okay, um one, mind ya business. And two, why are YOU leaving early?"

I chuckle, "I'm just trying to look out, I'm sorry. But I'm not feeling good. I tried to tell Jacobs, but he's not in his office."

"He left before you came to handle some stuff with his family. And if you must know, we're all leaving early today. I'm just the first one out here because I'm READY."

"Oh wow, I guess I didn't get the memo."

Wittily, "That's what happens when you're not in the talking mood."

"Anyway."

"Yeah, anyways. Before I forget, I bet you won't believe who I bumped into at the mall the other day!"

"Who?!"

"It was...." Her phone starts to ring. "It's him, I'll tell you another time. See you.", she says as she rushes off to her car.

Him? That was weird, but then again, it is Sharon.

I get in my car, grab some wings from my favorite wing spot to celebrate my tickets, then head home.

After I get home, I shower, eat, then lay in my bed.

Even though I got blessed with those tickets today, I'm still disheartened about Natalie. Today was supposed to be the day I officially met my wife. Today was supposed to be the day I would've finally known true happiness.

V

――――

I'M STILL HUNGOVER FROM THE DISAPPOINTMENT OF yesterday, but today's a new day. Today, I woke up with hope. I woke up hoping today was going to end the complete opposite of how it did yesterday. With me alone, heartbroken, and disappointed.

I get out of bed and do as I did yesterday. I took a long shower, I didn't leave the house until my head, teeth, and clothes looked perfect, and again, I waited for Natalie at The Spot.

After waiting about an hour or so, I came to the realization that she wasn't coming. My mood changed and I began to just sit there, miserably scrolling through my phone.

"Why the long face?", Chino says as he walks over to my table. "Maan look, if you keep letting her stress you out, you're gonna be bald like me by the end of the week."

I chuckle a bit. "You know I usually don't stress over women Chino, but she's been on my mind since the first time I saw her. I don't know what it is man. I don't know anything about her except that she's God's greatest creation. But at the same time, it's like I don't need to know her to know that she's the one for me. I know it's cliché, but I think it really is love at first sight." Chino starts rubbing his index finger against his thumb. Curious, I ask, "Chino, what the hell are you doing?"

"Oh, I'm just playing the world's smallest violin to help soothe you during your woman troubles." We both laugh.

"Maaaan get out of here!"

"No, YOU get out of here. You sound like one of those crazy stalkers they make movies about. Gonna have me on the news saying, 'He was honestly a good kid, but one day I guess he drunk some crazy juice and snapped." I stare at him with a blank face then he continues to say, "You know what? Now that I think about it, I could use some publicity for the diner. Go crazy, but not toooo crazy."

I smirk. "Nah man. I'm not about to follow her home or nothing crazy like that. I just want to genuinely get to know her. You know how it is when you're crushing on somebody."

"Look man, in all seriousness, if it's meant to be, it'll be. Stop stressing over what you can't control and live your life." His phone starts to ring. "I gotta go run and handle some business real quick, and if I see her, I'll make sure to relay your message for you." After he looked at his phone, he immediately left out the door.

He ran out before I could tell him not to tell Natalie how I feel. Chino's the last person I want telling her anything. You never know what's going to come out of that man's mouth. I don't need Natalie thinking I'm something that I'm not.

After moping for a couple of minutes, I decide it's time to head to work.

I walk in and I'm immediately met by Sharon at the door.

"About time you show up. Where the hell you been at Winston?!"

Dumbfounded, "What are you talking about woman?!"

"You're late for your meeting with Jacobs and the people inquiring about that resort by the lake."

"Meeting?! I was never informed about a meeting. Did this just come up?"

"No fool, they called yesterday and left a couple messages. You said you'd check them later, so I didn't say anything then."

I give a long sigh full of frustration as I drop my head. "Where they at?"

"They're in conference room 3J on the fifth floor. I hope you have a good excuse, for your sake."

I hope so too. "Thanks, wish me luck."

As I exit the elevator and rush towards the conference room, I see them walking my way. My heart drops to my stomach. *Ain't no way I missed the whole meeting. I'm definitely done for. It's curtains for me.*

It's Mr. Jacobs and two other suit wearers with him. Mr. Jacobs, wearing his famous navy blue meeting suit, sees me and says, "Winston! I see you've handled that emergency on the East side you had to tend to. This is Mr. Schroeder and Mrs. Merrimam." Mr. Schroeder looks like he's maybe in his early forties. He's a short and stocky German man in a grey suit. Mrs. Merrimam is an older black woman that reminds me of my auntie. She's wearing a burgundy dress suit.

Jacobs waves me closer and introduces us. "This is Winston Williams. He's one of the studs of the office."

"Good morning, it's a pleasure to meet you both.", I say as I shake their hands.

"They're from Degan Industries. They're interested in buying that resort by the lake, but I'm sure you already know that. Anything you'd like to tell them before they leave, or would you prefer trying to schedule another meeting?"

He's clearly pissed, but I'm sure he isn't going to say anything in front of them because it'll ruin our name. Maybe I can just ask them for another meeting so I'm better prepared and won't sound stupid.

"Mrs. Merrimam, Mr. Schroeder, would you all be able to schedule another meeting? This emergency I had threw me off, and I wouldn't want to short change you on anything."

I look to Mr. Schroeder and he points to Mrs. Merrimam. "It's her call son. I'm just the muscle."

Mrs. Merrimam looks at me and says, "We understand that things do happen. Life is completely full of unexpected surprises, but we're on a tight schedule. We had another offer to buy the

Burlington estate on the south side from another firm, and today is the deadline for our decision. Due to us being given more information and better pricing from the other guys, we'll just have to go with them. It's nothing personal Mr. Jacobs, Mr. Williams, strictly business. You all have a great day."

VI

———

M RS. MERRIMAM AND MR. SCHROEDER SHAKE OUR hands and begin to get on the elevator to leave. As soon as the elevator door closes, Mr. Jacobs's face turns as red as a stop sign.

"Where the hell were you Winston?! Do you have any idea how big that account was?! You better have a damn good excuse for not being here!"

I'm stuck. My heart's beating fast and I'm lost for words. I know if I say the wrong thing I'm fired on the spot. I take a deep breath and say the only thing that comes to my mind.

"I had a breakfast meeting that ran longer than expected. I'm sorry sir."

"Another breakfast meeting, hmph? That's three straight days. Who was the client this time?"

The client?! What the hell am I going to say now? Whatever I tell him, he'll do some in-depth research into. I can't believe it. I'm about to lose my job over a woman I've yet to have a conversation with. A woman I don't even know. A woman that had me sitting foolish and alone for two straight days. I was lost as to what to say. Then it hit me. "I was meeting with Mr. Otis Jenkins. He owns this local diner called The Spot. He wanted to know how big of a possibility it would be to expand, and where'd be the most profitable place to expand to. He got a call from his wife midway through the meeting and it caused us to run late. Something about her not being able to find the remote for the bed. They have one of those beds that..."

"Ok, ok I get it. You're on thin ice buddy! Mr. Langston spoke very highly of you when he recommended you. So far, you've been proving him right. Keep it that way. I'd hate for you to be the person that makes him look bad. He's a very powerful man that knows very powerful people. Next time, at least give a courtesy call or something so I'm not completely blindsided. Another blunder like this and I might have to find your replacement." He pauses for a moment, then says. "You may find it hard to believe, but you're not as indispensable as you think. You're not even a full ninety days in yet. Get it together. We're supposed to be in the business of making money, not watching it leave off on the elevator."

"Yes sir, I'm on it."

"And could you let me see Mr. Jenkins's paperwork? I'd like to help if I can."

Damn. "Thanks Mr. Jacobs, but I actually gave him all the papers to look over with his wife and forgot to make copies."

"Hmmm, that's not like you Winston. You're usually on top of those types of things. That's a part of the reason why you were able to move up so quickly."

"Hey, everyone has an off night every now and then, right?"

"I suppose." We walk towards the elevator and stand there in silence while we wait for its arrival. As it finally comes, he says, "Are you lying to me Winston? I've given you waaaay more freedom and leeway than anyone else in this firm. I basically let you do what you please as long as you show up on time and get your work done. I'd hate for that generosity to get taken advantage of."

We enter the elevator and I say, "C'mon now Mr. Jacobs. You know me. I'm one of the best at my job and it's very rewarding. Do you really think I'd risk an account that big or even my job over a lie? I've come way too far for that."

"You're right, but you must admit everything does sound peculiar."

Sarcastically, "Well that's life for ya." I shrug my shoulders. "You never know what the future may hold for ya Mr. Jacobs."

As the elevator begins to descend, he looks at me and says, "Winston, could you forward me Mr. Jenkins's information. I'd like to do a follow up about your meeting with him this morning. Just to make sure you didn't have an *off night*. We can't afford anymore mistakes this month, especially after what just happened." The elevator stops. "I'll be expecting it soon." We both exit the elevator.

As I walk inside my office, Sharon walks in behind me and says, "So do you still have a job? I see y'all lost the account."

I smirk as I take a seat at my desk and say, "For now. I told him I had a meeting with Chino about expanding his restaurant and it ran late."

She closes my door then steps towards my desk. "Who the hell is Chino?"

"Chino's my friend that owns The Spot. You remember him? He's short, dark, and bald with a beard. He was the only person I could think of."

"Oh yeah, I remember now. Well I know Jacobs didn't fall for that simplistic, juvenile bullshit. He's been a real asshole lately. He's been having woman troubles and that's making him act worse than usual."

"I meeeaan, I finessed some more stuff in there too, but you're right. He asked me to forward Chino's information to him ASAP. And how you know about his lady issues?"

"I'm the secretary, I know eeeeverything. I even know about Henry having an affair with the cleaning lady and Steve doing booger sugar in the bathroom during his lunch breaks." My face drops in shock and disbelief. She continues to say, "That stuff is for another day though. Mr. Jacobs has a lot of meetings today and he's about to go to lunch in a few minutes. That should give you enough time to do what you have to."

"Thanks, Sharon. I..."

"Yeah, yeah. Look Winston, you gotta get your shit together. I don't know what's been up with you these past couple of days, but you gotta tighten up. You don't look like the smart and ambitious guy I saw when you first got here. I know we agreed to just be friends, and that's why I'm saying this. You trippin." The office phone starts to ring. "I gotta take that. Get your shit together Winston." She exits swiftly as her black skirt blows in the wind behind her.

Seconds after she leaves, Mr. Jacobs stops by my office before he heads out to lunch, "I need that info waiting for me when I get back."

Still stunned from Sharon. "I-I'm sending it now sir."

As soon as he leaves, I call Chino. He doesn't pick up. I call again, still no answer. Twenty minutes goes by and still not a word. I call three more times and still no answer. I say forget it and just use a fake number. That'll give me more than enough time to get me and Chino on the same page.

Now, an hour has passed. I see Mr. Jacobs entering the office. He goes to Sharon's desk and I can see him tell Sharon to get me. She gets my attention and points to her phone. She calls me and says, "Mr. Jacobs wants you in his office, good luck."

"Thanks.", all I can say before I hang up. I get up from my desk and start to walk over to his office. As I pass by Sharon, she goes, "If it makes you feel any better, he looked like he was in a good mood."

I continue to walk. I get to his door, take a deep breath, and walk in.

"Sit down.", he says. I sit and he continues to say, "So, I went over to The Spot for lunch."

———

*T*HE SPOT?! MAN IT'S NO WAY HE'S TALKING ABOUT *thee The Spot. That must explain why he looks like he's in a good mood. He's excited to fire me.* I became nervous as I started to anticipate him say, "Winston, you're fired."

I give a fake smile then ask, "How was it? The food's great right?"

He smiles back and says, "Yeah, the food was awesome, but I'm more impressed with the people that work there. Specifically, Mr. Jenkins, or Chino as he goes by."

My heart drops. Nervously, "Well, um, what did he say when you talked to him?" My heart starts beating faster. I start to feel a bead of sweat slowly drip down my forehead.

Mr. Jacobs clears his throat, "He said he's excited to see where this goes. Said he's been trying to find somebody that can help him expand for awhile now and that your plans were the most impressive ones he's seen by far. Good work Winston."

I breathe a huge sigh of relief. "Just doing my job sir, that's all." *Maybe I should let Chino talk to Natalie for me after all. He's not too bad at improvising.*

"Sorry for doubting you Winston. I just had to be sure. We all have to be extra cautious now after our loss earlier. We were already counting that fish as caught. Well, you know what they say, 'Don't count your chickens before they hatch, or you'll end up farmless at the farmer's meat market." He starts to laugh then I laugh as well, even though the joke wasn't funny or even made any sense.

"Good one Mr. Jacobs, I never heard that one before."

"I know right. I should write a book. Jokes by Jacobs is what I'd call it. What you think?"

I think naming it Corny jokes by King Cornball would be a more suitable fit honestly, but for the sake of my job I'll just agree.

"Great idea, you should really look into it." He types it in his phone. "Is that all you needed from me sir? I have a couple more clients to follow up with before I leave."

"Yeah, you're good." As I get up and exit his office he says, "Hey Winston!"

"Yes sir?"

"Remember, no more off days."

"I got you. You have a good one."

"You do the same."

I walk to my office and give the "ok" sign to Sharon as I walk by while she's packing her stuff. She walks into my office to say goodbye before she leaves. "Where are you going?", I ask.

"I have a big date I have to get ready for tonight."

"With whoooo?!"

"When the time is right you'll know." She winks at me. "You should be getting ready to leave too. You know traffic is *three* crazy when it's a game day. You really should be leaving with me or at least within the next hour or so if you want any chance of being on time. You know you stay on the completely opposite side of the arena."

She was right. With everything that happened today, I entirely forgot about the game tonight. "Thanks for reminding me. I forgot all about the game. I'll just finish sending these emails. I can do everything else tomorrow."

Sharon rolls her eyes, "I really stay saving your ass Winston.

When are you ever gonna do something for me? That's a part of the reason we...never mind. Enjoy yourself Winston and be safe." She slams my door as she walks out. I sat at my desk in awe. *In a way, she was right. I wasn't ready for the type of relationship she wanted, so it did get a little one-sided at times. I can admit that, but that wasn't the main reason we broke up.*

Forty-five minutes goes by, and I'm ready to leave. I get up, turn my lights off, and walk out. As I'm about to get in my car, I catch a glimpse of my reflection in the window. I started to think.

I'm a young, black, educated and successful businessman that almost lost his job chasing after a fantasy. Am I crazy? A stalker? Deranged? Hopeless? Pitiful? Or am I just a lonely man determined to find the love of his life? The only thing I know for sure is that she has me sprung. I need to clear my mind and get my priorities in order. Like Chino said, 'If it's meant to be, it'll be.' This game is just what I needed. The best thing that's happened to me all week.

As I'm driving home, I get a phone call. It's Chino. I answer, "Aye man! Why you got the police raiding my spot asking about you?!"

I laugh, "I tried calling you to let you know my boss was tripping and he might be contacting you. I called like ten times to give you a heads up, but you didn't answer. You were probably busy with customers or something. I appreciate you looking out though."

"You'll get my bill in the mail sometime next week, don't worry."

I grin, "I'll make sure to keep an eye out for it."

"I gotta go, I'll make sure to follow up tomorrow morning about our new found business adventure."

"Alright Chino."

We hang up the phone as I pull into my parking spot at my apartment. It's about two and a half hours until tip off. Ideally, it's about a thirty or even forty-five minute drive from my house to the arena, but that's on a normal day. On game days, that time can be anywhere from an hour and a half to two hours.

I get out of the car, go up to my place, and start to get ready. I shower, brush my teeth, then get dressed. By the time I'm ready to go, it's two hours until tip off. I walk out wearing my white and red Wardogs jersey, the white and red shoes to match, and khaki cargo shorts. I then get in my car and drive away.

Traffic is even worse than I expected. I thought I'd at least have time to get a couple snacks from the concession stands before the game, but by the looks of it, I won't be there until a few minutes after the tip off, if that.

After swerving in and out of traffic and having on and off stand stills for about two hours, I finally arrive at the arena. It's now five minutes until tip off, and I still have to find a parking spot.

Man, traffic is even crazier in the parking lot. And I know damn well these folks ain't charging $150 for a parking spot! TUH! If it ain't free, it ain't for me.

I finally find a free parking spot about a mile from the arena. Luckily, I was just in time for the War Bus, the shuttle that takes people to and from the parking lot to the arena, so the most I'd miss is five minutes of the first quarter. As I get inside, I hear an announcement saying that the game is being delayed because they're having technical difficulties. Due to a speaker malfunction inside the arena, they're not able to play the national anthem, or even music. No national anthem, no music, no commentators, no game. Tonight's game is also nationally televised, so that doesn't make things any better for them, but for me, it's great news. An uncontrollable smile starts to take over my face. *Happy day, happy day. This gives me time to go get some things from the concessions.*

A couple moments later, my hands are filled with popcorn, nachos, and a white cherry slushy while I search for my seat.

After walking around the arena for a few minutes, I finally find where I'm supposed to be, and just in time. They seem to have figured out the issue with the speakers and are ready to get the game started. I enter the gate and greet the usher. She checks my ticket. "Right this way Mr. Winston, we've been expecting you. Mr. Langston told me to take good care of you." She walks me down to my seat. "Enjoy."

No way this is all for me. I owe Mr. Langston bigtime if it is.

My seat is in the front row and on the court. Shocked and

confused, I ask the usher, "Excuse me, mam! Are you sure this is the right spot?". She smiles and says, "Yes sir, If you need anything just let me know. My name is Helda."

I smile back. "Thank you, I will." She walks back up the stairs.

I'm in awe. *Great seats, good food, and I'm watching my favorite team play. How can it possibly get any better than this?*

I look up across from me and nearly drop everything. Who do I see? Natalie. *The girl of my dreams has once again appeared in my reality. She's looking even better than when I last saw her. She even has a Wardogs shirt on. She's not only into sports, but she's a Wardogs fan! She's definitely my very own melanin angel sent straight from heaven.*

She's sitting a few rows up across from me. She's close enough that I can admire her, but far enough that it won't be obvious. As the game goes on, I stare and stare, barely, if at all, paying attention to the basketball game that was literally happening right in front of me. Natalie's peerless beauty had me in a trance. It was impossible for me to look away.

Her smile is perfect. Her hair is perfect. Everything about her is perfect. I need her.

Halftime comes and I expect her to go to the concessions, or maybe even just want to walk around for a little bit to stretch. *That will be my chance.* I sit in my seat waiting for her to get up, but she never does. She sat in her seat for the full 20 minute half time break. Yeah, watching dogs do tricks and people jump off trampolines is cool, but I would much rather have been conversing with my future wife.

The horn sounds. Half time is up and the game resumes. As I continue to sit there captivated, I pray that we make eye contact, but nothing. Time passes and it's now the 4th quarter. The game was almost over and I hadn't even noticed. I was too busy admiring my melanin angel. *I'm probably never going to get this opportunity again. I should just find her and talk to her after the game, regardless if she notices me or not. I can't miss this chance.*

Now it's 1:24 left in the game. As I'm looking at her across the court, I begin to plan what I'm going to say, what I'm going to do. Then I suddenly realize that I don't have any gum or even mints in my pocket. I sigh as I rub my hand across my head. *First impressions are everything. She's with her friends too, I REFUSE to be known as the stank breath guy.* I look up one last time and an usher comes into my sight. *Maybe Helda has something I can use.* I raise my hand and call her over. "Do you have any gum or maybe a mint?", I ask her.

"Yes, take both. Is that all?", she asks.

"Yes mam, thank you." She nods her head and walks away.

I wasn't sure if she was just being very generous or if she was politely trying to tell me my breath stunk, but it's not important. I got what I needed, and now I'm ready to talk to my angel. I look Natalie's way again and I notice her friend is upset. She talks to Natalie for a bit, then they all get up and leave. *Damn.* I see her walk out the tunnel with about thirty seconds left to go in the game. *The game is tied, so it must've been something urgent.* I sigh. *Any sensible man knows the timing isn't right now. To go chase her and try to talk to her while she has to comfort her friend is just setting myself up for failure.* Once again, I let her go. All I can do is think about Chino's words earlier, "If it's meant to be, it'll be."

VIII

———

AS I SIT THERE NUMB, DEPLETED, AND SURROUNDED by yelling chaotic fans, the buzzer sounds, indicating the game is over. The Wardogs lose by 3. The fans that were upbeat and cheering seconds prior, are now exiting the building with a sad, dismal look because James Love, our best player, missed the tying three pointer in the game's final seconds. I'm sad too, but for a completely different reason. I missed my shot to talk to my melanin angel...again. I was now 0-2, and losing the game horribly.

I begin to gather my things and walk up the stairs towards the exit.

"There's been an incident blocking the exits. It'll probably be at least an hour before you'll be able to get out of here. I suggest you go to the arcade instead of just waiting in line going nowhere.", Helda says.

"Thanks, I'll check it out. You have a good night."

"You too, just make a left and it's right across from the bathrooms. Be safe."

I wave goodbye then begin to make my way through the sea of doleful and upset fans.

After about five minutes of bumping into and rubbing shoulders with random people, I finally reach the arcade. Before I go in, I make a pitstop in the bathroom.

"Hey Winston!", I hear as I'm walking out. I pay it no attention and continue to walk into the arcade. Seconds later, I hear the door open behind me and the same voice say, "Winston, I know your bighead ass heard me call you!". I turn and it's Sharon. She's wearing a dress with the Wardogs's colors on it, red, black, and silver. She comes and gives me a hug. Her mood is the complete opposite of how it was when I last saw her. "I'm sorry, my head is all over the place. Wassup?"

"Yeah, this game has everyone acting crazy."

I laugh and say, "Yeah, the game. It's crazy how it ended. What you doing here though? I thought you had a date."

"I did, well, I do. This is my date."

Curious and puzzled, "Sooo where is he?"

She smiles then says, "Like I told you before, when the time is right you'll meet my *mystery man*."

"Understood. By the looks of it, you had a pretty good time tonight."

"It was alright, but the real date doesn't start until I leave here."

Even more confused, I say, "What you mean? So you came to a Wardogs game by yourself?! Nah, that doesn't sound like the Sharon I know. Since when were you into sports? Where were you sitting?"

She laughs, "Winston you're asking too many questions. When the time is right you'll know. Just mind your business, pimp."

Sarcastically I say, "Well excuse me for trying to be a good friend." She laughs then gets a phone call. She walks off to answer it. *I still can't believe she's here. She wasn't into sports while we were dating. I couldn't even get her to watch a Wardogs game on TV let alone actually attend one. Her new boyfriend must be somebody special if he has her doing all of this.*

"Winston, I'm about to go. Do you want a ride to your car? A golf cart is on the way to pick me up", she says as she walks back over.

"Sure, but what about all these people? It's still packed in here."

"Don't worry about it. Like I said, you're asking too many questions. Come on, it's outside." We walk outside and it's a security officer on a golf cart waiting for us. We get on, he turns on his lights and sirens, then we drive straight through the sea of fans. A thirty/forty-five minute walk became a ten minute ride. As I'm in the back riding, I can't help but ponder on who Sharon came to the game for. *She could be dating one of the players, but then again, you only hear about them dating models or celebrities. Never any "normal folk". Maybe she's messing with one of the old owners. Then that doesn't even sound like her. I doubt one of the workers in the arena has any pull to authorize a golf cart escort. I guess I'll just have to wait until "the time is right" to find out.*

She's very beautiful. She has dark, chocolate, melanin skin with short hair and a perfect smile. She could be a model if she really put her mind to it honestly, but her attitude always gets in her way. She's 5'4 and feisty.

"Where are you parked?", the driver asks.

"Out in J37", I respond.

"Sheesh, I hope we have enough gas to make it that far.", he jokingly says.

"Damn Winston, with floor seats you'd think you'd have better parking."

"Ha, ha, ha funny. How did you know I had floor seats? You stalking me now?"

"No, but it seems like YOU was stalking somebody. I couldn't tell who exactly from the skybox."

I blush and try to change the subject. "The skybox?!?! How you get there?"

"You'll know when the time comes Mr. Williams. Just know staring at someone for an entire basketball game isn't going to get their attention."

"Yeah, yeah. My car is the third one after you make that next left."

"That blue hoopty with the back window missing?"

"No, the burgundy car across from it, goofy. You know what I drive."

"With the way you've been acting lately, I thought it got repoed or something."

"You just think you're quite the comedian today, huh? Here's some advice, don't quit your day job."

"I think Bubba here would beg to differ, but since you don't find anything funny you can get off sir."

Bubba laughs and says, "I'm just doing my job. My name is Bennet and I ain't in it.", as he turns the corner.

"It's cool Bubba, he's a big boy. He can take it.", Sharon says.

We arrive at my car, so I had no choice but to get off. "I'm getting off because I want to go home, not because you said so."

"Mhhmm, okay. You have a good night."

"You too, and thanks for the ride."

Sharon and Bubba wave as they drive off. *What a night.*

I get in my car and head home. I get there, eat the burger I picked up, take a shower, then go to sleep. Or at least I try to. It was around 11:00 when I laid down.

Now, it's 1:00am and I'm wide awake. I close my eyes and lay in silence in an attempt to fall asleep, but I'm constantly tossing and turning.

I had a long day at work, did a lot of driving because of the game, and even ate great when I got home. You'd think I would've passed out as soon as my head hit my pillow. Why can't I sleep? Well, that's obvious. Natalie. I just can't stop thinking about her. About us. I know I said if it's meant to be, it'll be, but I still can't help but to think what if. What if we locked eyes and instantly had a connection? What if we had sat right next to each other and just talked throughout the entire night? What if I ran into her at the concessions and I got her number? What if......what if I just walked over to her in the middle of the game instead of just stare at her the whole time? That was my one chance to make up for freezing at The Spot and I folded. I folded like a lawn chair at a barbeque after someone has had one too many plates. What if she gets a boyfriend before I can see her again? But, what if I never see her again? Then what? Man, I have to stop stressing myself over her and try to move on. I'm going to worry myself to death if I don't relax and stop thinking about her. Or worse, I'll be bald like Chino.

In an attempt to clear my mind, I took a deep breath, closed my eyes, and exhaled. When that didn't work, I watched TV until I drifted off to sleep.

IX

———

T ODAY, I WOKE UP WITH A NEW ATTITUDE AND mindset. I felt like I had been reborn. I realized I didn't need Natalie, or anybody else, to solidify my life. It sounds crazy and surreal, but I had had an epiphany. I had a dream that I was an African king. A rich, powerful ruler of many nations. I laid awake and thought about it for a while before I realized my dream was actually my reality. I may not have an army or a room full of gold, but I'm still rich in who I am, in what I am. And that's an educated, hardworking, sophisticated, and dapper individual. Yes I'm a successful financial advisor, but I'm also rich in my family and heritage. The weight and value that has is incomparable and priceless. And power, the color of my skin is all the power I need. I'm feared by many men, groups, and even countries solely because I have a darker skin complexion than them. Feared to the point that I can be targeted and killed without having a weapon, committed a crime, or even being any type of threat. Now that's power.

That dream gave me exactly what I needed to get over Natalie.

It gave me the slap of reality that I needed. Now, instead of feeling depressed, I felt empowered. Feeling completely refreshed, I was excited to start my day. After my alarm woke me up at seven, I got out of bed, took a shower, got dressed, and left my apartment around seven forty. I didn't intend on waiting for her at The Spot either. I get there around eight wearing a white button up and khakis.

I walk in and hear Chino's voice. Smiling, "Aye man! You gon' have the feds coming in today? We're cooking up some white birds in the back and I need to know if my chef needs to clean up or not. Wink, wink."

We both laugh. I take my seat at the counter. "You're good to handle your *business*. My boss was just tripping yesterday. I appreciate that again Chino. I thought I was going to get fired, but you really came through in the clutch for me."

"You know me, I always come through in the clutch, unlike ya boy James Love last night. The man couldn't hit the ocean with a rock. Cost me about two thousand messing around with him. We should've left that man in North Carolina instead of trading for him."

"Give him a break, everybody has an off night. And I told you about all that gambling. You need to stop before Shareeda puts you out and you're sleeping on my couch."

"First off, Shareeda will neeeevver kick me out. She knows who brings the bacon home."

"Yeah, okay. Just know my couch will be waiting for you whenever Shareeda comes to her senses."

"Whatever. You gonna get you something to eat or are you waiting around for your imaginary meeting? I haven't seen her since Monday, just to let you know. Whatever you said must've really scared her off."

I smirk. "Yeah, get me a Rico Special, and I'm actually trying to be on time today. I don't plan on having any *meetings* any time soon. I'm over her, I saw her last night at the game and realized I was tripping."

"Woah, woah, woah! Wait a minute. What game? I know you not talking about the game last night?! You telling me you went to a Wardogs game without ME? Your boy? Your homeskillet? The audacity of some people, boy I tell you. Should've let ya squarehead ass boss fire you."

I couldn't help but to laugh. "C'mon man, it wasn't like that. Mr. Langston blessed me with a ticket, and I forgot about it until I was leaving work yesterday."

"Yeah, okay. You said you saw Natalie there? She curved you real good last night, huh? She told you to stop stalking her and to leave her alone, didn't she?"

I suck my teeth. "Stop trying me man. She was with her friends and left the game early, so I didn't even get a chance to talk to her."

He leans over the counter, looks me in my eyes, and says, "You froze again, didn't you?"

Appalled, I throw my head back. "Chino, why you act like I don't have game?"

"Cuz you don't! You're one of the shiest people I know. Until you change that, you're never going to have a chance, my brotha."

As much as I wanted to disagree, he was right. I was always the quiet, laid back, shy guy. Especially with women. I have a way with words and have no problems discussing business, or things of that nature, but as far as initiating conversation with a woman, I always get nervous and freeze. The only time I can recall I didn't, was the first time I saw Sharon, but that's a story for another time. Now, because of that dream I had last night, I'm a new me. I'm Winston Williams 2.0.

"Everyone has an opinion. And I'm done chasing and thinking about that woman. For real this time. Is my food ready yet? I really have to get to work."

"Yeah, okay I hear you. I'm just trying to help. And yeah it's ready, you need anything else?"

"I appreciate it Chino, and let me get a cup of apple juice to go."

He goes and gathers everything together then brings it to the counter. "$6.34."

I swipe my card, grab my food then leave. "I'll see you tomorrow Chino.", I say as I leave out The Spot.

"Stay up, brotha!", he responds.

I get to work, and I'm prompt for the first time all week. I get settled in my office and notice Sharon didn't make it in. *She was probably too tired from her date.* Without her here, my day was really quiet, but also banal. Finalizing contracts, calling clients, and getting caught up on emails all day isn't as fun without a distraction.

Time passes and it's time to clock out. As I was getting ready to go home, Mr. Jacobs calls my phone. "Hey Winston, can you come to my office before you leave please? We have to discuss some things for tomorrow."

"Okay." I hang up the phone, finish putting my things in my briefcase, and head to his office.

I knock on his door. "Come in Winston." I open the door and walk inside.

"What's up Mr. Jacobs? Is everything ok?"

"Yeah, everything's great. I just got off the phone with Mike Gonzalez. He's an investor that's new to the area, and he's inquiring about potential advantageous investments. I need my top guy here and on time. He scheduled a meeting for tomorrow morning. It's at nine, but I need you here by eight thirty to gameplan. Please don't be late."

"I got you Mr. Jacobs, I'll start up my plan as soon as I get home."

"Thank you, this is a big one. According to my research, he has big bucks. And like I told you yesterday, we can't afford any more off nights."

"Yes sir, we're good. You don't have to worry."

"Good, I'll see you first thing in the morning."

"See you then, enjoy the rest of your day." I say as I go shake his hand.

"You too." I leave his office and head to my car to go home.

I get home, and take a couple burgers out of my refrigerator to cook later. Then I do a quick thirty minute workout I found on the internet. Dripping in sweat, I hop in the shower. When I get out, I hear my phone ding. I don't pay it any mind. I figured if it was important they'd just call me. After I dry off and put on some purple gym shorts and a black t-shirt, I check my phone. I look and I have three missed calls and ten text messages from Sharon. *What the hell?!* I panic and immediately call her.

"Winston!", she says as she answers the phone, "Are you busy?! I need a huuuuge favor from you." I'm shook. More worried than anything though. She wasn't at work, the last time I saw her was last night before her date, and now she's randomly blowing up MY phone out of all people.

"What is it? Are you ok?", I say.

"Yeah, I'm fine. I need a ride from the chicken spot on Agnes and Paulhill. I think it's about ten or fifteen minutes from you."

"Rico's Finest?"

"Yeah. Can you come? Please, you owe me."

"I got you. Give me about twenty minutes and I'll be there."

"Thanks Winston.". I hang up the phone. *I know she's not my girl anymore, but we did agree to be friends. Friends are supposed to help each other out in tough times, right?* I grab my keys off of my dining room table, lock my door, and make my way to my car. I drive off into the dark and cloudy overcast and Sharon calls me again. "Are you ok? Be there in ten."

"Yeah, I'm good. I honestly just wanted to hear your voice."

Hear my voice?!?! I start to assume the worst. *Her date must've ended terribly wrong last night.*

"Just be cool, I'm on my way. If you haven't eaten yet, you can order us some food to go. I'll pay you back when I scoop you."

"Okay, barbeque with a dash of lemon pepper right?"

"Yeah, and get a large lemonade too please."

"Eight or ten piece?"

"Fifteen."

She laughs then says, "Oh my bad. I forgot how much you like to eat."

"Yeah, I haven't eaten since lunch so I'm pretty hungry."

"Alright, do you mind staying on the phone until you come?"

I hesitate for a little then say, "Yeah, it's no problem."

We stay on the phone for the next seven minutes. We didn't say a word. The only noise came from her loud background of customers and the employees. "I'm pulling up.", I tell her. She walks out and it starts to sprinkle. She's wearing the same dress from last night, her eyes are red, and her eyeliner is running. It's obvious she had been crying. I park, get out, and give her a hug. We embraced each other in the light rain for about thirty seconds. She whispers in my ear, "Thank you." I let her go, then walk her around to the passenger side. I open her door and help her get in. I get in the car and ask her, "Where am I taking you?"

She takes a deep breath then sighs it out. "To be honest Winston, I feel so lost right now. I don't know what to do."

I look over at her. She's in no shape to be by herself. Not only as a friend, but as a man, I wouldn't feel right just dropping her off home to be by herself all night with no one to talk to or console her. Especially in this storm that might take place. She'd just be miserable and drive herself crazy. With that being said, I did the only logical thing. "You want to come over to my place? We can have a movie night like the good ole days, except as friends this time."

She looks out the window. "Yeah, that's fine. I'm going to need to borrow a pair of your shorts and a shirt. I need to get out of this dress ASAP."

"That's cool, you know where they at." I start the car back up and we drive back to my place. She took a little nap and I just listened to music.

When we get to my apartment, she makes her way to the bathroom as I prepare everything in the living room.

Twenty-five minutes later, I have everything ready for our movie night. The food is heated and placed on the table, I have her favorite movie ready to play, and I have a warm blanket waiting for her.

"Thanks again Winston, I really appreciate it.", she says as she walks out the bathroom wearing my clothes.

"It's no problem, that's what friends are for right? You can just put your stuff by the door so you won't forget anything." She places her things by the door then checks her phone.

"The food and movie are ready too. The only thing that's missing is you."

She walks over and takes her seat by me on the couch. "So, who's going to bless the food? Me or you?"

I smile, "I really want to be blessed by your voice, so I think you should do it."

She laughs and rolls her eyes, "Uggghhh alright. Bow ya big ass head."

I drop my jaw, "C'mon man. Not before we pray."

"C'mon what? God knows he gave you a big ass head."

I bring my hands together and bow my head as I say, "Dear Lord, please forgive her for coming to you with this little booty energy. She doesn't know any better."

"I know you did not."

I laugh, "You gon' pray or what? Our food is getting cold."

"Ugh, you are so aggy. Dear Lord, thank you for this day, this food, and great friends. Please allow this food to nourish our bodies and bless the hands that made it. In Jesus's name I pray, amen."

I stand up and start to clap, "I almost shed a tear. Was that so hard?"

"You're really aggy, you know that? Shut up and play the movie before I slap you.", she playfully says.

We begin to eat and watch the movie. We finish our food a little over halfway through it. She puts her trash on the table, lays across my lap, and pulls the blanket on top of her. About twenty minutes pass and she blurts out, "He has a fucking girlfriend Winston! A whole fucking girlfriend. We were driving back to his house from lunch and she called him. I guess he forgot his phone was connected to the car. When he picked up, I heard her on the speaker letting him know she returned early from some type of business trip and she was waiting for him at the house. He immediately hung up, but it was too late. I told his driver to drop me off at Rico's Finest. That bastard had the nerve to tell me he loved me last night! He keeps calling and texting trying to explain, but I ain't hearing none of it."

"Damn, I'm sorry to hear that. You ok? Like, honestly."

"I've never felt so betrayed, so embarrassed, so abandoned. I'm heartbroken right now."

I pull her hair back, then start to rub her head. "I hate you had to experience that. You're really a great friend of mine and a great person. I hate that you feel that way."

The rain starts to pick up outside. "I mean, I'll get over it. Men come and go. I hate it ended like this because I really did genuinely like him, but that's life. I'll bounce back."

"Yeah, that's a fact. You're truly one of the strongest, nicest, most caring, loving, smartest, even sexiest women I know. Any man would be blessed just to be in your presence. You're a real queen and don't deserve to be treated like a peasant. You'll get the man you deserve, I believe in it."

Her eyes start to tear up. "Thanks, Winston. That really means a lot coming from you. You didn't even say stuff like that while we were together." We laugh then just look at each other. She then repositions her body in an upright position. She leans over to me, pulls my head to hers, and we kiss. Not a little peck, but a sensual, passionate kiss. We kissed as if we were two lovers that haven't seen each other in a while.

After kissing for a minute, I pull back. "Look Sharon, I don't think this is a good move, especially for our friendship. You're emotional and...". She puts her index finger on my lips, stopping me mid sentence. "Shut up and kiss me Winston.", she says as thunder begins to rumble. We begin to kiss again. She begins to take off my shirt. I take off hers. I begin to lick her breasts and she starts to squeeze my back as she lets off a soft moan. She then gets up, drops her shorts, and walks to my bedroom. She looks back and signals for me to follow her. In the heat of the moment, I didn't think twice about it. We get to my bedroom and she grabs me. She takes off my shorts, throws me on the bed, and starts to pleasure me orally. The thunder begins to rumble louder. When she finishes, she climbs on top of me and we begin to make love throughout the rest of the thunderous, stormy night.

X

———

I T'S SEVEN IN THE MORNING WHEN MY ALARM WAKES me. I yawn, then stretch across my bed. *What a night. I still can't believe what happened. I would've never thought we'd do that again.* As I stretched across my bed, I noticed Sharon wasn't lying next to me. "Yo, Sharon, you here?!", I yell out. I check for her in my bathroom first, and then my living room. Not a sign of her anywhere. I notice her stuff isn't by the door anymore, so now I'm certain she's gone. *Why'd she leave though? I woke up with the intentions of picking up where we left off last night, but I guess she had other plans.*

I then check my phone to see if she left me a message or something. I look, and there's nothing. Not a missed phone call or even a text. *Oh well, I guess I'll just see her at work. Work!* I slap my face with my hand. *I completely forgot! I was supposed to prepare a business plan for my meeting with Mr. Gonzalez and Mr. Jacobs. If I screw this up, I'm fired on the spot.*

Now, it's about seven thirty. I have less than an hour to throw something together. I open up my laptop and begin to look through old documents hoping I'll find something that'll help.

After forty minutes of copying and pasting old reports together, I was able to design a decent business plan containing some of Ricoville's finest attractions and a brief layout of the area. *It's not perfect, but it'll have to do. If I'm missing anything, I'll just talk my way out of it.*

With my plan being finished, I now have about five minutes to get dressed and fifteen to get to work. I brush my teeth, put on the first shirt and pair of pants I see, then rush out the house into my car.

My stomach grumbles. *I definitely don't have time to stop by The Spot. I'll just have to suck it up til lunch.* A few minutes after leaving my apartment, I'm stuck in a standstill. *With all this traffic, there's no way I'll be there by eight thirty. It's doubtful I'll even make it before nine.* I take a deep breath, and think. *Maybe Mr. Jacobs won't be mad if I give him a heads up.* I text Mr. Jacobs and tell him that there was an accident on the highway. The only thing he replied was "K". Not drive safe or even "okay", but the letter "K". I drop my head. *I'm definitely fired when he sees me.* A couple minutes later, he texts me, "J80", to let me know which conference room to meet him at. *Maybe I'm good.*

It's eight fifty when I finally pull in to work and eight fifty-three as I'm rushing into the conference room.

"Good morning Mr. Jacobs, traffic was crazy this morning."

"It's eight fifty-five and I asked you to be here at eight thirty. Traffic or not, you should've planned accordingly to avoid any mishaps."

I get agitated. His foolish statement topped off my hectic morning. "Mr. Jacobs, there's no way to plan for a random car accident. It's not like you can calculate exactly when a car accident is going to occur and how long the holdup is going to last. You sound stupid."

His face starts to turn red. "Excuse me?! Who the hell do you think you're talking to! I..".

As soon as he was about to let me have it, Mr. Gonzalez walks in wearing a dark brown suit and matching snakeskin shoes. Full of energy, "Good morning Mr. Jacobs, I know I'm a little early, but I'd rather be early than late."

Mr. Jacobs goes and greets Mr. Gonzalez with a firm handshake and says, "Good morning Mr. Gonzalez, I wish more people had that attitude. That mentality really goes a long way." He gives me a glare as he says that.

"And who is this fellow? Is this the star pupil you were telling me so much about?", Mr. Gonzalez says.

Mr. Jacobs hesitates a few seconds then answers, "Um, yes sir it is. Mr. Gonzalez, this is Winston Williams, he's one of the best at what he does."

I shake Mr. Gonzalez's hand. "Good morning sir, how's everything? You enjoying the city so far?"

"Morning, and yes. The city of Ricoville has a lot more to it than what people think. I'm familiar with the area, but I've only been living here for a week. Still looking for some fruitful investments."

"Have you checked out the resort by the lake yet? I personally think that has the most lucrative potential. That, and the area in the North Side city limits, it has the space for an athletic complex and all types of other attractions."

"I actually have not, but that's what this meeting is for, right?"

Mr. Jacobs butts in and says, "You're right. Shall we get started?"

All three of us take a seat at the table. Mr. Jacobs is sitting at the head, and Mr. Gonzalez and I are sitting directly across from each other. We spent about an hour and a half discussing Ricoville and all of its' advantageous assets before we concluded the meeting.

"And if you put at least $750,000 here, it'll return about a 350% profit within the next three years. You put down anything less and there will barely be anything left after you have to pay bills. I'll email you the contract as soon as we finish this meeting.", I say.

"Sounds like a big risk, but from what you all have shown and explained to me, the reward is greater. Email it then I'll get back with you.", Mr. Gonzalez replied. "Now, if this wraps up everything y'all have planned for me, I'd like to officially close the meeting. I enjoyed you guys's company, but I have to make my way to a brunch date with my wife. Happy wife, happy life."

Mr. Jacobs gets up and walks toward the door to open it. Mr. Gonzalez and I follow him.

Mr. Gonzalez shakes our hands and says, "Thanks for meeting with me. I'll make sure to call you personally to finalize the contract after I review it."

"We're grateful to have you Mr. Gonzalez, and safe travels.", Mr. Jacobs says.

"I think this meeting has made us comfortable enough to refer to each other on a first name basis, call me Mike."

"Well safe travels Mike, I'll make sure to be in touch."

"Actually Francis, I'd prefer to be in contact with Winston. I like the way he thinks. You make sure to keep him around. He just might be running his own firm in a few years."

Mr. Jacobs's face turns red. "Yeah, he has potential.", was all he could say.

"Well, I can't keep my wife waiting. Winston, I'll be in touch.", Mr. Gonzalez says as he walks onto the elevator.

"Yes sir, I'll be waiting for you. Have a good day.", I say as the elevator closes.

Mr. Jacobs comes over and grabs me by the shoulder. "Good job today Winston, we didn't have the best start, but we had a successful finish. I'm going to forget about what was said earlier and just move on from it."

I guess money makes you forget everything. "Sounds good to me Francis."

We get on the elevator and depart to our offices. As I walk to my office, I pass the secretary's desk and see Sharon's not here. "Sharon called in sick today?", I ask her substitute.

"I think she has the flu or something. She called in sick yesterday too."

"Oh okay, hope she feels better." I walk into my office, sit down, then check my phone. Still nothing from Sharon, but I have a text from Chino. It says, "You must have women repellent. You won't believe who came in today."

XI

———

I LAUGH. *AIN'T NO WAY HE'S TALKING ABOUT NATALIE.* *Out of all the times I've sat at The Spot to wait for her, she picks the day I didn't even come to show up.* I'm flabbergasted. I text Chino back, "LOL who?". After a few minutes, he replies back, "Natalie man. She came by around 8:30 looking fine as usual. Don't worry, I put in a good word for you ;). Come by later and I'll tell you what I said." *Chino didn't let me down before with Mr. Jacobs, so I hope he comes through again. I might just leave work at lunch time then stop by The Spot on my way home. I'm sure securing a new client is deserving of an early weekend.*

As I'm texting Chino to let him know that I'll be there soon, Sharon texts me. "Can I come over when you get off? I want to talk." I sigh. *I knew we shouldn't have done that. We were doing great just being friends, and now us having sex has messed it up. Sharon has a strong outer shell, but can be very vulnerable internally, especially when she's emotionally attached to someone or something. She probably never really got over us to begin with, and that's why she didn't want to stop. For both of us to completely move on and remain friends, we really have to talk and establish boundaries. It's a fact that you can't move on into a new relationship if you're still reminiscing and holding on to the last one. It'll never work. Her relationship with her mystery man was bound to fail for that reason alone.*

Now I have a dilemma. Do I go by Chino and see what's up with Natalie, or do I go clear things up with Sharon? I sit and think about it at my desk for a minute before I realize I have to take my own advice. I tell Chino I can't come by today and that I'll see him in the morning. Then, I tell Sharon to meet me at my place in about an hour.

I take a few quick phone calls then email the contract to Mr. Gonzalez before I gather my things and leave.

When I get to my apartment, Sharon is already in the parking lot waiting for me. She gets out of her car and greets me with a hug wearing black sweatpants and a white t-shirt with an elephant on it.

"Wassup, you okay Sharon? You weren't at work today.", I say as we walk towards the stairs to my apartment.

"I'm good, I just needed time to be alone, and think."

We get to my apartment and go in. "Do you want anything to drink?", I ask her.

"No, I'm good. I just have to speak my peace. It won't be long."

"Oh, cool. Well, you said you wanted to talk, so wassup? I'm listening."

She laughs, then takes a deep breath. "Right. I just wanted to apologize for yesterday. I was very emotional and should've listened to you when you tried to stop before it escalated. I was broken and you made me feel so complete. Not only was it the sweet things you said, but it was just the way I felt being around you. The truth is, I'm not completely over you Winston. And in order for me to start something with anyone else, we must first communicate as to what we are and what we're going to be. I personally think that we're great as friends and hope we can remain that way."

I laugh under my breath. *She said everything that I was thinking earlier.*

I smile. "I completely agree, couldn't have said it better myself."

"So, we're friends?"

"Yeah, always. It's possible for two adults of the opposite sex to have a completely platonic relationship. You know I got you."

She walks over and gives me a hug. "I'm glad we got that out the way."

"Yeah, me too. You're just going to have to start controlling yourself a little better. I know I'm irresistible and all, but remember, boundaries." I jokingly add.

Sharon scoffs and rolls her eyes. "Boy bye."

I laugh, " But seriously, I'd hate to lose you as a friend, Sharon. You always have my back. I'd be lost without you."

"Yeah, yeah, I know." We just smile at each other.

"Yo, I have to tell you about Francis?"

She chuckles, "Why you calling him that?!"

"We're on a first name basis now."

"What?! Since when?"

I tell her about the conversation I had with Mr. Jacobs prior and after the meeting with Mr. Gonzalez.

"I cannot believe you said that! I know his face was red.", she says while laughing.

"Apple red.", I say as she starts to laugh harder. "Do you want to order a pizza or something? I'm free the rest of the day."

She checks her phone then says, "Mmmm, maybe another time. I really have to go. But hey!" She grabs my hand. "I'm glad we can still be friends. I wouldn't want to lose you either Winston." She gives me a hug then leaves my apartment.

I check the time and it's only two thirty. *I'm off work early on a Friday, but I have no plans. I could go by The Spot, but Chino's going to be leaving soon. Once he clocks out, he goes into hibernation until the next day, especially if his wife's home. He'll never admit it, but we both know she runs things. I guess I'll just order a pizza and have a day to myself. A little self love never hurt anyone.*

About thirty minutes later, my pizza gets here. I lay on the couch and watch a couple movies while I eat it. I doze off midway through the second movie. I wake up around seven thirty to a call from an unsaved number. I don't answer. It calls again, but I still don't answer. Instead, I sit up and continue watching the rest of the current movie that's playing. *I've learned my lesson about picking up unknown numbers. The last time I did that, it ended up being a bill collector.*

Five minutes later, I get a text. It reads, "It's Mike Gonzalez, pick up." The phone rings not too long after that. I answer.

"Winston, wassuuup!?!?!?", Mike says. He's clearly drunk and at a party of some sort. I hear loud music in the background. "What you doing tonight?"

So much for my personal day. "Nothing, you ok? You called earlier than I expected to talk about that contract."

"No man, I like to get to know the people I'm doing business with. You seem like a cool and fun guy, unlike your uptight ass boss. My friend is throwing a mansion party in south Ricoville. I want you to come by. Loosen up and enjoy yourself. I'll send you the address as soon as I hang up and I'm not taking no for an answer.

XII

———

H E HANGS UP THE PHONE AND IMMEDIATELY SENDS the address. I put it in my phone to see how far it was from my apartment. *I really don't feel like driving an hour, but I do receive about two percent out of every deal I make. So driving about an hour for a potential $50,000 payout isn't too bad. Plus, it gives me something to do tonight.*

I take a shower, get dressed, and make my way to the mansion. Not sure if I should wear a suit or dress down, I just wear a navy blue button up with black slacks.

When I arrive at the party, it's about nine thirty. I drive up to a huge, two story house. They're playing music so loud you can hear it about three blocks away. Luckily, the mansion is secluded. The party probably would've been shut down already if it wasn't.

As I'm parking, I notice there aren't many cars in front of the house. My "this seems like trouble senses" start to go off, but I ignore them. I try to call Mike to let him know I'm outside, but my phone doesn't let me. A few seconds later, he walks out the door with a beer in his hand wearing the same brown suit he had on earlier. He gives me a big bear hug and wraps his arm around my shoulder. "Winston, come in! Let me show you around."

As soon as we walk in the door, I see at least thirty women in the living room. All of them gorgeous, you would've thought we were about to shoot some type of music video. He catches me staring and says, "Those are our guests. We'll come down and entertain them later. All of the fellas are upstairs. It's not many of us, so you'll have plenty to choose from. But let me introduce you to everyone first before you have your fun." He shakes my shoulders then we walk up the stairs. "I want you to enjoy yourself. Think of this as a thank you for all of the money you're about to make us. Um, uh, I-I mean me." He grins.

I'm still speechless. I've never been in an environment like this. I have no clue what to expect, or even who to expect. We get up the stairs and he takes me to this room filled with cigar smoke and the smell of liquor. I'm shocked as to what I see, or rather who I see. I stand still at the door, I'm hesitant to enter. "Come on Winston, I'm sure you know some of these people. You'll thank me later." He walks me to the center and gets everyone's attention. He clears his throat and says, "Everyone, this is Mr. Winston Williams! He's a great financial advisor with a golden thumb." He then proceeds to introduce me to all of the major people in the room, pointing at each of them as he says their names. "Winston I'm sure you know Mayor Payne, (the devious and ruthless ruler of the city) , Sheriff Brooks, (a middle aged do-boy that's Mayor Payne's money hungry right hand man) , Judge Taylor, (a vicious and fiesty woman that doesn't take anything from anyone), and Councilman Ingram, (the tall, dark and handsome poster child for the city of Ricoville)." He pulls me to the side and says, "These are some very powerful people. Make sure you get AND STAY on their good side."

I nod my head as I swallow the air in my mouth. "How'd you get involved in all of this so soon. Didn't you just move here?"

He pauses then says, "I got pulled over by Sheriff Brooks for speeding a while back. Another ticket would've suspended my license, so I tried to pay him off. He went to his car and came back with a piece of paper with a phone number on it. He gave me the paper, told me to call it, and drove off. I called it as soon as he left and it turned out to be the mayor. We talked for about an hour and here we are."

I'm not sure what type of business they have going on, but I'm 100% sure it's not all legal.

"I know you don't want to be up here with us old folks Winston. Councilman Ingram, why don't you take him down stairs. You kids enjoy yourselves. Most of these guys up here are married. Their wives would kill everyone in this house if they saw us with the women downstairs, even Judge Taylor's wife would throw a fit.", Mayor Payne jokingly says with his deep and vibrant voice.

Councilman Ingram gets up and says, "You gotta drink a cup of this first. It's a mix of a little bit of everything. You won't taste it that much because of all the juice, but you're sure as hell gonna feel it in about five minutes." He pours a glass and tries to give it to me.

"I don't really drink man.", I tell him.

"C'mon, you're partying with the big dogs! We're giving you thirty-five gorgeous women to choose from, that's the least you can do!", Sheriff Brooks yells out with his country accent.

"Don't be a wuss! Grow a pair and put some hair on your chest.", Judge Taylor added.

Mayor Payne gets up out of his chair, takes his cigar out of his mouth, and walks over to me and the councilman. He grabs the cup from the councilman and hands it to me. "Look son, relax. There's no cameras, no recording devices, and you're a single man. You are single, right?"

"Uuuhh, yes sir, I'm single."

"Good! Now a tall, handsome, and from what I've heard, successful cat like yourself deserves to feel and be treated like a king. Now take this glass, drink it, and enjoy yourself. Okay son?"

"Yes sir, I got you." I take the cup from him and drink it, all of it. Immediately, I started to feel the effects of the cup. At that point, I figured if I didn't drink it, I would deeply regret it.

Mike raises his fists in the air. "Yeeeaaaahhh!".

Mayor Payne pats me on the back, smiles at me, and says, "Now you kids go have fun."

The councilman and I leave the room and make our way downstairs. When the door closes, Mayor Payne goes to the middle of the room and looks at Mike. "Mike! What the hell do you think you're doing bringing an outsider in here?! Did I not tell you that we've been running a smooth operation for twenty plus years now with NO mishaps? We can get rid of you and nobody would bat an eye. A car accident is easy to pull off."

Mike frantically walks to Mayor Payne with his hands up saying, "Woah, woah, woah. No need for all that. You said you wanted more ideas about places to clean the money, so I brought you your best option. Like I said when I brought him in, he has a golden thumb. The kid knows how to make money."

The mayor gets close to Mike. He grabs him with his right hand and puts his cigar in his face with his left hand. "If he messes this thing up, that's your ass."

XIII

———

MEANWHILE, THE COUNCILMAN AND I ARE HAVING the time of our lives. We're in the middle of the living room surrounded by women, liquor, and music. I don't normally drink because of personal reasons, but tonight, I got wasted. One second, me and the councilman are back to back on the couch dancing, and the next thing I know, one girl comes up to me and gives me a shot. Then, I turn right around and have another girl give me one. That started what seemed like a never ending cycle of shots and women. After about an hour of this, I pass out in the middle of the living room. It's probably not even midnight yet, but I was out for the count.

When I wake up, it's Saturday evening. I sit up on the couch ,dazed and confused, as I look around the room. There's not a person in sight. I check my phone, and it's dead. I try to get up, but I can't. The room started to spin as I wobbled up, so I sat back down. My head is killing me, there's no one here, and my phone's dead. With the way I was feeling, I was convinced I was going to die here. I lay back down for about five minutes, then I get a tug on my arm. "Wake up man, you're about to sleep your life away. Here, drink this.", the mayor says as he passes me a sports drink and a can of ginger ale as I sit up. "I don't mind you staying here until you get yourself together, just don't throw up on my couch. I paid a lot of money for it."

"Yes sir, I appreciate it."

"No problem. You need anything before I leave? I gotta make a run and you might be gone when I get back."

My phone falls out of my pocket. "Uhhh, do you have a phone charger?"

"Yeah, let me go get it." He goes into a room around the corner. I just sit there and admire the beautiful house while he gets me a charger. The expensive art work and decor he has on his walls is definitely a sight to see.

A few minutes goes by and he hasn't came back yet. *He must've got lost in his own house.*

A couple more minutes pass by and suddenly I hear him yell, "For the fiftieth time, I'll get there when I get there!! You sweat me again and I'll fit you for a casket!" He slams the door as he walks out and makes his way towards me. He calmly says, "It's tough being the mayor of the glorious Ricoville, Winston. The work never stops. I have to constantly tend to the needs of hundreds, thousands even."

I crack a fake smile then say, "I can imagine. They have to realize you're not God."

He starts to puff out his chest as he's standing in front of me in his all black suit. "Oh Winston, I am. To many people, I'm the captain of their fate. The master of their soul. I'm a very powerful man, Winston. I'm a king, and Ricoville is my kingdom. It's the biggest city in the south and it's responsible for 65% of the state's revenue. Our hand is in everything, the agricultural business, transportation, tourism. Every way you can imagine to make money, we're in it. I'm in it. I provide jobs, housing, income, everything, to a lot of people, Winston."

"Wow. I didn't know that, Mayor Payne."

"Call me MP, but yes, in a sense, I am god." From that moment on, I knew I didn't want any parts of Mayor Payne. Any man that even thinks about comparing himself to God is insane. He throws me the charger as he leaves towards the door.

"Thanks."

"No problem, feel better." He stops walking and looks back at me. "And as for the great people you saw over here last night, we're all business partners. I've assigned them all specific jobs to do to help keep the economy in good standing. We meet about two times a month to discuss everyone's status. We like to be private so that the townspeople don't worry or interrupt things. That's why we meet here. At the city council meetings, there's a lot of chaos because everybody has an opinion and a new solution that they want to share. That leads to two hours of getting nothing accomplished. Here, I control the meeting, people say what they have to say, and we leave. Simple."

He turns around and continues to walk towards the door.

As he begins to open the door, I say, "You're just going to leave a stranger alone in your house while you're gone MP?"

He smirks, "The moment you took that cup out my hand and drank it, we became associates. Maybe one day we'll even become friends, or perhaps family. But as for now, just know we're going to keep in touch." He opens the door and walks out. Before he closes it, he looks me in my eyes and says, "Oh, and Winston."

"Yes?"

"Remember, I'm a god, I see everything." That sent a chill through my spine.

He leaves, and I plug my phone up. My curiosity is urging me to get up and explore the house while I wait for it to turn on. I was about to let my curiosity get the best of me, but I thought about the conversation I just had with MP. *He probably has cameras all over his house, and ten times out of ten, I'm going to find something that I'm not supposed to. Who knows what he'll do to me if I find something.*

So what do I do? I do what any sane person would do in this situation, I sit on the couch, motionless, until my phone is charged. I just periodically take sips from the sports drink and ginger ale MP gave me before he left.

It takes about ten minutes for my phone to turn on. The longest ten minutes of my life. As soon as my phone turns on, I immediately leave the house. When I get to my car, I realize my keys aren't in my pocket. My heart drops into my stomach, I lower my head, and lean on my car. *Damn!* I didn't want to go back into that house, but I didn't have a choice. I get in, then immediately find the bathroom. I knew my keys weren't in there, I just really had to pee.

After washing my hands, I come out to the living room to check the area and the couches, but there's no sign of my keys. Something tells me to look in the kitchen, so that's what I did. I check the counters and see nothing. Next, I check the dinner table. I didn't see my keys, but I did see a copy of the contract I sent Mike earlier. *He was probably just having MP or somebody look over it. He's still new to the area, he probably wanted to make sure our claims were legit.*

As I'm continuing the search for my keys, I begin to get frustrated. "My keys aren't anywhere in here!" I exclaim. As I begin to walk out, something catches my eye. A key rack. I examine it closely to see if my keys are on it. I look, and find them right in the middle of the rack under another pair of keys. *One of the girls must've hung them up for me after I passed out. I wish I would've been sober enough to get one of their numbers. That definitely would've helped with my Natalie situation.*

I grab my keys and leave. I didn't want to spend another second in that house that I didn't have to.

When I finally drive off, it's about eight o'clock, so it's a little dark outside. I get a few miles from the house, and my phone starts dinging. *Oh wow, guess I didn't have service in the house.* I check my phone while I'm at a red light. I have missed calls from Mr. Langston, Sharon, Chino, and Mike. Mike, Chino, and Mr. Langston left voicemails, Sharon just texted me. The light turns green and I continue to drive up the highway. I'm still checking my phone, and that causes me to swerve a little bit. I'm the only one on the road, so it wasn't a big deal, or so I thought. Seconds after my car veers off the road for a brief moment, I hear police sirens. I look up at my rearview mirror, I see red and blue lights light up on top of a white sheriff car. Not knowing what's about to happen, my heart starts to beat faster and faster. I was terrified. I'm the only person on the road, and on top of that, it's dark out. I pull my car over to the right side of the road, let my window down, turn my car off, put my hands at ten and two on my steering wheel, and drop my head as I pray. I hear the officer get out of his car and slam his door. As I feel him getting closer and closer, my hands start to sweat. I'm nervous. I'm scared. The officer approaches my car and knocks on the top of it to get my attention.

KNOCK. KNOCK.

I look up, and see it's Sheriff Brooks. He walks up wearing his brown uniform, matching cowboy hat, and black shades. "You must still be recovering from last night, huh? You was passed out on the couch when I left. From the looks of it, you really enjoyed yourself. "

I'm shocked it's him, but also somewhat relieved. "Yeah, I woke up not too long ago. I'm about to go home and lay in bed for the rest of the night. Whatever it was I drank last night really got to me."

"We call that drink The Nectar of the gods. It only comes out on celebratory occasions."

"Oh, cool. What was the occasion?"

He hesitates then says, "New business." He starts to smile as he reaches in his pocket. Not knowing what he's about to pull out, I slowly lean my body away from the window. "Go get yourself something good to eat. I'm sure you could use some food in your system after last night.", he says as he hands me the ten $100 dollar bills he just pulled out of his pocket.

I refuse to take it. "I appreciate it Sheriff Brooks, but I'm good. I have money."

"Look son, it's just an appreciation gift for coming out and partying with us last night. The least I can do is pay for your meal."

This definitely throws up a red flag in my head. *They're paying ME, for partying with THEM? Nah, that ain't right. What did I just get myself into?*

Sheriff Brooks continues to say, "Winston, right? Either you can take this gift, get you something nice to eat, and enjoy a nice, peaceful evening to yourself, or I can arrest you and put a nice DUI charge on your record. Valentine's Day is coming up right? I'm sure you have a nice young gal you want to treat right and impress. Here." He puts the money in front of my face. "I'm just trying to be generous. Just take it."

I grab the money. "Thank you."

"No problem!", he says with a smile. "I'll be seeing you around. You have a good one now." He slaps the top of my car two times then walks off.

He gets in his car and skrrts away.

The bright side is that I'm $1,000 richer, but what comes with that is still unknown. I fold the money, put it in an envelope I had in my car, then put it in my arm rest before I continue driving home.

I get about fifteen minutes from my apartment and my stomach starts to growl. I realize I haven't eaten all day and decide to get something to eat. I stop at Rico's Finest because it's the closest. I get an order of barbeque wings sprinkled in lemon pepper, a bacon cheeseburger, a side of fries, and a large lemonade to top it off. I get my food, get home, and relax in front of my tv in the living room. Before I start eating, I check my phone to see what I missed. Sharon texted me, "Hey, wassup? I was calling because I haven't heard from you today. You ok?"

I type back, "Long night. I'll tell you about it later.".

"Tomorrow afternoon?"

"Yeah, I'll call you when I get out of church."

"Ok :)"

Now I check my voicemails. Chino's is first. "She didn't come in today. She'll probably be back Monday morning though. That gives you plenty of time to get your wack ass game together. Stay up brotha."

That's crazy. Monday I could finally have the opportunity to officially meet Natalie and I'm not even excited. I guess the alluring fantasy I once had has quickly become a thing of the past.

Next, I listen to Mike's voicemail. With a slurred voice, "Hey man, call me whenever you get this. Just making sure you're ok."

I'll be better off calling him tomorrow, he's probably asleep and still hungover from yesterday.

I haven't talked to Mr. Langston in a while, I wonder what he wants.

"Hey Winston, just checking on you. Dinner tomorrow? Let me know before the wife makes plans. See ya." *It's nine o'clock so he's probably still awake.* He's a night owl that doesn't usually go to sleep until after eleven or twelve at the earliest, so I call him.

The phone rings about four times then he finally picks up. "Winston! I see you got my message. Is five at Little Peet's fine?"

"Hey Mr. Langston, yes that's fine."

"Good. I don't want to hold you up, I'll see you tomorrow."

"See you then." We hang up the phone. Our phone conversations usually don't last longer than three minutes. He likes to get straight to the point.

I now sit back, relax, and enjoy my food. I spend the rest of the night laying on my couch and watching movies until I fall asleep.

XIV

———

IT'S ALMOST NINE THIRTY WHEN THE SUN HITS MY EYES and wakes me up. Last night was quite mundane, but I was still exhausted from Friday's extravaganza. Still in awe and bewildered about what took place, I sit up on my couch and think about everything that transpired. The mayor, Mike, the women, getting pulled over by Sheriff Brooks, everything. *Something just isn't right. I can't exactly put my finger on it, but everything feels a little off. As if I unknowingly opened a giant can of worms.*

After sitting there for a while, I look at the time and begin to start my day. It's ten fifteen when I'm showered, dressed, and ready for church. I still have time to kill before service actually starts, so I decide to stop by The Spot for breakfast. Hopefully, Chino's there. Sometimes he works on Sundays, and sometimes he sleeps in.

I get there a little past ten thirty wearing a red polo shirt and brown slacks. As soon as I walk through the door, I see Chino behind the counter smiling from ear to ear. I'm curious and confused. "Wassup man?! Shareeda let you dip in the honey pot last night?"

Laughing, "Nah, my pills don't come in for another week. But

I might be able to help YOU with that problem." He then winks at me as he continues to smile.

Now I'm even more confused as I take my seat. *What the hell is he talking about?* "I'm not going on any more of your blind dates. The last one smelled funny. It was a mixture of cotton candy and moth balls."

Chuckling, Chino says, "At least you know she has a clean home. You couldn't handle Beatrice anyway. She would've had you in a corner crying for your mama. But, that's a story for another day. As for now, you wouldn't believe who actually came in this morning." I immediately start to blush. I figured the only person he could be talking about was Natalie. "They left not too long before you came in here actually. Probably around five, maybe ten minutes ago."

Anxiously, "Who?! Just spit it out Chino!"

"Calm down son, don't get your panties in a bunch. It was just your boss. He wanted to check in on our progress and see if you was doing your job right."

Disappointed, I slouch in my seat. "Damn, for real? What you said?"

Chino bursts out laughing. "Man I'm just playing with you. I just wanted to prove that all that 'I'm over her' stuff you were talking was bullshit."

Embarrassed, but also thrilled, I sit up in my seat. "Kiss my ass Chino! So was it Natalie or not man?"

"Woah, take it easy playa. Don't make me call your boss and tell him you're having a bad attitude."

I begin to get frustrated, "Forget it Chino, I don't even care anymore."

"You know you do."

I suck my teeth. "So who was it? Spit it out."

He starts laughing again. "You already know who it is. I don't know why you keep acting like you don't."

I sat there, shook. *Just a little earlier! If I would've set an alarm. If I didn't sit around earlier, I would've made it!* I couldn't believe it. My expression said it all.

"She said she had gone out of town for a couple of days to handle some business.", Chino says. "She said she'll be here tomorrow morning between eight thirty and nine."

My face lights up with joy. "Cool, as of now I don't have anything planned. I'm about to get her Chino."

"We'll see tomorrow morning, my brotha. Do you want an omelette? I'm about to make me and Shareeda one before I head out."

"Yes we will. And yeah, I'll take one. I need to eat something before I go to church anyway, ain't no telling how long we'll be in there. Why you leaving so early though? Don't you usually stay til twelve thirty on Sundays?"

"First off, don't be keeping tabs on me. I'm a grown ass man. Secondly, Shareeda wants to go to the mall around twelve to catch a movie and shop a little. She's trying to get those Valentine's Day deals before they end. You want me to get you the matching shoes while I'm there? What size you wear?"

"Ha, forget you."

Grinning, "Just trying to save you a trip man." Chino walks to the grill and starts making the omelettes.

"Hey Chino!"

"Hey Winston."

"No seriously, I have a question. Do you know anything about Mayor Payne?"

When I said Mayor Payne's name, Chino looked as if he'd seen a ghost. He turns to me and says, "What about him? I just know the same thing everyone else does. He's a powerful man that does a lot in the community. Why you asking about him?"

"You think he's involved in anything crazy? I met him this weekend. He was at a party with the sheriff, the councilman..."

Edgy, "Aye man, lower your voice. Don't put that man's business out like that. Whatever you did relating to the mayor and any of his people I don't want to know. As a matter of fact, tell no one, and I mean NO ONE. Look Winston, I know you're still somewhat new to the city, but you should know the Mayor and his people are not a game. If you're thinking about being an advisor for him or any of them, DON'T. That's all I'm going to say on that."

Suddenly, I felt like I had seen a ghost. Shocked and in dismay, I sit back in my chair. "Thanks for the warning." Now I'm even more skeptical about everything.

"No problem, just looking out. I know some people that weren't fortunate to receive that warning. Well, knew." He then goes to the grill to get my omelette. "Here ya go.", he says placing it in front of me.

As I'm still trying to comprehend and calculate what he just said, I dive into my omelette. Out the corner of my eye, I notice Chino start to fidget as he's packing up to leave.

"You okay over there Chino?", I ask.

"Yeah, I'm heading out. I'll see you tomorrow." He frantically walks out the back.

Softly, "See ya Chino."

I wonder what that was about? I hope it didn't have anything to do with what I said.

I leave when I finish eating my omelette and make my way to church,

St. John's First Missionary Baptist Church. A small, family oriented church I found when I first moved to Ricoville. Today's service didn't last that long, about an hour and a half, and the sermon was great. The pastor's message was about having faith, keeping it, and putting the work behind it. He started with Hebrews 11:1. It states: "Now faith is the substance of things hoped for, the evidence of things not seen." He went on to say that the Word focused on ensuring that we always have faith no matter the circumstance, situation, or surroundings. To have faith that God will always see us through. We just have to keep the faith and not quit. He then went on to James 2 . To sum it up, it says, "Faith without works is dead." The pastor, Pastor Lee, said, "We must not only have and maintain the faith, but also put forth a great effort behind it in order for anything to happen. God will ALWAYS do his part, we must be sure to do ours as well."

After hearing that message, I started to feel a little more at ease with everything going on. I was still a little nervous, but I had faith I was going to be alright.

As I'm leaving church and walking to my car, I hear a voice yell my name, "Winston!". I turn around and see it's Pastor Lee. "Winston, can you come here for a second? I want to share something with you." I walk over to him behind the church where his car is parked. He's wearing a baby blue suit and light brown shoes, as if it was Easter, and still has beads of sweat dripping from his head full of grey hair. He uses a white towel to wipe it off when I get close to him.

"Wassup pastor? I enjoyed your sermon today, it really hit home for me."

"I'm glad it did. If the Word touches at least one person when I preach, then I've done my job."

"Amen. Well, what is it that you wanted, Pastor?"

"Look Winston, don't panic or show any emotion when I say what I'm about to say please." I suddenly get hot and anxious as little beads of sweat form on my face. "I've been told by a high power to keep a close eye on you. I was directed not to tell you, but since you've been a consistent face in the church, I felt obligated by an even higher being to tell you. Please be safe and watch yourself Winston." Pastor Lee shakes my hand, gets into his car, and leaves. Bewildered, I walk to my car. I get in and just sit there with the AC blasting while I process what Pastor Lee just said. *I'm being watched by a high power? It must be the mayor. This man truly believes he's a god. But what does he want with me? That's the real question. I'm just a decent financial advisor that's bashful when it comes to women.*

My phone starts to ring as I'm thinking. It's Sharon. "You home from church yet? I'm dying to know why I didn't hear from you all Saturday.", she says.

"I'm about to be home in about twenty minutes. I have to leave around four thirty for a dinner meeting though, just to let you know."

"That's fine. It'll be about two when I get there, so that's plenty of time for you to tell me what happened."

"Okay cool. I'll see you there."

"Oaky dokey." I hang up the phone as I pull out of the church parking lot. Twenty minutes later, I arrive at my apartment.

"Hey Winston!" Sharon says greeting me with a hug as I get out of the car. "Ewww, why are you so sweaty?!"

I shrug my shoulders, "It was hot."

"Well that's gross Winston." We walk up the stairs and into my apartment.

"Hey Sharon, you want something to drink?"

"I know where it's at." She walks into the kitchen and opens the refrigerator. I go to my room to change shirts as she grabs a bottle of water. She then heads over to the couch and starts to watch TV.

"Soooooooo what happened Friday night that caused me not to hear from you?", she asks as I walk out of my room.

"Maaaaan…" As I was about to tell her about all of the events that transpired the past couple of days, I started to hear the voices of Chino and Pastor Lee in my head. "Don't tell ANYONE.", I hear Chino say in my left ear. "You're being watched.", I hear Pastor Lee tell me in my right ear. I realize I can't tell Sharon what actually happened. That's not only putting my life in danger, but hers as well. "I got bored and went over to Chino's house. He made me drink some crazy stuff from his wife's island. I was knocked out all night and didn't wake up until a little before I texted you back."

She rolls her eyes. "Woooowwww. You had me anxiously waiting to hear that boring ass shit?! You could've just texted me that."

"I'm sorry, it sounded way better in my head than how it came out." I go and try to give her a hug, but she pushes me away.

"Nah, I don't want that. I need some gas money for that lame ass story."

I chuckle. "You're not being serious."

She extends her hand with her palm up and fingers spread. "As a heart attack. Time is money, honey. And don't act like I stay the next door down. I have to drive a good couple of miles to get here. It's only right."

I laugh and say, "Okay, I got you. Your case is valid." I send her $20 via phone then sit on the couch next to her. We just chill and watch movies until about four o'clock.

My alarm starts to go off. "I guess that's my cue. I'm about to get out of your hair Winston. I'll see you tomorrow at work."

"Alright, I guess I'll start getting ready." We get up and walk to the door. She gives me a hug and leaves.

"Be safe Winston."

"You too."

I close the door and begin to get ready. Anything dealing with Mr. Langston is always business attire. That's just who he is. I shower and put on a black blazer with a white shirt underneath, black slacks, and matching shoes. It's about four thirty when I leave my apartment, and a few minutes past five when I get to the restaurant. I walk in and see Mr. Langston sitting at a table wearing an all white linen suit. He waves me over and I come. As I get closer, I notice that there's someone else sitting at the table as well. The waiter is blocking my view, so I can't tell who it is. When the waiter dispurses, I stop in my steps. It's Mayor Payne. He's dressed in all black. He has on a black collared shirt and black pants. My heart drops.

XV

———

"COME WINSTON, TAKE A SEAT.", MR. LANGSTON TELLS me in his smooth, calm voice as he points to my chair. I'm still in dismay as I'm standing there stunned and motionless from the mayor's unexpected appearance.

"Mr. Williams, I've heard so much about you. Please join us so we can enjoy this fine eatery on this lovely evening.", the Mayor says with a grin.

I take a big gulp and try to maintain a calm demeanor as I pull my chair out and take my seat. "Good evening Mr. Langston, Mayor Payne."

"Ha, I see you already know who this old geezer is Winston.", Mr. Langston jokingly says.

Little did he know I knew a lot more than what I hoped for. With a fake smile I say, "Yes sir. Who doesn't know about Mayor Payne?! He's basically the king of Ricoville, the whole state of Georgia really."

"Oh stop it, you're making me blush.", Mayor Payne pleaded. "I'm just a man trying to make an impact on society that'll behoove the current generation and the generations that will follow. He won't admit it, but Mr. Langston is the real king amongst us. He's been my role model for as long as I can remember. He taught me to always take what I want, don't let nothing or no one stop me." MP and Mr. Langston exchange looks.

"Now that's foolishness!", Mr. Langston teased. "Quit that bashful and humble act. We all know the boastful proud person you really are. You're amongst real people and not your *followers*, or citizens as you call them."

We laugh as the waiter comes with shrimp cocktails. We pass them around and we begin to eat.

"Ricky!" Mayor Payne yells as he signals for our server. "Can you bring us three glasses of our finest wine please."

Mr. Langston butts in. "The kid doesn't drink. Get him a raspberry tea instead. That's correct, isn't it Winston?"

I look at Mr. Langston, "Yes sir, I don't and the tea is fine."

Mayor Payne looks at the both of us. "C'mon, this is a congratulatory dinner Robert! We must celebrate."

"You don't necessarily need liquor to celebrate Frank. Please don't ruin the night trying to enforce your power. Respect the man's decision." Mr. Langston looks at the waiter and continues to say, "Two glasses of wine and one raspberry tea please." The waiter leaves to get the drinks.

There's an awkward silence at the table for a couple of minutes. Everyone was just looking at their phone or the giant TV that's mounted at the bar not too far from us.

"Well, what are we celebrating tonight?!", I blurt out to break the silence.

The mayor gets an astonished expression on his face. "You haven't told him yet Robert?!"

Mr. Langston clears his throat. "No, I haven't. I haven't told anyone yet actually. It's not official. That's really a part of the reason why I invited you to dinner Winston. I didn't expect king jackass to be here though."

The waiter returns with the drinks. Mayor Payne scoffs at Mr. Langston as he rolls his eyes and sips from his glass.

"Well, what's up Mr. Langston?", I ask him.

"I'd actually prefer to talk in private. Just me and you. How about I just swing by your office tomorrow morning."

"That's fine. Just let me know whenever you're on the way. I'll be free."

"Oh please.", the mayor sneered. "I already know what's going on. There's no need to hide anything. I know EVERYTHING."

"Well that's violating the discretion of our client privacy policy." Mr. Langston replied.

Boastfully, "Now you know better than anyone that I know how to work my way through a loophole or two.", the mayor adds as the waiters come to our table with food. "Now, when dining out with the king, you get treated like the king." They bring out a feast. It consisted of: steak, lobster, alfredo, chicken wings, baked potatoes, steamed broccoli, and shrimp. "Just get what you like, the options are endless."

In awe of the food that was brought out, all I could say was, "Thanks MP."

Mr. Langston immediately raises his brow and glares at me. "Winston, where does MP come from?"

Nervously, "Um, it's short for Mayor Payne, right?"

"Now now Robert, settle down. Very few know what it stands for. He probably heard someone call me that and assumed that MP is short for Mayor Payne like most people. It's a common mistake. Relax, don't be such a tightass all the time."

Mr. Langston waves him off and indulges in the food.

For the next fifteen minutes, we just eat and enjoy the ambience of the atmosphere.

When we finish eating, Mayor Payne sits up in his chair and clears his throat as he looks my way. "Winston, is it true what they say about you? That you have a golden thumb. I've heard so many positive things about you, and I want to ask you personally if it's all true. If so, I need to set up a meeting with you ASAP."

I begin to blush, "I mean, I guess you can say that. I just study and follow the algorithms of the market and the specific project. Not too much to it honestly."

"He's also very humble.", Mr. Langston adds.

"Yes he is. Well, I'll be sure to contact you for my appointment. We have a lot of business to discuss." He checks his phone and begins to rise up from the table. "I've enjoyed our dinner tonight. We must do it again Robert, Winston. Don't worry about the bill, it's covered. And Winston, I'll be in touch. You two enjoy the rest of your night, I have mayor stuff to do. Oh, and before I forget. If you Winston, and um, even you too Robert I suppose, would like to eat here for Valentine's Day just let me know and I'll take care of that bill too."

"Thanks Mayor Payne, I really appreciate that."

"You're welcome Winston. And you too Robert, your eyes say enough." He shakes our hands then exits the restaurant as he makes a phone call.

"He's quite the character, isn't he.", Mr. Langston chortled.

"Yeah, he's definitely one of a kind. That dinner might come in handy though.", I added.

"Don't trust it Winston, he always wants things in return....I had no clue he'd be here. He sat down probably five minutes before you walked in. He owns the place so I guess he just chose tonight to be the night to pop in and check on things."

That definitely wasn't a coincidence. I still don't know exactly what he wants, but I'm sure I'm about to find out soon. He's making it known that he's watching me. The question that still remains though, is why?

"Well Mr. Langston, a free meal of this caliber is always nice."

We both chuckle. "In all seriousness Winston, I want you to be careful in your dealings with him. Like I said earlier, he's VERY powerful. He has his hands in just about everything. We go way back. I know things about him that most don't. He's a great guy, but he's controlled by money and power. It's not my business to announce his to the world, so just take heed to what I'm saying. Be careful."

This is the third time I'm hearing this. Who I once thought was just a great, influential, and positive figure for the community has now been painted to be the exact opposite of that.

"So what am I supposed to do when he tries to schedule a meeting?"

"Act as you normally would. I'm just suggesting you move with caution when dealing with him. That is all. Are you ready to leave? I told my wife I wouldn't be more than two hours."

"Still whipped I see.", I joked.

"Hey now! Watch your mouth son. You can't whip a wild stallion."

We laugh as we get up from our table and walk outside to his car.

"Be safe Winston, and thanks for coming. I'll call you tomorrow when I'm heading to your office." He gets in his car, closes the door, and starts it.

"Thanks for having me Mr. Langston. Have a good night and I'll see you tomorrow."

"You too." He drives off. I then head to my car, get in, and drive home. I arrive at my apartment at about seven-thirty. I walk in, change clothes, and relax on my couch. I lay down and begin watching a movie. Not too long after the movie starts, I get a text from Chino: "Don't forget about tomorrow. She'll be here between eight thirty and nine."

XVI

I HAD COMPLETELY FORGOTTEN ABOUT THAT. I'M SORRY, *but Mr. Langston will have to wait. Tomorrow is going to be the day my melanin angel will finally be mine.* I text back: "Tomorrow is show time my boy."

Chino replies, "Yup, I hope you come wearing your track shoes."

I send back a laughing emoji and the conversation ends. As I attempt to go back to watching my movie, all of my focus and thoughts shift towards Natilie. *She's beautiful, smart, and soon to be mine.* All of the excitement and anxiousness I had when I first saw her reentered my mind. *Her voice, her hair, her physique, her demeanor. Everything about her is so enticing, so perfect. I know people say nobody or nothing is perfect, but Natalie is perfect in my eyes. I'm convinced she's a melanin angel sent straight from the heavens, and I refuse to let anything stop me from claiming my blessing.* I spent the rest of the night preparing for my big day. First, I took out the suit I was going to wear and pressed over it. I chose to wear my navy blue blazer and slacks with a white shirt and red tie. I also took out and shined my dark brown, snake skin shoes. I then memorized what I was going to say, and exactly how I planned on saying it. I was ready. I wasn't up much longer after I prepared everything. I fell asleep around eleven.

BEEP, BEEP, BEEP

My alarm goes off at seven thirty. I'm still a little tired when I wake up, so I just snooze it, or so I thought. Instead of hitting the snooze option on my phone, I mistakenly hit cancel. Not realizing the blunder I just made, I go back to sleep.

When I finally wake up, I roll over to check my phone. I'm expecting it to be seven forty-five, give or take a few minutes, but instead, it's nine o'seven. I'm dumbfounded, furious, heartbroken, and disappointed, just to name a few of the many emotions I was feeling.

"Stupid! Stupid! Stupid! How could I be so stupid?! I should've just woken up and gotten right in the shower.", I angrily shout.

Still hoping there's a chance, I quickly hop out of the bed and get ready. As I reach for my clothes, I see they somehow fell off of the hanger last night and onto the floor. I tried to iron them, but due to the time, I wasn't able to knock out all of the wrinkles and press it cleanly. It took me about five minutes to get ready. When I finished, I bolted out of my apartment with my clothes halfway ironed, teeth partially brushed, and face looking a mess. I got in my car and went straight to The Spot. At this point, I'm not caring about any stop signs, traffic lights, construction sites, or even cops. The only thing on my mind is getting to Natalie before she leaves. *I can't miss this chance, I can't miss this chance.*

I finally get there and notice that the same regular cars are parked outside of The Spot. *Maybe she took a bus or something today.* I burst through the doors and look around for Natalie.

"You're a little too late playa. She just left out not too long ago because she had a flight to catch. Before she left, she told me that her job is moving her to Florida for a better opportunity. I'm sorry man. I guess it wasn't meant."

Completely perturbed and heartbroken, I just walk to the counter and sink in my chair.

"Maybe if you had on your running shoes you would've caught her.", Chino adds.

Agitated, I say, "I'm not in the mood Chino."

"My bad, just trying to lighten the mood man. I know how much she meant to you. I feel for you, I really do. I'll just give you some space." Chino walks away and begins to tend to customers. Meanwhile, I'm sitting there numb. I can't move, my appetite is gone, and my mouth feels like it's full of cotton. I drop my head, close my eyes, take a deep breath, and pound the table in frustration.

Chino rushes back over. "Woah, woah, Winston! Relax! There's plenty of fish in the sea man. Now that I think about it, they're actually having a little event for singles at my church tomorrow night. You can come and I'll show you around and introduce you to everyone. It'll help you get your mind off of her."

I sigh, "Thanks, but no thanks Chino. Natalie was different. I don't know exactly how, but I just know she was different man. Plus, all the women at your church either smell like fish and perfume, look crazy, are crazy, or all three. I'm good on alllll that Chino."

He laughs. "You trippin young buck. You're missing out on some top quality, good ole southern women."

"Yeah, I've already seen them...and smelled them. I'll pass."

He smirks, "Whatever, stay lonely then. I tried." A customer calls Chino and he walks off, leaving me to be.

Time progresses and I'm still depressed and disheartened. I check my phone and decide it's time to head to work.

"See you tomorrow Chino!", I say as I begin to leave. He waves back and I continue walking.

As I'm walking out I hear, "Keep your head up Winston, we've all felt your pain before. You just need to go home, get yourself a beer, then go down to the strip club tonight. You'll be just fine." I turn to see who it is. It's my old high school principal Mr. Floyd.

Where the hell did he come from?! I just give him a thumbs up and continue to walk to my car.

As I'm about to open my door, I hear another voice. "He's right Winnie. Life's all about learning from your past situations and moving on from it. Don't take it as a loss, take it as a lesson for next time."

Only one person calls me that. I turn and I see my mother walking towards me. I'm astonished.

What the hell is going on here?! This is crazy! Who am I going to see next, Jesus? As I go give my mother a hug, I trip, fall, and bump my head. When I finally wake up, it's seven-thirty and my alarm is going off.

XVII

———

WHEN I WOKE UP THIS TIME, I WOKE UP WITH A SENSE of urgency and immediately hopped in the shower when my alarm went off. Not even thinking about hitting snooze or laying around in my bed. I learned from the mistake I made in my dream, and didn't waste any time getting up and getting ready. The opportunity to turn my yearning fantasy into my reality wasn't about to slip out of my hands this time.

It's eight o'three when I finish getting dressed. I'm ready to go. My teeth are brushed, suit is pressed, shoes shined, and my plan is off and underway. I look in the mirror before I leave and I'm confident. I walk out into the bright, sunny day, and down the stairs to my car. As I'm getting ready to pull off, I get a text from Chino. I look at my phone and it says, "She came in a little early today. She just walked in. And don't forget your running shoes.".

As soon as I read that, I suddenly became overwhelmed with anxiety and nervousness. My heart starts to pound in my chest. It's thumping as if someone was playing a bass drum inside of me. My body begins to get hot. I start to feel sweat percolate through my forehead and armpits. My hands start to shake. All of the confidence I just had goes out the window. *It's finally happening. I can't believe the moment I've been longing for all this time is finally here.* I start to hyperventilate. I'm having a panic attack. *What if she doesn't like me? What if she doesn't even give me the time of day? What if she's uninterested? What if I freeze again?* I turn up the AC in my car and try to relax. *Just breathe Winston, just breathe. You'll be fine.* I begin to slowly calm down. *She's just a woman. Your normal, every day woman. You're not a shy guy anymore. You're a king.* I take a couple of deep breaths, then I return to my normal state. I had never done this before. I'd never done it before a game when I played sports, before an important meeting, and definitely not before approaching a woman. It was surreal. Natalie had a hold on me that I couldn't escape from. No matter how hard I tried to fight it, I would still be sprung solely off of her existence.

I gather myself and begin to make my way to The Spot. As I get closer, I begin to practice what I'm going to say when I approach her. "Hey beautiful, how you doing today? My name's Winston, what's yours? Nah, that's basic. I think I'll just try to make her laugh with something corny. Hey beautiful, I have a question I just have to ask you! Did it hurt when you fell from heaven? Because I feel like I'm in the presence of an angel. Yeah, that's the one for sure." I repeat this again and again until I get to The Spot. And when I finally got there, I did it again about five or six more times before I got another text from Chino. "Where you at? She's waiting for you." At that moment, all of the nervousness I just got rid of came right back around as if it was a boomerang. *Relax Winston, just be cool. You've spent a week preparing for this moment, you got it.* I start inhaling and exhaling slowly. I look at my phone, it's eight thirty-six. I sit back in my seat, take a deep breath, then exhale. *I'm ready.* I put a mint in my mouth, spray my favorite cologne, and start making my way to the door. I walk in and I'm stopped in my tracks. There she is, my melanin angel. She's sitting at the counter talking to Chino so she doesn't see me walk in. She's wearing an elegant, bold, yellow dress that compliments and highlights her curvaceous physique, as if it was specifically handcrafted just for her. She was even wearing the yellow heels to match. Her curly long hair was perfectly placed and aligned over her shoulders. It could've been the light shining from the window by her, but from where I was standing, she was glowing. Her golden brown skin was shining from head to toe, as if someone took a brush and painted her body with baby oil. I just stood there and admired her. There she was, glowing like the melanin angel in which she is. After standing there for a few seconds, Chino waves to me to come over. Natalie turns around and smiles at me. I smile back. I walk up and say, "Wassup, Chino?" I then reach out my hand to grab Natalie's, look her in her alluring, light brown eyes, then say, "Good morning beautiful, my name is Winston."

XVIII

———

S HE STARTS TO BLUSH. I'M LOOKING AT HER SMILE AND
it's even more radiant and exquisite up close. Still holding my
hand, with a soft, gentle voice she says, "Good morning Mr.
Winston. My name's Natalie. It's nice to finally meet the
successful financial advisor that Unc has been talking about." She
lets go of my hand as I take a seat by her at the counter. "He didn't
mention how much of a looker you were though."

I smile and nod my head, but on the inside I was confused. *A
looker?! I've never heard that before. Is that her nice way of calling me
ugly?*

"I'll just leave you two to be.", Chino says as he starts to walk away.

"Wait Chino.", I say before I look at Natalie. "Have you eaten yet?"

She looks at me then says, "No, I actually haven't."

"Well, are you hungry?"

"I could eat."

"Okay, well let me treat you. Chino, let me get two Rico
specials please, and two cups of OJ."

"Thanks Winston, but what's a Rico special?"

"Just trust me, you'll enjoy it."

She smiles. "Ok, I'll trust you. This is your one chance to prove yourself."

I laugh then look at Chino. "Alright Chino, don't let me down. I need this one to be good."

Chino schoffs then says, "You must've forgot who you was talking to son. Like this ain't my establishment. When was the last time something came out of that kitchen that WASN'T top tier?! Oh wait, I'll tell you, NEVER! Boy I tell ya. Y'all give me a second, I'll be back with y'all stank ass orange juice.". He storms off away to put in our order and get our drinks.

"C'mon, don't be so sensitive, Chino. I didn't mean it like that.", I say as me and Natalie share a laugh.

Astounded, "I see he takes his food seriously."

"Yeah, his food is his soft spot, but that's why it's always packed in here."

As I'm sitting next to her, I'm still in awe. I was still trying to comprehend what was happening as I sat there, amazed and mesmerized at how beautiful she is. I couldn't believe I had finally gotten the chance to sit next to and talk to her, my melanin angel. After seeing her a week ago and freezing, then missing my chance with her again a few nights later at the Wardogs game, now, I was finally going to make things right. This felt RIGHT. I wasn't nervous like I thought I'd be. The longer I sat by her, the more comfortable I got.

I breathe, sit up in my seat, and say, "So, um, where you from Natalie? I don't think I've seen you around here before. I'm sure I would remember seeing a face as beautiful as yours."

That was smooth. Even though I was lying, I'd never tell her we had seen each other a week ago here and I immediately fell in love with her. Or that she's been on my mind ever since that moment. Or the real reason I didn't go approach her at the game was because I thought that she was out of my league.

She blushes. "Aawww, thank you. You're too sweet." *Not exactly the response I wanted, but I'll take it.* "I'm from North Carolina. I stayed home and went to college there too. When I graduated, I stayed home for a while before I finally left and moved here for my job. I haven't been here that long, so that's probably why you haven't seen me around. I'm still trying to move in and get situated."

"Oh, well yeah that would explain it. I hope I can help make your transition to the new area a little easier for you."

"We'll see. Call me crazy, but I'm getting this weird deja vu feeling like I've seen you before. Were you at a Wardogs game sometime last week? I went there with a couple of friends, but I left a little early because one had a baby daddy that felt like being aggy."

I gasp under my breath. *There's no way she spotted me. Right? Yeah, relax Winston. I mean, you were staring at her the entire night, you definitely would've noticed if she did.* I look at her and say, "Nah, after work I usually just go straight home and watch a movie or two before I go to sleep. I have been told by a few people that I have a familiar face, whatever that means."

"I guess, maybe I'm just tripping."

"Naaah, I'm definitely the one that's tripping Natalie."

She gets a confused look on her face as she chuckles a little bit, "What do you mean?"

"I'm just saying that earlier, when I first walked in I tripped…...and fell for you at first sight." I chortled trying to avoid showing the embarrassment I felt after saying that. *That sounded way better in my head.*

She laughs, "I know you did not just say that corny ass line. That sounds like something out of a romance novel. I'll admit it was cute though."

We both laugh as Chino comes back with our orange juice. "Here y'all go. The food should be ready in about five to ten minutes."

As he's placing the drinks down, Natalie says to me, "So is it really true?" Puzzled, I lean in closer to listen to what she has to say. "Chino told me you were an Olympic track star before you hurt yourself. Said you used to take off faster than anyone he's ever seen."

I look at Chino and give him a sarcastic stare as he walks away laughing.

"What else did he say?"

She laughs and says, "Nothing, it was just a joke. He told me to tell you that before you came in here. What does it mean?"

"Nothing, nothing. You know how he is. Always making terrible jokes."

"Mmmhhmmm, if you say so Mr. Winston." She checks her phone because she just got a text. After she reads it, her mood changes. She blows out a breath of frustration then gathers herself. "Well Winston, you know a little about me, so tell me something about you. Where are you from?"

"You ok Natalie?"

"Yeah, it's just aggravating work stuff, nothing serious. I'm sure you can relate. So, where you from?"

"Definitely understand that, and I'm from Normans. It's a small city in south Georgia. About two and a half hours from here. I went to college in Florida then moved here when I graduated in hopes of getting a good job. Things didn't go as planned to start, but eventually things worked out. And I met Chino in the process."

On cue, Chino comes with the food. "Yup, he came here a scared little boy looking for guidance, then once I started mentoring him, he turned into who he is now.", he says as he delivers two plates full of shredded hash browns, scrambled eggs, cheese, peppers, onions, spinach, and bacon topped off with his special garlic sauce. "Here, I hope everything will hold up to, if not go above and beyond, your standards my good sir.", he sarcastically says.

"I'm sure everything is superb."

Natalie immediately takes a bite out of her food. "Oh my gosh Unc! Why have you never recommended this to me?! This is amazing."

Chino starts grinning. "Well thank you Natalie, I'm glad SOMEBODY appreciates our food. Y'all let me know if you need anything.", he says as he walks to the kitchen.

"I guess I was right to trust you after all Mr. Winston.", Natalie says as she smiles at me.

"See, you can trust me."

Still smiling, she asks, "So you're good at what you do? Making money and what not?"

"Eeeh, some people think I'm great at what I do, but in my eyes it's really simple and banal."

"It's interesting to me. I always wanted to learn about markets and investing and stuff like that, but I could never find the right person to teach me how it works."

"Well, I'm actually offering a class. That is, if you're interested." She smirks.

As Natalie was fixing her mouth to reply, my phone starts to ring. I look and it's Mr. Langston. "Excuse me Natalie, I have to answer this." I say as I get up and walk outside to answer the phone.

"Good morning Mr. Langston. You on the way to my office?"

"Good morning Winston, and yes sir. I'll be there in about ten minutes."

"Okay, I'll see you then." I hang up the phone. Now is the moment of truth. *Do I ask for her number, or wait until who knows when to see her again? Maybe I should just go ahead and ask her out for Friday? Is it too soon?*

As I'm walking back to my seat, I catch Chino and tell him to bring me a to go box. Then, I proceed to take my seat next to Natalie as she finishes her food.

"Work?", she asks.

"Yeah, I gotta go actually. I have a meeting with a big client."

"Oh ok, well before you go, I want you to get my contact information."

I light up with glee. I couldn't believe she was the one initiating the number exchange. I was ecstatic, but also mind blown.

I should definitely ask her out now.

Chino walks back with my to go container as Natalie is in her chair going through her purse. "You about to head out now?", he asks.

As I pack up my food, I say, "Yeah, I have a meeting."

"I thought this was the meeting.", he jokingly says.

I suck my teeth. I then take my phone out of my pocket so I can put Natalie's number in it.

I go to hand her my phone and she says, "Found it! Here, I usually check my voicemails and emails before and after each work day." Out of her purse, she hands me a business card with her name, email, and work phone number on it. I felt...actually, I didn't know how I felt. I'm happy that I have a way of contacting her, yet, I was still disappointed that it wasn't her cell phone number.

I look at Chino and he's trying his hardest not to laugh. He looks at me then walks off to the back.

"I'd like to follow up on that class. I have some business questions I'd like to discuss, and from what Chino's told me, you're the man for the job."

Now I feel even more deceived. Did we actually click, or was she just trying to charm me to get what she wanted? Internally, I was in shambles.

XIX

———

W AS IT MY FAULT FOR HAVING MY EXPECTATIONS
so high? Was it my fault for believing things could've been
more than what they were? Was it my fault for placing her on such
a high pedestal? I didn't know the answers to those questions.
What I knew for sure, was that I was hurt. I felt like I played
myself. What I thought was going to be a good first date, actually
became an inquisition for a business meeting.

I hesitate at first, but I take her card. I read it, and in big bold
words it says, "Natalie Graves: Real Estate and Insurance Agent".
I'm still bewildered at the fact that she's giving me a card and not
her actual cell phone number. *I know she felt the connection, or at
least what I thought was a connection.*

She then says, "I'm available Monday thru Friday from eleven
in the morning to five in the evening. Please don't hesitate to leave
an email or voicemail if I don't answer your call. I'm looking
forward to hearing from you."

All I can do is laugh a little under my breath. "I'll see you
tomorrow Chino!", I yell out as he waves from the back still holding

in his laugh. I shake Natalie's hand and say, "I'll see you around." I then exit the Spot and get in my car. *I can't believe I played myself! I can't believe I waited a week to get friend zoned. Scratch that, associate zoned. I can't remember the last time I felt like this. I'm done chasing her.* I felt as if my heart was snatched right out of my body and beaten with a baseball bat. I was done with Natalie. I took it as a sign that it just wasn't meant to be. I remember what my mother told me in my dream. I didn't take it as a loss, but as a lesson.

As I'm pulling out of The Spot, I take a glimpse inside. Natalie's looking at her phone with a dejected expression on her face. I then turn up the music in my car and drive off.

It's about nine thirty when I pull into the parking lot at work. I didn't care about being late, or anything at that point.

I park my car then head to the office. As I'm walking in, I see Mr. Langston talking to Sharon. He's wearing a tan suit and Sharon's wearing a blue blouse with her black skirt. *What could they be talking about? Sharon's probably searching for a sugar daddy now that she's single.*

I walk up and greet Mr. Langston with a handshake. Intruding in their conversation, I say, "Good morning Mr. Langston, great to see you. And thanks again for dinner….."

As I was in mid sentence, Sharon sassisly blurts out, "Well hello and good morning to you too Winston, damn!"

I smile and laugh, "Hey Sharon, good morning. You look nice today."

"Yeah, yeah, I'll see you later Mr. Langston."

"He's married! He ain't got time to be playing sugar daddy with you.", I say as we walk away.

"You just jealous.", Sharon jokingly says as she sticks out her tongue.

We laugh as we walk into my office and take a seat.

"And before I forget again, thanks for the tickets the other day. I guess all that talking with the mayor made it slip my mind."

"No problem Winston, it was a pleasure having you at dinner and I'm glad you enjoyed the tickets. I hope Helda took great care of you."

"Yeah, she was great. She came to be really handy."

"That's good, I told her to take good care of you."

"Yes sir, that she did." There's a brief pause in our conversation, then I clear my throat to say, "Well, what is it that you wanted to talk about Mr. Langston?"

"It's actually what we were just talking about Winston."

In shock and disbelief I say, "Helda?!"

He laughs, "No you jive turkey. The Wardogs. I'm considering becoming a majority owner. Everything is in place, I just wanted to check with my advisor first."

"What all comes with being a majority owner?"

"I already forwarded you an email with the logistics, but to sum it up, I'll have majority say in everything, like contracts and deals. I actually played a big part in the North Carolina Cougars trade that got James Love to the Wardogs. It was a little under the table, so that's why not many people know about it. Oh, and I'll have season skybox seats."

Ecstatically, "You should've led with the season skybox seats! I'm sold already. And knowing you, I'm sure everything is in order, but I'll look over it later and get back to you ASAP."

"Thanks Winston."

"No problem Mr. Langston. Is that all?"

"No actually, I wanted to know if the mayor has gotten in touch with you recently. He told me he would be reaching out."

The mayor was starting to become an annoying gnat. I just kept hearing him buzz everywhere. I couldn't stop it no matter where I went.

"He hasn't yet, but I'll be looking for him."

"Let me know when he does and what he says."

Puzzled, "Okay."

KNOCK, KNOCK

It's Mr. Jacobs. He pokes his head in and says, "Morning Winston." He then spots Mr. Langston and says, "Hey, I thought I heard you in here. How you doing Robert?"

"Hey Francis, I'm good. Just came by to have a little talk with my financial advisor. His name is starting to become quite popular in the area. ", Mr. Langston says.

"Yeah he has. His rise to the top was very expeditious and impressive I must say."

"Yes sir, I'm still waiting for my thank you card and paycheck in the mail for giving you this gem."

Mr. Jacobs grins, "Oooh I sent that stuff a while ago. It must've gotten lost in the mail. You know how that stuff is."

Mr. Langston sits back in his seat, rolls his eyes, then sarcastically says, "Yeah, ok. I guess your next loan is going to get lost in the mail as well Francis."

He chortles, "Well that's a talk for another day Mr. Langston." He then shifts his attention towards me. "I actually came in to talk to you Winston."

Intrigued, I sit up in my seat. "What's up Mr. Jacobs?"

"The mayor's people came by looking for you earlier. They stopped by my office and told me he'll be calling at one. I've been trying to work with the mayor for years! I'm so excited. This is a big fish Winston!"

"I hear you boss."

Mr. Jacobs shakes our hands. "You guys have a good day. I have some calls to make." He walks out of my office.

Mr. Langston drops his head as his face turns pale. Under his breath he says, "And so it begins."

XX

———

I LET OUT A DEEP BREATH AFTER HEARING WHAT MR. Jacobs had said. I knew this moment was inevitable, but I still didn't want it to happen. *I get a cold chill that slowly runs up my spine whenever someone just mentions the mayor. Who knows what actually working with him will do. I was about to lose it when I was sitting across the table from him at dinner the other night. And that was at a public place with Mr. Langston there. I know I'll start to panic if I'm with him one on one. I wasn't nervous when I was at his house alone, but then again, I was partially intoxicated and hungover.*

"Winston, Winston.", Mr. Langtson says as he tries to get my attention after I've zoned out. "Winston, are you ok?"

Snapping back and stuttering, "Y-yes sir. Just was thinking about some stuff, that's all. What's up?"

"I'm staying with you until one. He won't tell me exactly what he needs with you, but I'm certain it's something you don't want to be involved with. Something I don't want you involved with."

I crack a smile then say, "I appreciate your concern Mr. Langston, but I'm sure I can handle a phone call. He's not some cartoon that has the ability to reach through the phone or anything like that. I'll be alright."

Mr. Langston bows his head then lowers it into his hands as if he was praying. "Winston, just listen to me. You know, me and my wife weren't able to have kids."

I sit up in my chair because I know he's about to say something serious. "Yes sir, you've told me."

He clears his throat. "Well, I never told you why." He then sits up in his chair and places his arms on my desk. "I'm sterile. After trying to have kids for years, we found out I suffer from azoospermia. It means that I have semen, but not any sperm. Only 1% of men have it. Preposterous, right? The doctors don't know specifically what caused it, but yeah, azoospermia. I told my wife I wouldn't mind getting a sperm donor or even adopting, but she said if that kid didn't have my DNA she didn't want it. I mean I respected her decision, but that still left me with an unfillable void. It left me without someone to carry on my last name. To not be able to fulfill my life's ultimate dream of having a family because I can't produce is heartbreaking." There's about a ten second silence as he tries to hold back his tears. "Winston, we've only known each other for a few months, but honestly, it's felt like years. The way you carry yourself, not just as a man, but as a black man, is very admirable. You're very intelligent, well mannered, charismatic, and even very handsome I must say. After talking to you and getting to know you when I was in the store looking for a gift for my wife that day, I just didn't see a store associate, I saw myself. That's why I recommended you for this job. I had to do some unspeakable things to get to where I'm at today. Nobody ever cut me a break, I started from under the bottom and had to crawl my way to the top. I carried so much weight on my back. I noticed your potential and didn't want that for you. I'm pretty sure you can guess what I'm trying to say. Winston, you're like a son to me, I refuse to let anyone or anything take that away." A tear falls from his face.

I choke up a little bit too. "Believe it or not, you've always been like a father to me Mr. Langston. It was always just me and my mom when I was growing up. My pops left us before I was born. She had to work two, sometimes three, jobs just to keep the lights on. Once I turned thirteen, I didn't think twice about getting a job to help her out. Long story short, my first job was working at one of your restaurant chains in Normans. You might not remember this, but I do. You came in wearing all black everything on a hot, summer day. You had on an all black suit, black shoes, black belt, and you were even carrying a black briefcase. The only thing that wasn't black, was a bold gold tie that you wore. You said the reason you wore it was to let everyone know that light will always shine in the darkness. To give everyone around you hope. Give them a sense of great belief in themselves. After you finished your speech, you ordered something to eat. I'll never forget this. You came to the register, my register, and ordered one cheeseburger. Your total came out to be $1.05. You paid with a one hundred dollar bill and a nickel. You said, 'Let this change be your first deposit on a greater life. Don't spend it all in one place. As a matter of fact, don't spend it at all. Invest it and make you some more money. You just might be rich as me one day.', then you walked away to handle your business. Ever since that moment, I became intrigued with business and making money. That was also the moment you became my role model. Seeing your face on billboards, in commercials, on tv shows, just made me hungrier to study and take care of my business. When I saw you walk in the store that day a few months ago, I paid my coworker $50 to switch zones with me. We started talking and the rest was history. So even though you didn't produce me, I still feel like you raised me. You were always that father figure I looked up to."

He takes a deep breath and gives me a hug. "I'm about to go run some errands. I'll be back at one.", Mr. Langston says as he gets up wiping tears from his eyes. "I'll see you later Winston." I wave goodbye as he walks out of my office.

I check the time and it's only ten thirty. I reach in my pocket to pull out my phone and Natalie's card falls out. The heart to heart I just had with Mr. Langston made me forget all about her and how foolish she made me feel.

Just rip it up Winston. I start to tear it, then I stop. *But at the same time, I know I'm not crazy. The way she smiled at me, looked at me, even the way she shook my hand, I can tell she's interested in being more than just business partners, or whatever she claims she wants. Maybe I'll give her a call and we can go out to lunch or something. Who knows?*

I check my phone and see I have ten texts from Chino. *Maybe Natalie said something about me when I left. Maybe she confessed her real feelings.*

I open my phone, and it's ten messages of laughing emojis. Not in the mood, I roll my eyes, and send him the middle finger emoji.

He then texts back, "You wouldn't believe what she said when you left playa."

Excited and anxious, I quickly reply, "What?!"

"Guess", he responded

"Just tell me man, stop playing."

"Do you really want to know?"

I start to get agitated, "Yeah!!"

"I'm just playing, she ain't say nothing." I slam my phone on the desk.

KNOCK, KNOCK.

It's Sharon. "You okay Winston? It looks like you and Mr. Langston had a bad break up. He walks out wiping tears from his face, and now you in here trying to slam your phone through your desk. Y'all straight??"

I laugh, "We're good. It's just a lot going on right now."

"Okay, cause I don't want to hurt nobody over my sugar daddy." We both laugh. "Well do you want to go get lunch? Since you have so much going on, you can provide me with some tea. I also have to tell you about mystery man."

"So the time is right now, huh? Y'all back together?"

"Long story, but to eliminate the suspense, yes." I just shake my head at her. "It's a long story Winston. And you will never guess who it is either. I'll bet you lunch you won't guess."

"Stop playing and tell me.".

"Ugh, you're no fun. Okay, it's..." As she is about to tell me who her mystery man was, Mr. Jacobs calls her into his office.

XXI

———

THE TIME WAS CLOSE TO ELEVEN WHEN SHE WENT IN, and now it's approaching twelve. *She's taking too long, I'm hungry.* I leave to go to a burger joint up the street. I get there, and choose to dine in. I get my food then take my seat at a secluded booth in a corner. I wanted to be alone. I needed space to clear my head and prepare myself for anything that the mayor was going to say. Nobody ever tells me specifically what's bad about him, only that he's trouble, dangerous, and that I should stay away from him. Although I'm a little scared and nervous to work with him, there's a small piece of me that thinks he's genuinely a good person. After all, great people do bad things sometimes.

As I'm eating, I notice a poster of the mayor on the window across from me. It's from his Feed My People project that focuses on feeding the homeless and low income families. He's wearing an all white suit standing on a stage in front of a crowd of people. He has a loaf of bread in his left hand and a fish in the other. I laugh. *He really believes he's a god.* I believe the mayor's intentions are good, but his approach may be a little deranged.

As I'm in the middle of my lunch, Sharon texts me. "Wooow you left me?"

I reply, "It's 12:30, I wasn't waiting an hour and a half for you."

"Lol I know. I'm just playing. Mr. Jacobs wanted me to review all the files on the mayor. He's really amped about getting him as a client, he's doing the most right now"

"Guess it's a lot riding on me, huh?"

"You'll be fine, you always come through."

"Thanks, it means a lot."

"No problem :)"

"You want me to bring you some food back?"

"Nah, I'm good. Mystery man had some food delivered for me."

"Ok, I'll be back soon."

"Okay."

I finish my food then return to my office. It's twelve fifty when I get off of the elevator. I walk in and see there's a giant bouquet of roses on Sharon's desk with three red heart shaped balloons tied to them.

"This the doing of the mystery man?", I ask as I approach her desk.

With a huge smile on her face, "Yup, he's the best. I can't wait to see what he does Friday."

"Friday? Oh, right, it's Valentine's Day. Well, I'm glad you're happy Sharon."

Jokingly, "Thanks Winston. Maybe one day you'll find someone to replace me."

I laugh at her then sarcastically say, "Oh how will I ever manage to do that? Hopefully one day I'll be able to find somebody to take me out of my misery.", and walk away.

As I take my seat in my office, Mr. Langston walks in and shuts the door behind him. "Are you ready?", he asks.

It's not like I had a choice. The mayor is unavoidable.

"Yes sir.", I respond.

My phone begins to ring. It's one on the dot. I look at Mr. Langston as he looks at me. "Put it on speaker.", he says as I answer the phone.

"Hello?", I nervously say.

"Hello, Winston! Good afternoon, how are you?", the mayor says with enthusiasm.

"I'm doing well sir, and yourself?"

"That's good and I'm doing fine, can't complain. Now look, I'm not going to keep you long. Would you mind stopping by my house tomorrow night around seven? I prefer to talk business in person and in the comforts of my home. Is that okay with you? I just wanted to personally call you to make sure you got the message."

"That's fine. I'm available."

"Good, it won't be noisy or chaotic like it was during your last visit. Do you remember where I live or do you need the address again?"

I take a big gulp as Mr. Langston gives me an intense, aggressive glare. "Yes sir, I remember."

"Okay, I'll see you tomorrow at seven. Have a good one."

"You too." We hang up the phone.

"You went to his house and didn't tell me?!?!", Mr. Langston rages, "What were you doing there, were you there alone, are you okay?"

I take a deep breath and think. *Should I ignore all the warnings and tell Mr. Langston everything that happened? I mean, he is the one trying to protect me. If I tell him, he might be able to help escape all this.*

I exhale and tell Mr. Langston everything that happened. From Mike calling me that Friday night to the $1,000 that sheriff Brooks gave me.

"Then he just handed it to me, walked to his car, and left."

Appalled and still trying to comprehend what he just heard, Mr. Langston just sits there. "You okay sir?", I ask him.

Still stunned, he just stares off into space.

"Mr. Langston, you with me?!", I say as I snap my fingers trying to get his attention.

"I-I'm here."

"Well, are you okay?"

"You already know too much Winston. Sheriff Brooks, Judge Taylor, and Councilman Ingram are all counterparts working for the mayor. The Sheriff is the muscle, Judge Taylor is in charge of the logistics, and the councilman is just a pretty face they use for events and publicity. They are ruthless people that will do anything to get what they want, money."

Flummoxed, I say, "How do you know all of this Mr. Langston?"

He sits up in his chair and looks me dead in my eyes, "I used to be a part of it." I'm blown away. "Like I told you earlier, I came from the very bottom and had to do some things that I'm not proud of to get to where I am today. I'm not going to get into details right now, but I know as well as anybody what the mayor really does behind the scenes."

How can you claim you want to protect me, but keep me from the truth?

"I thought I could trust you.", I tell Mr. Langston.

"What are you talking about Winston?"

I raise my voice and say, "You're being a hypocrite! How can you be bad mouthing the mayor and telling me to stay away from him when you're just as guilty of doing everything he's doing, if not more?"

He scoffs, "I'm a changed man Winston. Life is about growth and that's what I did. I've grown immensely mentally and spiritually since then. I'm nowhere close to being the same person I was back then. That was years ago. And as much as I want to completely erase my ties with the mayor, I can't! We're connected for the rest of our lives because of the things we've done. I'm trying to help you avoid experiencing anything like this Winston. Just listen to me."

Frustrated, "You have to tell me everything first. And I mean EVERYTHING. I've already been dragged into all this no matter how much you want to deny it. Tell me who the mayor really is!"

This causes a brief pause in our conversation. Mr. Langston looks down at the floor, then looks up at me. "Look Winston, what I'm about to tell you, you must never repeat. You understand?"

"Yes sir, I understand you."

He gets up to close the blinds on my window then sits back down. "About thirty years ago, before Ricoville became the great and powerful city that it is now, it was a very rural area. Believe it or not, me and the mayor used to be deep in the drug game when we were younger. We were yin and yang. I had his back and he had mine. We used to sell everything from marijuana to crack cocaine. We were "trap stars" as the kids say. Then one day, our connect introduced us to some Guatemalans. When me and the mayor met with them, we told them that we wanted more. So, they gave it to us. Things were smooth for about a month. Then the mayor got greedy, we got greedy. We double crossed our connect and the Guatemalans. We started killing our connect's people and blaming it on the Guatemalans, and killing the Guatemalans and blaming it on our connect. Eventually, they started taking each other out. Being the "informants" blanketed us with immunity so nobody touched us. We outsmarted them all. That led to both sides getting weak. Weak enough that we could take control of each side and combine them to all work for us. This started the emergence of the empire known as Ricoville. All the money we made, we invested it. We didn't spend it on cars, houses, clothes or things like that, we saved it. Then once we reached a specific number, we bought fields to grow crops and cannabis, buildings that turned into restaurants or clubs that we used to distribute our goods, and we were able to put high officials on our payroll. The business part was all me, and the mayor handled the other stuff. We ran a smooth operation until we had a misunderstanding one day. Ever since I left him, his business hasn't been able to sustain its success. It's actually started to disintegrate through the years and that's probably why he needs you. He's heard about your talent in the business world and wants to utilize it. He's spilled a lot of blood to get to where he is, and I'm sure he'll do the same to stay there. That's why I'm so cautious. I don't want anything to happen to you Winston."

"Wow.", the only thing I could say. It was a lot to take in. Just not about the mayor, but Mr. Langston. *Who would've known that my role model, my father figure, was the mastermind behind a billion dollar underground operation.*

Mr. Langston checks his phone then says, "I have some business to handle at one of my buildings. If you have any other questions, just call me."

"Yes sir, I will." He shakes my hand then walks out of my office. I get up to open my blinds back then sit back down. Still in shock, I check my emails to take my mind off of things and relax. Then, Mr. Jacobs walks in.

XXII

———

"SOOOOO, IS THE MAYOR OUR NEWEST CLIENT YET? How'd that phone call go? If we get him, we're set for the rest of the year. The next couple of years really.", Mr. Jacobs anxiously says, wearing a colorful green suit.

"Still not sure. He just called to set up a meeting for tomorrow. Did you change your suit?"

"Yeah, it's for an event I'm attending this afternoon. It's Italian. You like it? Sharon said it's eccentric. What do you think?" He starts to strut around my office brushing off his suit.

"Uumm, it's definitely something, sir. If you like it, I love it", I say with a smile on my face trying to hold in a laugh.

He stops strutting and stands in front of my desk. "Means a lot coming from a dapper fellow like yourself. So what time should I be here in the morning? Eight? Nine?"

I chuckle a little bit, "Umm about that, he actually wants me to meet with him tomorrow evening at his house. Just me and him. Alone."

His face becomes dejected, "Oh okay, well good. I'll just follow up with you Wednesday morning. I'm sure you'll do a splendid job. I'm about to be on my way. See you tomorrow."

"Yes sir, will do. Be safe." Mr. Jacobs nods his head as he walks out of my office and closes my door.

When he leaves, I get up to close my door then I let out a long, deep breath as I yawn and sit back down.

As I sit at my desk, I was still trying to wrap my head around what I had heard prior to Mr. Jacobs walking in. I was flabbergasted by what Mr. Langston had told me. My childhood superhero had actually turned out to be a villain. I couldn't believe it. His whole multimillion dollar empire is built off of drugs, lies, and spilled blood. It was a lot to take in. The thought of Mr. Langston taking a life, or even being a part of that lifestyle, just wouldn't process in my mind. I'm torn apart. I honestly didn't know how I felt, or even how I was supposed to feel. I've always profoundly respected and honored him because of his hustle. That part of him inspired me to be the man that I am today. Then on the other hand, I was horrified. The man that I looked up to and admired throughout the years, the man I thought I knew, the man that was the father figure in my life had suddenly become a mystery to me. I suddenly felt like I didn't know him at all. He became a mystery that I wasn't sure I wanted to solve.

"Winston I'm about to head out.", Sharon says as she knocks on my door.

"Already?! It's only two thirty. You usually stay til four."

"You're right, but I just got a text from mystery man. He said he has a limo on the way to pick me up. And Mr. Jacobs just left for the day, so everyone is working Winston hours today." She giggles.

Confused, "Winston hours?! What's that?"

"C'mon! Don't act like you don't know what we're talking about Winston. You basically leave as you please and Jacobs says NOTHING to you. The whole office notices. You know if Barney, Chester, or even Lizzy did that they'd all be fired on the spot."

I laugh then say, "I've also closed more accounts in three months than what they combined for all last year. To be honest, they're just dead weight. Jacobs should just fire them then distribute their commissions throughout the office ."

Sassily, "That'd be nice, but that's not the point, Winston. The point is that you get treated like royalty while everybody else gets ignored. From what I'm hearing, everyone is envious and upset."

I become confused and annoyed. *I don't bother anyone. I just show up and do my job. How can they be mad because I'm good at what I do?*

I start to pack up my things. "Well, maybe they should do their jobs better, Sharon. They can't be mad because I'm good at what I do!"

She puts her hands up and waves them as she's trying to calm me down. "Chill Winston, I'm on your side. Like I told you before, your drive was what attracted me to you. I'm all for you getting your money. I'm your biggest fan. That's why I'm telling you to your face." Her phone starts to ring. "That's my ride, I'll see you tomorrow love." She gives me a hug then walks out.

As I look out my window into the office, I see people packing up and leaving. Some wave goodbye to me as they walk by, and some just put their head down and walk straight past me.

Haters. All of them, haters. I laugh and shake my head as I gather my things. I exit the office and don't waste any time getting to my apartment. I'm flying down the highway in vexation. Triggered by the combination of Natalie, the mayor, Mr. Langston, and now my coworkers, it was like everything was hitting me at once. I didn't want to talk to anyone, see anyone, or be around anyone. I just wanted to be by myself so I can process everything in peace and solitude.

As I'm about to turn into my parking spot, a car speedily backs out in front of me and I almost hit him. Clearly, he was in the wrong, but he still felt the need to flick me off. "Watch where you're fucking going buddy!", he yells out of his black sports car with loud music playing in the background.

I take a deep breath as I'm trying to keep calm. I let my window down and say, "You shouldn't have backed out like that! Somebody could've gotten hurt."

Loud and rudely, "Fuck you, jackass!". He then spits towards my car and speeds off.

All of the anger, frustration, and irritation I had accumulated throughout the day had finally reached its tipping point. I snapped.

When he sped off, I went right behind him. I followed him to the stop sign at the back entrance of my complex. I honk my horn to get his attention. He notices it's me and parks his car. He then opens the door and gets out, I do the same.

When he gets out, he starts to briskly walk towards me. "What's your fucking problem bro?!", He says pointing his right index finger at me.

As he gets within an arm's length of me, I swing without any hesitation. I step and throw a right hook that creates a gash over his left eye, immediately knocking him out. I stoop down to check on him. He's completely unconscious and barely breathing.

XXIII

———

I START TO PANIC. THE CLOUDY, BREEZY AFTERNOON just got a lot colder. I begin to rapidly pace back and forth with my hands on the top of my head. "I'm going to jail. I'm about to go to jail. I just know I'm about to go to jail.", I frantically repeat. I squat back down to check on him. I shake his shoulder to try to wake him up, and he doesn't budge. I do it again, same result. I get up and get back to pacing. I start to sweat profusely from the nervousness and anxiety I'm receiving from the situation.

After going back and forth a few times, I decide to get back in my car to think. I close my door and blast the AC so I can cool down. I take out my phone and begin to go through my contacts. *Who can I call?! Who can I call?!* As I'm scrolling through my phone, I look out the corner of my eye and I see blue and red lights approaching. I sink into my seat and drop my head as I let out a deep breath of frustration. *Fuck.* The only word I could think of.

The police officer drives up and gets out of the car.

Just relax and don't make any sudden movements, Winston. You can avoid going to jail, but there's no escaping a coffin if I make the wrong move.

Before the officer does anything else, he says something in his radio as he looks at me. I assume he's calling for backup.

He walks towards my neighbor, then kneels down to check his pulse. He looks at him and talks into his radio again. I'm guessing he's calling for an ambulance this time.

He gets up, walks to my car, and motions me to let my window down. I let down my window and he says, "I got a call about some loud noises and arguing. Would that be what led to this man laying on the ground unconscious?"

I nervously laugh then say, "Yes sir. He pulled out in front of me, almost causing a wreck, then he flicked me off, cursed at me, and then spat at me."

"And that made you want to knock him out, nearly killing him? I hope you have a good lawyer boy, cause it looks like you're about to be facing battery, assault, and attempted murder charges?"

"Attempted murder?! Officer, we just got into a little scuffle and I got the best of him."

"We'll see how that holds up in court. From my eyes, it looks like you followed this innocent man to this back entrance, where there's little to no traffic, in an attempt to rob him. You then dragged him out of his car, and attacked him. Just wait until he wakes up and I can get a report. Luckily, a neighbor called it in before you could finish whatever it is you were about to do."

I'm appalled, "That doesn't make any sense, how could I have dragged him out of his car if his car is off? He got out of his car and approached me, officer."

"Watch your tone. Are you getting smart with me? Get out of the car!"

My heart drops and I feel like time has frozen around me. *Is this how it ends? No wife, no kids, no family? What about my mom?*

Suddenly, I hear ambulance sirens in the distance. As they get closer and closer, I breathe a sigh of relief. They drive up and park right in front of my neighbor.

The officer laughs under his breath. "Don't get too excited now.", he whispers as he walks away to talk to the medics.

As he's talking to one, two other medics are tending to my

neighbor and loading him onto the ambulance. I just sit in my car scared and motionless as all of this is happening.

After a few minutes, the ambulance drives off and the officer returns to my car.

He pounds on the top of my car.

BANG. BANG. BANG.

"I said get out!"

As I open my door, he grabs me out of my car and slams me up against it. "I didn't even do anything man!", I plead.

"You're trespassing in an area you have no business in and damn near killed a man. It's clearly a robbery gone wrong."

As he was cocking back his right hand to strike me, some more blue lights drive up. I couldn't see exactly what it was because my face was smushed against the car. Everything was blurry.

"Oh, you're in trouble now. Just wait until he gets a hold of you. You're done for, boy." I hear a car door slam and footsteps walking towards us. The officer then grabs me and shoves me towards whoever just arrived. I trip over his foot and fall. As I look up, I see the face of the new officer. It's Sheriff Brooks. The officer then grabs me off of the ground and starts to walk me over toward Sheriff Brooks.

Astounded, his face lights up. "What the hell are you doing? Let him go."

"Excuse me?", the officer says.

"Let him go, I'll take it from here. I heard them say that there's another disturbance over on 39th and Broadway. Why don't you go and check that out for me. I'll meet you there. I can finish up over here myself." The officer looks at Sheriff Brooks and fixes his mouth to try and rebuttal, but before he could say anything, Sheriff Brooks roared, "That's an order! Now go!"

The officer starts walking then stops to look back at Sheriff Brooks. He gave him a stern glare before he shook his head in disgust. He then continued to walk to his car. He got in, slammed his door, and drove off with the sirens on.

As I'm brushing myself off and gathering my thoughts, Sheriff Brooks comes over to help. "Winston, are you ok? I'm sorry you had to go through that. He's a real jackass."

I move away from him. "So if I wasn't known by the mayor and was just some regular guy you wouldn't have stopped it, huh? Who knows what else he would've done. What y'all would've done." Sheriff Brooks says nothing, he just stares at me in silence with a look of deep shame on his face. "That's what I thought." I shake my head and walk towards my car.

"You go ahead and enjoy your night Winston. I'll take care of everything."

I wave him off. "Yeah, whatever." I get in my car and drive back around to my apartment. I strip and go straight to the shower once I get there. I put my arms on the wall, drop my head, and just let the hot water run down my body as I'm hoping that my troubles follow. Since I was a kid, the shower has been my sanctuary.

XXIV

I SPENT ABOUT TWENTY-FIVE MINUTES SULKING IN THE
shower. When I finally got out, even though I was pruny, I felt
at ease. I was at peace. For the rest of the night at least, I was
relieved of all of my troubles and worries. For dinner, I ate a
frozen pizza I warmed up in the oven. I ate it on the couch and
fell asleep not too long after I had finished eating.

When I got out of bed, it was a little past seven. I wasn't in the
mood for The Spot today, so I took my time getting ready. I didn't
feel like being bothered by anyone, and I definitely didn't want to
risk seeing Natalie again. So for breakfast, I just ate three slices of
toast covered in grape jelly with a cup of orange juice on the side.
It was no Rico special, but it was breakfast.

When I finished eating, I got ready for work. "Hmm, I wonder
what joy today will bring me?", I sarcastically say as I look in the
mirror.

At eight twenty, I'm dressed and ready to be on my way to
work. Today I'm wearing a dark brown blazer with a white t-shirt
underneath, khaki slacks, and dark brown loafers. I wasn't in the

shirt and tie mood. When I leave my apartment and walk to my car, I notice my neighbor's car isn't in its usual parking spot. *There's no way he's still in the hospital. I didn't even hit him that hard. Maybe he just left early today.* I proceed to get in my car and head to work. The traffic was light, so I got there rather expeditiously. When I arrive, I walk straight to my office.

"Good morning, Winston. How are you?!", Sharon yelled as I walked by.

"Good.", I responded as I kept walking.

As I'm setting my briefcase down and taking my seat, Sharon walks in and shuts the door behind her.

"Okay, now what's wrong with you, Winston? You never just walk past me like that. One of these uptight jackasses said something to you? It was Steven, wasn't it? I've been waiting to get on his crusty ass since he started working here." I laugh a little. "There's a smile! Now tell me what's wrong, Winston." She sits down.

"It's nothing really, I just had a long day yesterday that's all. I'm still tired."

Sarcastically, "Mmmhhmmm, and I became the queen of England last night. Now tell me what's really wrong with you. You know you can always talk to me."

Playfully, "Well I'm honored to be in your presence, miss queen. It's nice to meet such a prestigious individual like yourself." I bow my head and extend my arm to her.

She laughs. "I'm serious, Winston. Talk to me." She places her hands on top of mine and gazes into my eyes. "Please, I don't like seeing you like this. It's all in your eyes."

I reposition my hands to be on top of hers. "Sharon, I promise you I'm good. I appreciate your concern though, sugar foot."

"Eeeww, what I told you about that name.", she says with a grin. "You remind me of one of those old school players whenever you say that."

I crack a smile. "Hmm, I bet if I was Mr. Langston calling you that you wouldn't mind." I wink at her.

She bursts out into laughter and rolls her eyes, "Boy bye. I got work to do." She gets up and heads out of my office. When she gets to the door, she stops, and looks back at me. "Seriously though Winston, I'm here if you need me."

"I know Sharon, thank you. But like I said, I'm fine."

"Just letting you know I'm here for you." She continues to walk out of my office and sits back down at her desk.

Speaking of Mr. Langston, I still have to email him about his contract. After I send the email, I check my phone. Chino texted me.

"Why you ain't come in today? Ol girl was asking bout you?"

I sit up in my chair, excited from the news, and text back, "What she say?"

"She just wanted to know when you was going to call her. She said it's important."

I slouch back in my chair, "Next time you see her, tell her I've been busy."

"Will do my boy. And some plan you got going on btw. My notepad's full."

"Just be patient, you'll see."

"Yeah ok."

I had actually forgotten about my plan and gave up on Natalie after yesterday. After she gave me her business card instead of her cell number, I decided to quit and throw in the towel. Who knows what the future holds though. I guess only time will tell. But as for now, my melanin angel is only a fantasy, nothing more than a hopeful dream.

As I'm sitting there drifting off into space, my phone rings. I look at Sharon and she says, "It's the mayor, pick up."

I throw my head back in frustration. *Now the day has officially started.*

I pick up, "Hello?"

Excited and enthused like always, "Good morning, Winston! How are you?"

"I'm doing good and yourself?"

"I'm just splendid. Are you still available for our meeting tonight?"

"Yes sir, I am. Is that the only reason you called? To confirm our meeting tonight."

He chuckles, "Now we both know that it's not it. I've heard

you've got quite the right hook, Winston. We might need to get you out of that office and into a boxing ring"

"That asshole deserved it."

"Did he deserve the concussion and laceration over his eye too?"

"Yes sir, he actually did."

"Well, I'm glad you're satisfied with your decision because he also thinks you're worthy of a couple things. A long jail sentence being one of them."

I raise my voice in anger, "He can't do that!"

"Oh, but he can Winston. There's video evidence showing YOU following HIM to that stop sign. Also, it shows that YOU struck HIM. So he can in fact do that, sir."

"So you're calling me to warn me? This your way of telling me that I need a lawyer?"

"No, no, no, quite the contrary actually. I was calling to tell you that it's all been taken care of. Just think of it as a downpayment for your services."

"A downpayment?"

"Yes, we'll discuss more tonight. I'm looking forward to your visit."

I pause for a moment then say, "That's not all we'll discuss."

"Well, what else do you have in mind?"

"We need to talk about how you allow your officers to harass innocent people."

He takes a deep breath before he calmly says, "I'll see you tonight, Winston."

We hang up the phone as I laugh. *I hope he knows that this conversation is far from finished. I'll see him tonight.*

When I hang up the phone, I get up and go to the bathroom. I pass by Sharon's desk to thank her for checking on me earlier, but she's not there. *She must've stepped out for a second.*

I begin to pick up my walking speed. The pizza that I ate last night wasn't sitting well. My stomach was starting to bubble. I burst through the bathroom door and rushed into a stall.

While I'm in the bathroom, I overhear a conversation between a couple of my colleagues at the water cooler not too far from the door. The voices sounded familiar, but I couldn't quite make them out.

"I can't believe he's getting the mayor too!?"

"I know right, it's like Jacobs looks past all of us and goes straight to Winston EVERY TIME."

"It's bullshit. He basically comes and goes as he pleases, automatically gets referred to the wealthiest people, and he's not even that qualified for this job."

"He was only hired because Mr. Langston owns the building. I think Langston even paid Jacobs to hire him too."

"I agree."

"Me and you, we need to get Winston out of here first, then Jacobs. Then we'll run this shit ourselves. We deserve better than this."

"My thoughts exactly. What you have in mind?"

"You still banging that cleaning lady?"

"Shhhhhhhh! Don't be so loud, Karen has ears everywhere, but yeah. Why do you ask?"

"Look, I have some blow in my desk. I keep it in the top drawer behind all my stuff. I'll give you the blow when everyone leaves, then you'll give it to the cleaning lady and tell her to plant it in Winston's desk somewhere."

"We call it in and BOOM. We're heroes and back at the top of the food chain."

"Exactly! What time do they usually come in?"

"Juanita gets here when we leave at four, but the rest comes in at six. It gives us enough time too…"

"Yeah, yeah I get it. I don't need the visual. Come to my office at four so we can do this."

"Cool."

"Hey! Be cool and don't say anything to anyone else."

I hear them walk away. I sat there lost for words. I didn't know people felt like that or even thought about doing things like that. *Who were they? I could just wait around the office and see who doesn't leave right away, but then that'll give them time to cover up their mess.* As I'm washing my hands, I try to think of a plan, but I couldn't think of anything. I exit the bathroom and walk back to my office. I look around to see if anyone has a suspicious demeanor or looks at me funny as I walk, but I didn't notice anything. I sit at my desk and attempt to think of a plan again, but I still drew blanks. I look around the office hoping to get inspired or hit with a clue, as if this was a cartoon, but nothing happens. I pull up the office roster to see if any names stand out, but I'm cool with everyone. Or so I thought.

I look out the window again and notice Sharon's back. I immediately text her, "Sharon, come here 911". She reads it and then she looks at me with a confused expression on her face. I wave her to come into my office, and she does. "What is it, Winston?! What's the emergency?"

Jittery I say, "Close the door and sit down! Hurry, hurry."

She closes the door and takes a seat. "So are you going to keep talking gibberish or are you going to tell me what the hell is going on?"

I take a deep breath, "Alright, so I was sitting on the toilet..."

She rolls her eyes, gets out of her chair, and motions to walk out. "Boy bye! I am not about to listen to you tell me how big of a shit you just took! I got work to do. You probably ate one of those frozen pizzas that I've been telling your ass to stop eating and.."

I grab her and laugh. "No, no. I mean I did eat one of those pizzas, but that's not what I wanted to tell you. Sit down, it's crazy."

She sits back down in her seat, "Well spit it out, I have work to finish by three."

"Okay, well like I was saying. I was in the bathroom and overheard two people outside at the water cooler talking about setting me up to get fired."

She gets a concerned look on her face. "What?! Who was it? What they say?"

"Well, that's what I need you for. They said they were going to get one of the cleaning ladies to plant some booger sugar in my desk whenever I leave, and then they'll call it in and get me arrested. You have any idea who that could be?"

"Did any of them happen to mention if they were screwing the cleaning lady?"

I raise my eyebrows and say, "Actually, yeah. That setting off alarms?"

"Boy that ain't nobody but Henry and Steve. Henry's been sleeping with that woman for as long as I can remember, and Steve's a borderline addict." I sit back in my seat in shock. "Those two have been getting on my nerves since before you got here. They're just some privileged Aholes that think they're entitled to everything just because they went to some fancy school and their families have money. Well, what do you want to do about all this Winston?"

I sit up, and think for a few seconds. "I have an idea. We're going to get them before they get me. Do you know anyone in security?"

Puzzled, "Yeeah. What you need?"

"Just text me the number and I'll handle the rest. Just sit back and enjoy the show that's about to take place. They're gonna get what they deserve." I wink at her and she blushes.

Her phone starts to ring at her desk. "I should probably get that. Just give me a warning before everything pops off so I can get my popcorn ready."

I smile at her and say, "Okay, I got you."

Now it's one thirty and everyone has returned from their lunch. I'm at my desk waiting for everything to occur. During that time period, I made a few calls and took a trip to the security office in the building.

I take a look out my window then text Sharon, "It's time."

She looks at me and smiles.

A few moments later, three police officers step off of the elevator and onto our floor. I just sit back and watch the show from my desk with my door open.

They approach Sharon's desk and ask her to point her in the direction of Steve's office. She points them in the direction then texts me, "OMG you didn't?!"

I reply back, "Chess not checkers."

A couple minutes later, Steve's getting dragged out of the office kicking and screaming, creating a huge scene. "Henry, you fucking rat! I hope you burn in hell you son of a bitch!", he yells as he's being taken out in handcuffs.

When the police leave, Sharon rushes to my office.

"You called the police on him?!"

"I had to get him before he got me. He can afford a good lawyer. He'll be okay."

She laughs, "So what's next?"

"Act two. You'll know when it's starting."

"I can't get a hint or anything?"

"Nope, patience is a virtue my dear."

"Ughhh!", she rolls her eyes and goes back to her desk.

After about twenty minutes passes by, a middle aged, brunette woman hops off of the elevator wearing a dingy, yellow sweater and khakis. "Where's Henry!", she exclaims as she walks towards Sharon's desk.

She points towards his office and says, "He's over there mam, but I believe he's in there talking to a client."

"Fuck him and that fucking client!", she yells as she storms into Henry's office. I walk over to Sharon's desk to watch what's about to take place. "You're cheating on me with a fucking cleaning lady. Henry?! You little pencil dick having motherfucker!" Henry's confused face turns red and he begins to babble. "Are you sure you want to do business with a lying cheat?! You can't trust this son of a bitch! I've been married to him for twenty years so I would know.", she angrily exclaims to his client.

His client gets up to leave, "I see you have a lot going on Henry. We'll just do this another time."

Henry tries to stop him from leaving, but his wife, Karen, gets in front of him and pushes him onto his desk and starts to hit him. "You fucking bastard! All those times you said you were working overtime you were really with the lady that cleans this place."

He gathers himself and places his hands on her shoulders trying to calm her down. "Honey, dear, Karebear, I love you. I'd never cheat on you and you know that. I made one mistake when we first got married, but I've been honest and faithful ever since. You know you're the only one for me." He hugs her and kisses her on the cheek. She just stares at him.

"This is about to get good.", I whisper to Sharon as she sits at the edge of her seat in anticipation of what's about to happen next.

"Honey bunches are you okay? We can leave and finish this discussion at home, in private.", Henry says with a soft voice.

She takes her phone out of her pocket. "What the hell are these you fucking liar?!" She shows him videos from the security footage of his affair. "These date back ten plus years you fucking lying piece of shit!" She slaps him, takes Henry's paperweight off of his desk, and throws it at his glass wall connecting to his door. The wall instantly shatters to pieces. "I flattened your tires too, so good luck getting home asshole." She then turns around to address the office. "You all have a great day. I'm sorry y'all had to witness that, but I'm sure you can understand my actions." She walks to the elevator and leaves the office. Sharen turns to me with her jaw dropped in awe.

"What thee fuck, Winston?!"

XXV

———

I JUST LOOK AT HER AND LAUGH. "LIKE I SAID, IT'S CHESS not checkers. I couldn't just let them get away with that."

She smirks. "I feel you. I probably would've done the same thing, or something worse. Sometimes I forget how smart you really are."

I shrug my shoulders and say, "Thanks, I guess." I walk around from behind her desk. "Well, I think I've accomplished enough for the day. Securing my job and getting rid of a couple of pompous jackasses is more than enough, right? I'm about to head out. You staying til four?"

"No, I'm right behind you. Mr. Jacobs isn't here so there's no need to stay. And everyone else looks ready to leave too."

Concerned, I ask, "Did Jacobs call in?"

"Weirdly, no. He just never came."

"Oh wow, that's odd. I hope he's ok."

"Yeah, me too." As Sharon begins to pack up her things, I get up and go back to my office to grab mine. When I'm about to leave my office, Chino calls me. *What does he want? He usually texts me.*

I'll just call him back when I get in the car. I let the phone ring and lock my door.

"Hurry up, Winston! I refuse to ride on this raggedy elevator by myself." Sharon yells as she's holding the elevator door open.

"I'm coming, I'm coming." I shout while I make a light jog to the elevator. "Whew!", I exclaim as I'm out of breath as I get in.

Jokingly, Sharon says, "You sound like you're a little out of shape there buddy. Might need to invest in a treadmill or something."

"Ha ha. I know you ain't talking."

"Uuuum, I am! I do yoga three times a week and do a three mile run at least two times. So thank you sir. How else do you think I'm able to keep this elegant figure?" The elevator stops. We get off in the parking lot and walk towards our cars.

"Yeah, yeah."

"I'm serious Winston, maybe my boyfriend can give you a pointer or two."

I smirk, "First off, I'm in great shape. You should know that from the other night." I wink at her. "And secondly, I could probably teach HIM a thing or two, whoever he is."

Sharon laughs. "Honey, I was acting to boost your little ego, so don't flatter yourself. And you still don't know who he is, huh?"

I give her a sarcastic glare, "Now we both know you weren't acting that night. I still have the scratch marks to prove it. You need to be in somebody's movie if you were acting that good. And nah, are you finally going to tell me who mystery man is? Or is the time still not right?"

She smiles, "Whatever, and you probably know him. I'm surprised you haven't figured it out yet. I'm dating…". My phone rings. It's Chino calling back. "You go ahead and answer that, I'll just tell you another time. I'll see you tomorrow, Winston." She gives me a hug and walks to her car as I finish walking to mine.

I answer my phone, "Wassup Chino, are you okay? I'm just leaving work."

"Maaaaaaan you gotta call Natalie!"

"Hold on Chino, about to get in my car." I get in my car and wait for the phone to connect before I continue the conversation.

"Okay, now what are you talking about?", I ask as I drive out the parking lot.

"She came in today looking sad and then started crying not too long after she sat down. I tried to talk to her and get her to open up, but she wouldn't. She kept saying it was just some personal stuff and she'll figure it out on her own. This could be your chance. Maybe you can get her to open up about what's bothering her, and then you could console her and take it from there."

At first I was excited, but then I started to think about how I felt when she handed me her business card. I realized my melanin angel was just a fantasy. And sadly, I had to let go of my hopes of making it into a reality.

"Thanks for trying to look out, but I'm good Chino. I'm over her. I don't even remember where her card is anyway."

There's about a five second pause before Chino says, "Winston, I'm saying this because you've become like a little brother to me over time." He pauses again then says, "Boy if you don't get out your damn feelings and man up! In the business world, you act like a big dog. But when it comes to these women, you're always turning into a scared little puppy. Okay, things didn't go your way the first time, but it's a new day, a new opportunity. I told you that you have to let go of that shy guy stuff if you want her. And we both know that you have her business card stashed away in your briefcase somewhere. You either call that woman when you get home or I'm banning you from The Spot."

I chuckle, "You're not serious Chino. You wouldn't ban ME out of all people. Especially over something like this."

His voice gets serious, "Try me. I'm deadass serious, Winston. Were you not the one saying you had a plan, and told me to just sit back and watch? Well, I've watched enough and you're failing, miserably. Valentine's Day is right around the corner. It's about to be game day and you don't even have a team. Now either you call her today when you get home, or find you another breakfast spot."

I was lost for words because deep inside, I knew he was right. *I've been lying to myself. Fooling myself to believe that my heart was broken when she handed me her business card, when in reality, I've just* been too scared to call. I can't hide the fact that my face lights up whenever Chino mentions her name, or I get butterflies in my stomach when I think of her. I had to search inside of myself and answer this question, why am I so scared to call her? Is it because I feared rejection? Am I afraid of being labeled not good enough for her, or not on her level? Or is it because I placed her on a pedestal so high, that I manipulated myself into thinking that she was an actual angel, and I could be nothing more than her peasant? Maybe it's because I'm not all the way over Sharon?

"Winston, you still there?"

"Y-y-yeah. I hear you Chino."

"I'm serious, man. I'm telling you this cause I love you. You're smart, successful, and you got your head on straight. I know I joke a lot, but if anybody deserves to be with a woman like Natalie, it's you. I know things with Sharon ended a little rough for you, but you can't let that stop you from getting back out there and getting what you deserve, happiness. When you come in tomorrow morning, I'm gonna be expecting a full rundown of everything that was said."

I didn't tell him, but what he just said meant a lot to me. It was the confidence boost I needed. "I got you Chino. I'll see you tomorrow morning."

"Aye man, I love you."

"Love you too Chino." We hang up the phone as I pull into my parking spot. As I'm getting out, my neighbor pulls into his spot. Stunned, I step back, then wave.

He rolls down his window and says, "Hey! It's Winston, right?"

Hesitantly, "Yeah?"

He gets out of his car and walks towards me with a black left eye. "I'm Aden. I just wanted to apologize for last night. I was out of line and in the wrong. I deserved this little gift you gave me"

I was caught off guard and didn't know what to say. *What the hell got into him? The last thing I was expecting to come out of his mouth was an apology.*

He extends out his right hand and says, "Truce? Let's just put this whole altercation behind us, and move on from it as happy neighbors."

I shake his hand and say, "Yeah, truce. I'm sorry about your eye too. I didn't mean to hit you that hard. I just had a rough day, that's all."

"It's cool man, I understand. I didn't make it any better I'm sure. But hey, have you ever thought about boxing? You'd probably be a natural. That was a hell of a hook." We laugh.

His girlfriend comes outside of his apartment and yells at him to come in. "I better get going. You enjoy the rest of your day."

"Thanks, you too. I'll see you around." We separate and walk to our apartments.

When I get in mine, I head straight to the couch and drop into its comfort. I take off my blazer and my shoes, then grab my briefcase and place it on my lap. I open it and grab Natalie's business card.

XXVI

———

I STARE AT NATALIE'S BUSINESS CARD AS I TWIDDLE IT in my hands. "Natalie Graves: Real Estate and Insurance Agent", it says in big bold letters.

What am I waiting for? Just call her, Winston! Chino's right. This is probably a golden opportunity. It's only two forty-five, she's probably still in her office. Just do it.

I take a deep breath as I look up at my ceiling, and exhale as I take my phone out of my pocket. I open my phone and go to the dialing pad. My hands start to get clammy, my heart starts to beat faster, and my mouth is as dry as the desert.

I can't do this! I need to get some water first. I go to my refrigerator, grab a bottle of water, then sit back down.

Okay, I'm ready. I do a shoulder shake to loosen up. *Let's do this.*

I take a sip of water and dial the number on the card.

This is it. Now, just relax Winston. Be cool. You got this. The phone begins to ring.

"Hello, thanks for calling Crenshaw Realty! This is Debbie, how can I help you?", their receptionist says with a nice and pleasant voice.

I clear my throat and say, "Hey, Debbie. Can you direct me to Ms. Natalie Graves please?"

"Okay, one second. Hold please.", she says as she redirects my call. About thirty seconds go by. "Hello?"

Confused, "Hey, is this Natalie?"

She giggles, "Haha no sir, this is still Debbie. I'm sorry, but Natalie left around one thirty because she wasn't feeling good."

I suck my teeth, "Okay, thanks Debbie."

"I'm sorry, would you like me to leave a message? She should be in around ten tomorrow morning."

"Umm. You can just tell her that Winston called."

"Last name?"

"Oh, umm, Winston Williams."

"Okay, and what was your purpose of calling?"

I sigh, "Sheeeesh, do y'all need my social too?"

"Haha I'm sorry Mr. Williams, it's just protocol. I promise this is the last question."

"Just tell her Winston Williams, the financial advisor from The Spot, called. She should know what you're talking about."

"Oaky dokey Mr. Williams. I'll make sure she gets your message and returns your call. You have a terrific Tuesday."

"Thanks, you too." We hang up the phone and I exhale a deep breath of frustration.

Uuuggghhhh! I guess it's just not meant to be. I get up from the couch and go to my room. I belly flop in my bed and just lay there. *Maybe this is a sign that we're not meant to be together. I'm not about to stress it though. I tried.* I lay in my bed and scroll through my phone for about five minutes before I doze off into a deep slumber.

I wake up to my phone buzzing. The mayor is calling me. I look out my window and it's dark out. I look at the time and it's seven o'one.

I slap my forehead. *I overslept!*

Phone still ringing, I answer it, "Winston! Do you know what time it is?! I'm a busy man with a strict schedule. Did you forget that we had a meeting tonight? At seven o'clock sharp."

Not knowing what else to say, I tell the truth. "I'm going to be honest with you, MP. I dozed off when I got in from work and overslept. I'm sorry."

He pauses for a second then says, "Honesty is hard to come across when you're in the business that I'm in. I respect and admire that, Winston. Can you be here by eight thirty?"

I release a breath of relief. "Yes sir. I'll be on my way in a few."

"Okay, see you soon."

He hangs up the phone and I immediately start getting ready. I take a quick shower then put on a blue button up with khakis. By seven twenty-four I was in the car and on the road.

I arrive at the mayor's house at around eight twenty. As I'm parking, he comes outside to greet me wearing a plush, silk black robe with a white t-shirt and black gym shorts underneath.

"Here, take a sip of this since you're an hour and a half late to the party." He gives me a white styrofoam cup that smells like there's liquor in it.

Surprised, I take the cup and say, "I thought this was a meeting, MP. If I would've known that you were throwing a pajama party, I would've worn my lion onesie."

He laughs and gets a big smile on his face. He then puts his arm around my shoulders, "There's nothing wrong with a little pleasure while you do business. It eradicates the tension and creates a relaxed mind. C'mon, let's go in." He walks me into the house and I see about twelve of the women that were here last time.

"Are the others here as well?", I nervously ask.

"No sir, it's just me and you." He winks at me. "But before we party, let's go into my office and discuss a couple things." We walk through the sea of women in the living room and go into his office.

"Take a seat.", he says as he pours himself some wine that he had sitting on his desk. "I would offer you some, but you haven't even finished what you already have."

I laugh and say, "You know I don't drink, MP."

"Just take a sip. For being late, it's the least you could do. I promise it's not poison." He chuckles. "It's just smooth, tasteful liquor. The good stuff." He looks and smiles at me while he waits for me to drink it. "Well, I'm waiting. Don't be a party pooper, Winston."

I look down at my drink, shake my cup around, and take a sip. "It's strong.", I say as I grimace.

He walks over to me and pats me on my left shoulder. "Don't insult me, go ahead and finish it. I poured you a little less than three shots. I'm sure you can down all of that. Relax, let loose a little bit, Winston."

I take a deep breath and finish the cup.

A big smile covers his face as he applauds me and says, "Good. Now we can talk."

XXVII

C OMBINING A LOW ALCOHOL TOLERANCE AND THE fact that I hadn't eaten since breakfast didn't make the situation any better. As soon as I drank whatever was in that cup, I immediately started to feel it. The room had gotten hotter, MP started to look blurry, and I began to feel free, as if I was buttnaked floating on top of a cloud. I felt relaxed and exuberant.

An uncontrollable smile starts to cover my face. My forehead and armpits begin to sweat.

MP laughs then says, "Are you okay, Winston?"

Slurred, "I'm fine."

"Okay, well let's begin. The reason I have my meetings at my home is because I prefer to be comfortable while I discuss business. It gives me a clear mind. What's a better haven than my home?"

"Gotcha."

"It also gives me a sense of control over everything. In my home, I know where everything is, so there aren't any surprises."

I just smile and nod my head.

He drinks from his wine glass, then begins to walk around the room. "Well Winston, I don't believe we've ever had a formal introduction yet. Tell me about yourself, where are you from?"

I smile, look him in his eyes, and say, "My momma."

We both laugh, "When's the last time you ate? There's no way you should be this tipsy from that little bit of liquor."

I wave my hands in a playful gesture, then with slurred words say, "I'm fiiinee, MP. I just wanted to tell a little jokey joke, that's all. I'm from the great city of Normans."

"Normans? I used to spend quite a bit of my time in Normans when I was younger. That's where I met Robert actually. I've made many great memories in that city throughout the years. It's always had an abundant amount of beautiful women. You still have family down there?"

"My moms is stills there. Her and my auntie dwells togethers."

"What about your father? I know he must be proud of the man you've become."

I burst out into laughter. "My mom is very proud of me."

He gets a puzzled look on his face. "Is your father not proud of you? I find that very hard to believe."

"Well you better believe it brother. I was so much of a disappointment to him that he left before I was even born. My mom had me young and raised me by herself."

MP drops his head for a second then says, "Well the way you've overcome such arduous circumstances is quite admirable. I'm sure you've suffered through some tough hardships, but you'd never be able to tell by the way you carry yourself. It's quite honorable and very admirable."

I chuckle, "Woah there, take it easy Mr. Mayor. Do you need me to get one of those women to give you a hug?" I put my hands up in a defense position. "You're getting a little TOO emotional for me buddy." I laugh.

He shakes his head, "Do you eat turkey Winston? You need some food in your system."

I nod my head, "Yeesh, gobble gobble."

He chuckles then calls one of the girls from outside into his office. He tells her to make me a sandwich and something to drink.

When she leaves out, the mayor gets a concerned look on his face. "Winston, if you don't mind me asking, what's your mother's name?"

"First and last?"

"Yes please, if you don't mind."

"Well, most people call her NB. That name sound familiar to you?"

"Um, no I'm sorry. That name doesn't ring a bell. What does it stand for?"

"Nunya Business.", I laugh as the mayor just stares at me unamused.

"I'll go check on your food. You want chips or anything to go with it?"

I smile, "All thee above please sir."

"Okay then." MP steps out of the room. "I'll be back, just make yourself comfortable.", he says walking out.

While he's gone, I just sit in my chair and bob my head to the music they're playing outside with a huge smile on my face.

After about two songs, I get up and start wobbling around his office. I look over at his bookshelf, but I don't find anything interesting. I then shift my focus to his desk. Under a bunch of other papers, I see a contract with the Georgia Department of Corrections on it. I attempt to read it, but as soon as I started to reach for it, I hear MP walking back in.

"I hope you like sour cream and onion chips. That's all I had. I've been so busy lately, I keep forgetting to send for groceries.", he says, entering the room with his back to me holding a tray with a sandwich, chips, pretzels and a soda on it.

Startled, I begin to dance and hope he doesn't notice me snooping around his desk.

I dance my way over to my seat and say, "That's fine. It's actually one of my favorite chips."

"Okay good." He places the tray in front of me, and sits down. "Enjoy."

"Thank you sir, I appreciate it."

"No problem." His phone begins to ring, but he ignores it.

"You gonna get that?", I say as I demolish my food.

"No, I'll call them back later. This is more important. Are you ready to discuss business?" He takes a quick look out of his office then says, "Actually, let me step out while you finish that." He takes his phone and walks back out.

About thirty minutes later, he comes back in a cheerful mood. He slaps his hands on the desk and with a big smile says, "Now, let's talk business, Winston. You ready?"

While sitting alone in his office for thirty minutes, I not only ate, but I started to sober up and read those papers that were on his desk. I became infuriated by what I saw, but I wasn't going to expose it just yet.

"Yes sir, just let me use the bathroom first. I have to make a little tinkle winkle."

MP shakes his head. "Use my office bathroom, it's right behind you."

I get up, use the bathroom, and gather my thoughts.

"You better now?", he asks as I walk out.

I chuckle, "A lot better. So, what's on ya mind?"

He clears his throat then sits up in his chair. "I'm a man that likes to get straight to the point. I'm sure you know by now that my job involves a lot more than what the typical citizen will assume I do." He looks me in my eyes. "Well, actually Winston, what is it that YOU think I do? And please remember, honesty is always the best policy with me."

"What do you mean MP? You're a mayor aren't you? Mayors are basically responsible for keeping the city intact. Making sure it runs smoothly and what not. Right?"

He laughs, "Winston, c'mon now. Between Robert and other people I'm sure you've talked to, I'm certain you've heard SOMETHING. Just tell me what it is and I'll confirm everything for you." He raises his right hand. "Word is bond. I won't lie. Don't be nervous."

I sit back in my chair and think for a second. I contemplate if I should share anything with him or just keep it to myself. Still a little buzzed, I blurt out, "Is it true that all of Ricoville is built off of drug money and bloodshed?"

He grins, "Don't forget wit and strategy too." He shrugs his shoulders then says, "But yes, all of that's true. From the Guatemalans to the incident that caused Robert and I to stop working together."

"What incident? He had a change of heart and wanted to turn his life around, right?"

He takes a deep breath as he sits back in his chair and smiles at me. "Winston, I said I was going to tell the truth, so that's what I'm going to do. The real reason we stopped working together is because his wife used to be my girlfriend, fiance` actually. You know, some rules you just don't break as a man. He just didn't care. Years of blood, sweat, and friendship, flushed down the toilet. I'll never forgive him for that. The only reason I'm cordial with him in public is for publicity purposes. Can't have two powerful black men publicly quarrelling with each other, that's just not a good look. The media would have a field day."

I'm blown away. "Wow, that's crazy. I would've never imagined that Mr. Langston would even think about doing that to someone, especially his best friend."

"Lesson learned, Winston. Never trust anyone. No matter if they're your best friend or even blood. The only thing you can trust is a dollar amount."

"Since we're being honest. Is that the reason you're so intrigued with me? You need someone to focus on all the business and financial aspects of what you're doing, so you can focus solely on the other things?"

He laughs under his breath and shakes his head. "He told you that too, huh? That he was the brains and I was the muscle? Robert is a sly dog I tell you. Well Winston, Mike Gonzalez has been handling my finances for years if you must know. He just didn't randomly move down here. I just decided it was time to bring him closer. You, Winston. You, I see myself in. Except for the wisdom and understanding that you have. That, I didn't get until I was about twice your age. If a police officer ever offered me $100, hell even $10, I would've taken it in a heartbeat. You turned down $1,000. You probably still haven't spent it. With that discipline and self respect, I want to mold you into being the next Mayor."

———

XXVIII

I SIT BACK IN MY CHAIR, LOST FOR WORDS. *HE DIDN'T just say that.*

"I know it's a lot to take in right now, Winston. Just give yourself a few days to take it in and think about it. I'll give you your space then follow up when I feel the time is right."

After sitting in my chair for a couple of seconds trying to gather my thoughts and comprehend everything, I say, "I'm truly honored, really MP. But, why me? Why not the sheriff, judge, the councilman, or even anybody else? Why me?"

He takes another sip of his wine then says, "It's obvious, Winston. With your brains, morals, demeanor, etc. I think you're the only person that is capable enough to take over my throne when I leave. Sheriff Brooks is too money hungry. For the right price, he'll do just about anything for anybody. The councilman, he's our face because of looks. And well, that's all he has. He's not nearly as intelligent as you. The only reason he's in the position he's in now is because he comes from a very powerful family. He's the only one left now though. They got in over their heads with the wrong people and well, you can fill in the blanks. So even if the councilman does want to run for mayor on his own, he won't stand a chance. And as far as the judge, that's just not her cup of tea."

"I'm flattered, really MP, but…"

He comes over and places his hand on my shoulder. "Winston, before you say anything else, just think about it first. I'll follow up later for an answer. So for now, just relax. Now, with that out of the way, is there anything else you'd like to discuss before I conclude this meeting?" He then walks back around his desk and takes his seat across from me.

Sitting there perplexed, completely baffled, and still slightly tipsy, I just sit there in silence with my head down and rub my temples.

MP, sitting back in his chair with his right leg crossed over his left, lights his cigar. He takes a couple of puffs then says, "Well if you don't have anything else to say, we can conclude this meeting. Feel free to hang around and party a little if you'd like. Mi casa es su casa. One thing about an MP party, we can party for as long as we want and as loud as we want because we'll never have to worry about the police shutting us down."

As soon as he said the word police, my head popped up with an expression of disgust.

"Did I say something, Winston? You're free to leave if you're not in the mood to party. There's no pressure to stay. I understand you do have work in the morning."

"Do you know?"

Confused, he asks, "Do I know what, Winston?"

"That your police force is out there harassing and abusing innocent civilians."

He chortles, "Winston, Winston, Winston. C'mon now. I can't babysit and monitor my officers 24/7. They're grown men, they don't need babysitters. They get paid to do their job and that's that. As far as I'm concerned, they're all doing a splendid job in the community."

My face cringes a little bit. "I'm not saying they need to be babysat, but they do need to be monitored to ensure they're not going around abusing their power. Who knows if I would be here if I didn't know you or Sheriff Brooks."

"Look Winston, I'm well aware of that situation. You knocked a man out with belligerent force because he pulled out in front of you. You needed to be detained. That was road rage at it's finest. If anything, you should be thanking us for not locking you up!"

"That's not the point! Your officers shouldn't feel the need to arrest me or even place their hands on me just because they THINK they have a clue of what's going on. If you required your officers to have their body cams on during their entire shift and have them reviewed each day, then you'd cut down on a lot of police brutality and these senseless arrests." MP begins to laugh. "What's so funny? I thought you'd understand where I'm coming from, where your people are coming from."

He shakes his head. "Winston, as you young folks say, 'there's levels to this.'"

"What do you mean?"

He puts his cigar out in the ashtray on his desk, takes a sip of wine, and begins to walk around his office. "First off Winston, *my people* are green. Since I was a little boy, the only people that I've depended on were the green presidents I carry around with me in my wallet. *Our people, as* you say, tried to rob me, beat me up, and shoot me every day, so stop it with that, *our people* nonsense. And secondly, the police are doing exactly what I pay them to do, stop crime and get me free labor to run all these crop fields. I give them all the freedom they desire as long as they do that without causing too big of a scene."

I shake my head in disgust. "How could you even fix your mouth or even think of saying something like that?! You have innocent people dying every day because of this *freedom* you're allowing. Not just black people, but all people. YOUR people, the people you swore an oath to protect and serve faithfully. Open your eyes MP! No amount of money is worth a dead life, or lives even."

"You'll understand one day. It's not all sunshine and rainbows in the real world, Winston. It's a business! It's eat or get eaten. I pride myself on running the most powerful city in the world, and that's what I'm going to continue to do."

"MP, as the mayor you have the power and say so to change all of this. You're more worried about how much money you make than the safety of your own people. You could actually provide jobs that pay people to work in the fields and what not instead of having innocent people do it for free. That's modern day slavery and you know it. How can you call yourself a *god*, or even a man if all you do is prey on the weak and innocent. You're supposed to be uplifting them. You have your cops focus on patrolling these low income areas because you know they don't have the proper education they need or the income to afford a good lawyer to escape false imprisonment. I didn't want to believe it, but I guess you really are as crooked as they say."

"Be careful, Winston! You do or say the wrong thing and.."

"And what?! You're gonna have me arrested? Or maybe even killed, huh? Yeah, I think this meeting is adjourned. I'm out." MP sits there with an irate look on his face as I get up from my seat, walk out of his office, and then the house. I get in my car and drive home.

XXIX

———

THE AUDACITY OF THAT INCOMPETENT JACKASS. HOW can anyone think like that? He's basically putting bounties on innocent people. That's down right inhumane. I don't want anything to do with him or anyone else around him if that's a part of his business.

I pull into my parking spot and walk up to my apartment. It's about eleven thirty. I walk in, take off my clothes, and take a nice relaxing shower to ease my mind.

I get out after about fifteen minutes. I then put on a pair of gym shorts and lay in my bed. I stare at my ceiling. *But, what if I do become the new mayor? I can actually be the person to change everything and do what's right. I can be the positive and influential change that the city needs. That the world needs.* I doze off to sleep fantasizing about all of the different possibilities that could happen if I'm in office.

When I wake up, it's seven thirty-five. My alarm didn't go off, so luckily, I didn't oversleep too much.

I get up and quickly begin to get ready to go to The Spot. I had woken up starving, there was no way I could survive another day on orange juice and toast.

After I wash my face and brush my teeth, I throw on a black t-shirt, a tan blazer and matching pants, then make my way out the door. I get to my car and notice there's a note under my left windshield wiper. It reads : "Just know I'm watching you. I hope you have a delightful day full of excitement and ecstasy:)".

I laugh and shake my head. *Nobody but the mayor.* I ball it up and throw it on my car floor as I get in. I then start my car, pull out, and make my way to The Spot.

I arrive there around eight twenty. As soon as I walk through the door, Chino comes from behind the counter to greet me. "Did you do it?", he asks as he places his hands on my shoulders with a smile on his face. "Cause if you didn't, you know I'll have to escort you out of here until it's done. Don't lie to me now. I told you I wasn't playing."

I laugh and jokingly push him out of my way. "Move man, I'm hungry and trying to be on time to work."

He slides in front of me as I try to walk to my seat. "Winston, did you do it? Don't make me have to get the strap."

"Yeah man, I did it. Sheesh."

He places his hands on his hips as he squints and looks me in my eyes. "Now did you REALLY call her, Winston? What y'all talked about?"

"I meean I called, but she wasn't there. I left a message with her secretary though. Hopefully she gets it and calls me back today. Can I sit down now?" I step aside and continue to walk to my seat. "Seriously though, let me get a Rico special to go. I'm hungry and running late."

"Mmmhmm, let me find out you lying and just chickened out. You gonna mess around and be sad and lonely Friday night, per usual."

"Chino, I'm far from lonely. I got women."

Chino smirks then says, "Yeah, okay."

"I'm serious, man."

"Ooookaayyy". He sarcastically says as he goes back to the kitchen. He stays back there for about ten minutes before he comes back with my plate. "Here you go, Winston."

"Thanks Chino, I'll see you tomorrow." He gets a big smile on his face then snatches my bag back as I try to grab it. "C'mon Chino, it's about to be eight forty."

"Be cool and take a seat. I forgot something."

I let out a sigh of frustration. "Hurry up, Chino."

As I sit back down and look at my phone to check the time, I get a tap on my shoulder. "Hey, um it's Winston right?" I turn and it's Natalie. She's looking beautiful and elegant as she always is. She has on a navy blue dress suit with white heels and her hair in a bun.

"Yeah, and it's Natalie, right?" *As if I didn't already know that.*

She takes her seat by me. "You must've been really busy at work these past couple of days for you not to give me a call."

I blush a little bit. "Honestly I have. I'm sorry to keep a beautiful woman like yourself waiting." She blushes. "But, I did make time and gave you a call yesterday afternoon. Your secretary said you had left early though."

"Yeah, I had left because I had some personal issues to resolve, but how about I just call you later around one. Does that fit into your busy schedule Mr. Winston?"

I grin. "Yeah, that's fine. Is everything okay with you though?"

"Yeah, I'm fine. Thanks for asking." She says with a smile.

She takes out her cellphone and goes to the dial pad. I start smiling. *We're finally about to exchange numbers!*

She looks at me and says, "What's your work number, Winston? And the extension too, if you have one?"

My mind exploded. *Not again.* "Um, you don't just want to exchange cell phone numbers? It'll make it a little easier for us to communicate if we just do that.", I say, trying to keep a straight face and avoid showing the disappointment I felt on the inside.

"To be honest Winston, don't take this the wrong way, but I try to keep business business. I've had some bad experiences in the past that lead to me having to get a new number. Ever since then, I rarely give my number out. Don't get me wrong now, you're quite the looker Winston, but my safety and peace is more important. Maybe we'll get there one day, who knows." She starts to grin.

The inner me breathes a sigh of relief. *A looker is definitely a good thing. And she's leaving the door open, so maybe I shouldn't give up on her just yet. Shooters shoot, right? C'mon Winston, you're a king.*

"I completely understand you. A woman as fine as you probably has weirdos coming left and right, but look at you, can you blame them though?" *She's smiling Winston, go for it.* "To be honest, I think you're absolutely gorgeous and I'd love to take you out. Not for a business dinner, but a date dinner. Friday night to be exact. Valentine's Day."

She blushes and twirls a strand of hair that's hanging over her forehead.

Before she could answer, Chino brings our food. "Here y'all two lovely people go. Call in number eleven belongs to the lovely lady, and here's your Rico special, Winston. I hope I didn't interrupt anything."

I shake my head and give Chino a sarcastic stare as Natalie says, "Oh, thanks Unc. Now I gotta get going, but first, what's your number Winston?"

"Uuhhh it's 912-331-8004 with extension thirty one."

"Okay, got it. I'll call you at one. Thanks again Unc, y'all have a good day." She grabs her food and leaves.

Chino places his arms on the counter as he looks at me and says, "I got perfect timing, huh? I see you finally exchanged numbers. I'm proud of you son."

I suck my teeth. "You interrupted me asking her on a date for Friday you dingus. You threw off her train of thought so she just asked for my number. Some timing you got." I sarcastically say as I grab my food and walk towards the door.

"Man, I saved your ass from a rejection! You should be grateful!" He jokingly yells as I wave him off as I leave and go to my car.

XXX

———

A S I'M PARKING, I NOTICE THREE POLICE CARS SITTING in front of the building. *What in the hell is going on?* My calm demeanor instantly becomes nervous, panicky. *MP sent his boys to come get me. Our little disagreement must've really made him mad. I'm sure he knows I was tipsy though…..maaaaaan, I'm done for. They're going to kill me. I have to go. I have to leave town, no, the state. Maybe the country.* I pull my phone out of my pocket. *I have to call my mother. I have to call Mr. Langston. I have to…* My phone buzzes, it's a text from Sharon: "Where are you? It's crazy up here, they're doing a full out investigation on Steve." I exhale.

I'm shocked, starled, but most importantly, relieved. I put my phone back in my pocket then get out of my car, grabbing my briefcase and food, and make my way to the elevator.

When I get off, I see about five police officers scattered throughout the office questioning my coworkers. One is talking to Sharon as I walk in. We exchange waves then I go to my office and get myself situated.

I get a knock on my door as soon as I sit down. I look, and it's the same police officer that tried to arrest me the other night at my apartment.

With a big smile on his face, he says, "Well looka what we got here. Whenever you get done cleaning your boss's fancy office, let me holla at ya for a second."

I chuckle a little bit under my breath and raise my eyebrows. "Excuse me? Can you say that again? I don't believe I heard you correctly."

He steps into my office and raises his hands in a defensive position as he laughs and says, "Woah, woah, easy there now bucko. It was just a joke man. I recognized your name on the employees list and thought I'd be the one to interview you."

"Man first off, give me one good reason why I shouldn't make a scene in here right now and report you? I'm amongst my people so they'll attest to everything I say in court."

He laughs. "Because we both know the man in charge doesn't give a rat's ass about what we do to common folk like yourself, and from what I've heard, you're on his bad side, right? So I dare you to do something, I double dog dare ya."

I swallow my tongue and sit back in my chair. I didn't want the images I was fearing moments prior to come true. "Let's get this over with man, I got stuff to do."

He smiles then takes his seat across from me. "Now that's more I like it. This will be quick. Shouldn't take no more than five minutes." He takes out a notepad and a pen. "Before we begin, let me properly introduce myself, my name is Officer Taylor Russo."

He reaches out to shake my hand. I look at him, look at his hand, then back at him. I reach out and give him a fist bump. "You know, germs man. No offense."

"Haha yeah, I understand. None taken." He clears his throat and sits up in his chair. "Well let's get this started now, shall we? Were you aware that your colleague, Steve Walton, was using and even selling drugs on the premises?"

"Oh wow, what drugs?"

"Well, when they raided his house and searched his desk and car, they found cocaine, marijuana, percocets, oxycontin, and ecstasy to name a few."

I chuckle. "Daaamn Steve, didn't know he was getting down like that. I was unaware he was selling, but I did always think he was on something."

"So you DID know he was a user? Correct?"

"I mean, he'd have mood shifts throughout the day and he'd even have some powder on his nose here and there, but I just minded my business. Just because someone acts weird you can't automatically assume they're on drugs. It's unfair to the person. They could just be experiencing life problems like everyone else."

"Mmmhhmm." He says as he nods his head and writes something in his notepad.

I sit up in my seat to try and get a glimpse of what he wrote. "What you mmhhmming and writing about over there Officer Russo?"

"Just some notes. Would you pass a drug test right now if you were to randomly receive one?"

"Look man, I ain't on drugs. Next question."

"Hmm, that's a very quick transition from relaxed to hostile when asked about a drug test." He nods his head and writes some more. "Have you, or are you currently selling drugs? Are you his supplier?"

I suck my teeth. "Look Officer Russo, just because I'm black that doesn't mean I sell drugs. How dare you ev..."

When I was mid sentence, another officer knocks on my door, peeks his head in, and says, "Hey Russo, we gotta go. It's a ten fifty-four."

Officer Russo gets up. "I'm sure I have all I need. It was nice talking to you, Winston. Stay hydrated." He nods his head and walks out of my office to join the other officers before they swiftly exit the building.

No more than thirty seconds pass before Mr. Jacobs walks into my office. He's wearing a bright red suit as if he was Santa Clause. He knocks on my door and walks in. "So, do we have the mayor yet? How did the meeting go last night?"

I exhale then say, "To be honest, I don't think he'll be working with us. Well, at least I don't believe I will. I just can't work with someone who has such malicious and materialistic values. I can't do it, Mr. Jacobs."

Firmly, "Look Winston. I don't give a damn about your morals or ethics, or whatever it is. Put all that sunshine and rainbow stuff to the side and get the job done. I just lost my second best advisor. And on top of that, we're not just losing all of his clients, but clients throughout the entire firm. They refuse to associate themselves with a company that hired a drug fiend. Once the investigations end and the news gets out, I'm sure we'll continue to lose more and more. Then on top of THAT mess, we have clients spreading rumors that we're unprofessional and have crazy wives coming in and out of here breaking windows. Like what the hell happened yesterday, Winston?! I stay home sick one time and this place turns to shit. You know what, I gotta take a walk to cool off." He starts to hyperventilate.

I try to comfort and cool him down by fanning him with papers off of my desk. "Relax sir, it's all gonna be okay."

Breathing heavy and beginning to sweat, "We'll continue this later." He walks out of my office and goes into his.

Sharon texts me. "Is everything okay?"

I text back, "Yeah, Jacobs is just on one right now. He was probably one of Steve's biggest consumers lol."

"LMAO I can believe it.", she replies.

We laugh and make eye contact through my glass wall. She smiles at me then gets up and walks into my office. "You want to go get lunch today?", she asks.

"I still have this Rico special I gotta eat. Maybe tomorrow, if that's fine with you."

"Winston, come on. For us to be *best friends* we barely spend time together. At least just come and talk to me. Please?"

"Fine, we just have to be back by one. I'm expecting a very important call."

"Oouuuu, who is it?"

I laugh then say, "When the time is right, you'll know."

"Uuuggh, you're so aggravating." She rolls her eyes then walks out my door.

"Haha Wait! What time are you trying to leave for lunch?"

She looks back and says, "When the time is right you'll know, Winston." She laughs then walks to her desk.

I sit back in my chair and let out a yawn as I stretch my arms to the sky. *Finally, some peace and quiet. So much has happened and it's not even twelve yet.* My stomach growls. *I'm starving, now's the perfect time to eat.*

I get up and take my food to the microwave to warm it up. I walk past Sharon and she's on the phone. I walk past Henry's office, and maintenance is working on repairing his glass wall that his wife shattered while he's in there trying to salvage his clientele. I get to the microwave, warm my food up, and make my way back to my office.

As I'm walking, Mr. Jacobs calls me, "Hey Winston, my office!" I turn around and he sees the food in my hand. "Whenever you're done eating. Don't take long."

"Yes sir, give me thirty minutes."

"Twenty, it's urgent."

"Okay, I got you." I walk back to my office and begin to eat. I finished my food in about seven minutes, and took the rest of the time to relax. That is, until Mr. Jacobs walked by and motioned me to come to his office.

I release a sigh of frustration as I get up to go follow him. "Do you have any clue what he wants?", I ask Sharon as I'm walking by.

Sarcastically, "When the time is right, you'll know."

I laugh and keep walking. I get to his office and take a seat. "Well, what's up?", I ask.

"I just got a call from the police department. They said they want pee samples from everyone in the office."

Puzzled, "Okay, so why are you telling me and not the entire office?"

XXXI

———

I SIT BACK IN MY CHAIR ANTICIPATING HIS RESPONSE. I just knew he was about to say some foolishness.

His face turns red and he repositions himself in his chair.

As soon as he's about to speak, Sharon knocks on the door, walks in and says, "Excuse me guys, I hope I'm not interrupting anything."

"No, no, you're good Sharon. What is it? Is there someone here for me?", Mr. Jacobs quickly says.

"It's actually for Winston. Mr. Langston is here to see you. He's in your office waiting for you."

I turn around. "Okay, tell him I'll be in there in a second."

"Alright.", she says walking away.

"You should probably go handle that, Winston. Don't wanna keep a man like Robert Langston waiting.", Mr. Jacobs says with a grin.

"Yeah, iight." I get up and walk to my office.

I walk in, and Sharon is conversing with Mr. Langston. They're giggling and laughing. He's sitting down wearing a yellow linen suit, and Sharon's wearing her favorite pink sweater and her black skirt.

"I'll leave you two to be. Congrats again Robert." Sharon says as she walks out.

"What's up Mr. Langston, what do I owe the pleasure?", I say as I sit down at my desk. "And what's up with the champagne?!"

Mr. Langston sits back in his chair as a big smile begins to cover his face. "First and foremost Winston, I wanted to apologize for the way we left things the other day. I hope we can have a fresh start."

"It's all good, you know you're my guy, Mr. Langston. What else is there? I know you didn't bring this champagne just to say sorry, knowing I don't drink."

He laughs, "I also wanted to give you tickets to tonight's game. You'll be able to watch them in the skybox."

I'm blown away. "The skybox?! How'd you manage to get these on such short notice?....You're the owner now?!"

With a bigger smile, "Yes, Winston, season-long skybox seats are just one of the many perks of being the new majority owner of the Ricoville Wardogs."

"Ah man. Congrats Mr. Langston, I'm happy for you!", I say as I get up and shake his hand across my desk.

"Thanks, Winston. Everything is still being finalized, but yeah, I'm the majority owner of the Wardogs now. This news was too big to tell you over the phone, so I decided to drop in and tell you in person. And as far as the champagne, just save it for a rainy day. You never know when a special moment might occur and you'll need it."

"Yeah, you're right. I appreciate it, I'll stash it here in my office."

"Yes sir." He begins to chuckle. "Well Winston, that's really the only reason why I stopped by. I was in the area and like I said, this was news I just had to share in person." He begins to get up out of his seat.

"Congrats again Mr. Langston. I'm really proud of you, seriously. You're a real inspiration. And once again, thanks for the tickets. It's a big game tonight."

"Oh, that reminds me. The game tips off at eight thirty, so please be there an hour early. I want you to be with me at my introduction. My wife is out of town visiting her family and you're the next best thing."

"I'd be honored, Mr. Langston. What exactly do I need to wear?"

"Hhmmm, if you could find a black suit and red tie to wear that'd be perfect."

"Okay, I got you."

"Excellent! Well, you have your tickets and passes, I'll see you tonight, Winston. I'm looking forward to it."

"Likewise, Mr. Langston." He shakes my hand and he exits my office.

Now it's about eleven thirty. When Mr. Langston leaves, I check in with a few clients and look through my emails until twelve. When twelve hits, I go outside to see if Sharon is ready to leave. When I get to her desk, I see she already has food.

"Damn, so just forget about having lunch together, huh?", I say as she's preparing to eat her food.

"I'm sorry, my boo thang surprised me with lunch today." She says blushing. "I just know he's doing something special Friday. But hey, there's plenty if you want some."

"Aaaaw, that's so sweet. Hashtag goals.", I sarcastically say. "Thank you, but I'm good. I'll just order takeout or something. I have work to do anyway. Plus, mystery man got that for you, I wouldn't want to take away from his chivalrous gesture. It wouldn't be as special."

"Yeah, yeah. More for me. You excited about tonight though? When I was talking to my sugar daddy earlier, he told me about how he's the new majority owner and the tickets he got you."

"You do know he's a married man right?"

"That doesn't have anything to do with me, hunty."

I shake my head and laugh. "Is Mr. Langston really your mystery man?"

She doesn't say anything, she just sticks her tongue out and winks at me. "And on that note, I'm going to wait for my food in my office. I don't even wanna know anymore." I shake my head again, and walk back to my office.

"As my bestie, you're obligated to support me and my sugar

daddy's relationship, Winston!", she jokingly yells as I'm walking away.

I get to my desk and order my food from my phone. It's twelve-ten when I order it, and it's twelve-fifty when it gets delivered.

KNOCK, KNOCK.

The delivery man comes in with my food. I get up to greet him at my door. "Tip?", he asks with his hand out.

Tip?! Y'all are five minutes away and it took y'all forty minutes to get here. How can you expect a tip?

"I got a tip for you, never put all your eggs in one basket.", I say as I grab my food.

He sucks his teeth, "Cheapskate.", he mumbles under his breath as he walks out.

I ignore it and prepare to eat my food. It's chicken, steak, and rice from a hibachi spot down the street.

Halfway through my lunch, Mr. Jacobs comes into my office. "You've been hungry today haven't ya?"

I finish chewing the food that's in my mouth. "You just have bad timing today. What's up?"

"I need you to pee in this cup by one-thirty. There's someone from the police department here to watch you to make sure it's really yours."

I raise my eyebrows in shock. "Umm, aren't there rules against that? I'm almost a thousand percent sure y'all breaking about five or six laws man."

"Hey, I'm just telling you what the police told me. Most of everyone is already finished, so the bathroom should be empty if you want your privacy. Well, privacy with the observer of course." He chuckles.

Still confused. "And everyone did it?"

"Yes Winston, they were direct orders from the police department. I'll just place this cup right here." He places a clear plastic cup on my desk. "I have a few phone calls to make. Remember, before one thirty." Mr. Jacobs says as he walks out of my office.

I'll finish this later. I close my food. *If I go now. I'll be back in time for Natalie's call. It's twelve-fifty eight now, I doubt she'll call me exactly at one.* I get up, grab my cup, and go to the bathroom.

"Hope you ain't been smoking. Let me find out you were one of Steve's regulars.", Sharon jokes as I pass by.

I walk in the bathroom and nod my head at the man standing in the corner waiting for me. "Just whip it out and release.", he says.

"Aye man, it's just you and me in here. How about I just turn around and do all that. I'm not comfortable with all this."

"I'm sorry pal, but it's protocol. With a case this serious, we can't take any chances with anyone switching their piss.", he says as he shrugs his shoulders.

After an awkward silence, I pee in the cup then hand it to him.

"Thank you, that wasn't so bad, was it? We'll have the results in the morning."

I cringe then wash my hands "You have a good one." He nods his head and I exit out the bathroom to return to my desk.

"Did I have any calls?", I ask Sharon.

"No, why? Are you expecting someone? Hmmm?"

"I told you, it's business."

"Mmhhmm, okay, Winston. Whatever you say." I anxiously walk to my office and close my door.

It's one fifteen, what's taking her so long? Eeh, she's probably busy today, Winston.

I sit at my desk waiting, anticipating, yearning to hear her voice on the other side of the phone. Five minutes past, then ten, then twenty, and then thirty. *It's one forty-five, if she doesn't call by two I'm leaving.* I lean back in my chair, and play on my cell phone for about fifteen minutes. I check the time, and it's two o'two.

Forget it. I'm going home to get ready for the game.

I pack up my things and begin to walk out. As soon as I go to close my door, the phone rings.

———

XXXII

I IMMEDIATELY RUSH TO ANSWER THE PHONE. THE CALL I've been waiting all day for. To hear Natalie's voice on the other side of the phone would mean more to me than receiving the tickets to the game tonight. I pick up the phone anticipating to hear her sweet, pleasant, angelic voice.

"Hello, Natalie? I see you were the busy one today.", I nervously say.

I anxiously wait for her to respond. "Hello, are you satisfied with your current car insurance provider?", the automated message says.

I instantly hang up the phone. I grab my things and leave my office with a face full of disappointment and a heart full of crushed dreams.

"Bye Winston, I hope you enjoy the game tonight!", Sharon says as I walk past her.

"Thanks.", I nod my head and wave at her.

"Hold on Winston! Come here, what's up with you? You don't look too excited for tonight's game. I may not be too into sports, but I do remember Mr. Langston saying this is a nationally televised, rivalry game. And on top of that, you're going to be watching it in the skybox with a bunch of millionaires, maybe even some billionaires too. That's big! That's so much opportunity waiting for you. What's wrong?"

I turn around and put a fake smile on my face. "I'm good Sharon, I promise. I'm screaming with excitement on the inside, trust me."

"Mmhhmm, how'd that call go?"

I shrug and say, "Eeeh it was alright. Shorter than I expected, but it's cool. There's always tomorrow."

She scrunches her eyes then looks me up and down as she says, "Winston, are you having lady issues? Be honest with me."

I scoff. "Me? Lady issues? You out of all people should know better than that."

"Yeah, whatever. If she's right for you, she'll come right to you."

"You read that in a fortune cookie or something?"

She giggles, "No silly. It's just a fact. If you have to constantly chase something, then it's not destined for you. When it's meant for you, you just know. Remember, the rabbit didn't chase the tortoise, he ate the carrot."

I put my things down and grab Sharon's hands as I look her into her eyes. "Look Sharon, that made zero sense, but I really and sincerely appreciate the effort, honestly." We start to laugh. "Now I'm about to go. And you, you gotta lay off of those crazy, dramatic soap operas you be watching out here."

"Boy get out my face." I let go of her hands, and pick up my things as I laugh.

"I'm just trying to look out for you. They're making you talk crazier than usual."

"Whatever." She rolls her eyes.

"I'm out, for real this time. I'll see you." I begin to make my way to the elevator.

"Be safe and enjoy, Winston."

I wave back at her as I enter the elevator. I get off in the parking lot and get in my car to go home.

Maybe she'll call me tomorrow. She could've just had some personal stuff going on again. Maybe I should call her when I get home. Nah, that'll make me look thirsty. But if I wait, that call might never happen. Ugh, the balls in her court now. I'll just wait for her to call me then just go from there.

It's a little past three when I pull into my parking spot. That gives me about an hour and a half to two hours to relax before I have to get ready for the game.

I get in my apartment, change clothes, warm up my leftover hibachi, and relax in my favorite spot, the couch.

I put on a TV show, and decide to take a nap to make sure that I'm well rested for tonight. Who knows what may happen or who I'll meet.

As I'm laying down with my eyes closed, on the verge of taking my nap, my phone rings. I look to see who's calling. *Chino, this better be important.*

I answer and with a sleepy voice say, "Hello? What's good, Chino?"

"Man, I know you're not over there crying! Well I guess you just have to respect her decision and move on from it. My church is having another singles event tomorrow night after service. You should come."

"Maaaan, I told you I'm done with your church. At the last service I went to, a lady grabbed my butt when I was walking by for the offering. Then another tried to smother me with her breasts when we were doing the meet and greet. I'm straight man."

"Winston! The Lord said you shall lay hands on thine neighbor. You can't get mad at those women for being obedient servants of the Lord."

I laugh and say, "Whatever man, I still ain't going back."

"We'll see, but how that call went? Did she say no to the date? That's the reason you over there crying, ain't it."

"First off, I was asleep. I was trying to take a little nap because I'm going to the Wardogs game tonight. And she didn't even call Chino. I think I'm about to just say forget it."

"Mr. Langston might as well be your daddy, Winston. I know

he's the one that gave you the tickets. And you say that every day sucka. Just give her some time and be ready whenever she does call you. She has a life too, the world doesn't solely revolve around you, son."

"Chill man, that's just the OG. He's always looking out. And I got you, but a man can only have so much patience."

"To consider yourself a man, you sure do be acting like a little puppy when it comes to Natalie." He laughs.

"And on that note, I'm going back to sleep."

Firmly, "You can't handle the truth! Keep playing. I see sad and lonely in your near future."

"Whatever, Chino."

"Be safe tonight Winston, and bring me a t-shirt or something."

"I got you." I hang up the phone, set an alarm, then lay back down. Not too long after I lay my head down, I drift off to sleep.

I wake up to the sound of my alarm at five. I already have a black suit that's pressed and ready to be worn, so I just hop in the shower, brush my teeth, then get dressed.

It's around five-thirty when I'm dressed and ready. I stare at myself in the mirror for a few seconds, then I grab my keys as I walk towards my door. As I'm walking out, my phone rings. I don't recognize the number, so I let it go to voicemail. It calls again, and I do the same thing. I get inside my car, and the number calls for a third time. I decide to pick it up. *This better be about money.*

"Hello?", I say.

"Hey Mr. Winston, it's Natalie."

XXXIII

———

C AUGHT OFF GUARD AND LOST FOR WORDS, I DON'T say anything.

"Um hello, Winston? Are you there? It's Natalie, Natalie Graves. The woman from The Spot."

"Hi, hey Natalie. What's up? You just caught me a little off guard that's all."

Very apologetic, "Oh, I'm so sorry Winston. I got caught up with work. I was trying to close a deal with an expecting married couple and it took a lot longer than I anticipated. I tried calling your office, but no luck. I figured you probably left, so I just got this number from the secretary, and yeah. I hope this isn't a bad time. Are you free?"

Hmm, I should probably make it sound like I'm busy.

"It's all good Natalie, but I'm actually driving to a meeting right now."

"Oh, okay. I'll let you go. I'm actually about to leave my office and get ready for one myself. I just figured it'd be either now or never if I was going to call you today."

I fake laugh. "Yeah, I understand. How about we just meet at The Spot early Friday morning. That fine for you?"

"Um yeah, sure. That's fine, especially since we can't figure out this phone situation. What time is good for you? I don't have to be at work until ten."

"I can do anything between eight and eight forty. I have to be in at nine."

"Hmmm, let's do eight-fifteen. It shouldn't take no more than thirty minutes."

"Okay, that's fine."

"Great, I'll see you then. Have a good.."

"Wait Natalie." I take a deep breath. "You never answered my question earlier. Would you mind if I take you out....on a date?"

She waits a few seconds then says, "I'm getting another call Winston, I'll see you Friday?"

Disheartened, "Yeah, Friday."

"I hope you enjoy the rest of your day, Winston, see you then."

"Thanks, you too." We hang up the phone and I drive off and make my way to the arena.

You'll see her Friday, Winston, don't worry about it. She'll come around.

After ducking and dodging traffic for about an hour and a half, I finally arrive at the arena at seven twenty. And because Mr. Langston gave me a parking pass, I can park in the arena.

When I pull into the gate, I present my badge to the security guard and park in my designated parking spot. I call Mr. Langston to let him know I'm here.

"Hello, Mr. Langston? Can you hear me?"

"Hey Winston. Are you here? I'm in the sound room right now."

"Yes sir. Where should I go?"

"You're parked in A-12, correct?"

"Yes sir."

"Get on the elevator, take it to C-11, and there will be somebody waiting for you. I'll see you soon."

"Okay, thanks." I hang up the phone, get out of my car, and walk to the elevator. I get on, then I go to C-11. When I get off of the elevator, I see a big muscular security guard waiting for me with a red collared shirt and khakis. He's at least 6'8, 285lbs. If he wasn't a security guard, I'm almost sure he'd be a world champion wrestler or either an All-Pro lineman.

"Right this way Mr. Williams.", he says as he greets me with a deep, heavy voice. We get on a golf cart and he drives me around the corner to meet Mr. Langston. I was in awe at how sturdy the golf cart was. I was expecting it to lean a little when we got in.

"Just go through those doors right there and make that first left.", he tells me as he stops the golf cart and I get off.

"Alright, thanks man. Have a good one."

"My pleasure, you enjoy the game." He drives off. As I walk through the double doors, I see Mr. Langston standing there waiting for me.

"There he is!", he says as he greets me with a hug.

"Yes sir, right on time. How long til show time?"

"We're going to walk out around eight ten. It'll be just before warmups. We're going to walk out, wave, then I'll say a couple words and that's it. It's party time after that."

"Sounds like a plan."

"Indeed, I want to thank you again for coming, Winston. I really appreciate you being here with me. It means a lot." He begins to tear up.

"No, it's an honor for me really. To just be here to experience all of this is incredible. To know where you came from and to see you here now is truly amazing. You beat the stereotype, rewrote the narrative, that's remarkable to see and be a part of Mr. Langston. Coming from where you did, you were supposed to be dead or in jail. Instead, you're one of the most successful businessmen in the country. And now, you're a majority owner of the Ricoville Wardogs, one of the most prominent franchises in sports."

He hugs me again as tears fall from his eyes. "That means a lot coming from you Winston, son."

We embrace each other for a couple of seconds before one of the event directors calls us over to discuss a few things about the ceremony.

We talked for about twenty minutes before he got a call letting us know that it was time to line up and get started. He then escorts us down to the court, and we wait by the basketball goal until it's time for them to call us out. As time progresses, I look around the arena and notice the crowd starting to get bigger and bigger. I begin to get nervous. My body begins to get hot, my hands start to get clammy, and beads of sweat start to form on my forehead.

Mr. Langston notices and bumps me with his elbow. "Relax Winston, just breathe. I'm the one that has to speak and do the real stuff. You have the easy part. Just stand there and look pretty." We both laugh.

"Yes sir, I got you." He hands me some napkins out of his pocket to wipe my face.

Now it's eight thirty, it's showtime. The lights begin to scatter across the arena as the announcer begins to introduce Mr. Langston.

"Goooood evening Wardogs nation!!! Shift your attention to the center of the court and help me in introducing the newest, majority owner of our Ricoville Wardogs!!! Everybody stand to your feet and make some noise for the legendary, one and only, Mr. Robert! Jonathan! Langston! He's accompanied by his son, Winston Williams. Give them a warm welcome as they make their way to center court." The crowd begins to go crazy as we begin walking to half court. The screams of 40,000 people shake the arena. "Mr. Langston, welcome to the Wardog family!", he continues.

We get to the center of the court and they hand Mr. Langston a mic.

He waves to the crowd then says, "Thank you so much Wardog nation! I'm honored to be a part of such a distinguished and historic franchise. I hope to add a lot more trophies to that trophy case while I'm here. Let's goooo Wardogs!" He drops the mic and we exit the court. "Whew", he says as he turns and looks at me with a smile.

We're then greeted by a couple of arena workers, and they take us up to the skybox. In the skybox, there's a big congratulatory celebration awaiting for Mr. Langston. A giant room full of rich and prominent people. Some elected officials, some ex-ball players, and some other well known businessmen.

Before we enter the room, Mr. Langston turns to me and says, "Prepare yourself for a long night with some arrogant, ignorant, and obnoxious snobs, Winston. Just stay close to me, and we'll make it through." He grins then gives a slight chuckle. "Let's go."

We enter the room, and we're immediately greeted by balloons, streamers, and confetti. "Congratulations!", they all say. Everyone comes up and shakes our hands.

Mr. Langston then walks to the center of the room and says, "Thank you everyone. I really appreciate the love and support from the bottom of my heart. Now that that's out of the way, I want everyone to grab a beer and enjoy this basketball game. The business is over with, now lets play."

The room starts to applaud. I get a tap on the shoulder, and I hear someone say, "It's good seeing you again, Winston." I turn to see who it is, and it's the mayor. He's wearing an all black suit and a red and white striped tie. "Don't look so surprised to see me. I know you didn't think I'd miss my friend's big day?"

Mr. Langston comes over, "Hey MP, what a pleasant surprise." They exchange handshakes. "Thanks for stopping by. You staying for the entire game?"

"No, I just came to show my face and personally congratulate you. Well, the two of you." Me and Mr. Langston both get a confused look on our faces.

"What are you congratulating Winston for?", Mr. Langston asks.

MP pauses for a moment. Then with a grin he says, "Opportunity.", as he raises his beer bottle. "I'm certain you'll understand shortly.", he looks at his watch, "Now if you excuse me, I must get going. I have a city to run. Congratulations again you two." He shakes our hands and exits the room.

Mr. Langston turns to me. "Do you know what that was about?"

"No sir, no clue. I told him I wouldn't work with him after we had our meeting, but that's it."

Mr. Langston shakes his head and laughs, "He doesn't know how to take no for an answer, be careful. But this is a celebration, Winston, we'll worry about him tomorrow."

And that's what we did. After the mayor left, we conversed

with a few people then sat back in our chairs and enjoyed the game. There's about two minutes left before halftime when Mr. Langston turned to me and began to say, "You know what, Winston? I can't believe that with all the food they have in here, they don't have any nachos. I guess these people are too upscale for that. Would you mind taking my card and getting me some? You can get whatever you like as well."

"Yeah, I don't mind, I could use some fresh air and a break from all this anyway."

"I understand you completely, I think I've just become immune to all of it over time. Oh, and I don't know why, but this spot over by D-34 is never packed so it shouldn't take you no longer than ten minutes to get everything. It's a concession stand, but it's also like a sports bar. The food is a little high priced, but it's amazing. I'm planning on building a couple of franchises in the city. But anyway, you're going to make a right when you leave here, go down a level, then make a left and it'll be right there. You'll know it when you see it."

"Alright, I got you." I get up and leave the room. I find the place Mr. Langston was referring to, and he was right. There are hardly any people in line and as I look at the menu, I see he was downplaying the prices a little. As I'm making my way up the line to order, I hear a couple of people behind me having a conversation. I raise my eyebrows because one of the voices sounds very familiar. I pretend to stretch, so it's not obvious that I'm looking at them. When I turn around, my face lights up and I'm astounded by who I see. It's Natalie, she's with two other friends, but I only notice her. She has her long, curly hair down, and she's wearing a white Wardogs t-shirt with jeans, that are gracefully hugging her voluptuous legs, and white tennis shoes. She makes the basics look exquisite. *This must be fate.* She has her back turned as she's talking to her friends, so she doesn't see me as I'm looking at her. *This is my chance. I'm wearing a nice suit, I'm in the skybox, this is the perfect opportunity.*

I step out of line and let the two couples behind me take my place. I then walk up to Natalie and her friends and I tap her on her shoulder. Her friends stare with confused expressions on their faces. When I get her attention, I smile then say, "Hey Natalie, some meeting huh?"

XXXIV

H ER FACE LIGHTS UP AND SHE STARTS TO BLUSH. Before she could even think about saying anything, one of her friends steps up and says, "Are you thee, Winston? The fine ass financial advisor she's been playing hard to get with? We heard them say your name in that ceremony before the game, but we didn't know if that was really you. Natalie never told us Robert Langston was your father."

Now I begin to blush because I'm in disbelief of what I had just heard. Bashfully, "Um, I don't know about the other stuff, but yes my name is Winston and I'm a financial advisor. And Mr. Langston isn't my dad dad. He's just been a really good mentor and our relationship just grew from that."

"Aaawww", her friends say.

I shake their hands and smile as I introduce myself. "But anyway. Hey, it's nice to meet y'all."

"Mmhmm, I got ya. Well hey Mr. Winston, I'm Keisha and this is Celeste." Keisha says as she points to Celeste. Keisha has dark caramel skin with short, straight hair and is wearing a black

Wardog jersey dress, and Celeste is light skinned with long brown hair and is wearing a red Wardogs jersey and shorts. Both are also extremely beautiful. Celeste is slim with an hourglass figure, and Keisha has more of a curvy body type . "Now look friend, you may not believe it, but Natalie is always talking about you. She's been out the game so long, that she doesn't really know how to come off as approachable to the opposite sex. We tried to tell her that stuck up, playing hard to get boujie shit wasn't gonna work. But, anyywayy, we're gonna move up some and give y'all room to talk. Soooo, bye."

We both nervously laugh. "Some friends you got.", I sarcastically say as I smile at her while she looks down in embarrassment.

She looks up at me and says, "I'm sorry, I can't take them anywhere. They're so extra. I really can't believe Keisha just said that with her single ass, always trying to hook somebody else up. Ugh."

I chuckle. "Relax Natalie. Everything happens for a reason. Maybe it was destined for this to happen. God was like, 'Maaaaaan y'all two are playing waaay too much. Ima just position y'all riiight here, and y'all gon' meet like this. BOOM." She starts to laugh.

"Yeah, that could be it."

"I love your smile by the way. I think it's your best curve honestly." She smiles and blushes at me. "Soooo is it true what they said?"

"What you mean?", she bites her lip.

"I know you're not gonna act like your friends didn't just put you on blast thirty seconds ago?" She looks down and laughs. "Is it true you talk about me and have been playing hard to get all this time?"

"Hey you two lovebirds, what y'all want?! It's our turn to order.", Keisha yells back as I sigh.

"Y'all hurry up, I'm hungry.", Celeste adds.

Natalie laughs then with a big smile says, "C'mon let's go, I'm hungry too." She walks up to the cash register and I follow behind her.

I let all three of them order then I step up and say, "I got it. My treat." I look up at the menu, then place my order, "Can you add two orders of the grande nachos to that too please? Extra beef and cheese."

"Well shit, if I would've known he was gonna be Mr. Money man, I would've got more.", Keisha says.

"Girl, shut up!", Celeste says as she nudges her. "Thank you, Winston. We appreciate it."

"But this food is to die for!", Keisha exclaims.

I laugh, "Get what y'all want. It's no problem."

"See, closed mouths don't get fed y'all. Thank you, I'm team Winston all day.", Keisha says as she steps up to add onto the order.

"Don't thank me, thank Mr. Langston.", I humbly say. "It's his treat."

"Aaaww, that's nice of him to give you his card.", Natalie adds.

"That'll be $133.75 sir.", the cashier says as she has a perplexed look on her face.

I reach into my pocket, grab the card, and hand it to her. "Here you go."

"Thank you!" She grabs my card and swipes it. "Um, could you enter the pin please."

I enter the wrong pin twice, foolishly thinking it was my card. "Wrong pin, please try again sir.".

Unaware of my surroundings, I blurt out. "Damn, I forgot this wasn't my card." The cashier raises her eyebrows. "One second please." I tell her as I pull out my phone to call Mr. Langston. Simultaneously, the cashier asks me for my ID. I give her my drivers license as I'm calling Mr. Langston. He doesn't pick up, his phone goes straight to voicemail. *He must not have service in here.*

"Excuse me sir, can you step aside please?", the cashier says before she leaves to go to the back. Still focused on trying to call Mr. Langston, I just take a few steps to the left.

"Everything okay?", Natalie asks.

"Yeah, just forgot to get the pin like a dummy."

"I can cover it. It's cool, really."

"No, it's fine I...", As I'm talking to Natalie, I get tackled by two security guards.

"That's him officers!", the cashier yells as she's pointing at me while she's walking back to her register.

"We gotcha now!", one of the officers shout.

The girls frighteningly step back, "Winston, are you ok?! Need me to do anything?", Natalie frantically asks.

Keisha and Celeste pull out their phones and start recording. "I wish y'all would! Fake ass mall cops.", Keisha viciously threatens.

"Get off of him. Y'all doing too much!", Celeste adds.

"Go get Mr. Langston! He's in suite A-31.", I tell Natalie as one guard holds me on the ground with my arms behind my back. The other is kneeled down in front of my face mushing my head into the floor.

Natalie takes off in a sprint to get Mr. Langston.

"Y'all not even the real police! Y'all wannabees can't be doing all that!", Keisha yells.

"He's very dangerous ma'am, please calm down and back away. He's been robbing and scamming people in this building for years. The Bankcard Bandit! We finally got him!", guard one says.

Guard two adds, "Listen to my partner, we don't want anyone to get hurt."

"Y'all have the wrong guy! I'm trying to tell you. Search me!", I scream.

Guard one pushes my face harder into the ground. "Shut it!"

Guard two pauses as he notices the concerned crowd forming around us. He whispers to guard one, "Stand him up. More people are starting to show up with cameras. Let's just take him in. I can hear that promotion calling our name now." He then turns to the cashier and says, "Thanks for notifying us mam."

They slap handcuffs on me, pick me up, then start to walk me towards their golf cart.

"We're gonna get you out of this, Winston! Don't worry.", yells Celeste.

"Yeah, these dumbasses are about to get fired.", Keisha added.

As they're loading me onto the golf cart and getting ready to pull off, I hear Mr. Langston. "Stop! Don't you move that golf cart an inch! Let that man go, immediately!"

"And who the hell are you?!", guard one asks.

Mr. Langston chortles. "Okay, I see you guys missed my induction, so let me inform you. I'm the new majority owner of the Wardogs. And since you two are security guards in this here arena, that makes me your damn boss! So like I said, let him go you ignorant, incompetent imbeciles."

"But this is the Bankcard Bandit! We caught him trying to use your card, sir. We've been trying to catch this con artist for years.", guard one replies.

Mr. Langston scoffs, "This isn't the damn Bankcard Bandit! This is my son. Uncuff him immediately!

Guard two speedily hops out of the passenger seat and walks over to me to take off my handcuffs. "We're sorry about that sir. It was an honest mistake."

"Yeah, we're so, so, so sorry sir. I can't afford to lose this job. Spare us sir, we were just doing our job.", pleads guard one.

I shake my head.

Mr. Langston walks over to me as I'm brushing myself off, "Winston, are you okay? I'm sorry you had to go through that."

"We're so sorry, man. Please forgive us.", guard two begs. "We were just reporting the call and trying to do our jobs."

I ignore them and shake my head again as I walk away holding in my frustration and anger.

"I'll handle this later with you guy's supervisor. But as of now, you too get out of my sight. You're lucky I don't fire you on the spot for negligence and assaulting an innocent civilian!"

The guards shamefully hop on their golf cart and drive off as the crowd slowly disperses.

Mr. Langston pulls me aside then asks, "Are you okay, Winston? Seriously?"

I hesitate to answer, then I say, "Do you think it would've went down like that if my skin was lighter?"

Mr. Langston grins, "I think we both know the answer to that. It's really tragic that that's the sad truth. It's a shame that things are still this way. It's been like this since I can remember. Even in my father's time, and during his father's."

"You're absolutely right. It's not going to change until we all see each other as equal human beings and children of God and stop judging one another on cliche' stereotypes based off of skin color."

Mr. Langston nods his head in agreeance. "Couldn't have said it better myself, Winston. I was already starting to worry because you were taking longer than I expected. Then when your girlfriend came running into the suite calling for me, I just knew it was trouble. She quickly explained everything, and now here we are."

"I'm just glad you came when you did, and she's not my girl. She's just a friend. An associate really."

We look over at Natalie as she's talking to Keisha and Celeste. "How genuinely concerned and anxious she was when she barged into my suite made me think otherwise. She's damn sure a fox, Winston. You sure you just want her to be your *associate* looking like that?" He taps me on the chest. "I know what the truth is, don't worry."

I smile then ask him, "And what's that?"

"You just don't have any game.", we laugh and walk over to Natalie and her friends.

XXXV

———

N ATALIE RUNS OVER TO GREET ME WITH A HUG, "ARE you okay, Winston? Did they hurt you?"

"Nah, they just dusted my suit a little bit. Other than that, I'm fine. Me and Mr. Langston will handle all the paperwork later. Thank you for going to get him too, I owe you."

"Well I'll just add it to your tab."

"I owe you too.", Mr. Langston adds. "I probably would've blown the whole arena up if something happened to Winston because of those idiots."

"Oh, don't worry. I'll make sure to add it to your tab as well." Me, Mr. Langston, and Natalie chuckle.

As we're talking, we look over at Keisha and she is still upset.

"And we got something for yo little mophead ass too, Ms. Becky!", Keisha yells at the cashier as she tries to approach her.

"Girl, calm your ass down and come on.", Celeste says as she goes to grab Keisha to bring her over to me, Natalie, and Mr. Langston.

Still upset and hostile, Keisha continues, "I'm telling you, somebody needs to beat her ass! She wanna call the police for no reason. Well I'll give her goofy ass a reason to call the damn police."

Mr. Langston goes up to her and places his hands on her shoulders as he attempts to calm her down, "Keisha, right?" She nods her head. "Relax sugar foot, I promise she'll be dealt with. Let me handle it." He looks at everyone then says, "Now, lets not allow all of this foolishness to ruin our night. How about you ladies come join me and Winston back at my suite. Y'all can enjoy the rest of the game there with us. C'mon." He puts his arms out for Celeste and Keisha to grab.

"Oouuu, Mr. Langston got game." Keisha mutters as she wraps her arms around his.

"He's real strong too. You work out Mr. Langston?", Celeste comments as she wraps her arms around his other arm.

"Ladies, ladies, call me Robert." Mr. Langston smoothly says as they walk out in front of me and Natalie, leaving us behind.

We laugh. "They're a trip." Natalie jokingly says.

"Are they always like this?"

"Unfortunately, yes. They're always getting me into trouble. It's been like this since college."

"C'mon, don't wanna get too far behind." I say as we start to follow behind Mr. Langston. "So all y'all from North Carolina?"

"No, only me. Keisha's from Chicago and Celeste is from Cali."

"I love Chicago, it's beautiful there. It doesn't get enough credit honestly. The media is always highlighting the negative. It makes people forget how beautiful and prominent the city really is."

"I concur. I love Chicago, and Cali is so pretty too. Not just the beaches and LA, but places like Inglewood and Compton are pulchritudinous as well."

"Okay, okay, I see you with the little vocabulary flex. I like how you just sprinkled concur in there to start it, and then you just dropped pulchritudinous to finish it off. We get it, you're not just fine as hell, but smart as hell too."

She laughs and blushes. "You're so sweet Winston. I honestly didn't take you for the smooth type. I expected you to be more of a shy guy really."

I chuckle under my breath. "What makes you say that? I came off as a shy guy when you first met me?"

"Uhh yeah, well, I mean not really. You just weren't as aggressive as I thought you'd be, or what I'm used to I should say. But I can't really talk though." She giggles. "After we talked Monday, I realized I *did* actually see you before."

My heart drops. *Please don't tell me you saw me staring at you last week at the game.*

I clear my throat. "Oh, really? Where?", I ask.

"Okay, promise not to look at me any differently though."

I grin. "I won't."

"Promise?"

"Haha yeah, promise. Spit it out."

"Okay, alright. Well, before I officially met you this week, I think we crossed paths last Monday." My eyebrows jump. "I was at The Spot waiting for my food to come. I was scrolling through my phone, then all of a sudden I looked up and I saw this fine ass man walking my way. I didn't know what to do, so I just stayed on my phone. Then for some reason, I decided to look up. I was so nervous. But anyway, when I looked at him, we said good morning to each other. I feared I wouldn't know what to say if he started talking to me. I got so nervous and scared that I faked like I was on the phone and left. Don't laugh."

I just smile. "Wow, that's crazy."

She playfully nudges me, "Don't make fun of me. And I didn't recognize your face at first, but I did recognize your voice. I know it's weird, but yeah. Don't judge me."

"I'm not. And since we're being honest, I just wanted to say..."

"Natalie, you gotta come see this. This shit is NICE.", Keisha exclaims.

Natalie sighs, "Like I said, I can't take them anywhere."

We get to the suite and walk in. "I think your friends will be fine. Let's go down there." I grab her hand and take her to some secluded seats in the lower right hand corner of the suite. Most of the big timers that were here had left. There were only about fifteen other people in the suite excluding me, Natalie, Keisha, Celeste, and Mr. Langston.

Now it's the start of the fourth quarter. The score is tied at seventy.

"Out of all the basketball games I've been to, this is the first time I've ever been in a skybox suite.", Natalie says to me as we sit down.

"Yeah, mine too. This whole night has been so surreal."

"I know. It's like something out of a book."

"Yeah, some first date huh?"

She laughs, "Now what were you saying earlier Mr. Since We're Being Honest?"

I blush. "Oh, yeah. Since you confessed, I figured I might as well do the same. And like you said, it's a judge free zone, right?"

"It's only fair."

"Alright, well that was in fact me. I remember it like it was yesterday. You were wearing this red dress that was looking TOO good on you." Natalie starts to smile. "I saw you as soon as I walked out of the bathroom. You were sitting in my seat actually, but anyway, as I started walking, I made up a whole plan on how I was going to approach you and get your number."

She bursts out laughing. "Not a plan! You did not."

"Hey, hey, hey. What happened to no judging?"

Still laughing, "Okay I'm sorry, please continue."

I clear my throat. "As I was saying, I had this whole plan I was gonna follow. It was good too. But, as soon as I got to you, I was lost for words. I don't know if it was a piece of the ceiling missing or a broken window somewhere or what, but the way the light was hitting you, you looked like an angel sent straight from heaven."

"Boy stop, I ain't nothing spectacular. You're just being corny now."

I suck my teeth. "I'm serious, look in the mirror. You're a gorgeous queen that's absolutely flawless. If nobody's told you that, I'll be the one to do it."

She smiles and blushes. "Thank you, Winston. You really make me feel how you say I look. I'm sorry if I don't react the way you expect. I'm just not used to all of the chivalry and compliments."

"That's a shame. A queen like you deserves to be treated like one."

"Thank you, Winston. I genuinely appreciate that." She wraps her arm around mine and places her head on my shoulder. "So, continue with your story."

"Ummm, well it's really the end. I got to you and froze like a deer in headlights. And when you looked at me, Loooord, I melted. All I could do was wave and say good morning. And yup, here we are now."

"Wow. And I thought I was the scaredy cat." She sarcastically says.

We laugh. "Remember all of this the next time you want to get sentimental and what not."

"Yeah, yeah, I'm so scared."

"Oh you will be, trust me."

"Mmhmm." She repositions herself and lays on me while we watch the game.

A couple minutes pass, and we're still cuddled up in our seats. "Natalie."

"Yes, Mr. Winston?"

"Ever since I saw you at The Spot, I've been dreaming of this moment."

She pauses then looks up at me and replies, "Me too."

———

XXXVI

S HE SNUGGLES CLOSER TO ME AS I RUN MY HAND through her thick curly hair as she lays on me while we watch the game. It's about six minutes left in the fourth quarter and the Wardogs are losing seventy-seven to ninety.

"Do you think it's over?", Natalie asks.

"Eeeh, it's too early to tell. There's still plenty of time left. What do you think?"

"They can, but they're being stupid. They went cold from the three point line and they still keep shooting them like idiots. They need to attack the paint and get some easy looks close to the basket to get going. And on top of that, James Love is bricking everything with his nonshooting ass. He really irks me sometimes."

Her comment catches me off guard and I begin to smile. "Whaaat?! You sound like you know a little something about basketball. Look at you talking about attacking the paint to get easy looks at the basket. Let me find out that you're an ex-hooper."

She blushes. "I know a little something. I'm definitely not a hooper though." She giggles. "I was a track girl when I was an athlete back in the day. My dad's the reason I know so much about basketball. He'd watch it all the time when I was younger. He played pro for a few years before he quit. He stopped playing so he could raise me, my little sister, and my big brother when my mother left us when my little sister was born."

"Oh damn, I'm sorry to hear that. Your dad sounds like a real one."

"It's all good, and he is. He held it down for the most part, but he couldn't do anything with me and my sister's hair. Luckily, my step-mom came in and saved the day. But anyway, you'd be surprised about what you'd find out about me."

"You wouldn't happen to be a crazy serial killer, huh?"

She makes a weird face as she looks at me. "I guess you'll just have to find out for yourself, Mr. Winston." She laughs.

I move her head off of my lap and scoot away from her in my chair. "I think it's best if we keep our space from here on out." I joke.

She grabs me and pulls me back to her. "Stop playing and come back here. I'm just kidding, sheesh." She places her head back on my lap as she lays across the seats. "Or am I?" She playfully says.

I put my arm around her. "Keep playing, I'm going to go get Ms. Becky to call the police on you."

"Winston, that's not funny. You really could've gotten hurt, or worse."

"Laughter is good for the soul. If you can't laugh at things, you'll just be mean and miserable all the time."

"Yeah, yeah, yeah."

I caress her head with my hand. "So, what's your favorite color?"

"Uuuuum purple, but red is a very close second. What about you?"

"Green and purple. Money's green and purple is the color of royalty. You have a favorite chocolate/candy?"

"Hmmm, you really bringing the heat. I'd say the cookies and cream chocolate bars are my favorite chocolate, and sour gummy worms would be my overall favorite candy. Are these questions a part of your serial killer survey or something?"

"Haha, nah. I'm just trying to get to know you, that's all. But since you don't like them, this will be the last one for the night."

"I never said I didn't like them, but shoot."

"It was implied." She rolls her eyes. "What's your favorite animal?"

"Really?! That's your final question? Out of all the things you could've asked?"

I grin. "YES, now answer it please."

"Okaayy. Let me think. It's a toss up between elephants and dolphins. But, if it was a life or death situation I'd choose dolphins."

"Okay, noted."

The score is now eighty-six to ninety-two with three minutes left in the game. James Love misses a three pointer to make it a one possession game. The other team gets the rebound and calls a timeout.

"Now, everyone direct your attention to the jumbotron for our Kiss-Cam!", the announcer says over the microphone.

The camera goes through about six couples before...

"Y'all gotta do it!", one person yells.

"Girl, you better kiss him!", Keisha adds.

Natalie sits up and we look into each other's eyes. She pulls her hair back, I lick my lips, then magic. We lock lips for the kiss of the century. Well, it was to me at least. It felt like a lifetime of ecstasy was jammed into a three second kiss. *If the world was to end at this exact moment, I'd be content.*

Everyone claps, the horn sounds, and the game resumes.

She lays back down in my lap as we just smile and nervously look away from each other.

As the game continues, James Love misses another three.

"Uuugggghhhh, why did he shoot that stupid shit?! He really gets on my nerves.", Natalie yells in frustration as she sits up in her seat.

"Damn, what he do to you? Everybody misses shots."

Under her breath. "If only you knew."

"What you say?"

"We went to the same college and he was just aggy. I'll always support him because of our alma mater, but other than that, he's just, ugh. Gets on my nerves. And some of the dumb plays he makes just exasperate me. Sometimes I question how he even got into the league."

I nervously laugh under my breath. "Wow, that's kind of dope. That was harsh, but still dope. He's my favorite player. Y'all dated?"

She begins to blush.

"Girl you better not throw up in here!", Keisha yells at Celeste as she's standing over a trash can.

Natalie gets up and rushes over to her friends. I take my time and follow behind her.

"What's wrong with her?!", Natalie asks.

Mr. Langston walks up with two small bottles of ginger ale. "She ate and drank a little too much. She should be fine though.", he says.

"Just take me home.", Celeste mumbles. "I need my bed." She then throws up a little bit in front of Mr. Langston.

Keisha sucks her teeth. "Ugh, now we ain't ever coming back. Your ass can never hold your liquor." She points at Natalie. "Grab her purse so we can go."

"I just called a cart, it should be outside shortly.", Mr. Langston says. "Don't worry about the mess, it'll get cleaned up. And Keisha, I enjoyed y'all's company. Y'all will always be welcomed as long as I'm here."

Keisha smiles and gives him a hug. "Aaaww, thank you Mr. Langston. With your sweet ass. If you looking for a little sugar baby to be in your life, I'm here for it. Allll of it." She winks at Mr. Langston then grabs Celeste to walk outside to the cart.

Natalie shakes her head then gives me a hug. "I'll call you sometime tomorrow. I probably won't be making it to The Spot in the morning. I really enjoyed tonight, Winston. And thank you again for everything Mr. Langston."

"Anytime." Mr. Langston says.

Natalie kisses me on the cheek then leaves out with her friends.

Mr. Langston nudges me with his elbow and sarcastically says, "Just associates, huh?"

"I guess I got game after all", I reply as I shrug my shoulders.

"C'mon, let's finish watching the game. I have a surprise for you, but it'll only be a good one if we win."

"Well, what is it?"

"Winston, if I tell you, it wouldn't be a surprise now would it?"

"Yeah yeah."

We walk down to the lower seats in the suite to enjoy the last minute of the game. The Wardogs are still losing, but the score is close. It's ninety-four to ninety-six. Both teams are missing shots as time elapses. Now, it's ten seconds left and the score is the same. Mr. Langston and I sit on the edge of our seats.

It's the Wardogs's ball, and James Love has it at the top of the key. The crowd starts to count down, "Ten, nine, eight,..".

James Love takes one hard dribble to the right then crosses over back to his left as he steps back. "Three, two,..". He shoots as the time runs out and hits the game winning three. The crowd goes crazy and me and Mr. Langston begin to celebrate. The ten people left in the suite are jumping and hollering as well.

We look out onto the court and see the players rush the floor and celebrate.

"What a way to start off your ownership!", I exclaimed.

"It is indeed Winston. And it's only the beginning. Wooh!"

A worker from the arena comes into the suite and tells Mr. Langston that he has a couple of newspapers and TV stations waiting to interview him.

"What a comeback, what a game!", Mr. Langston yells. "I'll be back in a few Winston, hopefully this won't take long. Stay put."

"Go handle your business, Big Time."

I take a seat and look out onto the court as I wait. About twenty minutes pass and I begin to get drowsy. I get up and walk around to keep myself awake.

A couple minutes pass. "Winston.", Mr. Langston says as he walks back in. "Follow me."

We walk out of the suite and go into a tunnel leading to an area filled with photographers, journalists, and players. Mr. Langston takes out his phone to send a text.

About twenty seconds later, he says, "Turn around Winston, I have someone I want you to meet."

I turn and see James Love walking towards me with a woman

around his arm. He's far so I can't exactly make out what the woman looks like yet, but I definitely recognized James Love. His 6'9 frame is almost impossible to miss.

"This is crazy Mr. Langtson! I'm a huge fan."

"I know, I figured it was only right that you meet him."

As James Love gets closer, I start to see him more clearly. I'm blown away and lost for words when I'm finally able to make out the woman.

Sharon?!

———

XXXVII

B EFORE THEY GET TO US, THEY STOP AND KISS AS A
photographer takes their picture. Sharon is wearing a white
number five James Love jersey, and James just has on an all black
team sweatsuit. I squint then rub my eyes to assure myself that
I'm not seeing things. *There's no way I just saw Sharon kiss James
Love. There's no way the secretary of the office, my best friend, my ex, is
dating thee James Love! I refuse to believe he was the mystery man all
this time. My brain won't allow it.*

I turn to Mr. Langston for confirmation and ask, "Is that Sharon
with James Love, or am I seeing things?"

He looks at me. "Yup, that's Sharon. It was her idea for you to
meet him actually. I knew you were a huge Wardogs fan, but I
had no clue how big of a James Love fan you were. Sharon told
me about it when I came in earlier today. I told her that I wanted
you to be the one here with me at the game, and then she
mentioned that you'd always talked about wanting to meet James.
She said she would set it up because she knew him, and she'd text
me when they were ready. She never mentioned they were dating

though. It's kind of a weird addition to the surprise, don't you think?"

I'm still flabbergasted. *Who would've thought?! She's not only dating my favorite player, but arranged for us to meet.*

I didn't know if I should feel flattered, intimidated, or played.

"Hey Winston!", she says as she gives me a hug. "Hey Mr. Langston, congratulations again." She then hugs Mr. Langston.

"Thank you Sharon. And hell of a game James, y'all had us all nervous in the first half. The whole game really, especially in the end." Mr. Langston shakes James's hand. "And James, this is my son Winston. He's a big fan. Winston, this is James Love."

I reach my hand out to shake James's, and it gets completely swallowed. His hands are huge. I had never felt so small. I'm 6'2, but next to him I felt 5'2.

He looks at me and says, "What's up Winston, I've heard a lot about you. I'll have a jersey for you the next time I see you." He then shifts his attention to Mr. Langston. "I didn't know you had a son."

"He's my unbiological biological son." Mr. Langston replies.

"Oh, okay. Well nice to finally meet you Winston. Sharon's always talking about her best friend."

Sharon begins to blush. "I wouldn't say all that now. I mention him here and there.", she rebuttals.

James gives me a sarcastic stare then we share a laugh.

He checks his phone. "I don't mean to cut this short or be rude, but we have to get up out of here. Sharon, you wanna take our pic real quick?"

"Okay, who's phone y'all want me to use?", she asks.

"Just use yours and send them to us. Come on." James says as he places his arm across my shoulder.

"Say cheese!", Sharon says as she takes the pictures. "Okay, that's it. Mr. Langston, do you want to hop in one?"

"Yeah, come on...pops.", I say as I wave him over.

"Put James in the middle, Winston you go on the left, and Mr. Langston you come around to James's right side. There you go. Now cheese on three. One, two, three, cheese." Sharon takes the pictures and James walks over to her to look at them.

"Yeah, these pics are fire. Send these ASAP.", he excitedly says.

"Let me see.", I say as I walk over to her.

She snatches her phone back and says, "You'll see them when the time is right."

I suck my teeth, "Don't start with that again."

"Okay, well again, it was nice meeting you Winston and congrats again Mr. Langston. I look forward to working with you." James says as he shakes our hands.

"Likewise, it's an honor. And good luck with the rest of the season if I don't see you again.", I say.

"Thanks, hopefully this will be the spark to a bigger fire.", he replies.

"I'd like to hope too." Mr. Langston adds. "I meant it when I said I planned on adding to the trophy cases. But, we can get into that another time. Y'all better get going. Thanks again. Y'all be safe."

"Yes sir, we will. Y'all too."

"See you in the morning, Winston." Sharon says as she waves goodbye. James then grabs her hand and they exit out of a door to the side of us.

"Well, I hope you enjoyed your night, Winston. I know it's one I won't forget for a while. And that Keisha is something else, isn't she? Her personality is definitely one of a kind.", Mr. Langston says as he puts his arm around me as we walk towards the parking lot.

"Yeah, she seems like she can have a bit of a wild side to her."

"Oh, that's what I like, Winston.", he says with a smile.

"Okay, let Mrs. Langston find out. You're gonna be sleeping in one of your hotels instead of just managing them."

He laughs, "So what did you think of tonight?"

"Besides that mixup earlier, the night was perfect. It all worked out for the best to be honest. I feel like me and Natalie really bonded."

He stops in his tracks. "I honestly forgot all about that mindless incident Winston. I guess that's my age showing. You go ahead and head home. I need to get all of this handled immediately before I forget again. I'll call you if I need anything from you, although the video from the cameras should be enough."

"Oh, yeah. I guess I did too with everything else that was happening. Thank you again for everything. It was really a night I'll remember for a long time."

"Likewise. I'll keep you posted with everything that's going on."

"Okay, I'll be by my phone. Thank you again for everything."

"Thank you, be safe going home."

"You too." Mr Langston embraces me and we part ways.

XXXVIII

———

I GO THROUGH ABOUT FOUR OR FIVE DIFFERENT DOORS and hallways before I reach the parking garage. When I finally find my car, I get in and make my way home.

I exhale a deep breath of relief as I pull out of the arena. *What a night. I finally had my moment with Natalie. The golden moment I've been fantasizing about since the first time I laid my eyes on her. The moment I've been yearning for. Just wait until Chino hears this. I can't wait to see his face after I tell him what happened, I know he's not going to believe it.*

After forty-five minutes of driving, I'm home walking into my apartment. It's about one o'three when I make it to my room. I throw my phone and keys on the bed, take my clothes off, and get in the shower. As I'm in the shower, I hear my phone go off a couple times. *Who wants to talk to me this late?*

When I get out of the shower, I dry off, get dressed, brush my teeth, and then check my phone. I have five text messages, three from Sharon, one from Mr. Langston, and one from an unsaved number.

I lay in my bed then read Mr. Langston's first. "It's all taken care of. The two guards were suspended indefinitely, and they said that they have to further investigate the cashier because the restaurant is its own separate franchise. They'll get back to me when it's finished. And thanks again for coming, I'll give you a call sometime tomorrow."

I still don't feel like that was enough of a punishment, but I guess something is better than nothing. The whole situation was absurd. Now, let's see what Sharon wants. I lay in the bed and pull the covers over my legs.

I open the messages and they read: "Surprise! That's my mystery man lol", "Hope you made it home safely and enjoyed everything", "I know your bighead ass is probably asleep by now or at least in the bed so I'll just talk to you tomorrow morning. Goodnight bestie :)".

That whole situation is still mind-boggling. I'm still having trouble processing that part of the night. It doesn't make any sense. There are so many unanswered questions. I'm going to need her to explain all of the details tomorrow at work.

Now, I get to the unsaved number. It has an area code I don't recognize. I look it up, seven zero four, and discover it's a North Carolina area code. "It couldn't be.", I tentatively say.

I open the message and it reads, "Hey Winston it's Natalie. I know we didn't exactly exchange numbers, but my secretary wrote your cell phone number down on a sticky note when she gave it to me earlier. Keisha made me find it whenever we got home and yeah lol. I hope you made it home safely and I really enjoyed tonight. I know you're probably asleep so just hit me up in the morning I guess. Sweet dreams Mr. Softlips ;p."

After I finish reading Natalie's text, I immediately hop up with excitement. I take about two minutes to think about what I'm going to say before I reply, "Hey, glad you made it safe. How is Celeste doing?". A couple seconds later I also send, "And tell Keisha that I said thank you too lol we wouldn't have had that moment without her ;)."

About ten minutes go by as I'm anxiously waiting for her reply. *I shouldn't have sent that last text. It was too corny.*

Thirty more minutes pass. Nothing. *She's probably asleep. I guess I should do the same. It's almost three and I do have work in the morning.*

I turn my alarm on, put my phone on the charger, and go to sleep.

My phone begins to ring. I wipe my eyes then I grab my phone to check it. When I pick it up, I notice it's not my alarm, but a phone call. It's six-thirty in the morning and the caller ID says it's unknown. *What the hell?* I decline it and go back to sleep. A couple seconds goes by and an unknown number calls again. I suck my teeth as I look at my phone then decline the call. I put my phone on my nightstand, and lay back down to enjoy the thirty minutes of peace I have before I have to get up and get ready for work.

Five minutes pass, and I'm back sound asleep. That is, until my phone starts ringing and it wakes me back up. I'm grouchy and aggravated as I check my phone. For the third time, it's an unknown number. I answer, "What?! Who is this calling me this early in the morning?!". I wait for an answer and hear them laughing. "Is this some type of joke?! A prank call? Stop calling me!" I hang up.

At this point, I don't even bother going back to sleep. I grab my phone and go sit on my couch to watch a little bit of TV before I have to get ready. As soon as I sit down, the unknown number calls me again. Tired and irate, "Stop calling…"

"Wait Winston! Don't hang up yet.", they say.

That voice sounds familiar. "MP? Is that you?"

He laughs, "Yes, I see that you're not much of a morning person."

"What you want man? I told you I'm not interested in working with you."

"I gave you time to think about it and you still feel that way?"

"Yes! I'm not getting involved with you or your world. There's nothing you can do to change my mind. Whether you would've given me a couple days, a week, a month, whatever, the answer is NO."

"Okay Winston. I guess I'll just call back later and see if you're still feeling the same way."

"Don't bother, it's still going to be the same answer."

"We'll see about that." He hangs up the phone.

XXXIX

———

I NEED TO TELL MR. LANGSTON ABOUT MY MP PROBLEM.
He just won't stop, and I'm tired of it. Hopefully, Mr. Langston can
help me get him off of my case. I see he wasn't lying when he told me that
MP doesn't take no for an answer.

The mayor's morning shenanigans irked me. I knew my whole day
would be ruined if I didn't relax and change my attitude. So, with the
little time I had left, I chose to hop in the shower to ease my mind.

I get out when my alarm goes off. I brush my teeth then begin
to get dressed. I decide to wear a lavender suit with a white shirt
and no tie. I put on my brown dress shoes, grab my phone and
keys, then make my way out the door and to my car. As I'm
getting in, I hear my neighbor and his girlfriend arguing. All I
hear is loud noises and yelling. No words were clear, so I don't
pay it any mind and just carried on about my business. I continue
on, and head to The Spot.

I get there and walk in with a big smile on my face.

"What you so happy for? You must've been in somebody's
nooks and crannies last night.", Chino playfully says.

I shake my head then take my seat at the counter. "You're not gonna believe my night. It was too crazy."

"How was the game? I saw you and ya daddy on TV. And what's up with my jersey? Did you get it?"

I laugh. "My bad Chino, I forgot all about it. I got you next time."

"Maaaannn dudes get fifteen seconds of TV time and all of a sudden they become Hollywood. Boy I tell you. I ask for ONE thing and you can't remember..."

"I was with Natalie."

His face lights up with confusion and excitement. "W-what you just said?!"

I start to grin. "I was with Natalie last night, that's why I forgot about your stank ass jersey, Chino."

"So she called you and y'all met up at the game?"

"Nah, I mean she did call me, but the conversation wasn't bout nothing. Long story short, we ran into each other at the concession stands at half time then spent the rest of the night cuddled up in Mr. Langston's suite."

Chino puffs his lips up and squints his eyebrows. "Boy, stop lying to me. You know I was just playing about banning you if you ain't talk to her. You my boy. I was just trying to motivate you."

"Chino, I promise I'm not lying to you. It was a wild night. We even kissed."

"Kissed?! Winston, please tell me you didn't harass that woman."

"No man. We just happened to get caught on the kiss cam, and yeah." I begin to grin.

"So you just expect me to believe y'all *randomly* ran into each other at a concession stand, started talking, and y'all was just two lovebirds the rest of the night? Oh, and kissed on the kiss cam. Nah playa. One, life don't work like that. This ain't of those fairytale, princess, kiddie movies. And two, Mr. Langston is one of those old school playas on the low. Most people don't peep, but game recognize game. Ain't no way he just sat there by himself twiddling his thumbs while you were with her the whole night. Especially on HIS big night."

"Okay now what are YOU talking about? Mr. Langston has a whole wife."

"Yeah that's for y'all to see. He got married so he'll look good in the public's eye. I'll bet this building and my house that they're probably having some type of marriage issues. What was he doing while you and Natalie were caked up, huh? I'll wait."

"He was hanging out with Natalie's two friends."

Chino bursts out laughing and points at me. "I told you, game recognizes game playa. But anyway, back to this Natalie thing. What all y'all was talking about? You got in them nooks and crannies?"

"Nah, she had to leave the game a little early because one of her friends got sick. And we were just talking about regular stuff I guess. We would be watching the game and stuff would just pop up. She went to the same college as Jame Love. Oh, and I even met him last night. Yo, Sharon's dating him now. That's crazy as hell, right?"

"Mhhm."

I chuckle. "What now Chino?"

"That man is definitely slam dunking both of your women." He starts laughing. "Just monkey dunking both of them like aarrggghh.", he says as he mimics a slam dunk.

I suck my teeth and look away. "Man, go get my food ready. You know what I get." He doesn't move and just stares at me. I sigh, "Go get my food ready, please."

He smiles. "That's what I thought. I know your daddy Mr. Langston taught you some manners."

"Whatever man, can you get my food please?"

"Don't hate the messenger. I'm just keeping it real with you. It's for here or to go?"

"To go."

"Daaaamn, you don't ever eat with ya boy no more. That's that Hollywood nonsense." He goes to tell one of the workers to make my order then returns. "Back to the topic. Seriously though, I wouldn't lie to you Winston. The facts are there."

"First off, Sharon's not my girl anymore. We're just friends now. She can do what she pleases, especially if it gives me a chance to meet my favorite player. Secondly, I asked Natalie straight up if they dated and she said they didn't. She even said he was annoying."

"Hmmm *annoying*. Yeah, okay playa. Either way, I'm happy you finally manned up and talked to her. I hope it all works out for you. You and James have a little girl swap thing going on. Who would've thought?" He laughs and I ignore him. He then goes to get my food and brings it to me. "So you finally got her number?"

"I mean, she texted me last night. I replied and I'm still waiting for her to text me back."

"Tsk, tsk, tsk." He says as he shakes his head.

"What now man."

"And James Love comes down the lane on a fast break and BOOM, another dunk. The crowd goes wild." He starts chuckling and grinning.

"Whatever man, she fell asleep. It was like two in the morning and she has work today too."

"It's eight-forty. She should've been up by now, correct?"

My phone buzzes. I look at it and I smile. "Well look who it is."

"What, your momma texted you? Tell her I said, 'Heyyyyy'."

"Don't make me tear up this lovely building of yours, Chino."

He laughs. "Who is it?"

"It's Natalie. She said, 'Good morning Winston, I'm sorry I fell asleep on you. I hope you have a great day.' So ha, I'm going to take my food and be on my way to work, good sir."

"Just pay attention to the signs my brotha."

"Yeah, the signs of a hater." I grab my food, wave at Chino, and begin to walk to my car.

As I'm leaving out, Chino yells out, "I'm not a hater, just the messenger!"

I walk out and get in my car to leave. Before I drive off, I text Natalie back, "It's all good, I knocked out too. And good morning beautiful, how are you doing today?"

After I send the text, I head to work.

I pull into the parking lot and my phone buzzes. I think it's a text from Natalie, but it's Sharon. "Mr. Jacobs is over here having one of his temper tantrums and he's asking about you. You did something?"

Perplexed, I reply, "Nah, but I'm coming up."

I get out of my car with my food and briefcase, then walk to the elevator. I get off on our floor and immediately go to Sharon. "What's good with him?", I ask.

"No clue, he told me to tell you to just go straight to his office whenever you got here."

"Oh damn, okay. And thanks again for last night, I really appreciate it."

She smiles, "No problem bestie. Now get back there. It sounds pretty serious."

I nod my head and walk back to Mr. Jacobs's office. I get there and knock on the door.

KNOCK, KNOCK.

With a stern and fierceful tone he says, "Come Winston, sit."

"Good morning sir, what's up? Is it because of the mayor?"

"No, no. Far worse Winston. I must inform you that you're fired. Or at least suspended indefinitely without pay."

"Fired?! For what?! I'm the best here!"

"The urine samples came back. Everyone's results came back clean. Well, everyone except yours. They found traces of molly in your sample Winston."

XL

———

"MOLLY?!", I YELL. "MR. JACOBS C'MON MAN, YOU know me. I don't even drink. I can't believe you're accusing me of doing molly. You know that doesn't sound like me. I wouldn't jeopardize all of this for a stupid drug!"

"I'm sorry Winston. It's not me. Rules are rules. No exceptions. Hopefully they'll overturn it soon, but as of now, there's nothing I can do other than to dismiss you out of the building."

I slam my hands on his desk as I stand up. "Run those tests again! I'll take another one! The first ones had to have been wrong. Jacobs you know me, you know I don't do that type of shit!"

He motions his hands trying to get me to calm down and sit. "Winston, calm down now. Don't make a scene. Just sit down and relax. We can't do another test because now, I'm not saying that you are, but, if you were using, you would've had an ample amount of time to cleanse your body and get that stuff out of your system."

"No! It's all a mistake. And now you're making it seem like I'm just a random druggy off the street or something. How many times do I have to tell you that I don't do that shit! Never have! I don't even have a clue how it got in my system. You have to believe me."

"Okay, okay just relax. Were you at a bar or club recently? Somebody could've slipped it in your drink while you weren't looking."

I tap my index finger on my forehead as I think. "I haven't been to any clubs or..." I stop mid sentence as it hits me.

"What is it Winston?"

"I have to step outside and make a phone call real quick Mr. Jacobs."

"I'm sorry Winston, but as soon as you step outside of my office, I'll need you out of here ASAP, company policy. Also, the police will be here soon to talk about the results, so unless you feel like getting interrogated and possibly arrested, I suggest you leave now while you can. And maybe consider getting a lawyer." I look at him with a face full of anger and disappointment. "I'm sorry Winston. Hopefully we'll be able to work through this."

Piqued and flustered, I grab my things then storm out to my car.

"What's wrong Winston? Where you going?", Sharon says as I walk by her desk.

"I'll tell you later.", I quickly respond.

I get on the elevator and shake my head at Sharon as the doors close. When the elevator gets to the parking lot, I get off and go sit in my car.

I punch the steering wheel. "I can't believe the mayor drugged me! Aaaargh!"

I grab my phone to call him. As I scroll through my phone, I realize I don't even have his number. Every time that he's called me, he's used an unknown number, so there's no way I can contact him.

I sit back and think. *Mr. Langston probably knows how I can get in contact with him. It'll probably infuriate him, but at this point, he needs to be stopped before the whole situation gets worse. If that's even possible.*

I scroll through my phone to find his number. As I'm about to dial it, an unknown number calls me.

I exhale a sigh of frustration and answer it, "MP."

Enthuzed, "Heeey Winston, how are you?"

"Why'd you drug me? I lost my job. You happy now?!"

He chuckles. "It's chess not checkers, Wintson. Right now I have you in check. The next move you make decides whether it'll be checkmate or not. So, think wisely."

"There's no way you planned all of this? This incident at my office happened Tuesday afternoon, hours before our meeting Tuesday night. And on top of that, I didn't even mention it. So there's no way you could've known."

"Well based on your urine results, it's very possible that you were highly intoxicated Tuesday night, so there's no telling what you did or didn't mention." He chuckles then sighs. "Now Winston, you must realize that I'm everywhere at all times. I'm omnipresent. One of the officers on the scene recognized you and informed me of the incident with your coworker. I recognized that I had an opportunity and took full advantage of it. Now that you're in dire need of a new job, I think it's a perfect time to inform you that I have a position for you."

"Look MP, this little sick, evil, twisted game that you're trying to play with me, cut it out. I don't want to have to take it to another level, but I will."

Nonchalantly, "Winston, what are you talking about? I'm just trying to expand my business ventures with a smart, intelligent, and sophisticated person like yourself. It's synergy, Winston. Do you know what synergy is?

"Yeah, it's basically one plus one equals three, but…"

"Exactly! Now listen Winston, I put some deep thought into what you said at our meeting. And, you're right. I need to change the way I do some things. I thought a little harder, then came to the conclusion that the best person to help me with that would be you. All these years of doing this and that, and nobody's even bat an eye. Then you come along and immediately seek change. That's admirable and why I want you to take my throne and run things how YOU think they should be ran. So here's what's gonna happen. I'm going to give you some time to reconsider my counteroffer then go from there. Oh and remember, make your next move your best move." He hangs up the phone.

I throw my phone into the passenger's seat as I sit and think about what I'm going to do next. *Can't do that, just no. But what if...uugghhh. Mr. Langston would probably know what to do. He knows him just as good as anybody. He'll know if MP is sincere or up to something. But, it'll probably start a war I don't think I'm ready for.*

I hear my phone go off, but I don't check it. I sit back, rub my hand across my head, and think about my next move.

As I'm sitting here, my stomach rumbles from the smell of my food. I reach over to grab it, and begin to eat it. About halfway through my meal, I get startled and spill it all over my lap and my seat. As I was sitting there eating, two police cars drove up. In fear that they might see me, I immediately reclined my seat back. I waited a few seconds, then I peaked my head up to see if they had recognized me or my car. They didn't, so as soon as the three policemen got into the elevator, I drove off.

My phone buzzes again.

I ignore it again because I'm still deciding what to do and where I should go. And on top of that, I'm vexed from spilling my food.

If I go to The Spot, Chino's going to be asking questions. I don't need to get him sucked into this. And if I go home, there's probably going to be someone there waiting for me.

I drive about ten minutes up the street and find a ducked off secluded area to park at. I get out of the car to clean my suit and my seat. When I finish, I reach over to the passenger seat and grab my phone. I see that I have a text from Sharon and Natalie. I instantly get an idea. I ignore Sharon and go straight to Natalie's text. "I'm doing good, I'm already ready to go. I wish I was in bed sleeping though lol How are you Mr. Winston?."

I reply, "Lol same, and I'm okay, but honestly I'd be feeling a lot better if I saw your beautiful face. Bless me with your presence and let me take you out to lunch."

XLI

———

I CAN'T HELP BUT TO LAUGH AT MYSELF. *WINSTON, you're really a smooth criminal, you know that? I just know she's going to say yes. There's no way anyone can say no to that. That was something out of a romance novel.*

While I'm waiting for Natalie's reply, I see what Sharon sent me.

"Winston, what the hell is going on?", "Jacobs told me what happened. Are you ok?", "Call me whenever you feel like talking, I'm here for you bestie:)."

I ignore them. I appreciate Sharon's concern, but I wasn't in the mood to talk about work or anything related to it. I just let my seat back and wait for Natalie to text me back. Ten minutes go by, then twenty, then thirty, and now an hour passes.

Uuugghhh I can't just sit here. I have to do something.

I do the only thing I can do in this situation. I call my mother. My whole life she's been the only person that can make any sense out of the abnormal. She always knows the right things to say. She's my anchor and I wouldn't be the man that I am now without her.

I dial her number. It rings about three times and she picks up. "Hello?"

"Wassup mom, how you doing?"

"Hey Winnie! I'm all good over here. I'm just at home, sitting on the couch and watching TV. I'm waiting for your aunt to get home from the doctor so we can go to the store. How's my baby doing?"

"I'm good, I just have a lot going on right now."

"What's wrong? Me and your aunt Lo don't need to pull up to Ricoville with our steel do we? You know the way we drive, two and a half hours ain't nothing."

I laugh. "Nah mom, y'all good where y'all at."

"Well, what is it?"

"I got fired from my job today."

She pauses for a second. "It's okay Winnie, it's their loss. Everything happens for a reason, you just have to trust God's process. I know He has a big plan for you."

"Yeah, I hear you mom. I trust Him."

"When one door closes, a bigger one opens. Believe that."

"Yes ma'am."

"What was their reason for firing you?" I chuckle a little bit. Not because I found the situation funny, but because I knew how my mother was about to react when I told her. "I hope I'll be laughing too. Spit it out boy."

"We got drug tested and my pee came back dirty."

"Boy, what the hell is wrong with you?! I see you woke up stupid and decided to throw all of your success and dreams away to get HIGH. It better have been worth it! I know damn well I didn't break my back every day, work three jobs, and sacrifice my golden years to put you in a position to succeed just for you to piss it all away for some drugs. You know damn well I ain't raise you like that! What was it? Crack? Cocaine? Marijuana? What?!"

"Relax mom, I don't do drugs. Any type, you know that's how you raised me up. Up until I was sixteen you told me my dad wasn't around because he overdosed on drugs before I was born. Even though it wasn't true, that always stuck with me in the back of my head."

"Mmmhhmm, then explain to me how the hell they found drugs in your pee? I know they just ain't magically get there. And you still ain't tell me what they found exactly."

I exhale, "They found molly in my pee mom. I promise I ain't do it though."

"Boy, who the hell is molly? What she got to do with you having dirty pee pee. I told you to leave them fast tail girls alone." I couldn't help but to laugh. "Boy, I don't see shit funny. Now tell me who the hell molly is."

"Molly isn't a person mom. It's a drug. It's what people call ecstasy nowadays."

"Winnie, now why in the hell were you taking ecstasy? You were trying to get your hunch on?"

"Haha no mom. I was, I was at a club with some friends and I think somebody slipped it in my drink when I wasn't looking."

"Now don't I always tell you to make sure you watch your cup whenever you're at the club or a party. Once you leave it, throw it away. Been telling you that since you were young."

"Yes ma'am."

"Now what you gone do now since you're jobless? You can afford your apartment still?"

"Yes ma'am, I have plenty of money saved, and you know I have a lot of investments also. It's not about the money mom, it's just the way everything happened that's bothering me."

"Well, what you gon' do about it? You know I always taught you to fight for what's right and to stand stern on what you believe in. You've always done that. I know whatever happened, you're not going out without some type of fight."

I begin to smile because at that moment, I realized what I needed to do. "Yes mam, you know it."

"Well, your auntie Lo just walked in."

"Oh, okay mom. I'll let you go and get ready then. Tell her I said hey."

She yells, "Winnie said hi Lo!", to my aunt. "She said hey. And okay Winnie. Remember, it'll all work out in your favor, you're anointed. Even when you think you're alone, He's there right with you. You're one of God's special children, He has a tight grip around you. I love you Winnie."

"Thank you, I love you too mom."

"I'm always here if you need me."

"I know mom." We hang up the phone.

When I get off the phone with my mother, I immediately call Mr. Langston. His phone goes straight to voicemail. I call him again, and it's the same result. I assume he's in a meeting, so I just text him. "Hey Mr. Langtson, call me whenever you get a chance. It's important." After I send it, I sit back in my seat and wait for him to reply.

About a minute after I sent that text, my phone buzzes. Assuming it's Mr. Langston, I instantly picked my phone up. When I looked at it, I realized it wasn't Mr. Langston, it was Natalie.

"Aawwww Winston you're really the sweetest. I'd honestly love to go to lunch with you. I'm actually about to take my lunch break in a few minutes, so just let me know where ;p", it reads.

My face lights up with glee. I wait a few seconds, then I call her.

"Hey Winston, where should I meet you?", she says when she answers the phone.

"Uhhh, well what you have a taste for?"

"Um, just something good. Surprise me. You're one and zero so far. You have to keep the streak going."

"Haha, I got you. Well where is your building located?"

"It's on the west side. By 5th Ave and Crosstown. You know where that's at?"

"Yeah, it's like twenty from where I am now. Meet me at Eazy E's. It's about halfway between us. I'll go now to get a table. I'll see you whenever you get there."

"Okay, sounds like a plan."

"Drive safe."

"Thanks, you too." We hang up the phone and I make my way to Eazy E's.

After about a twelve minute drive, I arrive. I park my car and walk in to get our table.

"Good afternoon. Right this way sir.", the hostess says as she greets me and escorts me to my seat. "Someone should be with you shortly.", she adds.

I was only waiting at the table for no less than five minutes before Natalie walks in looking gorgeous as always. Her hair elegantly blows with the wind as she walks through the door. She's wearing a dress suit that's the same color lavender that I'm wearing.

"Wooow, you talked to me for one night and I'm already your role model. I'm flattered.", I jokingly say.

"Haha, you're clearly just a big stalker." I stand up and pull her chair out when she approaches the table. "Oouuu a gentleman too?"

"A queen deserves nothing less, right?", I say with a smile.

She blushes. "Yeah, I guess you're right.

Our waiter comes up to our table and says, "Oouuu twinsies. I like it, you guys must really be in love." We look at each other and laugh. "Do you guys know what you want to drink yet?"

"Yes, can I get a raspberry tea with extra lemons please?", Natalie requests.

"Yes ma'am, and for you sir?", our waiter says as he writes her order.

"Can I get a..". My phone starts to ring, I check to see who it is. It's Mr. Langston returning my call.

"Hold on, one second please.", I tell the waiter.

"Aht aht.", Natalie says as she sees me about to answer my phone. "No phones at the table Mr. Winston. It can wait."

"But it's Mr. Langston. I gotta take this. Just order me whatever you get. I trust you." I give her a wink as I get up from the table. Before I leave, I tell the waiter, "I'll take a raspberry tea as well."

I walk outside to take the call. "Hey Mr. Langston." I hear talking in the background. "Are you busy?"

"Hello Winston, I have a few minutes to spare. I, um, I've been in meetings all day. I saw you called me and read your text. What's up?"

I take a deep breath, "It's about MP."

"What about him? Is it about your meeting you had with him the other night? I was so caught up with my ownership stuff that I forgot to ask about it when I came by your office."

"Long story short, he wants me to work with him. He plans to mold me into being the new mayor when he's out of office. He even got me fired from my job."

"What?! That must be why Jacobs was blowing my phone up earlier. Look Winston, I only have one more meeting today. You meet me at my house at three, and we can talk then."

"Sounds like a plan. I'll see you there."

"And Winston, it'll be okay."

"I know it will." We hang up the phone and I walk back inside to my table.

"Well, welcome back stranger. How was your *important* secret call you just had to take?", Natalie sarcastically asks as she squints her eyes as she looks at me.

I chuckle, "Um, it was good. Are you okay?"

"Mmmhmm." She rolls her eyes and takes a sip from her tea.

"Natalie, what's wrong? It was an important call from Mr. Langston that I had to take. And I was gone no more than five minutes, so what's the issue?"

"You sure that wasn't one of your *bitches*?"

I'm flabbergasted and lost for words at the fact that she even thought of saying that. "Excuse me?"

"You know what, I'll just say it. Our original waiter had to leave and we got another one. I guess he recognized you when you came in, and when he came over to bring us our drinks, he called me Sharon. He immediately apologized after I corrected him. He said it was because he forgot his contacts at home and there's bad lighting in here. But anyway, who the hell is Sharon, Winston?! I'm not like one of these other women that likes to share their man or even stand for being anything less than number one in your life, excluding your mother and other family of course. Now speak! I demand answers and you better not lie."

"Okay, but first, can you relax for me? I promise you it's not what you think."

"I am relaxed! Now speak, Winston."

I sigh. "Sharon is the secretary at my office and my best friend. We come here for lunch sometimes. That's it."

"Mhhmmm, y'all men will say anything."

"Look Natalie, I don't know what happened in your last relationship or with any of the other previous men you've dated, but I'm not them. In my eyes, you're a melanin angel. Gorgeous, smart, funny, well just all around flawless really. When I first laid my eyes on you, I knew you were special. You were, and still are, all I think about. And now that I have the privilege of actually getting to know you, I'll be damned if I mess it up, especially over anything stupid. You're just not the number one woman I'm talking to, you're the one and only."

She blushes. "I'm sorry. It's just…"

"You've been heartbroken, betrayed, taken advantage of, etc., I understand. I understand you still need time to heal, that's okay. But at the same time, you're going to miss out on the present if you never let go of the past. I'm here to help you heal and protect you, not hurt you."

"Hey Mr. Williams, how are you?", the waiter says as he comes to the table.

"I'm good, and yourself Rufus?"

"I'm good, same old stuff. Just school and work. Here's two cajun shrimp pastas for ya. Be careful, they're hot.", Rufus says as he places our plates on the table.

"Thanks man.", I tell him.

"No problem, you guys enjoy. And sorry again for that mixup Ms. Graves. I found a pair of glasses in the back and can see clearly now." Natalie rolls her eyes. "Good seeing you Mr. Williams.", he says as he walks back into the kitchen ashamed and embarrassed.

"He's really a good kid. Smart too. He just turned sixteen and he's already a college freshman. Just can't see without his glasses."

She just looks down and plays with her food.

"Sharon, what's wrong?"

"Excuse me?!"

I feel as if my soul had just been snatched out of my body. *I didn't just say that?!*

"Winston! What did you just call me?"

"N-Natalie is your name correct?", I say, trying to play off my mistake.

"Yes, that's my name, but that's not what you said. You called me Sharon. It was as clear as day. I was stupid for even thinking this could be anything more than a business relationship." She signals Rufus to come to our table. "Hey Rufus, can I get a to go container please?"

"Yes ma'am, that's fine. You need one too Mr. Williams?"

"Uh yeah, please." Rufus walks off and I shift my attention to Natalie. "I'm sorry, you know what, wait." I pull out my phone and video call Sharon. "It's one-twelve, so she should be free." The phone starts to ring.

Natalie rolls her eyes. "Who you calling now? You calling your other side chick?"

"You'll see. I don't want you to have any doubts and think it's something that it's not."

After about four rings, Sharon picks up. "Hey Winston, are you okay?! How the hell did they find…"

Everything that had occurred at the office just a few hours prior to my lunch date with Natalie had completely slipped my mind until Sharon started talking.

"Hey, hey, Sharon hey. Look, I'm on a date right now."

"A date?! You taking your left hand out to eat? That's so sweet of you. I'm glad you're finally rewarding her for her hard work." Natalie giggles and I blush. "That sounds like a woman's laugh, let me see." I position my phone to where she's looking at Natalie. "Oh, she cute Winston. She must not know about…"

I put the camera back on me. "Sharon, I just called so you can tell her that we're just friends. I'm at Eazy E's. Rufus forgot his contacts and thought she was you."

"Oh Ima beat Rufus's ass next time I see his scrawny butt. But yeah honey, me and Winston are just friends. Best friends actually, I have a whole boyfriend too. So you don't have anything to worry about." I hear Mr. Jacobs begin to say something to her. "I gotta go Winston, I'll text you."

"Okay." We hang up the phone and I smile at Natalie. A few seconds later, Sharon texts me, "Don't trust her Winston. She looks really familiar."

XLII

———

I PAY SHARON'S MESSAGE NO MIND, SHE ALWAYS SAYS crazy stuff. *She's probably just jealous that I'm with another woman. If it's something that I need to know, I'm sure I'll find it out eventually. The truth always comes out.*

"Hmmm, everything okay Winston? You're quiet over there.", Natalie says.

"Yeah, just thinking. That's all."

"Okay. Well, before we go, I just want to apologize for my behavior earlier. You're right, I can't be judging you based on my past situations. That was wrong of me and very unfair to you. And for that, I'm truly sorry Winston. I just had a flashback and..."

"It's fine really."

"No, no, no. I also think that I've been moving just a little bit too fast."

"What you mean?"

"Like the way I was just acting for example. I mean, we're just friends and I'm acting as if we're a married couple or something. I know we had a little kiss last night, but it was just a show for the people. I think with everything that's going on in my life, it's just all adding up and boiling over. You know how it is. A person can only take so much of something before they snap. And, I'm sorry for snapping at you. I hope it doesn't change the way you look at me because I really think this could be the beginning of something great."

She starts putting her food in her container. *I hear what she's saying, but I stopped listening when she said we're just friends. This doesn't feel like a "just friends" type of vibe that we have. That kiss felt like it was way more than just some show for the crowd. This is all much more and she knows it. What if she's just doing all of this to hide something? What if Sharon might be on to something? What if..."*

"Here's the to go box and the check Mr. Williams.", Rufus says as he hands me the container and folder for the check.

Natalie grabs it and says, "I'll take care of it. It's the least I can do for being so childish earlier." She places a hundred dollar bill in it and hands it back to Rufus. "Keep the change and keep up the great work, there might be a lot more of these swimming around in your pockets in a few years."

"Thanks ma'am, I will. You two have a great day. And thank you again Ms. Graves." He starts to walk away.

"Hey, hold on Rufus."

"Yes sir?

"Do you mind taking our picture? I know you probably can't see it, but we're matching today."

"HA very funny Mr. Williams." I hand him my phone and he takes our picture. "Here ya go. I took a lot."

"Okay, we appreciate you Rufus."

He holds his hand out. "That'll be extra Mr. Williams."

I suck my teeth and Natalie laughs. "Man, we just gave you like an eighty dollar tip."

"Correction, SHE just gave me like an eighty dollar tip. It's your turn."

I tilt my head, "C'mon now Rufus."

Natalie giggles then goes in her purse, pulls out a twenty, and hands it to him. "There you go Rufus. Now get your slick self outta here before I get my belt."

He laughs, "Yes ma'am. And thank you, I truly appreciate it."
He leaves the table and walks back to the cash register.

"You big bank ain't it? What you wanted me for?", I
sarcastically say.

"You said he was a great kid so I wanted to reward him. And
also, thanks for reminding me. I totally forgot about that. You're
like a super wizard genius when it comes to money, correct?"

I humbly say, "I mean, I'm alright. Nobody too special. What
you need?"

"Umm, okay. So could you, like, trace the activity and history
of an account for me? There's been a great deal of money being
taken out and I want to know why."

I chuckle a lit bit then sarcastically say, "Um, you never heard of
a bank Natalie? I'm sure even if your bank is based in North Carolina
you should be able to find SOMEBODY to help you down here."

She rolls her eyes then says, "First off smart ass, don't jump to
the conclusion before you know the facts. Didn't you hear that
when you assume it only makes an ass out of you and me?"

I laugh. "Oh, the irony, but please continue, I'm listening."

"HA, HA. Well anyway, I share an account with my, um,
brother, and I believe he might be doing some illegal activity. If it
turns out he is, then not only could he go to jail, but I might too.
Then the money will be gone as well. I use that money to take care
of my dad Winston. I don't know what to do."

"First off, relax. It's going to be just fine. Second, I might be
able to ask around and see if anyone can help you out. It's all
going to be okay, just keep the faith.", I say with a smile.

The alarm on her phone starts to go off. "Oh, my lunch break's
up, I must be on my way back."

"Aren't you a real estate agent?"

"Yes, and an insurance agent. What's your point? We're on a
schedule just like everybody else. And shouldn't you be heading
to work too?"

"Well *excuse* me. You learn something new everyday I guess. I
always thought y'all just came and went as y'all pleased. And um,
yeah of course. I'm just trying to be a gentleman and make sure

you're on your way first." I say as we get up from the table and begin to walk out.

"Aww, how sweet. But, um, Winston? I have to ask you something.", she says hesitantly.

"What's up Natalie?"

"What the hell is that on your pants?! I guess I was too upset to notice it earlier, but I can see it clearly now."

I laugh. "It's my breakfast. I was eating in the car and I...hit a speed bump or something and yeah. Haven't been able to make it home yet to change because...you know, work."

"Mmmmhhmm, okay. Your next investment just might need to be a bib." She giggles as we walk towards her car. "But anyway, thanks again for lunch Winston, I enjoyed it."

"Even though you paid for it and then some." I laugh.

"Well it's the thought that counts with me." I open her car door and she gets in. "Thank you. And I guess since you already know what I need, there's no need to meet tomorrow."

Quick on my feet, I say, "But there is."

Perplexed, "And that would be?"

"To have a follow up of our thing tonight."

She blushes and giggles. 'What's tonight Winston?"

"Oh, I guess you didn't get the email I sent you." I slap my face with my hand. "Ugh, well I guess I'll just tell you now. We're having a movie night tonight at eight."

She smiles. "Yeah, I guess I didn't get that one. Umm, well I actually…"

"Before you respond, think about it. There's always going to be a million reasons not to do something Natalie. If it makes you feel better, I used the term movie night and not date. It'll just be two *friends* hanging out. Harmless."

"Ugghh, you don't take no for an answer do you?" I just smile and admire her. "How about I go back to my office, check my calendar, and I'll call you later?"

"Cool, I'll be waiting."

"Okay, thanks again Winston. It was fun." She starts her car and heads back to work.

XLIII

———

I LOOK AT MY PHONE AND IT'S BARELY ONE THIRTY. *What am I supposed to do for an hour? I can't go home, I can't go to The Spot, and I damn sure can't go to work. I might as well just go to Mr. Langston's house and wait for him there.*

I get in my car, then I get on my way to his house. It's only about twenty-five minutes from my current location, so it's not that far of a drive.

The time is one-fifty eight when I make it to his house. He lives in a secluded upscale neighborhood where the cheapest house is a million dollars, and all of his neighbors are at least 100 yards apart. When I get to his house, I notice his car is parked in the driveway in front of his house. I also notice there's another car parked by his, but I don't recognize it. Assuming he's in a meeting, I park my car around the side of his house by his mailbox because I don't want to block anybody in. Then, I just sit in my car until it's time for me to go in.

I play on my phone, take a little cat nap, and observe a family of ducks roam the area to try and kill time. After doing all of this, the time is still only two-thirty.

I start to get anxious. *It's Mr. Langston. He's not going to mind if I'm a couple minutes early. I mean, it's practically my second home anyway. I'm the last person he'd kick out of his house. Well, second to his wife.*

As I prepare myself to get out of the car, his front door opens. He doesn't walk straight out though, he just stands there with the door open and looks out into his neighborhood, as if he was looking for someone. He glances at my car, but pays it no mind. His dealership drops cars off at his house a couple times a month for test drives, so a car sitting in front of his house isn't alarming to him. Also, my windows are tinted pretty dark, so it's hard to tell if someone's in here or not, especially since Mr. Langston doesn't have his glasses on. He's also not wearing his usual suit and tie. He's wearing his beige plush bathrobe that he lounges around the house in. I think nothing of it. I just assume he finished his meeting a lot earlier than expected, and came home to wind down and relax until I came over. *But who's car is that?*

As I see him walk out, I get out of my car.

"Mr. Langston!", I yell as I'm walking around towards the front of his driveway to greet him.

His face turns pale, as if he was looking at a ghost. Jittery and nervously, he says, "H-hey, uh, Winston. You're a little early aren't you? Shouldn't you be at work or something right now?"

I raise my eyebrows, "Um, I got fired Mr. Langston. You know this. That's kind of like the whole reason I'm over here. Well, a part of it."

"Oh yeah, that's right. It slipped my mind."

"You okay Mr. Langston? You're acting funny. What's up? Talk to me."

"I'm good, Winston." A door in his house slams. He hears it and his eyes bulge open. "You know what Winston, can you do me a favor and make a store run for me please? I'm tired and really don't feel like leaving to go anywhere. I'll pay you whenever you get back."

"I got you, but is Mrs. Langston back? I heard a door close."

"It's complicated Winston, we can talk about it whenever you get back."

Footsteps start to come down the stairs. "Well if that's her, I don't want to be rude and not say anything. You know how she is."

I reach to push the door open so I can go in and he stops me.

"No Winston, she's under the weather and will understand. She just wants peace and quiet right now so she can rest and recover from her trip. Just go up the street to that store on the corner, and I'll text you a list when you get there."

I raise my eyebrows again and shake my head. "So is she sick or is she tired from her trip?"

"Both, now could you hurry and go please?"

"Whatever you say Mr. Langston. Start texting me the list now, you know how you be forgetting stuff."

As soon as I turn around to walk back to my car, I hear, "Hey Winston!" I expeditiously turn around because that voice doesn't sound like Mrs. Langston's. When I turn, I see that it's Keisha. She's standing there wearing one of his t-shirts and black biker shorts, and holding her purse in her hand. "You ain't tell me we were having company Robby. I thought you had to be somewhere by three?"

I make a face at Mr. Langston, and he makes one at me. We then make eye contact with one another, and he motions his eyes to tell me to just go along with it.

"I, um, yeah, heeey Keisha.", I say as I wave. "He does, actually. I just came by to ask him a few quick questions. We finished right before you came out here, so I'm leaving now."

"Ummmm, ain't you supposed to be at work or something Winston? Or at least that's where you told Natalie you were going after y'all little lunch date."

I look at Mr. Langston for help and he just shrugs his shoulders. "This *is* work, Keisha. Mr. Langston is one of my biggest clients and my phone was tripping. We believe in only having the best customer service where I work, so I came all the way out here to ask him the questions."

She rolls her eyes then says, "Mmhmm, whatever. Well I'll go ahead and let y'all handle y'all business. I don't want to interrupt. Good seeing you Winston, and it's always good seeing you

Daddy." She gives Mr. Langston a hug and a kiss on the cheek before she gets into her car and drives off.

When she leaves, I look at Mr. Langston and facetiously say, "So you weren't gonna tell me you and Keisha were a thing?"

He laughs then grins as he says, "We're nothing more than *associates* Winston, calm down."

"That looked like y'all were a lot more than associates. I mean c'mon Mr. Langston, she called you "Daddy"."

He wraps his arm around my shoulder as we walk into his house and says, "When you got game like I got son, that's the only name they'll ever call you."

XLIV

———

W E LAUGH AS WE WALK IN THE HOUSE. "JUST TAKE a seat in the living room, I'll be in there shortly." He says as he walks into his kitchen. "You want something to drink or anything? Oh, wait. I forgot you just had a lunch date with your associate not too long ago." He grabs a beer then comes into the living room to sit by me.

I chuckle, "Mr. Langston, you're the last person that needs to be talking. I see you didn't waste any time."

He grins. "Well Winston, when you get to be up in age like myself, you begin to realize that you're running low on time. You realize that you have to start making every second count. After years of not doing what I wanted, I finally decided to only focus on what made me happy. I love Meridith, Winston, I truly do. But, I'm just not happy with her anymore. We're not happy. Life's too short to be anything but happy, son. We've been separated for months and before last night, I can't remember the last time I've felt a spark like that."

"Oh wow, I definitely understand where you're coming from.

You actually like her, or do you think it'll be a one night stand type of thing?"

"I'm not sure yet. I mean, she's real eccentric. A type of person that I'm not used to being with. Somebody new and refreshing. Meredith is a great woman, but she can be too soft spoken and conservative for my liking. Now Keisha, she's so wild and rambunctious. Being with her is so invigorating Winston. I mean she did some things last night and this afternoon that I didn't even know women could do. It was special, miraculous even. I mean, whew. She did this one thing where she put her leg over..."

"Yeah, yeah I get it. You're happy. I don't need the visual. I'm good on all that."

"Oh don't act like you're five, but suit yourself. I'm just saying that the night was magical. I'll probably give her some space to let her miss me, then I'll give her a call in a few days."

"You sure that's going to work? I'm not sure you know how women operate nowadays."

"Hmph, and you do? But anyway, proceed son."

I chuckle. "Let me inform you before you get a window busted or something. If you ghost her after the *magical* and *miraculous* night y'all just had, one of these two things is going to happen. She's either going to one, block you to where you'll never be able to contact her again, or two, she's going to bust your door down and see why you aren't talking to her." Mr. Langston looks at me with a confused look and I laugh. "You better get with the times, man. You're not as indispensable as you think you are. This ain't the eighties and nineties no more, the game's changed. Women have options now. They can post one picture, then BOOM, five minutes later she has a hundred dudes asking to take her out. I suggest you take this time to send her a text to let her know that you're thinking about her and you hope she makes it home safe."

"Thanks for the advice Winston. You know what we used to call people like you back in the day?"

Intrigued, "Nah, what?"

He grins then says, "A sucka." I just sit there and look at him with an unamused expression on my face while he laughs. "Just sit back and watch the master work. I've been doing this since before you were in diapers, young buck."

"Whatever you say. Just don't call me when she's banging down your door at three in the morning. I already see it coming."

"Yeah, yeah, we'll see. Now let's quit talking about my night life and focus on the real reason we're here. Now, tell me exactly what's going on with MP. How did MP get you fired?"

I suck my teeth. "Man, where do I start?!"

"Tell me everything, don't leave out any details."

I spend about twenty-five minutes telling Mr. Langston everything that happened, from the police incident to me getting fired.

Infuriated, "That mother fucker! We have to do something about this before he takes it too far. These are merely warnings. He'll stop at nothing to get what he wants."

"But Mr. Langston, why me? I've barely known the man for a week."

"Who knows with him. Ever since we were young, he's been a little off the wall."

"Mr. Langston, I can't go to work, I can't go home, I have nowhere to go right now. I don't know what to do."

"You'll always have a spot here, Winston. Just lay low here and I'll go take care of him tonight."

"By yourself?"

"Yeah, I can handle him by myself." He gets up out of his seat. "You know what, I'll go take care of that now. I'm going to put an end to this."

"I'll go with you."

"No Winston. It's better if I go by myself. Trust me. I'll go get ready now. You just stay here and occupy yourself. Don't leave. I shouldn't take more than a few hours."

Mr. Langston goes upstairs to get dressed while I stay in the living room and watch TV. As I'm sitting there, I check my phone and see that I have messages from Natalie and Sharon.

I read Natalie's first: "Thank you again for lunch Winston. And again I'm sorry for having an attitude earlier."

I reply, "It's all good really. But if you're still feeling bad....make it up to me with the movies tonight?"

I check Sharon's messages while I wait for Natalie to reply: "Winston are you ok?! The word on the street is that the police are looking for you and they say you're not at your house. You don't have to tell me where you are, just let me know you're okay."

"I figured, but yeah I'm good. Just hiding out until everything is resolved."

"Okay stay safe, I'm here if you need me:)"

Mr. Langston comes down stairs wearing a black suit and tie. "I'll be back in a few, Winston. We're going to get this mess under control."

"Let me know if you need me."

"I'll keep you posted." Mr. Langston walks out of the house and heads to the Mayor's place.

When he leaves, I just continue to sit downstairs and watch TV. After about thirty minutes, there's suddenly a loud banging on the door. It startles me because I wasn't expecting anyone, or anything for that matter. I ignore it and just hope it goes away. It stops for a couple minutes, then it continues, but louder.

BANG, BANG, BANG.

"Winston, we know you're in there! Either you come out, or we're coming inside and fucking up this beautiful big house you're in. Make a choice!"

I'm frozen solid with fear. I don't know what to do.

BANG. BANG.

"Open up Winston! There's no more running!"

I grab my phone to call Mr. Langston, but it goes straight to voicemail. I try calling again and it's the same thing.

"We're coming in! Three! Two! One!"

XLV

———

T HEY'RE ABOUT TO BURST INTO THE HOUSE, I HAVE TO think quick. *If I dart up the stairs to hide, they'll eventually find me and I'll have nowhere to run. My best bet will be to run out the back and hide out until I can get to my car.*

I grab my phone and keys then burst through the living room and out the back door. Simultaneously, they kick down the front door and rush in.

"Where are you Winston?!", one of them says.

"You can't hide forever!", goes another one.

Who are these people? Can't be anyone else but the mayor, but how'd he know I was here. I wasn't followed. Well, at least I don't think I was. Mr. Langston would never sell me out. Would he?

They begin to search the house, but little did they know I was already outside.

As I'm outside catching my breath, I hear footsteps coming on both sides of the house. *Now what do I do?! There's only one other place to go, and that's in the lake behind his house. If I do that, one shot and I'm drowning in the water and left for dead.*

I hear the footsteps get closer and closer. Then suddenly, I hear their radios say, "Everyone in the house, we need all hands on deck searching inside. We need him found pronto."

I breathe a sigh of relief. I wait a few seconds, then I take off running around the right corner of the house. As soon as I turn the corner, WHAM. I'm tackled by a masked man in all black.

"I got him!", he yells while I wrestle with him trying to escape.

We tussle for a minute, then I'm able to roll him over onto his back and punch him, causing him to set me free.

I get up and begin to run towards my car, but as soon as I got up, I turned right into the arms of another masked man. He smothers me with a chloroform covered rag and I immediately pass out.

When I wake up, I don't have any sense of the time or my location. All I know is that I'm tied up in some vehicle with a potato sack around my head.

"Where am I?! Who are you?!", I exclaim, trying to break free. "Let me go, I didn't do anything."

"He's up", man number one says. "You better relax, you're only making your restraints tighter."

"Put him back to sleep, we're not there yet and I don't want to hear his mouth. I don't want to shoot him. Our orders are to deliver him alive, not dead.", replies man number two.

"A shot to the foot won't kill him.", says man number one.

"Wa-wa-wait a minute. Y'all don't have too..."

"All of you, shut up! Just shut him up and put him back to sleep.", a third man yells.

"You got it.", says man number one. "Hand me the bottle."

He sprays my bag with chloroform and I pass back out.

When I wake up, I'm dazed and confused laying in what feels like a field somewhere.

"Why would you even spray it on the bag you moron?! I thought you were putting it on another rag or something."

"I was just trying to make sure he wasn't waking back up."

"You both are idiots."

I hear voices, but I can't see anything.

"Go check him, make sure he's not dead." I hear his footsteps walk over so I just pretend I'm still asleep. He comes over, puts his hands on my neck to check my pulse, then walks away. "He's alive."

"Good, the big man would kill us. He should be here soon. He said he was about ten minutes away when I got off the phone with him."

"How long ago was that?"

"About fifteen minutes ago."

"Ugh, he got about ten more minutes before I just throw him in the middle of nowhere and leave him there."

"Nah, then we'll all be dead. Along with our families too."

"Just think about the money."

"What does he even want with him?"

"Who knows man, you know that man always has some weird shit up his sleeve."

I start coughing and shivering. "Aye! Can one of y'all take this bag off me?! I gotta throw up!"

"Why you just standing there? Go handle that!"

"Me?! You handle that! I ain't no babysitter."

"Aye, one of you two go take care of that before it's a mess everywhere."

"Iight, remember this shit."

"Aye, make sure you hold his hair out of his face and rub his back too." Two of them laugh while the other takes my mask off. I immediately get on my knees and throw up. When I finished, I tried to look around to see who it was, but they still have their masks on. When he takes my mask off, I also realize that I'm not in a field, but an old empty barn.

"Aye, he's pulling up, put the bag back on him and stand him up."

"No! He'll just pass out again, idiot. Just take his jacket off and wrap it around his eyes."

"Turn around.", he demands as he unties me and takes off my jacket. He wraps it around my head, reties my hands, then walks me over to stand by him and his two other accomplices.

I hear a car pull up and two doors slam, there's a pause, then I hear another door slam.

"They're here."

Frantically, "Stand up straight, stand up straight. The boss is coming."

I hear two sets of footsteps start to walk towards us. I also hear a sound that sounds like something's being dragged across the ground.

I hear the barn doors open, "Howdy, howdy. I'm guessing everything went as expected." This voice sounds like it came from Sheriff Brooks, but I'm still unsure.

"Yes sir, it was a smooth operation."

"You didn't hurt him, did you?"

"No sir, he's good." The new man comes over to inspect me. "He checks out. Everything's fine, now where's our money man."

"It's on the way."

"And where's the big guy, I thought he was supposed to be coming too."

"He's on the way. Now enough with all these damn questions. And why do y'all dumb asses have his jacket tied around his head? Y'all couldn't find a bag or mask or something? I thought y'all were professionals?" He takes my jacket off of my head and hands it to me. I realize that it's Sheriff Brooks standing in front of me, and Officer Russo is the other person he came in with. He's standing in front of the door with a big black trash bag at his feet.

"We spilled chloroform on it.", one of the other masked gentlemen says.

Sheriff Brooks sighs. "Well, anyway, howdy, Winston. MP will be here in a minute. He had some stuff to take care of."

"What do y'all want with me?", I ask. "I haven't told anyone about anything, and I mind my own business."

"We honestly can't tell ya Winston. We just follow orders."

The head masked man starts to get impatient. "Now what about our money?! I'm not going to ask again. Y'all said y'all were going to pay us $105,000 if we got him delivered unharmed and on time. And since both of those are checked off..." POW. Officer

Russo shoots him in the foot. "Aaahgghhh!!! What the fuck man?!?!"

Officer Russo hops over the bag and runs over to the man he shot. "You say another gah damn word about that money and I'll shoot your lips off next. Consider that a warning shot." He looks back at the other two masked men. "Y'all have anything to say about the money?" They shake their heads no.

Sheriff Brooks starts to untie me and brush me off. Officer Russo walks over, "You know we have a warrant out for your arrest, right? You're failing to comply with our investigation. Your piss was dirty Winston. That automatically makes you a person of interest in this whole drug scandal. I know you didn't think running away and not going home would just make everything disappear."

I just stand there, frozen, tightly gripping my jacket. On the outside, my face was emotionless, but on the inside, I was terrified. I didn't know what MP wanted with me, what, or who, was in that bag, or if I was even making it out of this barn alive.

"Relax Russo. Actually, just go bring that bag over here." Sheriff Brooks says with a smile.

As officer Russo goes over to grab the black bag, another car pulls up. "It's show time." He says as he looks back at me.

A door closes, footsteps walk towards the barn door, and MP walks in wearing a red suit with black pinstripes and a black fur coat. He grins at me and says, "Running from it will not save you Winston."

XLVI

———

"NEITHER WILL RUNNING FROM PAYING US MP! WE DID the job and then some. And now, we're raising our rates from thirty-five thousand a head to fifty thousand since your people want to get trigger happy.", the head masked man sternly says.

MP walks over to him, looks him up and down, and then stomps on his foot. The masked man releases a loud howl full of pain. "How about I just subtract thirty-five instead. I don't like being harassed or nagged, especially about money. I'm a man of my word. Now, do I need to break that down some more so your puny, asinine, and idotic brain can comprehend, or are you good?"

He spits down at MP's feet then says "Fuck you, now where's our damn money? The jobs done."

MP chuckles. He takes a few steps towards me, pulls out a pistol that was tucked in the back of his pants, then turns around and shoots him in the head. POW. The masked man drops dead and everyone stands around in awe. MP tucks his gun back into his pants, walks over to the dead body, and says, "Now there's one thing I won't tolerate, and that's disrespect." He stares down at the body. "I am who I am and you should know that by now." He spits on him then looks at his two subordinates. "You two just got an extra thirty-five thousand dollars to split. One of you go get that briefcase out of my backseat and the other come here." They stand there confused. "Now!"

One of the masked men runs to MP's car and the other runs to MP. MP takes a handkerchief out of his pocket and hands it to him. "Wipe the blood off of my face and hands, then wipe my shoes."

"Well, somebody was eventually gonna do it.", Officer Russo jokingly says.

"That ungrateful prick had it coming to him. You want me to go ahead and wrap it up, MP?", Sheriff Brooks adds.

"That's enough." He tells the masked man wiping him off. He then looks over to me. "Put your jacket on. Aren't you cold?" He walks over to me, grabs my lavender jacket out of my hand, shakes it out, and hands it back to me. "Now, put it on. Can't have my new business partner out here getting sick." He then turns to Officer Russo. "Russo, bring that black bag over here. I want Winston to see something." Officer Russo goes to get the bag, then drags it in front of me, MP, the masked man, and Sheriff Brooks.

"Brace yourself for what's in this bag, Winston. Well, who's in it I should say.", Sheriff Brooks says.

I instantly think it's Mr. Langston because the last time I saw him, he said he was going to MP's place. My heart drops into my stomach and I begin to tear up.

MP looks over at me, "You okay over there, Winston? You don't look too well." I throw up again.

The masked man returns with the briefcase. "You two take that and get out of here. It was a pleasure doing business with you. I'll call you if I need your services again."

"Yes sir, likewise.", one of them says as they start to exit out of the barn.

"Hey!", MP yells, stopping them in their tracks. "Take this trash with you."

They come back to get their partner's body, drag it outside, get in their van, and leave.

I'm still standing there lightheaded and queasy, fearful that it's Mr. Langston in the bag. The longer I stood in front of that bag, the sicker I got.

"Winston, if you had to take a guess, who do you think is in that bag? You probably think it's Mr. Langston, don't you? Well, that's a very big possibility. It'll also be real easy to frame you too. You know, since your DNA can probably already be found throughout his house.", Sheriff Brooks jokes.

"Nah, he probably thinks it's his buddy that owns that diner he goes to almost every morning. What's his name? Um, it's Chino, right? He's already creeping up on death anyway, so no one will really think twice about him *dying in his sleep*.", Officer Russo adds.

I just stand there in awe of what they're saying. I refuse to believe it's any of them in that bag.

MP puts his arm around me, "You guys relax. Y'all are scaring the poor boy." He looks at me. "Your man Mr. Langston, well Robert, paid me a visit today, but I'm sure you already knew that. He was pretty upset about the promotion I offered you. I take it you didn't tell the story properly."

I get triggered and snatch away. "What?! What the hell is wrong with you? You drugged me and got me fired from my job, MP! How the hell is that a promotion?!"

"Hey, watch your tone there now, son!", Officer Russo exclaims.

"Simmer down Russo. He's good.", MP tells him. "Relax."

"We gonna crack this thing open or what? I'm tired of waiting. I want to see the look on the kid's face whenever we open up this sucker.", Sheriff Brooks impatiently says.

"Patience is a virtue, Brooks. That goes for you as well, Russo. I'm trying to prepare Winston's mind for what he's about to see." He turns to me. "Like I said earlier, I don't tolerate disrespect. Betrayal, now that's one of the highest forms of disrespect. To have someone that was not only a business partner, but was also considered a true friend, a brother, turn around and stab you in the back when you're not looking is tragic. Ugh, it's so heartbreaking. You ever felt that type of heartbreak, Winston?"

I don't say anything, I just stand there and stare at the ground. The assurance of it being Mr. Langston in that big black trash bag starts to sink into my brain. *He's the only one that MP could be talking about. They were very close growing up, best friends even. They were business partners as well. Then Mr. Langston stabbed him in the back and took his girl, his fiance. That's the heartbreak. There's not another person connected like that to MP.*

My hands begin to shake, and my knees get weak. The barn began to shrink as tears slowly started to fall from my eyes. This cold, dark, windy night had just gotten a lot colder, and a lot darker. I felt as if I had lost a piece of me.

I throw up again. "Winston, Winston are you okay?", MP asks.

"I think it's time MP, he's about to lose it. Just look at him.", Sheriff Brooks.

MP turns and looks at Officer Russo. "It's time, we have to show him what happens to people that don't cooperate and try to cross us.", Officer Russo tells him.

He then looks back at me. "Wipe your tears son. Death is really a beautiful thing when you think about it. It's the true judgement of one's life. If you lived a great, impactful life worth living, then your legacy will never die, and in actuality, you'll live forever. But, if you're like the worthless scum that's in this bag. Your life will be worthless and you'll be forgotten as quick as you came. Such a waste of life. Albert Pines once said, 'What we do for ourselves dies with us. What we do for others and the world remains and is immortal."

———

XLVII

M P LOOKS AT THE ANGUISH IN MY FACE. "RUSSO, CUT it open."

Officer Russo whips out a pocket knife from his pocket. "Finally.", he mutters.

He bends down and stabs the bag at its head, and drags the knife down through its opposite end causing the bag to split open down the middle. As the bag opens, a rank, foul, putrescent smell fills the area.

"This shit fucking stinks!", Officer Russo yells as he quickly backs away from the bag with his arm covering his mouth.

No way that's Mr. Langston. His body wouldn't be smelling like that in less than a day. Especially on a breezy day like today was.

"Go ahead Winston, go look inside the bag and see what's in there. I know the suspense is killing you. Go see what happens when my grace and mercy run out.", MP says as he gives me a little push in the back.

I look over at Sheriff Brooks and he's just smiling at me, waiting for me to look inside.

I walk up slowly. "C'mon now, we ain't got all night!", Officer Russo murmurs.

I take a deep breath, put my arm over my mouth and nose, and brace myself for what I'm about to see. I pull the bag back a little so I can look inside, and I'm stupefied by what I see. Well, who I see exactly.

It's the body of Mike Gonzalez. He's wearing the same brown suit he was wearing last Friday, and he has a bullet hole right between his eyes.

Puzzled, I ask MP, "Tuesday, didn't you say Mike was the one handling all your business operations? What did Mike do to deserve this?"

MP chuckles, "Well Winston, indeed he *was*. But, Friday night he got so drunk that he started telling Sheriff Brooks here about how he'd been stealing from me through the years. He had direct access to my money. The agreement we had was for him to just cash the checks and deposit the money I'd receive at the end of each week from all of my businesses into the proper accounts. What I didn't know, was that he'd take his shares out before he dispersed the rest. With most of it being cash, there wasn't really a way I could keep track of him taking a little piece of the pie here and there as he was doing it. He got me. And after he got done telling on himself, he had the audacity to try and persuade Brooks to get in on it too. I mean really?! Out of all people? But anyway Winston, I like to consider myself to be a real merciful being at times, especially towards ones in my inner circle. So, I called Mike and met with him after our dinner Sunday night to give him a chance to come clean. I guess he never went home because he was wearing the same clothes he was wearing Friday night. We sat down in my office, face to face as men should meet to discuss matters like this. I got straight to the point. I asked him if he'd been stealing from me, and of course, he denied it. I then showed him some bank statements, and he still denied it. He said they were wrong and that it wasn't him. Winston, understand our relationship. I took this man in when he was struggling five years ago. He had gotten fired for trying to make a little extra money by falsifying some accounts at his other job. He lost everything and didn't have a dime to his name. He couldn't provide for his wife and kids. They were borderline homeless. But, I helped him and made it possible because he helped me with a couple lucrative business deals when we initially met. Back to the story, I then call Sheriff Brooks into my office and he asks him about the money for a third time. Mike claimed to not remember anything from that night. He said that he must've just blacked out and started randomly making it up, but the bank statements I had didn't lie. My deposits that were being made were thousands of dollars short. Mike swore up and down he didn't do it. My inner gut told me he was lying, so I pulled out my gun and popped him in between the eyes. He betrayed me, lied to me, and stole from me, Winston. After all I had done to help him and his family. That hurt me more than it hurt him, but that's life."

"He deserved it, I can't believe he had the balls or was even stupid enough to take to over $100,000.00 from you. Almost eleven percent every week. Man, that money hungry bastard.", Sheriff Brooks comments.

MP gets a concerned look on his face. "I never showed YOU the bank statements. How do you know the exact percentage he was stealing from me? When you told me about Mike, you only mentioned that he was taking thousands, never an exact amount."

"Lucky guess.", Sheriff Brooks says as he shrugs his shoulders. "You know I've had my fair share of lucky guesses."

"Can we close this bag up yet? My stomach's starting to flip.", Officer Russo says as he interrupts.

"We'll continue this conversation another time, Brooks. Actually, I think it's best if you leave. You too Russo. And take Mike with you and dispose of him properly."

"MP, you know I'd never steal from you. I..." Officer Russo grabs Sheriff Brooks as he attempts to plead to MP.

"Leave. Now.", MP demands.

"Let's just go, you can explain yourself tomorrow.", Officer Russo tells Sheriff Brooks as they grab Mike's body and exit the barn.

MP looks at me when they leave. "Winston, you know too

much for me to just let you go and walk away freely. That's why we're here. Like I've told you before, it's chess. I'm always three moves ahead of my opponent. I knew you wouldn't go home because that would be the first place the police looked for you. The safest place for you to hide would be at Roberts's. Most people don't know just how close y'all are, but I do. I hired a team to set up surveillance there and bring you in when the time was right."

We hear their car drive off.

"But why?! Why MP?! Why me?! I've done nothing to you. I've told no one besides Mr. Langston about what I've seen, and what I know. You've gotten me fired from my job, and got me kidnapped and brought here to some old barn in the middle of nowhere. Why?!"

MP takes a deep breath, pauses for a second, then looks me dead in my eyes. "Either you come over and work for me, or you're gonna end up like our friend Mike. I'm tired of being lenient."

———

XLVIII

"**N**O.", I FIRMLY SAY.
 He pulls his gun back out and shoves the barrel in my face while grabbing my shirt with his other hand. "I'm going to give you one more chance. Now take a deep breath, and think wisely about the next thing that's going to come out your mouth." He takes the safety off of his gun. "It works Winston, you've seen it for yourself."

For some reason, I wasn't scared, nervous, or even worried. I was calm. Deep inside, I knew he'd never hurt me.

I look at him, "If you were *really* going to kill me, you would've done it already."

He pushes the gun deeper into my face. "You think you're funny, huh?" A car pulls up to the barn. "I thought I told those idiots to leave. Well, at least now I won't have to clean up the mess."

A car door slams and footsteps rapidly walk towards the barn.

"MP, let him go!", the voice ferociously yells out.

MP looks at me and smiles. Mr. Langston then walks into the barn wearing the same suit he had on earlier.

"Nice of you to join us Robert.", MP says as he looks at Mr.

Langston and puts his finger on the trigger. "I hope you enjoy the show."

"MP let him go. I thought we had an agreement earlier. What the hell is this?!"

He lets me go and walks over to Mr. Langston waving his gun in his face. "You really think I'd believe anything you say Robert? Ever since Meridith, your word means nothing to me. You backstabbing bastard!"

"Woah, woah, relax MP! Put the gun down and let's talk like men."

MP looks back at me and points his gun towards the door, "Go get in the car. We'll resume this another time."

I hesitate to leave. I look at Mr. Langston to get a sign of confirmation and he nods his head. "I'll be fine. Get in the car and keep it running."

MP shoots at my feet and says, "Hurry before I change my mind and put bullets in the both of you."

I expeditiously exit out of the barn and get in the driver's side of Mr. Langston's car.

MP looks at Mr. Langston, tucks his gun in his pants and says, "You got sixty seconds to tell me why I shouldn't blow your brains out right now Robert. You know I owe you."

"Look MP, I know you're still mad about Meridith and will probably never let it go, but like I've said a hundred times before, it was what was best."

"Stop saying that bullshit! You got fifty seconds before I fill you with this lead!"

"Just wait MP! I'm sorry for how everything played out that night, but you know y'all wasn't happy together. Especially Meredith. She was constantly feeling abandoned, and felt like she was second and even third place in your life. She was always hurt that you'd constantly put work and business ahead of her. And don't act like she didn't know you were dealing with three, four, five other women at the time either."

MP takes out his gun and holds it in front of his belt with his right hand and crosses his left hand over it. "Forty, thirty-nine, thirty-eight."

"She threatened to report you to the police! That's how fed up she was with you man."

Confused and troubled, "What?! She'd never! Stop with all this lying!"

"I had stopped by your house to smoke with you and have some drinks, but you weren't there. I had the key to your house, so, I just walked in to wait on you. When I got in, I heard Meredith on the phone with someone crying and telling them how she was going to turn you in and that she had all this evidence against you. I immediately rushed to your bedroom where she was. She hung up the phone and looked at me. I told her that if she went through with it, she'd not only be putting you in jail, but me too. I also told her that she'd be putting her life in jeopardy as well by affecting the lives of hundreds, and even thousands, of other people. She got scared then began to cry and pour out all of her emotions, thoughts, and feelings onto me. At that moment, I did what most men would do when they see a crying woman, I gave her a hug. I then asked where you were. She said you probably wouldn't be home for a few hours. I told her I'd come back then, but she saw the liquor bottles in the bag I had and wanted some. She said she needed a shot to help her ease her mind. I told her it wasn't a good idea, but she threatened to pick up the phone again if I left. She turned on some music and then we took a shot. One shot turned into two, two into three, three into four, then all of a sudden we're in the bed making love. Because of the music, we couldn't hear you come in. I still regret it til this day, but who knows where we would be if that didn't happen. I know continuing to date her and eventually marry her made it worse, but she threatened to tell everything if I left her. Everything!"

"So why are you just telling me this now? After almost twenty-five years?! It's cause you're lying to me Robert!" MP cocks his gun and points it at Mr. Langston.

"No, no, no! Promise to God I'm not lying MP! I didn't tell you because I know you would've probably killed her out of anger without considering any of the consequences. You were one trigger happy loose cannoned joker back in the day. If she didn't show up to her mother's house you know that would've been trouble for us. Mrs. Johnson ain't play about her daughter, and she's always had it out for you. She would've had the police swarming us in minutes. Just please forgive me. Yes it was wrong. I never wanted to ruin our business or our friendship especially, but in the bigger picture, it had to be done. I love you like a brother MP. I always will."

"Shut up!", MP yells as he waves his gun. "Shut it with the lies!"

"MP, just listen to me. We don't have to be friends, but we can still be business partners. I know your business ain't been running the same. Like I said earlier when we met, I'll run everything, just like the good old days, even better really. Just spare me right now and promise to leave Winston alone. Please, he's innocent in all this. Taking him from me isn't the same as the Meredith situation. He's not going to the authorities, or anyone for that matter. If he was, he would've ran to them already. Just listen to me. With me being the new owner of the Wardogs, you can generate even more revenue by distributing your stuff in the arena during the games. Just think about it." MP puts his gun to his side. "Now, we're gonna go, you're going to call your people off of Winston, and we're going to continue this business meeting at another time after you've processed everything and your head is clear."

MP stands there for a second. He then raises his gun, points it towards Mr. Langston, and fires it.

POW. POW. POW. POW.

XLIX

———

MY HEART DROPS AND SHATTERS WHEN I HEAR THE gunshots fire. I sink deep in my seat and realize I have a decision to make. Do I drive off in hopes to extend *my* life, at least for another night, or do I go back inside to view Mr. Langston's body one last time? I think about it for a second, take a deep breath, then put my face in my hands. *I wouldn't be the man I am today if it wasn't for Mr. Langston, it's the least I could do. I can't just leave him.* I then exhale as I get out of the car and rush back inside to the barn as the cold, brisk wind brushes against my face. I burst through the doors then come to an immediate halt. I'm flummoxed and astonished. I'm lost for words and my breath is taken away. I couldn't believe what I was looking at. There he was, Mr. Langston, standing there in front of MP untouched with four bullet holes in the wall behind him. I'm in awe.

MP tucks his gun back inside his pants and says, "He just saved your life Robert. Now go."

"Thank you MP."

"Leave! I'll contact you when I'm ready to conduct business."

Mr. Langston pats MP on the back as he walks away. We exit the barn and we walk to the car.

"I'll drive.", Mr. Langston says as we get to the car.

We begin to drive down a long, dark and narrow road. "What the hell was that about? I thought you were gone Mr. Langston. Thank God you're alive."

"Business Winston. I made a deal with him."

"But why did he say I saved you? What I do?"

"That's a question for another day. Let's just thank the man upstairs for sparing our lives and letting us see another day. We'll leave it at that."

I look at the clock in the car and see the time is twelve forty-two, it was indeed another day.

We ride in silence for the rest of the hour plus it was before we arrived back at his house.

We finally pull into the driveway and I clear my throat. "Thank you Mr. Langston, for everything."

"No problem Winston. You know I got your back."

I smile and nod my head. "How'd you know that's where we were?"

"Some things never change, Winston. When I came back home, I saw that my door was kicked in. I also saw that your car was here and you weren't. I checked through the house and outside for clues. I found your phone and keys on the side of the house and knew it was no one else but MP. I stood my door up then made my way to his barn. He's been doing his dirt there since the late eighties."

"You think it's safe for me to go home now?"

"Yeah, but I want you to get some rest first. Go inside, shower, and try to get some sleep. You can head back in the morning."

He parks the car. "Yes sir."

"Oh, and before I forget..." He goes into his arm rest, pulls out my phone and keys, then hands them to me. "There you go. It was buzzing like hell earlier, but it's probably dead now."

We begin to get out of the car and walk towards the door. Puzzled, "Did you happen to see who was calling me? I don't think I had somewhere to be or anything."

We walk up to the door then enter the house. "Remind me to call somebody to get this fixed in the morning." He says as he moves the unhinged door to the size. "And to answer your question, I think it was Sharon calling you if I'm not mistaken."

"Ehh, I'll call her tomorrow. She probably just wants to make sure I'm alright." I say as I sit in the living room.

He walks into his kitchen and grabs a beer and a bottle of water. "You know what, Winston, I think Sharon still likes you."

"What?! She's dating James Love, man. I'm just an average financial advisor. He's one of if not the best basketball player in the entire world. He makes six figures a game. You're tripping Mr. Langston, I think those gunshots got you discombobulated."

He chuckles and hands me the bottle of water as he sits down and cracks open his beer. "Winston, Winston, Winston. Money doesn't buy happiness. You can buy a woman all the diamonds in the world, but if you don't spend any time with her, she's just going to be miserable. I didn't always have money, Winston, but I did always have women. Not because I'd buy them this or that, cause the Lord knows I couldn't afford it, but because I took the time to genuinely get to know them and I spent quality time with them."

"Okay? You're saying all of that to say what?"

"A guy like James Love probably has women coming in and out his life like air circulates through his body. Yeah Sharon's at the games, but who knows when else they're together. He's probably not there for her the way you were emotionally and mentally. Hmm, what actually caused y'all's break up?"

I sigh. "I'm sure she's happy. She's just being a good concerned friend by calling and checking up on me. You're reading too deep into it."

He laughs. "I asked you a question, Winston. Why did y'all break up?"

I get up and walk upstairs to go to the guest room. "Life man. I'm about to shower and go to sleep. I'm sleepy."

Sarcastically, "Yeah, sure you are. Make sure you brush your teeth, too. Your breath smells terrible."

I shake my head and continue to walk upstairs. "Whatever. Night."

"Night, son."

I get in the room, plug my phone up to the charger he left in the wall, then go to the bathroom to take a shower.

When I get out, I brush my teeth, put on some shorts I found in the drawer, and lay in the bed.

I roll over to check my phone to see if it's turned on. It's on and it shows that I have seven missed calls and ten angry texts from Natalie.

I slap my palm on my forehead. *Tonight was supposed to be our movie night. I completely forgot with everything that happened. It's not like it was my fault, but still. There's nothing I can do now though. I'll just have to make it up to her tomorrow.* I sigh then put my phone on the nightstand by the bed.

I look up at the ceiling as I think about how crazy of a night I had. Everything still seemed so surreal. From being kidnapped, to seeing Mike's dead body, almost dying myself, and then almost losing Mr. Langston. It was a lot to take in. I begin to tear up and think about what Mr. Langston said when we left the barn. Before I doze off, I say a quick prayer. *Lord, I know we don't talk as much as we should, but I know you're watching over me. And for that, I just want to say thank you. Thank you for having your hand over me and Mr. Langston tonight. Please continue to guide our steps, watch over us, and protect us. In Jesus's name I pray, amen.*

L

———

I WAKE UP AROUND EIGHT THIRTY TO THE BOLD distinctive smell of bacon. My stomach growls. I quickly get up and go downstairs into the kitchen to see what's cooking.

"Good morning, honey. About time you woke up. Happy Valentine's Day, Boo! And what happened to your door? It's all bent and what not. I didn't want to wake you with the doorbell, so I just walked in. Anyway, I made breakfast for you. Bacon and eggs, your favorite." She turns around. "Oop, I'm sorry. I thought it was Robert coming down the stairs. Good morning though."

"Haha it's cool. Good morning to you too Keisha, the food smells good."

I reach for a piece of bacon from a plate sitting on the oven and she slaps my hand away. "Aht, aht now. That's for my baby."

"Daaaamn, it's like that?"

Sassily, "Mmmhhm, yup. What's for my man is for MY man. You on your own for breakfast, Mr. Ghost."

I chuckle. "Mr. Ghost?!"

"Yup! Your name is Mr. Ghost until further notice."

"What I do? Last time I checked, I'm alive and chocolate. Not dead and pale."

"Well I can't tell the difference with the way you ghosted Natalie last night. On Valentine's Day Eve too. I really can't believe you! I was rooting for you and everything. I guess all y'all men the same. Well, except for my man Robert. I know he'd never do me like that."

"Look Keisha, I care for Natalie, honestly. I was looking forward to going to the movies with her, but something came up last night that I couldn't control."

"Mmhhm, yeah, yeah, yeah. You was probably with that chick who's name you said at y'all lil lunch date yesterday."

I suck my teeth. "Man, it wasn't even like that."

"Boy bye, go somewhere with that goofiness. We see right through that wannabe player foolishness. You know damn well we are too old to be playing these little high school games. Now, how about you actually make yourself useful and go wake my man up so he can eat his breakfast while it's hot and fresh."

"Seriously Keisha. I was looking forward to our movie night, really. Something came up and Mr. Langston can attest to that whenever he gets down here. She was mad last night?"

"What?! Mad is an understatement. She called me around nine crying. She said she was blowing your phone up and you were just ignoring her and sending her calls straight to voicemail. We ended up calling Celeste and spending the night watching movies and eating pizza at my place. Safe to say she's done with you. You had your shot and you blew it. I'd be surprised if you ever hear from her again."

My heart dropped. I didn't want to believe that Natalie was just out of my life. Especially over something that wasn't my fault. I didn't want to believe our relationship was over before it really even started. I didn't know what to say. "Keisha, can you…"

"Can I help you make it up to her?! Umm, let me think…nope! It's one thing to stand her up, but to blatantly ignore her when she's blowing your phone up, that's just dirty. She was really worried and concerned about you. Like I said Winston, we all grown. We don't tolerate that kiddie play play shit."

"But…"

"Aht, aht. Go get my man."

I sigh, then I turn to head out the kitchen to go upstairs and get Mr. Langston. Before I leave, I get an idea. I quickly turn around and say, "Hey Keisha."

"What, Mr. Ghost? You letting my baby's food get cold."

"You really like Mr. Langston, huh?"

"I mean I ain't ever pop up at a man's house in a bomb ass dress just to cook breakfast for him after only one night, if that's what you mean. Holiday or not."

"What if I said I could make the feeling mutual?"

"Boy what is you talking about?!"

"Okay look, I really like Natalie, and you really like Mr. Langston. I'll help you if you help me."

"You sound desperate and stupid. First off, I don't need any help getting or keeping a man. I mean look at me Winston, tuh. Just wait til he sees me in this dress. He loves the color of crimson too. He's probably gonna kick you out the house as soon as he comes down. And second, we've moved on from you. All it takes is one screw up to get cut from the team. She was already on the edge about you. Last night just helped make her decision. So even if I DID want to help you, it'd be no point."

I sit in one of the chairs at the kitchen's island. "Keisha, Keisha, Keisha, let me kick some game to you real quick."

She rolls her eyes. "What, man?!"

"Okay, yes or no answers only. Now, did Mr. Langston know you were coming over this morning?"

"No, but..."

I wag my finger. "Aht, aht, aht. Yes or no answers only. Next question, did Mr. Langston text you after you left here yesterday afternoon?"

She sighs in frustration, "No."

"Now lastly, do you have a key to his house?"

"No."

"Okay, now if I don't go up there and tell Mr. Langston that I thought it was a good idea for you to come over, and that I was the one that let you in, he's going to think you're crazy and a stalker. You're technically trespassing and can also get arrested for breaking and entering. And if you add all of that to the crazy night we had last night, I'm sure this will be your last visit at this house. Regardless if it's Valentine's Day or not."

She thinks for a second then says, "Uuughh, what you want?"

I grin, "Just convince Natalie to give me one more chance. I'll make it up to her tonight."

"What you gon' do?"

"I'm going to invite her over to my place and do something for her there."

She laughs, "That's your plan? For Valentine's Day?! You setting your own self up for failure, but ok. Whenever she asks me what to do I'll help you out. Now go up there and get my baby."

I get up out of the chair, and make my way upstairs to Mr. Langston's room. I knock on his door.

"Come in.", he says.

I expected him to just be getting out of bed like I was, but he's standing in front of his mirror fully dressed and ready to go. I'm standing there in basketball shorts and he's wearing a dapper, mint colored suit. "Where you headed?", I curiously ask.

"I have meetings to attend and business to handle. Hopefully I can even have your job back by Monday."

"I appreciate it, but do you really think I should go back? Mr. Jacobs didn't even attempt to question my results or resist from firing me."

"Winston, business is business. Those results would've been made public to those in charge of Jacobs. They see that you're still working there and then what? Both of y'all are gone along with the rest of the firm. At least now you're in a position to get it back. I'll work on all that stuff today."

"I guess, you need me to do anything?"

"Nah, just clean up before you leave and wait for the guy to fix the door. I'm surprised you were up early enough to make breakfast. What you make?"

I laugh a little bit, "Oh, um, about that. That's why I came up here actually."

He raises his left eyebrow. "You didn't break anything did you? What did you burn?"

"Nah, everything's fine."

"Well, what is it? I have to be walking out the house soon."

I smile as I say, "Keisha's here."

"What?!?! What the hell is she doing over here?! I didn't invite her, hell, I haven't even talked to her since she left. She has to leave, ASAP."

"Calm down Mr. Langston, I invited her and it's Valentine's Day."

"You what?!"

"I thought you'd be tired and worn out from last night, so I told her to come. You know, to help you relax. And she thought it would be a great way to start off Valentine's Day. Don't get mad at her. It was my fault."

"Why do you keep saying that? Today isn't V Day."

"Check your phone."

He checks his phone and begins to laugh and scratch his head. "I guess I was mistaken."

"She made you breakfast. Bacon and eggs, your favorite."

"Look Winston, I appreciate the thought, but next time check with me first. I've told you about my past. Last night was just a typical night. I still have work to do, nothing's changed. And as far as V Day goes, I'll just make it up to her later. Watch the master work."

I chuckle, "Yes sir."

"Now hand me that gold watch off of the dresser so I can go."

———

LI

I HAND HIM HIS WATCH AND HE PUTS IT ON AS HE EXITS the room. I follow behind him.

"Now I gotta clean up the mess you've made.", Mr. Langston says as we walk down the stairs and into the kitchen.

Keisha greets Mr. Langston with a hug. "Good morning honey, it's about time you got up. Happy Valentine's Day! I made your favorite."

"Hey Keisha, good morning and Happy Valentine's Day to you too. And thank you, It looks good."

"I missed you. And I was worried about you last night. I thought that since you ain't text me yesterday something had happened to you."

Mr. Langston winks at me then says, "Yeah, me and Winston got caught up in a very long business meeting. As soon as we got out, we came straight home and went to sleep."

"Yeah, it was intense", I added.

"But I really must be on my way. Thank you again Keisha, it's nice seeing your beautiful face to start my day. And remember, don't leave until my door's fixed, Winston. He should be here around ten."

"Yes sir, I got you."

Mr. Langston grabs his keys and walks to his broken front door. Before he opens the door, Keisha grabs him, kisses him on the cheek, and says, "Have a great day Robert, I'll be thinking about you. I'll see you later right?"

"I'll call you Keisha." Mr. Langston smiles and exits through the door.

I laugh and Keisha eyes me. "What the hell you over there laughing at Mr. Ghost?!"

I grin and say, "You just don't seem like the lovey dovey type that's all. He has you bent."

"Well don't judge a book by it's cover. It takes a lot to crack my shell and let me tell you, Robert has it. I know he's a little older, but the way he moves, the way he acts, the way he touches me..."

"Alright, alright, I get it. He makes you happy."

"Not just happy, he completes me. He makes me want better for myself, for us. Like I know we only spent one day together, but I've felt more alive with him in those few hours than I have my other twenty-seven years of living."

"Damn, Mr. Langston must've laid that blue pill on ya."

She bursts out laughing. "Shut up. It's not always about sex you know. Even though he's far from lacking in that area, it's the way he touches me emotionally and spiritually."

I suck my teeth. "Y'all was together for a day. Really like sixteen hours, if that."

"Well, whatever Robert's doing, you need to write it down in a notebook and study it in order to have any chance with Natalie tonight. He's super busy now, but I know he probably has something wild planned later. And as for you, whatever goofy thing you got planned, it better work. It's Valentine's Day too, so you better bring it."

"Girl stop, I got game."

"Boy, what game?! You must be talking about video games."

"Natalie don't be talking about me in y'all group texts?"

She smirks, "And on that note, I'm going to head out. Feel free to eat all that since Robert's too busy for it." She grabs a piece of bacon then walks out of the kitchen. "Oh, and good luck tonight Winston. Hopefully some of Robert rubs off on you."

"Wait, tell me what she says about me!"

"Eeeh, I really gotta go, Winston. And remember, if she curves you tonight, it's not because of me. You just don't have game."

"Yeah, yeah. You'll see."

"Mhmm, bye, Winston. Make sure you get this door fixed too. Wouldn't want your daddy to whoop you." Keisha waves goodbye as she walks out giggling through the broken door.

When she leaves, I warm the food in the microwave, and sit in the living room as I eat.

As I finish my food and watch TV, time progresses. It's around ten-thirty when I hear the doorbell ring. I look to see who it is, and it's the repair man.

I answer the door. "Good morning sir and happy love day to ya. I'm Charles Bates from KnockKnock and I'm here to fix your door." He examines it. "Sheesh man, did you have a crazy girlfriend try to break in or something?!"

"Uh, good morning. I'm Winston, and yeah, it's a long story but I guess you can say that."

"Ah damn man. I suggest you get a restraining order. You gotta be a real psycho to do some crazy damage like this."

"If only you knew man. But hey, Charles right? You just do what you need to do. How long you think it'll take?"

"Um, it's no telling right now. Everythings pretty dented and beat in pretty bad. I'm surprised y'all got it to hold through the night. Especially with the winds we've been getting lately. Well, I have to measure it then go get the right door and all that fun stuff. Eeeehh, it shouldn't take no more than an hour. An hour and thirty at most. Two if I have to make any adjustments."

"Well okay, if you need me just ring the doorbell."

"Yes sir, will do."

I leave Charles to tend to his work as I go upstairs to get my phone. I grab it and come back downstairs to watch TV in the living room. I look through it and see what all I missed. Four messages and two missed calls from Sharon, seven missed calls and ten texts from Natalie, and one message from Mr. Langston. Since Mr. Langston's is the most recent, I look to see what he said. "Make sure that woman is out my house. And call me when the door man is done."

I laugh a little then just exit out of his message thread.

Next, I check Natalie's so I can go ahead and set up our date for tonight. Hopefully Keisha can come through. But first, I nervously read the messages she sent me last night.

"Hey Winston, I was thinking about it and I'm saying yes to the movies. It'd be fun."

"It's almost 8, where do you want me to meet you at?"

"I'm ready for our movie night. What we watching?"

"Heeellllooooooooo"

"Wow, how you gonna invite me to the movies then flake on me?"

"Asshole."

"I know you see me calling you."

"You're really about to ignore me?"

"I didn't think you was like that Winston"

"Don't bother texting or calling me ever again. You're probably with Sharon. I hope y'all enjoy each other. Just delete my number Winston. I'm over it."

I sigh. *Yeah, she's definitely angry. I'll make it up to her though. I just hope she didn't block me, that'll ruin everything.*

I sit back in the recliner and text her, "Good morning beautiful and Happy Valentine's Day. I'm sooo sorry about standing you up and ghosting you last night. I swear it wasn't intentional. I promise I'll explain everything when I see you. I'm truly sorry Natalie. I'll make it up to you tonight, I swear. Just give me another chance. Trust me, I promise you won't regret it." I send the message and it returns back to me. She blocked my number.

LII

———

I TRY RESENDING MY MESSAGE AGAIN AND AGAIN AND again, praying that something different happens each time, but it's the same result.

"Uuugghhhh!", I bellow in frustration.

"You okay in there, Mr.Winston? That didn't sound too pleasant.", Charles says as he's working on the door.

"Yeah I'm good man. Just women, ya know."

"A little Valentine's Day blues? Yeah man, I can relate. I got dumped like a week ago for wearing underwear."

I chuckle and become intrigued. I get up out of the recliner and walk towards the door. "What?! That's crazy man, what happened? Your girl a nudist or something?", I jokingly say.

Charles sucks his teeth. "No man. She caught me wearing her underwear. I know it was wrong to touch her belongings without her permission, but they're just so soft and they really hold everything together. It's the perfect feeling of comfort. You know what I mean, Mr. Winston? Well, anyway, now I'm all alone on this beautiful day of love."

A dismayed look covers my face. *This dude can't be serious.* I then pretend my phone's ringing. "Um, excuse me. I gotta answer this."

"It's fine, gotta go pick up the new door anyway. I'll be back in a jiff."

Charles gets in his truck to leave and I go sit back down on the couch to get back to my Natalie situation.

Should I just try calling her office? That's my only hope at this point. It's after eleven so she should be in.

I sit up and scroll through my phone for the number to her office. I find it and dial it. The phone rings, and rings, and rings. I let the phone ring for about fifteen more seconds before I hang up.

I lean back on the couch and exhale. *All this must be a sign that me and Natalie aren't meant to be.*

I put my phone down, and just watch TV. A commercial for workout equipment is on. I normally zone out during commercials, but this one said something that caught my attention. They said, "Anything worth having, will require a great amount of work, dedication, and persistence. Just because the path you're on is a little bumpy, that doesn't mean it's the wrong one."

Of course they were talking about working out and fitness goals, but I took it as a sign that I just needed to try a little harder with Natalie.

I had gotten an idea of what I wanted to do, but it'd have to wait. I couldn't leave the house wide open with Charles here. Who knows what he'd do.

I wait for him to get back and finish with the door. It's about eleven forty-five when he's done with everything.

He rings the doorbell and I go see what he wants.

"We're all finished here, Mr. Winston."

"Thanks man, it looks great. You have a good day."

He chuckles then says, "Thanks, you too Winston, but first, I need to know how you'll be paying us. It'll be twenty-three ninety-two."

"Um, excuse me? It's not already paid for by a Mr. Robert Langston?"

"Let me double check." He pulls out his tablet and scrolls through it for a few seconds. "Uh, no sir. It only says that a Mr. Robert Langston scheduled the appointment. If you look here under payment, it says TBD."

I laugh. *He set me up. That's why he wanted me to stay. He probably doesn't even have a meeting this morning.* I look at Charles. "One second, I have to make a phone call."

"Okay sure, but could you kind of not take your time please? I have another appointment at twelve thirty."

"Okay, just give me a moment."

"Alright, I'll run to the truck real quick."

Charles walks to his truck as I take my phone out my pocket to call Mr. Langston. The phone rings for about thirty seconds with no answer. I hang up, and try again. The same thing happens. I wave Charles back over.

"You know what, I'll just cover it. You said it was twenty-three ninety-two right?"

"Yeah, but as in $2,392.00."

"What?! All that for a door?!"

"This one was custom made. They normally run $1,911.00 but all the extra stuff adds up. And then you have to add the service charges so yeah, it'll be $2,392.00. How will you be paying? Cash, credit, or check?"

I think for a second. *There's no way he intentionally did this. This is a lot of money, especially for a door. I'm sure he'll pay me back later. I'll just try calling him again when I leave.*

"Can I pay with my phone?", I ask.

"Yeah, here." He takes out the device and I pay. "Would you like to leave a tip?"

Sarcastically, "A tip after paying $2,392? Yeah I got one, stop wearing ya girl's panties man."

He sucks his teeth, and walks to his truck. "Whatever, I'm not the only man that finds them comfortable."

I grin and shake my head. I then check my phone when he leaves and it says that the payment didn't go through. I crack a smile. *Well, that's between Charles and Mr. Langston, he told me to stay, not to pay. And panty boy should've double checked instead of worrying about a tip.*

A few minutes after he leaves, I leave too. I open my car door and I'm attacked by the smell of the leftovers from my lunch with Natalie yesterday. I throw them into a trash can behind me and make my way home.

After I'm about five minutes from the house, my phone starts buzzing like crazy. I get to a red light, and see why.

I have a text from my phone company and five texts from Natalie.

"We apologize for the disruption of your service and any inconvenience we've caused. The problem has been fixed and we'll bypass this month's payment to compensate. Thank you for your patience, and have a great day."

Wow, that's crazy. I guess she didn't block me. There's still hope.

I immediately go to her messages. They read:

"Good morning Winston and same to you. And all that sounds sweet, but I'll really have to think about it."

"I said I'll think about it."

"Stop sending me the same message."

"It's getting annoying, Winston."

"You're about to get blocked."

The car behind me honks their horn as I sit at the green light dumbfounded. This whole time I thought I was blocked, but in actuality, my service was just in shambles. That meant my window was still open. I knew with what I had planned, she had no choice to not only forgive me, but to completely render herself to my love.

I arrive at my complex at around one. I park my car, walk up to my apartment, and go straight to my room where I immediately collapse in my bed. I had never felt so happy to be home. I lay and swaddle in my bed for about fifteen minutes before I get up, take a shower, and officially start my day.

LIII

———

I T'S ONE THIRTY-SEVEN WHEN I GET OUT OF THE shower. *Natalie's probably finishing up her lunch break and on the way back to her office if she isn't already there.* After I dry off and brush my teeth, I sit in my bed and make a couple of phone calls. In order for tonight to work, everything must be perfect. When I get off the phone, I throw on a white t-shirt and grey sweatpants, grab a bottle of water out of the refrigerator, then make my way out of my apartment. As I'm walking down the stairs, I hear arguing. It's Aden and his girlfriend. They have a window open so everyone outside can hear everything.

"Fuck you, I'm leaving!"

"No the hell you're not! I won't let you. Especially not today!"

"Watch me. I'm done putting up with this mess! My mother was right about you."

"Come here!"

"No, I'm leaving."

The door starts to open. But, just as quickly as it had opened, it was slammed shut just as fast.

"I told you, you're not going anywhere!" A loud noise comes from the house.

BOOM.

I don't think much of it at the time and continue to walk to my car because this behavior is normal from them. As I'm opening my car door, I hear another loud noise.

BOOM.

Surrounding neighbors begin to get curious and peek their heads out of their doors. A few step completely outside of their homes to get a better glimpse of what's going on.

"I said you're not leaving! Now come here, I don't want to hurt you. I just want to love you and be happy."

"You're going to kill me, stop! You need help."

Now I start to get concerned, I call the police and report the domestic disturbance.

I guess one of my neighbors already beat me to it because an officer arrives at the scene a few moments after I call.

"You're such a piece of shit! Why are you leaving me?! Am I not enough for you now?"

"We both know this relationship has been over. I know I'm not the only one. I saw the messages in your phone and this isn't the first time I caught you cheating. This toxic shit isn't love."

"That doesn't matter. Those were just sexual impulses, mistakes. You're the one for me, the ONLY one for me! And you always will be." They say as the officer approaches me.

"Hey, I'm officer Lopez. Do you have any idea what's going on?", he asks.

"No sir, I was just getting in my car to leave and heard them arguing."

"Is this a frequent occurrence?"

"Sadly yes, they argue all the time. But never anything physical though."

"Well, what made someone call the police?"

"Sounds like things are crazy in there today. We all heard a couple of loud noises. Sounded like they threw something big."

The yelling gets louder. "Don't do it! Put it down! Please, please. I'll stay. We can love again and be happy."

"Shut up, you're lying! If I can't have you, nobody will."

BANG.

"Agh!"

Officer Lopez rushes up their apartment. He bangs on the door, "Police!", he screams out. Officer Lopez then kicks in the door and enters their apartment. "Put it down. I don't want to hurt you."

"Oh, you think the police are going to bail you out?!"

"He's here to help. Just put the gun down so we can get out of here and love again, please babe."

Scoffs, "No, you're lying again, *babe.* There's honestly no point in living anymore if I no longer have the love of my life...we must try this again our next time on Earth."

"No! Don't do it, put it down!"

BANG.

BANG.

I'm standing there in awe and terror, along with the rest of my neighbors that came outside. We're all stunned and confused. Nobody has come outside of the apartment, or even made a sound since that last shot went off. I'm looking at my neighbors, and my neighbors are looking at me. Another police car pulls up to the scene and there's an ambulance not too far behind it.

The officer expeditiously hops out of his car and looks at us, "Where is it?!"

"Up there, on the right. Door 209.", one of my neighbors points and says.

As the officer begins to run up the stairs, Officer Lopez walks out carrying the man's girlfriend. She's covered in blood. It looks like she'd been shot in the shoulder.

He hands her off to one of the EMTs and says, "There's a man passed out up there. He's been shot in the leg and arm. I wrapped shirts around his leg and arm to try and stop the bleeding."

Officer Lopez walks over to us and I ask, "So what happened? Are they going to be ok?"

"They'll be fine. From what I was able to observe, the woman was cheating and the man broke up with her. As he was trying to leave, the woman got infuriated. She threw a couple of boxes filled with his stuff at him to try to stop him, but I guess it didn't phase him. When she saw that wasn't working, she pulled out a gun and shot him in the arm. That's when I came in. I tried to persuade her to drop the gun, but I saw the look in her eyes and knew there was no stopping her. I was a millisecond too late. I shot her in the arm, but she had already fired off and shot him again in the leg.....I didn't want to kill her. If she wasn't jittery and had terrible aim, the guy might've been dead. I should've shot her sooner, but I wanted to give her help, not a death certificate." Everyone's shocked. "But, that's another day in the badge I guess. People need help, but unfortunately, not everyone is provided the same resources as others to get it. And hey, before you all go, we're going to need statements from you all. And Happy Valentine's Day to everyone by the way. I hope this didn't shoot down anyone's holiday spirits." I crack a smile, but nobody else laughs. He then clears his throat and points at me. "You first."

We walk away from the crowd, and I tell him everything that I saw happen.

"Alright, thank you. You enjoy the rest of your day." He says.

"You too. And thanks, you made cops look like real heroes today. Don't be down on yourself. They're BOTH alive and that's the important part."

He blushes and nods his head as I walk away and get into my car.

I look at my phone and see I have two messages from Natalie. With all the excitement going on, I didn't hear it go off.

"Thank you for the flowers, they're so beautiful. And I loved the poem you wrote too. It was cute. I didn't know you had such a way with words. :)"

"What's the plan for tonight? I've been convinced to give you one more shot."

A big smile overwhelms my face. My plan was off to the perfect start. When I got out of the shower, I called a local florist and made an order to get a dozen roses delivered to Natalie's office with a poem I wrote attached to it. It wrote:

Roses are red and violets are blue

Natalie, the only person I can see myself with is you

I'm sorry for last night, please let me make it up

I promise you won't regret this night, so wassup

Come bless me with your beauty and all your other marvelous assets

We'll make plenty of memories, that we'll never forget

I hope this leaves you smiling, because just thinking about you brings glee to me

Let me know when you read this and hopefully I'll see you tonight between 8 and 8:30

> *With love, passion, and great remorse*
> *Winston Willyoubemine? Williams*

"I want you to come over to my apartment tonight. I want to treat you like the queen you are and show you how truly sorry I am.", I reply.

She immediately texts back, "Address?"

"9660 West Brentwood Drive. Apartment 208."

"Okay, I'll call you when I'm outside."

I text back, "Alright, see you then beautiful."

It's two-twenty two. That gives me about five and a half hours to get everything I need. *After tonight, Natalie won't have a choice but to fall in love. She won't have any other choice but to be mine.*

LIV

———

I DRIVE OUT OF THE PARKING LOT AND GO PICK UP everything I need for tonight. It doesn't take too long. I'm back home by six.

The parking lot is clear of police cars, ambulances, and nosy neighbors when I return to my apartment.

It's six. That gives me about two hours to get ready and set everything up.

I get the bags out of the car and head upstairs to my apartment.

Hmmm, should I shower or set up first? There's no telling how long this will take to set up. I can always just take a shorter shower if I need to.

I place the bags by my couch and begin to get to work. I finish setting everything up around seven thirty. I step back and observe my work. *Perfect.*

I hop in the shower for about ten minutes and then get dressed. A black buttoned down shirt with white polka dots, black slacks, and black loafers was my outfit choice. It's seven fifty-eight when I'm done getting ready. "Right on time.", I say as I look at myself in my bathroom mirror. I walk out of my room and go into the kitchen. I take the big bottle of wine I bought earlier out of the freezer, and place it on my kitchen counter. I then take two wine glasses out of my cabinet and place them on the counter next to the bottle.

KNOCK. KNOCK.

I look at the time and it's eight o'clock on the dot. *She has perfect timing.*

I look through the peephole and see it's not Natalie, but the food I ordered on the phone earlier.

I open the door. "Happy Valentine's Day, Winston Williams?", the delivery man asks.

"Yes sir. I see y'all are very prompt. You got it with extra cheese, right?"

"Yes sir, it's all here. Just the way you asked."

"Alright, thanks. You have a good night."

"You too."

I grab the food and close my door. I walk to the kitchen and place the food in the oven so it doesn't get cold. I then sit on the couch and check my phone. It's eight o'seven and I don't have a call or even a text from Natalie. I don't sweat it. I just sit back on my couch and watch TV.

As I sit, show after show goes on and off, minutes continue to speedily pass by. It's nine-twenty nine now. I check my phone, and I still don't have any type of notification from Natalie.

Should I call her? Or maybe text her? I contemplate. *I don't want to sweat her, but at the same time I'm a bit concerned.*

As soon as I'm about to text her, I get another knock on the door.

I breathe out a sigh of relief as I get up and go answer it. *It's nine thirty, but it's better late than never, Winston.*

Anxious and excited to see Natalie, I rush to look through my peephole. I'm startled by what I see, or rather who I see.

KNOCK, KNOCK, KNOCK.

I hesitate to open the door. I just stare through the peephole and hope they will go away.

KNOCK, KNOCK, KNOCK, KNOCK.

"Winston, open the door! Your car is parked outside, I know you're in there.

KNOCK, KNOCK.

Open up, you can't ignore me forever!"

I crack the door open and stand where I can block her view of the inside, "Wassup Sharon?! It's a little late to be doing pop-up house visits isn't it? Shouldn't you be with your boyfriend or something? I mean, it is Valentine's Day."

I rarely see Sharon out of her work clothes. She had on a red and white strapless dress, red heels, and her hair was straightened out. As much as I didn't want to admit it, Sharon had it going on tonight.

"I mean, you weren't returning my calls or texts, soooo I decided to stop by and make sure you didn't do anything crazy to yourself since you got fired. Depression and suicide is serious. I was concerned so I decided to come check up on you. And the team is still out of town. They're on the way back from their little road trip out west."

"Oh yeah that's right. Well, thank you Sharon, I really appreciate it. It means a lot. And as you can see, I'm alive and well." I smile at her.

"Mmhhmm.", she looks me up and down, "Where you going? And why you blocking the door?"

"W-what you mean? I just got home from a meeting."

"You really gonna lie to me, Winston?" She pushes the door open and barges her way into my apartment. "Wooooow Winston, you been blowing me off all this time for some random piece of pussy?! I see how it is. You had all this time to set this corny shit up, but you can't return a phone call or even text me back? That's crazy. It takes less than ten seconds to send a damn text. And here I was, over here truly concerned for your well-being. You know what, fuck you!" She tries to storm out, but I grab her arm before she can leave.

"Look Sharon, I promise it's not like that. I just have a lot going on right now."

She snatches away from my grasp. "Whatever Winston. I'm tired of showing you nothing but love and only getting shown your ass to kiss in return. I'm over it. Tell the hoe you got coming over to help you with all your problems from here on out. I hope your trifling ass catch something. Happy Valentine's Day." She then walks out of my apartment and slams the door.

"Uuuggh.", I moan as I rub my hand across my head. "She'll be alright. I'll just deal with her tomorrow."

I go grab my phone off of the couch and sit back down. It's nine forty-five and I still haven't heard a word from Natalie. I sink down into my couch as I'm ready to call it a night.

I guess she had better things to do.

A few minutes pass by.

KNOCK, KNOCK.

KNOCK, KNOCK, KNOCK.

At this point, I'm not even excited to answer the door anymore. It could be Chino, Mr. Langston, or even MP for all I know.

KNOCK, KNOCK.

"I'm comin, I'm comin.", I mutter.

I get to the door, look through the peephole, and see it's Natalie.

KNOCK, KNOCK, KNOCK.

"Winston, can you open up? I have to pee."

LV

———

I OPEN THE DOOR AND NATALIE RUSHES IN. "IT'S OVER there on the right.", I say as I point to my guest bathroom.

She runs over and crushes the hundreds of rose petals I've placed throughout the floor as she scurries to the bathroom.

"You okay? I started to get worried about you.", I ask as I walk around lighting the vanilla scented candles I bought for her.

"Yeah, something came up. I was going to call but my phone died, I'm sorry."

"It's all good. I'm just glad that you're ok."

"Yeah, it's a long story. Crazy really."

There's a brief pause. I raise my eyebrow, "Yeah, I bet. Can't wait to hear it. You already knew how to get over here?"

The toilet flushes, she washes her hands, exits the bathroom and says, "It smells soooo good in here. How'd you know I love vanilla?"

"Uuh the fragrance you were wearing at the game and when we went out to lunch had a strong vanilla scent in it. I put two and two together and yeah. Not too hard to figure out."

She blushes then walks over to the couch as she looks around my apartment. "Aaaaawwww, I didn't even notice all these rose petals earlier. I can't believe I stepped on them. And these purple balloons, oh, my, gosh! You even have chocolate hearts everywhere too." She's standing behind my couch with her hands over her mouth in amazement.

She's looking absolutely irresistible and exquisite. She has on a brown leather jacket with matching boots, and a white blouse and dark blue jeans that fully embrace her curves. Her hair is curled, lips fully glossed, and her smile is lighting up the room. I try not to stare, but I can't help but to admire her. The Lord knows how hard it is not to.

"Close your eyes, I wanted to give it to you at the door when you first came in, but you surprised me."

"Ugh, okay. I hate surprises. Don't try nothing stupid. People know I'm here."

I laugh, "Relax, I'm sure you'll like it." I leave to go get her gift out of my room then come back to the living room. "Okay, open your eyes. Here, Happy Valentine's Day Natalie."

"Aww this is so sweet. I feel so bad because I'm empty handed. But Happy Valentine's Day to you too. "

"It's all good. Don't sweat it. I wasn't expecting anything after last night anyway." I say as I hand her a stuffed animal and a bouquet of six red and six purple roses.

"Are, are these flowers fake?"

"Haha, yeah. They're fake flowers."

"I'm not trying to be boujie or anything, but don't you think we're a little too old for fake flowers? I mean, you already sent me real ones earlier, so wassup? Why the switch up?"

I grin, "I really think it should be the opposite honestly." She has a confused expression on her face. "Think about it, hear me out. Flowers die, that bouquet of roses I got you earlier, you were in love with them when you first got them, but they're going to die within the next two weeks, if that. When you're young, it's the exact same thing with relationships. They die just as fast. You meet somebody, things are great, y'all talk for like a week, two weeks, a couple months at most, and then….it dies. Just like those past relationships, real flowers will die and quickly get replaced by some new ones. I wanted to personally give you these FAKE flowers because they will never die. Hopefully, just like this thing between me and you."

"Aww, I'm sorry if I came off as stuck up. I've just never heard that before. I guess I'm basic. I've only been given real ones…"

"It's cool, I understand. I just want you to see that I'm different. You like your stuffed animal?"

"Yeah, I was getting to that next. I love it actually. I've never seen a customized stuffed dolphin like this. It's a purple dolphin wearing my college's track uniform, and it even has my last name on the back. Even has red cleats like the ones I used to wear. How'd you know? You been stalking my social media pics?"

I chuckle, "Nah, I figured your cleats were either red or purple. The dolphin was already purple so yeah." I move closer to Natalie and grab her hand. "I pay attention to you Natalie, that's all."

"Mmmm, that sounds like some stalker shit to me."

We laugh. "Maaan relax, I just like you that's all. If you want something, you're going to do everything in your power to get it, right? I'm done playing, I want YOU Natalie."

"Nah, you just like the thought of getting in between these thick legs of mine, that's all. I see right through your sweet words and little romantic gestures." I suck my teeth and just stare at her with a perturbed face. "So I'm lying? It's all the same game, just different names."

Annoyed, "You serious? That's really how you feel? Like, you deadass think I did all of this only to fuck you?"

She looks me dead in my eyes and says, "Yes, I really do."

I was hurt. I drop my head down, walk over to the door, and open it. "If that's what you really think, then you should leave Natalie. That's crazy." She stands there shocked and confused. "I'm serious, you can go."

"You really about to kick me out Winston? Seriously?"

"Look Natalie, like I said, I like you. That's why I did all of this. Not because I'm trying to hit, but because I want to grow with you. Do you not see everything I did? Just for you. I know it's not a horse and carriage or anything crazy like that, but I got you things that show you that I care and actually pay attention to what's inside of you, not just your physical features. Candles, roses, stuffed animals, balloons, food, I even got your favorite candy over there in the kitchen. I got these things from paying attention to you. To YOU. If I JUST wanted to have sex with you, you really think I'd be able to do all of this? Don't confuse chivalry with horny. I think it's time for you to go."

"Wait Winston, I..."

"Nah Natalie, I see what you really think of me. I'm just another youngin looking for a nut, huh? Why did you even come if you thought that? Would you even have came over if Keisha ain't cosign?"

"How did you..."

"Yes or no Natalie."

"I mean, I was curious about you, honestly. I really enjoyed the night we had at the game. The kiss especially. It felt right, then after our lunch date, I started questioning you. Then on top of that, you ghosted me. And I wasn't going to say anything, but I did see Shannon leaving out of your apartment when I was driving up. I recognized her face. So, explain that. I'm just your night shift chick tonight, huh?"

"First off, some shit happened at my job and she came by to check on me because that's what FRIENDS do. She had been calling and texting me all day, but I was so busy setting stuff up for YOU, that I was ignoring her. She popped up on me. And you were supposed to be here at eight anyway, so how would that have worked if I *planned* that? Really? And her name's Sharon." She looks down at the floor with a dejected look on her face. "Like I told you at lunch, you have to let go of the past if you ever want to attain true happiness in your present and future. You said we're too old for the fake flowers, but if we're being honest, we're really too old to be holding grudges and stopping blessings. So I'm going to say this and let you make the final choice. If you really think I'm like the dudes you've messed with in your past, you can leave. If you're ready to let go, truly be happy, and get treated like a queen, then you can stay. The choice is yours."

LVI

———

W E STAND IN SILENCE FOR A FEW SECONDS.
          "Okay.", Natalie says before she walks towards me.
     I stand there still, leaning up against the door while I hold it wide open. Was she about to leave or stay? A question I had no answer to.

     She gets to me, and gives me a hug. "Thanks for everything Winston, it was really nice and sweet, honestly. Even though it may not seem like it, I deeply and truly appreciate it. By far the best Valentine's Day gifts I've received in a while." She squeezes me tight for a quick second then releases me. She then grabs the door from me and closes it. "Let's try it. I'm tired of being unhappy, and I'm sorry for being difficult. I really don't mean to, but sometimes I just be getting in my own way. I hinder myself from seeing the truth. I'm so stuck on my past that I just, ugh! I'm hurt, my heart's been torn, I'm broken. I..."

     I kiss her mid-sentence then say, "Let me heal you."

     I gaze into her light brown eyes as she stares back into mine. I gently grab her head, and slowly bring it closer for another kiss.

My lips begin to mash against her lips. So soft, glossy, and succulent. The taste of strawberry lip gloss began to fill my mouth. As our tongues wrestle, she presses me against the door and kisses me harder. She caresses my head as she bites my bottom lip. I aggressively grope and squeeze her butt as she wraps her arms around my neck.

"Wait.", she says. "Lets have something to drink first. I love this!"

"Oh, I forgot all about that. I didn't know what to get. I guess the lady that worked there has good taste."

She walks over to my kitchen counter and fills our glasses with the wine I bought. I join her and she hands me my glass.

She drinks the first one pretty quickly then pours another glass.

"You gon' be okay?", I jokingly ask.

"Yeah, we have to celebrate the beginning of something new and special, right?", she answers with a smile.

"Yeah, I guess you're right."

I couldn't believe it. My plan had worked to perfection. My melanin angel was officially mine.

In awe of the moment and still trying to process everything, I zone out for a second as I stare into my wine glass. Natalie begins to move closer to me and says, "Loosen up Winston. Have a little fun. Cheers! To happiness, fun, and love." We toast our drinks. I finish my glass and she finishes her second one. She then walks over to me and kisses me. "I want you.", she whispers in my ear. She then begins to rub around my penis as if it was a genie lamp. "Seems like you want me too.", she says with a grin. Natalie stops kissing me and begins to strut towards the couch. She takes off her jacket and throws it at me. She then sits down and begins to take off her boots.

I walk over to the couch and sit next to her. "You sure you want to do this? A few minutes ago you thought this was all I wanted."

"You're not going to stop talking to me after tonight are you?"

"Hell no.", I quickly say.

"If you're all mine, then this is all yours. Come here and kiss me daddy."

She grabs me by my shirt and brings me between her thick, long legs. I take off my shirt then begin to kiss and lick on her neck before I bite and suck on it.

"Wait.", she says pushing me off of her.

What now?! "I'm sorry, I bit you too hard?"

"No, no, you're fine. I love it to be honest."

"Then what's the problem?"

"I wanna strip for you."

I scoff, "Strip?! Why you trying to tease me? I'm right here and ready for you. My little soldier is ready for war. What you stalling for?"

She moves her index and middle finger down my lips, "Shhhh, relax and enjoy the show. Your little soldier is going to need all the energy in the world to swim across this ocean, boy." She begins to move her body sensually and seductively.

"You don't want any music?"

"I move to the beat of my own drum. Now shut up and sit back."

She puts her hands on my shoulders as she pushes me back and gets on top of me. She begins to kiss and lick all over my shirtless body. She runs her nails over my head and bites me on my neck. I jerk away as she smiles at me then bites her lip. "Too hard for you zaddy?"

I laugh, "Nah, you good. Continue with the show."

She takes her shirt off and throws it behind me. The top half of her body was definitely a sight to see. Her perfect breasts were being held together by a white laced bra, and she had a small dolphin tattoo on the left side of her torso, just below her rib cage. She starts to grind on me. The way she was moving her waist, you'd think she was a professional belly dancer. She then gets up, and begins to unbutton her jeans. She turns around and slowly pulls them down her thick, curvaceous figure as she bends over. She has seven stars tattooed on her back. Starting at her neck and ending at her lower back, right above her matching white panties.

She looks back at me, "You like the view?".

I bite my lip then say, "Yeah, but you're about to like this even better."

When she finishes taking off her jeans, I pick her up and take her to my bedroom. I slam her on the bed and begin to lick and kiss her all over, from her neck to her toes. I go back and stop in the middle, I slide her panties off then grab her breast. A few seconds in, she vigorously and aggressively sinks her white nails into my head. The sound of her moans quickly begin to fill my apartment. The more I lick, the more she twitches and squirms in my bed.

"Oh, Winston!", she loudly moans. "I want it! Put it in!" I get up, wipe my face, and drop my pants. I reach into my drawer to get a condom. As I'm about to put it on, she stops me, "No, I want to feel every inch of what you got."

I stop for a second to think about it, but before I could get a clear train of thought, she crawls over to me, knocks the condom out of my hand, and tackles me. She climbs on top of me, kisses me for a bit, then sticks it in. As much as I wanted to be the responsible, model citizen that I had always been and stop it, I couldn't. It felt too good to stop. I felt as if I was in fact being touched by an angel, my melanin angel.

LVII

———

I WAKE UP SATURDAY MORNING AROUND EIGHT THIRTY to the sound of Natalie's phone ringing on the dresser. I ignore it and go back to sleep. A couple seconds later, it rings again. I look over, and Natalie's still curled up and asleep on the other side of the bed. I get curious. I grab her phone to see who's calling her. The number is saved as "J".

J?! J could be short for Jasmin, Janae, Jennifer, or anything. They probably have breakfast or a brunch planned.

Her phone buzzes again, this time it's a text. I try not to be nosy and look, but I can't help it. I grab her phone.

It's a text from J, "Good morning Nat! I know you're probably tired and exhausted from your girls night so you're still asleep. I just wanted to tell you that I miss you babe. I thought about what you said the other day, and you're absolutely right. I've completely changed, for you. I want to work it out and try it again. I'm willing to do whatever it takes for this to happen. I love you."

I'm lost for words. I didn't know what to say, do, or even think.

I just continued to lay in my bed, numb. I wasn't mad, sad, hurt, or anything, just numb.

She starts to move and roll over. I get nervous and put her phone back. I try to lay down and go back to sleep, but I can't. I get out of bed and begin to pace back and forth in the living room.

I begin to argue with myself and get deep in thought about how I should assess the situation.

Should I just let it slide? I mean, we did JUST make a verbal and physical commitment to one another. From the text, it sounds like he's an ex or something. I can tell she's been hurt and broken in her previous relationships, so I'm sure she doesn't want to go back to any of that. I trust her. If it's important or a problem, I'm sure she'd tell me. Look at her. If she was my ex, I'd probably send her roses and call her every day until I got her back. Yeah, I'm not going to say anything. It's just a text. And my mom always said, "What's done in the dark will always come to the light." Although, she did lie about where she was at last night. But, she also could've been with her friends before she was with me. Who knows, maybe I'm just overthinking all of it. I take a deep breath in and release it. *It'll be okay.* I sigh. *I feel like I've waited forever for this exact moment, waking up and seeing Natalie's beautiful face in my bed after a night of passionate love making. My melanin angel, the girl of my dreams, my girlfriend. The moment I thought would make me the happiest man alive. The moment I thought would give me the feeling of true happiness, the ultimate fulfillment. Yet, I still feel incomplete. What's missing?*

I sit down on my couch and begin to watch TV as I think.

Minutes later, Natalie walks in wearing one of my t-shirts and hugs me as she sits in my lap. "Good morning babe. How you sleep?"

Without hesitating or even thinking, I blurt out, "Who's J?"

She gets up out of my lap and takes a step back. "Um, who?! You been going through my phone while I was sleeping? What the hell, Winston?! You don't trust me now or something? We can't start this if we don't trust each other. You out of all people should know that!"

"Look Natalie, I do trust you." I grab her arm, and pull her back into my lap. "That's why I asked you calmly and not mad or with an attitude. We have to be open with each other, right? I wasn't going through your phone. They called twice earlier and it woke me up. At first I ignored it, but I got curious on the second call. I just glanced to see who it was and that was it. While I was looking, he texted you too. I'm sorry for looking, but if the situation was reversed, I'm sure you would've done the same thing."

She kisses me on my cheek. "You're wrong, I probably would've spazzed."

"Probably?! There's no probably, you would've thrown my phone at me as soon as you read it."

We both laugh and she rolls her eyes. "Whatever, but for clarification, J is just an ex. He cheated multiple times and was just doing grimy shit. He was immature and basically a little boy during our whole relationship. I guess he finally realized what he had and how he messed it up, but it's a little too late for that. Right boo?"

I kiss her, "Right."

"What are you doing today?"

"Um, to be honest I have no clue. You want to go get breakfast? The Spot? I haven't been there in a few days."

"Sure, right now?"

"Yeah, Chino should be there. It's only nine."

"Okay, just let me get ready. You remember where you put my panties?"

"Haha nah, check the sheets or under the bed."

"Okay, c'mon. I'm hungry." She drags me off of the couch and into my room to get ready.

Twenty minutes later, we're heading out the door. She's wearing what she had on last night, and I just put on some black sweat pants and a purple t-shirt.

"Whose car are we taking?", I ask as we walk out the door.

"Um, I thought we were driving ourselves. I have to shower. I feel dirty, especially after everything we did last night." She grins and bites her lip.

I smirk. "Well now I guess you know to bring a night bag."

We start to walk downstairs, "Daaaamn Winston, I can't even get a drawer?! I'm on the night bag level still? Wow."

"I ain't mean it like that. I..."

"I'm just playing, don't be so sensitive." She gives me a hug and kiss on the cheek. "I'll meet you at The Spot, drive safe boo."

"You too."

I continue to walk with her to her car. "What you doing? We're taking separate cars silly."

"I can't open your door? I told you I was going to treat you like a queen." I open her door and she gets in.

She blushes, "You're really my blessing, huh?"

I smile and kiss her, "I guess only time will tell. Drive safe."

We get to The Spot around nine thirty. She got there first, so I parked next to her.

We get out of our cars and she comes around to mine. She grabs my hand. "C'mon babe, I'm starving."

We reach the door, I open it, and she walks in in front of me. She then reaches for my hand again as we walk towards a booth and take our seats.

No more than thirty seconds after we sit down, Chino comes over to us, slaps his hands on our table, and with a giant smile says, "Well, well, well, what do we have here?!" Me and Natalie look at each other and just smile. "So y'all was just gonna walk in here all lovey dovey and expect nobody to say anything?! And you Winston, I'm appalled. I thought we were boys. S.M.H., you think you know somebody. So this is why I haven't been seeing you these past couple of days. With all that late night bumping and grinding, I guess you ain't have the energy or time to come stop by and see your boy. It's cool though. I'm alright. I'll manage.", Chino sarcastically says.

I shake my head and laugh. "Relax Chino, THIS just happened. If you want to be technical, you're the first person that actually knows we're a thing."

"Yeah Unc, it hasn't even been twenty-four hours yet. Barely twelve.", Natalie adds to make him feel better.

"Yeah, yeah. Well anyway, what y'all two young lovebirds ordering on this lovely morning? Two Rico specials?", Chino asks.

"Yessir, and two lemonades please." Chino nods his head and goes to the kitchen to put our order in. I then look at Natalie and grab her hands. I look into her eyes and say, "You're absolutely gorgeous, you know that?"

She blushes, "Stop it, I'm just average. I appreciate the compliment though."

I suck my teeth, "Now you know you're far from average. You really look like something out of a magazine. Better, honestly. Those models have nothing on you. I mean, look at you. Even now, you're basically fresh out of bed and you're still the centerpiece of the room."

She blushes again as Chino comes back with our lemonades. "Hmm, what has you cheesing so hard mam? You laughing at Winston's corny no game having ass? It's just pitiful. I know she be telling all her friends about you. You probably just a big joke to all her friends. Tsk, tsk, tsk, a damn shame.", Chino jokes.

"Chino, you're just a hater. Natalie, tell this man I got game."

Natalie laughs and starts to choke. "See, she can't help but to laugh at that.", Chino teases.

Natalie takes a sip of her lemonade and clears her throat, "Hold up, hold up. Let me speak." She coughs. "Now, truth be told, Winston can be a little corny sometimes."

"I told ya.", Chino blurts.

"BUT, he can be a smooth criminal too. I can't lie about that. I wouldn't be with him if it wasn't for his sweet, smooth talking, romantic side.", Natalie adds.

I smile and wink at Chino, "Like I said, I. Got. Game."

Chino puts his hand on Natalie's shoulder, "Mam, if he's holding a gun to you and forcing you to say these things, just blink two times and I'll handle it."

We all laugh. "Chino, what you gon' do? Flip me with your spatula?", I sarcastically say.

"It's cool, just know I have security right under that counter."

"Since when?!"

He puts his index finger over his lips, "Don't worry about that son, just know I'm prepared for any and everything. Now, let me go check on y'all's food." Chino leaves the table and walks back to the kitchen.

"That man is a trip. He always has me laughing whenever I come in here.", Natalie says.

"Yeah, Chino's quite the character."

There's a brief silence. She then smiles and says, "You know, I'm glad he introduced us. Even though I was difficult at first, I'm happy it all worked out." Natalie's phone starts to ring. "I have to answer this, let me just step outside real quick."

"Okay, do your thing."

As she leaves, Chino comes back with our food. "Where she go?"

"She stepped out for a phone call."

"Her real boyfriend called, huh?"

"Man, chill out. It's probably work or one of her friends."

"Mhhmm."

With an attitude, "You going to drop our food or what? I know it's hot."

"Sheesh, I'm just playing. You always get so sensitive when we talking about Natalie. You know I'm proud of you. Walking in with her and what not. Aye..." He puts our plates on our table and slides into the booth opposite of me. He leans in and asks, "How did the championship go?.....You hit that?" I immediately start blushing and smiling from ear to ear. "Ooooouuuu, how was it? Don't tell me you was a one pump chump, minuteman, speedy Gonzalez..."

I chuckle, "I wasn't, I took care of business. And to answer your question, it was amazing. Probably the best I ever had to be real. And Natalie naked, my Lord. God definitely knew what he was doing when He put her together. A masterpiece." Chino's jaw drops. "Wipe that drool you got coming out your mouth. This is why I can't tell you nothing."

Chino wipes his face. "Whew, I can only imagine. I'm proud of you Winston. Since I'm a happily married man, I'm glad I'm able to live through you." I laugh at him. "Seriously though, I'm proud, man. I can just look at you and see you're not that shy guy I met a while back. You said you were going to do something, and you did it. Hell, proved me *and* the guys all the way wrong."

"The guys?!"

Natalie walks back in, "Chino, can I get a to go container, please? I have to leave."

"Yes ma'am.", Chino says.

"Is everything okay?", I ask.

"Yeah, girl problems. Can you please put my food up when Chino comes back, I have to use the lady's room." She puts her phone on the table, next to her keys, then goes to the bathroom.

"Yeah, I got you."

Chino comes back with the container. "She okay?"

"Yeah, just using the bathroom. She said she has to go handle some girl problems."

Her phone buzzes on the table. Me and Chino both look at it since it's facing up. It's a text from J, "I'll be there in about ten minutes. See you there."

Chino looks at me and asks, "J one of her girlfriends?"

I sigh, "No, not at all. It's an ex of hers."

"Mmm, *girl problems*, huh.", Chino sarcastically says.

Natalie walks out of the bathroom and begins to head back to our booth.

"What do I do Chino? She's coming."

"Just act normal. I'll talk to you when she leaves."

I begin to put her food in the to go container.

She comes back to the table and gives me a kiss. "Thanks babe. I'll text you when I get there." She grabs her food, phone, and keys. "And thanks Unc."

I grab her hand before she walks off. "One more kiss."

"Okay, but I have to go."

We kiss. "And where'd you say you had to go again?"

"I have to go help a friend out."

"Okay, drive safely, beautiful."

"You know I will. Bye Chino."

She waves goodbye and walks out of the restaurant. When she gets to her car, she checks her phone and looks startled, like a deer when they see headlights. She looks at me through the window, then continues to get in her car and drive off.

LVIII

———

I LET OUT A LONG SIGH AND DROP MY HEAD. I WASN'T upset, just disappointed.

"Do you trust her?", Chino asks.

I lift my head up, "I mean, I did."

"Why past tense? What did she do that made you change your mind?"

"One, she just lied about where she was going. Before we came, we made it clear that we'd be honest and open with each other. Not even two hours passed by before she went against it. She's already showing me she can't be trusted. How are we supposed to be in a relationship with no trust Chino?"

"I understand what you're saying and where you're coming from, but I say give her the benefit of the doubt. Just this one time."

"What?! You can't be serious right now."

"Hear me out. From talking to her and getting to know her these past weeks, she doesn't take me for the lie just to lie type. The way she looks at you and acts towards you is genuine. You can't fake that. I'm not saying that lying is justifiable, because it's wrong period, but maybe it's a reason she didn't tell you exactly where she was going. Don't rush to conclusions without talking to her first, whatever is done in the dark will always come to light. Trust me Winston, don't think too hard into this one."

"Yeah, yeah, yeah. I guess I'll just talk to her about it later."

"Now that that's settled, I have PAYING customers to tend to."

"Hey! I pay."

Sarcastically, "Once every couple of weeks don't count."

"It's the Winston Williams discount.", I jokingly say. "That's what I get for recommending you to so many of my clients. It's only right."

"True, those stiffs love coming here for brunch and whatnot. Oh, that reminds me, tell your boxheaded boss to stop calling me. Tell him I'm not interested any more."

"You don't want to open the new location anymore? What happened?"

"No offense, but your boss is a corny prick. And he's trying to get over on me. He just assumes I don't know anything about this business stuff. Why you can't handle it?"

"Haha, sounds about right. And I can, it just won't be for Mr. Jacobs."

"What you mean?" I pause for a second. "Well, spit it out!"

"I got fired."

"Man, how the hell YOU got fired? Ain't you like the star over there? Boy wonder? Why they let you go? You and the secretary got caught making whoopie on the desk?"

"No Chino, me and Sharon are just friends. We got drug tested the other day and my pee came back dirty."

"Dirty?! You?! You mean to tell me you've been lying to me all this time about not smoking? I've been bamboozled!"

"I don't smoke though."

"Then explain yourself."

"They found molly in my…"

"Molly?! I'm telling your momma. What the hell you was doing taking molly?! You was feeling impetent and needed help getting your soldiers to march? My blue thangs came in the mail yesterday if you need them."

"Maaaan, no. I'm good in that area, trust me. I was set up."

"Set up?! Sit your paranoid ass down somewhere. Who would want to set you up?"

"I can't really say. It's a long story."

Make up your mind. You can't say or it's a long story? You know what, forget it. Those drugs have you tripping already."

"How am I tripping if I'm sitting down Chino?", I jokingly say.

"And on that note, if you'll excuse me, I have a restaurant to run. You going crazy." Chino walks off.

"Didn't like my joke?", Chino ignores me.

I sit there and finish my food. Well, I try to, but the thought of Natalie lying to me has my stomach in shambles.

What if she's at his house? What if they're planning on getting back together? What if they're having sex right now? Oh, the agony.

I grab my phone and send a text. Then, I force myself to finish my breakfast.

As I get up from my seat and get ready to walk out, Chino stops me. "Hey." He says getting my attention. "Remember, benefit of the doubt."

"I got you."

"And watch your back. *They* might be watching. You don't want to get *set up* again.", he jokes.

I shake my head then walk out.

When I get in my car, I get a text from Sharon, "So now you want to hang out? That chick you had over must not have been it for you huh"

I smirk then text back, "It's not like that. You were right about everything you said last night. And I admit I was dead wrong. You show nothing but love and I do the opposite. I'm sorry for being a terrible friend. I'm free today so I wanted to spend the day with you."

"I'm glad you can acknowledge that. And you're free every day. You got fired, remember lol"

"Seriously, I want to see you."

"Yeah, yeah." I start typing to reply then she texts, "What time should I come?"

"I'll be on my way back home from The Spot soon. So probably in like an hour"

"Okay, I'll be over there"

I drive out of the parking lot and head home with my thoughts in a frenzy.

Why did I just invite Sharon over? Because regardless of what Chino said, I still felt betrayed, played, lied to, and hurt. Sharon has a way of making me feel better during my darkest moments. If there's anyone I can talk to about this Natalie situation and make me feel better, it's Sharon. She's easy to talk to and understands me. That's why she's my best friend. She deeply and genuinely cares for my well-being. Even though she's dating James, I know she still has feelings for me. And even though I don't show it, the feeling is mutual. Maybe Natalie was just an encounter to show me how much I really cared about Sharon.

As I'm pulling into my complex, I see Natalie's car parked next to my parking spot. *What's she doing back here?*

I get out of my car and she rushes to me to hug me. "I know you probably don't trust me now, but I swear I was going to tell you later after it happened. I knew if I told you where I was actually going, you'd get mad. I promise I just went to meet him so I could break things off between us. For good. It was the only way he was going to get the message. I want you, and only you, Winston."

LIX

———

I WAS LOST FOR WORDS. AS NATALIE WAS STANDING there with her arms wrapped tight around me, I just stood there puzzled, dumbfounded. For some reason, I felt guilty. Whether it was because I doubted her and automatically assumed the worst of her, or because I had already invited Sharon over with venereal intentions of revenge, a great feeling of guilt began to surge through my veins.

"When I left him, I went by my place to grab some clothes. Then I rushed over here to catch you before you went inside your apartment. Are you mad at me?"

I swallow the air in my mouth then clear my throat, "Um, no. Do I have a reason to be?"

"No, well yes, but not really. I just figured you were upset because I lied about where I was actually going. I know you read that message when I was in the bathroom. He called me during our breakfast and I knew then that I had to put a stop to it. I told him I'd meet him at a coffee place by my house to talk. I had to address it because there's no avoiding him. He knows where I work, live, everything. He sends the occasional love note, bouquet of flowers, my favorite foods here and there, and I'm tired of it, Winston. I knew I couldn't move on with you if he was still clinging to what we had."

A question hit's me and I raise my eyebrow, "Wait, didn't you just move down here? Like a month ago?"

"Yeah, two months actually. He moved down from North Carolina with me. We were deep into our relationship and living together. About a week after we moved, we started having troubles. I was starting to suspect that he had met someone else. He was on some shady stuff before we moved too, but I thought it would all go away when we came here. Boy was I wrong. Well anyway, I confronted him about it, and of course, he denied it and told me I was trippin. A few weeks later, Keisha and Celeste moved down here too for a fresh start. When I told them what was going on, we turned into Ricoville's finest. After a few days of *detective work*, we found him cheating on me with some short haired bimbo. We couldn't see her face, but we did see her leaving our house one morning. I told him I was going out of town for a girls trip, then we sat outside my house to see if he was doing anything. I was distraught. I couldn't help but to cry because of how heartbroken I was. I had packed up everything to come down here and be with him. And Keisha, she was ready to throw a brick at that girl's car. But after we all calmed down, we just gathered my things and moved them out into an apartment about twenty minutes from here. So I guess now you understand why I was how I was."

I hug her tight, "You'll never be anything other than number one with me Natalie, I promise you that." She grabs my head then pulls me towards her to kiss me. "Let's go upstairs. I'll grab your bag." I grab her travel bag out of her car and we head upstairs. "I see you took my advice about the night bag."

We laugh as we walk up to my apartment. "Yup, until you consider me worthy enough of a drawer. Whenever that will be."

"Baby steps, baby steps.", I say as we walk in.

"I guess, can I get a towel and a washcloth please so I can shower? Ugh, I feel so dirty."

"Yeah I got you, one second." I get her a towel and washcloth out of my side closet as she goes into my bathroom and starts her shower.

"Your bathroom is surprisingly clean. You sure you stay by yourself?", she questionably says.

"Single as a pringle."

"See, that's that corny stuff Chino was referring to earlier."

"Shut up, you know you love my corniness, well, smoothness. And my mom was a clean freak when I was growing up. Some habits you just can't break I guess."

"You're right, it's definitely one of my favorite qualities of yours. And aww, that's cute. I figured your guest bathroom was clean because you barely use it, but I guess that's just how you are."

"Yeah, that's me. Winston the clean man." I knock on the door to hand her a towel and washcloth.

"Come in, I'm already in the shower!" I walk in and put her towel on the toilet then try to hand her her washcloth. She pulls back the shower curtain. Even though I saw her naked heavenly body last night, seeing it now, wet and glistening is a whole nother story. I stood there in awe and just admired her curvaceous, elegant figure. After a few seconds of staring, she splashes me. "You just gon' stare, or you gon' get in?"

I didn't waste any time in stripping off my clothes and hopping in the shower to join her.

After about twenty five minutes pass, we get out of the shower and begin to get dressed.

"Mmm, that was one of the best showers I've ever had. Wooh."

I smile and look back at her getting out of the shower as I'm drying off, "Wish I could say the same. Somebody wanted to hog all the water and leave me in the back freezing."

She laughs, "Don't act like you ain't enjoy the view."

I smirk, "I'm sure my actions speak for themself." She bites her lip and smiles. "What do those stars mean anyway? And you better not give me a cliche' basic meaning like, 'It's a reminder that I should always shoot for the stars." I walk out the bathroom and sit on my bed as I search through my drawers trying to decide what I'm going to wear.

"Haha, yes and no. That's the meaning I tell random people that ask, but it's deeper than that. Seven not only represents perfection, but intuition, inner wisdom and deep inward knowing. I'm a real deep thinker and a bit of a perfectionist. And for the stars, yes it's a reminder to keep my goals as high as they are, but stars also symbolize clearness, truth, and the light showing you the path God has set for you."

"Oh, that's definitely not a basic or cliche' meaning. All of that is pretty deep and dope honestly.

She smiles, "Thank you, and the dolphin is kind of self-explanatory. I love dolphins."

"Why though?"

"They're always so happy. They live so free and they're always filled with joy. That's how I try to live."

"I feel you on that. So you're spiritual? We kind of got into this thing pretty fast. There's still a lot we have to learn about each other."

"Yeah, I totally agree. And to answer your question, I do believe in a higher being. Like I know there's a God and I pray to him, but I don't go to church. I went all the time when I was younger, but as I grew up, I discovered it was more of a business than a place of worship. I haven't been in years."

"Hmm."

She walks out the bathroom wearing pink shorts and a white tank top. "What you hmming about Mr. Winston?"

"You want to go to church with me tomorrow? I promise they're not all about money. It's not one of those mega churches. It's a small, big family type of deal. It's St. John's First Missionary Baptist Church. And the choir is great. You'll love it. It's like twenty minutes from here, across the street from that new grocery store and Lil P's BBQ."

"Uughh." I grab her arm and sit her on my lap. "Um, can you at least put some clothes on before we just sit here and talk about church please?"

I laugh. She gets up and hands me a pair of purple shorts out of my drawer. "Thanks, but seriously. Come with me, I'm sure you'd like it. Then we can go out to dinner after that."

She sighs, "Uuugghh, I guess. Only because you're like three and zero when I let you make decisions."

I smile. "Bet, service is at eleven so we'll have plenty of time to stop by your place and get you a dress or something to put on."

"Yeah, yeah." She looks in the mirror. "Ugh, my hair. It looks a mess."

"Shush, you look beautiful."

She rolls her eyes, "You're going to tell me that regardless."

"Because it's the truth."

"Yeah, I need to fix this." She gets her bag, goes into the bathroom, and begins to play with her hair.

KNOCK, KNOCK, KNOCK.

"You expecting company babe?"

"Um no? I don't think so. It's probably someone at the wrong house. They should go away."

"Okay."

KNOCK, KNOCK......KNOCK, KNOCK.

"Just go check it, I don't think they're going anywhere."

"Ugh, okay."

I get up to go answer the door. When I walk in the living room, I hear my phone buzzing. I pick it up and see it's Sharon calling me. I have three other missed calls and five text messages from her:

"Hey I'll be leaving in like five"

"I'm otw"

"Ten minutes away"

"Pulling up"

"Open your door."

KNOCK, KNOCK, KNOCK.

"Babe, get the door! It's getting annoying.", Natalie yells from the bathroom.

I'm stuck. *If I open it, Natalie's going to flip. She's going to automatically assume the worst. And if I don't open it, the situation could only get worse. Sharon's not leaving.*

KNOCK, KNOCK.

What do I do?

LX

———

I OPEN THE DOOR AND SHARON'S STANDING THERE with her hands on her hips. Even though she's only wearing a brown tank top and jean shorts, I must admit that she does look beautiful, especially in the light. With her hair put up into a puffy ponytail, I can clearly see her flawless face. "About damn time you open the door. You was in the shower or something?"

"Yeah, I just got out."

"I can tell, you still have water on your back and shit." She wipes it off.

Nervously, "Y-yeah, you know me."

"Winston, why you acting weird? Well, weirder than usual. Let me in, you got me standing out here in this heat. You know chocolate melts." She opens the door, moves me aside and walks in. "You still ain't clean up from your night with the floozy I see."

I close the door. "Um, about that. I..."

From the bathroom Natalie yells, "Babe, who was that at the door?! Did they have the right apartment?" She then turns on her hair dryer.

Sharon's face lights up in awe, "That bitch is still here?! I thought you said you were free? You made it seem like you were home by yourself. Why would you invite me over here? You want my blessing or something?"

I put my hands on her shoulders. "Sharon, relax. Lower your voice and let me explain."

She snatches away from me, "No Winston, there's nothing to explain. You messed around and double booked yourself, huh? I don't wanna hear it. As a matter of fact, I don't want to hear from you ever again. Friends, best friends, whatever, you know this ain't right. I'm tired of you treating me like shit. Like I'm just a nobody."

She walks towards the door and I grab her arm to stop her. "Sharon stop, don't be like that. You know you're not a nobody."

She starts to tear up. She clears her throat and says, "I don't even know why I'm so emotional right now. I'm trippin. I have a boyfriend to get home to. They got back from their trip late last night and he's probably up now waiting around for me."

She tries to tug away, but I'm still keeping hold of her arm. "Sharon, wait."

"Let go of me Winston. And since we don't work together anymore, this is it. There's no longer a need to communicate. I wish you and whoever that is in there the absolute best. Goodbye Winston." I slowly and hesitantly release her arm and she walks out of my door and slams it behind her.

I sigh, put my hand on the door, then turn around to walk back in my room to Natalie. *I hope she didn't hear any of that.*

I suddenly realize that Natalie's hair dryer isn't blowing anymore. When I turn, I stop and freeze. Natalie's standing at the doorway looking at me with a despondent face and watery eyes.

"Babe...", She slams and closes my door. "Babe..."

"Don't call me that shit no more, Winston! I'm over here ending things and cutting people off so we can be together, and you just pulled this shit?! You say this and that about being truthful, honest, open, and all this other foolishness then this happens. Wow, let me guess, you thought I was cheating so you made your own *play* as soon as I left? And when I popped up here, you were so surprised and thrown off that you forgot to cancel. Hmph, last night you had me fooled I see. Mmhhmm, y'all best friends alright. Y'all men are just UUGGHHHH!! Damn hypocrites."

As much as I wanted to say the *right thing*, something that would magically make everything better, something that would make her stop being upset, something that would simply and quickly defuse the whole situation, I couldn't say anything. My mouth was dry, it hurt for me to swallow, and my tongue was numb. She was right, absolutely, one hundred percent right about the whole situation. There was no lie I could fabricate to get me out of this. So, after a few moments of silence, I decided to tell the truth.

"Look Natalie, you don't have to say anything, I just want you to listen, please. The first time I saw you at The Spot, I knew it was love at first sight. I remember it like it was yesterday. You were wearing a red dress that magnified every inch of your perfect body. Oh and your smile, easily your best curve, was so bright and radiant. It looked as if you had stars for teeth. And your eyes…"

"You going to keep going on and on about how pretty you think I am, or are you going to say some real shit? Because now, I'm ready to run up out of here and delete your number. You got thirty seconds to change my mind."

I clear my throat, "I said all of that to say this. I knew I wanted to live out the rest of my life with you after the first time I saw you. Yeah I messed up, but I was hurt. If the situation was reversed how would you have reacted? Be honest. And it's not like I planned on having sex with her, I just needed someone to comfort me. She's my FRIEND. Why she reacted the way she did, who knows. And how I reacted to her? Well, she's truly a friend of mine. I couldn't just let her walk out of my life without a fight. You're my woman, she's my friend. Natalie please don't end this over a misunderstanding. I know we literally just started dating, but I love you, Natalie." I wait about thirty seconds for her response. "Natalie, talk to me, please." I still don't get a reply. I slide down the door and feel her body on the opposite side. "Natalie, let's work through this. I know you feel the same way."

A few minutes pass and Natalie finally speaks, "You know Winston, I've heard the same shit time and time again. And to be honest, I'm tired of repeating the same cycle and giving people chances that sure as hell don't deserve them."

"So what are you saying Natalie?"

She gets up and opens the door with her bag in her hand. "I'm leaving, Winston." She kisses me on the cheek and walks towards the door. I grab her arm and stop her. She looks at me then fiercely says, "Don't you even try that shit with me. Let me go before I press charges." I release her arm and she walks out of my door.

LXI

———

I STAND THERE IN THE MIDDLE OF MY LIVING ROOM with my head hung low. I'm sad, hurt, lonely, and full of false hopes that she'll return to me. *Sharon, she's just a friend. Friends come and go. But Natalie, she's the love of my life. Since the moment I first saw her, not a second went by that she didn't cross my mind. I don't know what I'd do if I lost her for good. She'll come back, she has to come back. Maybe she forgot something, her phone, hair gel, SOMETHING. She has to come back. She just has to.*

I text her, she doesn't reply. I try calling her phone, but she sends me straight to voicemail every time. *Is this it? Is it really over between us? It can't be.* My knees begin to get weak, chest starts to hurt. I walk around and sit on the couch with my head hanging low. As tears start to form in my eyes, I begin to pray. *Lord please, don't allow me to lose the love of my life. I promise if she comes back I'll do right by her. Whatever circumstances and situations that may appear in our journey of life, I'll stand by her and only her. Lord please...*I drop to my knees and begin to shed tears. *I'm sorry for doubting her and doubting You. I'm begging, pleading, please don't let me lose her.*

KNOCK, KNOCK.

I wipe my tears and instantly rush to the door to answer it.

KNOCK, KNOCK, KNOCK.

I gather myself then open the door.

"Hey."

Perplexed, I say, "What's up Sharon? You okay? I didn't expect to be seeing you again. Especially after what you said before you left."

"I know, I know, I was an ass and doing waaay too much. Can I come in? I want to apologize for how I acted earlier." She comes in and I close the door behind her. "Where's your girl? I wanted to apologize to the both of you."

I grin and rub my hand across my head, "She uh, she left about fifteen minutes after you."

"Oh my gosh! I'm so sorry Winston. I didn't mean to mess up anything between the two of you. Ugh, I'm so sorry. I guess that explains why you've been crying."

I suck my teeth and look away, "Man, ain't nobody been crying."

"Mmhmm, I guess your eyes are just red and puffy for no reason. You need a tissue to blow your nose?"

I sniff, "I have a cold, relax."

"You weren't sick earlier, but anyway, I'm sorry for throwing a fit. It wasn't right or fair. You supported my relationship with James, and it's only right I return the favor...no matter who the floozy may be."

"First off, Natalie isn't a floozy. And secondly, it's cool. You were just jealous and mad because someone else was getting the good old Winston weiner, I understand. If I was in your shoes, I would've probably reacted the exact same way."

She laughs, "Boy bye, don't nobody want that lil gummy worm."

Under my breath I say, "You wasn't acting like it was a lil gummy worm when we were sexing."

"Huh?! You say something?"

I chuckle, "Nah, nah. I ain't say anything."

"Thought so." She walks over to the couch and sits.

"What happened to having a boyfriend at home to tend to?"

"He had treatment for his knee to go to. I took that as a sign that I needed to come back and apologize. While I was driving, I realized how immature and juvenile I must've sounded. We're friends. No way a friend should've acted like that. You're free to screw whoever and vice versa. Although, a warning would've been nice, but it's cool. I'm a big girl. You probably just wanted to formally introduce us and I blew it way out of proportion. And for the last time today, I promise, I'm sorry." She gets up, walks towards me still standing by the door, and gives me a hug.

I wrap my arms around her and hug her back.

Should I tell her the truth and admit I really did just want to be with her? Or should I just continue to let her think that I wanted to introduce the two of them?

I look down at her face on my stomach and say, "It's cool, what's done is done. And you're just not my friend, you're my best friend." She squeezes me tighter then lets me go. "You hungry? When's James supposed to finish his treatment?"

"He should be done by one."

"Well, it's eleven forty-two now. You want some grilled chicken, steamed broccoli, and scalloped potatoes?"

"Wow, you're really trying to feed me your leftovers from a date with another woman? That's really low, Winston."

"Technically, they aren't leftovers. They haven't even been touched. I put them in the oven last night when they got delivered and forgot all about it."

"Uumm, I'm good. I'll just pick up something later."

"Suit yourself, more for me."

Sarcastically she says, "Yeah, I know all that crying built up quite the appetite. You need to build your energy back up."

I smirk as I walk into the kitchen and warm my food up in the microwave. "So what's it like dating a superstar? I know it has to be lit."

"To be honest Winston, it's not all glitz and glamour like you'd think."

"What you mean?"

"Sometimes, I just feel like I'm just a show girl. It was all sweet when we first started talking, but now, it's like he overcompensates for not spending time with me by buying me stuff. Like we barely know anything about each other, and on top of that, I think he's cheating on me."

"What makes you say that?"

"He thinks I don't notice, but he gets texts and calls all through the night from an unsaved number. I never get a long enough glimpse to memorize it, but when I do, it's on."

"Well, how do you know it's not his agent or anything business related?"

"Winston, really? I'm not stupid."

"I guess. Well, do what's going to make YOU happy. If you think he's playing you then leave. You know your worth."

"You're right. It's just complicated because I really like him."

"If the energy isn't being reciprocated, leave."

She scoffs at me then sarcastically says, "You're one to talk aren't you." We both smile.

"I meeeeeaaaan, you did leave me, didn't you?", I jokingly reply. "You want to have a movie day? I'm sure James can wait. I could really use my best friend right now."

"Aaaww…" Her phone dings. "Speaking of the devil. He said he's finished his treatment early and wants to meet me for lunch at twelve thirty." She looks at the time. "I should get going." She walks into the kitchen.

"Oh, well I guess maybe another time then. You know I'm free."

"Yeah, I know. You aren't going to look for another job?"

"Um, I'm good on money right now. I invested my first few big checks into some prosperous properties so I'm good. I really might open my own thing since I do have majority of the top clients."

"Yeah that's true, people have been dropping left and right since they found out you no longer work there." Her phone dings again. "I really must get going." She gives me a hug then walks towards the door. "I'm glad we could settle things out, friend."

I go open the door to let her out. "Best friend."

She smiles and walks away.

I then take my food out of the microwave and sit on the couch.

For the remainder of the day, it was just me, my couch, and the TV. Even though Sharon stopped by, she wasn't Natalie. When Natalie left out the door, I felt as if she had taken a piece of my existence with her.

It's now ten o'clock and I'm still in denial. I'm strung out. Every few minutes, I look at the door with hopes of seeing Natalie walk through. I constantly check my phone hoping she replies to my messages or returns my calls. False hopes and fake dreams constantly filled my head. I couldn't stop them. When I said that I loved Natalie, I absolutely meant it. To lose her meant to lose my heart, my soul.

LXII

———

I GET IN MY BED TO TRY AND GO TO SLEEP, BUT I CAN'T. I constantly toss and turn throughout the night. Images of Natalie just won't leave my brain. Thoughts of her smile, her voice, her touch. Memories of the first time I saw her, our night at the basketball game, and last night. All the hopes and dreams I had for our future had been destroyed. My heart was broken.

Despondent and uneasy, I watch a couple episodes of my favorite show on the couch as an attempt to calm my mind, but it doesn't work. Now, it's five past one, and nothing's changed. My stomach grumbles. I walk to my kitchen to find something to eat. I remember I still have food in the oven, Natalie's untouched portion of dinner.

As I take it out of the oven and put it in the microwave, I see the bottle of wine on the counter.

This should help ease my mind. I'm glad I got the big one.

I grab the bottle and pour myself a glass. One turns into two, then two expeditiously turns into the rest of the bottle. Fifteen minutes later, I'm sitting on the couch staring at the TV talking to myself.

"I don't need her! I was doing just fine before I met her. We're good over here. There's a plethora of women to choose from. She's easily replaceable."

"She needs me! I don't need her. It's her loss."

"She'll come back. They always come back."

"Natalie, why'd you have to leave?! My melanin angel...Come back!"

While I'm scrolling through pictures of her on her social media, "Natalie!! I miss you baby, I love you. I don't think I'll ever be able to get over you. You were perfect. We were perfect!"

I repeated this cycle of mixed emotions until I passed out around four thirty.

I wake up the next day with a full bladder. I quickly stand on my feet to rush to the bathroom. *Ugh!* I stumble across the dying rose petals for a few seconds before gravity vigorously sits me back down.

I gather myself, then try again, slowly.

When I finish washing my hands, I take a deep look at myself in the mirror. My hair is messy, face looks rough and crusty, eyes are red and puffy, and then the taste of the wine is still strong in my mouth.

Winston, you look a mess. That woman wasn't your life, she was only a part of it. Get your shit together before THIS becomes a habit. You're better than this. I splash water in my face then look at myself again. *Although, on the other hand, drinking did help ease the pain and help me sleep. I'm sure just one more bottle won't hurt or make me an alcoholic.*

I stare at myself for a while, then a thought overwhelms me. It was pushing me to go to church. *Hmm, maybe that's God trying to tell me something. I guess I'll go. I mean, I can always go to the liquor store after.*

I take a quick shower and brush my teeth. After, I throw on a white collared shirt and khakis, then make my way to my door. When I get to the door to leave, I realize I don't have my phone in my pocket. I look around for it, but I can't find it anywhere. I check the time on my TV and see that it's already eleven twenty. I quit looking for it and decide to leave without it. I speed off to church and get there around eleven forty-five. I don't want to be seen coming in late, so I sneak up stairs and sit up on the balcony because it's mostly empty.

I get there just as they're finishing the offering. I look down into the congregation as everyone is returning to their seats. My face lights up with glee the moment I spot a familiar face. It's Natalie. She's sitting in the back right corner wearing a yellow sundress and white sandals with her hair in a ponytail.

This must be why He wanted me here. The second chance I prayed for had come into fruition. My angel is coming back home.

From the time I spotted Natalie until the moment service ended, I was thinking about what I was going to say. I wanted everything that was going to come out of my mouth to be perfect. I wasn't messing this up.

As soon as the benediction ended and service was officially over, I darted down to meet Natalie before she left. I refused to let this opportunity slip.

I rush outside to search for her in the sea of people standing around socializing after church. I mistakenly turn around about three different women wearing yellow sundresses before I finally see Natalie inside talking to the pastor.

I escape the hot and sunny day, and go sit down in the back while I wait for her to finish. She notices me and starts to smile, I smile back.

She wraps up her conversation and begins to walk towards me. I begin to get nervous. My forehead begins to sweat, hands start to become clammy, and my mouth is dry.

She's getting closer and closer. *I should've gone to the water fountain or maybe the bathroom to get myself together instead of just sit here.*

She walks up to me, "Hey Winston, I was hoping I'd see you here. You were right about this church. It's amazing."

"H-hey Natalie." I clear my throat. "Glad you liked it. I see you found the church."

"Yeah, after you said it was across the street from that grocery store and the BBQ restaurant, I knew what you were talking about. I don't stay too far from here."

"Well that's good. You know…..we can still go out to dinner. My treat."

"Um Winston, actually, I'm going to pass on that. After that sermon today, I'm really glad I saw you. I need to lift this burden off of my spirit." I stand there with a puzzled look because Lord knows I wasn't paying attention to anything but her the whole time. She shakes her head. "You probably weren't even paying attention. Good thing I wrote it down. Luke 6:37: 'Judge not, and ye shall not be judged. Do not condemn, and you will not be condemned. Forgive, and you will be forgiven.' After I heard Pastor Lee's sermon on that, I knew it was meant for me to see you and talk to you."

"What you mean?"

"Well, long story short, I'm not going to judge the actions you committed yesterday. That's not my place. You have the right to do what you want. Although this one is hard, I won't condemn you for breaking my heart. And lastly, you're forgiven. I forgive you Winston, for everything. I'm not mad anymore. I prayed and released my pain unto the Lord."

Internally, I was ecstatic. Smiling from ear to ear, "I'm sorry for everything Natalie. I truly and genuinely care about you girl. I can't wait to pick this back up. I…"

"Wait Winston, I know I said I forgive you and what not, but there's no this. This, this is closure. We're done. I just wanted to let you know that there aren't any hard feelings between us. Well at least not on my end. I've said what I needed to say and I can be at peace now."

"Natalie...I love you."

She rests her right hand on my face, "No Winston, you love the thought of me."

I grab around her waist and pull her closer to me. "But…"

She steps back out of my reach. "Winston, you're a great person. Smart, handsome, a real gentleman, but, you're not for me. I've realized that now. We can still be friends. My spirit would be pleased with that."

I look her in her eyes, "I can't just be your friend Natalie. You mean too much to me."

Natalie gives me a hug, kisses me on the cheek, then says, "Okay, I guess I'll see you around." She gently pats my chest then walks out into the sunlight. I stand there alone in the back of the church distraught, dismayed, and dejected.

LXIII

I WATCH HER WALK AWAY FOR POSSIBLY THE LAST time. Deep inside, I wanted to drop to my knees and cry. I was devastated. Nothing compares to the intense, miserable, gut wrenching pain of heartbreak. That moment, I felt as if someone had stabbed my heart with a knife and bludgeoned it with a sledgehammer.

As I'm ogling Natalie as she's walking away, Pastor Lee walks up behind me and rests his hand on my shoulder. "She's a work of art, isn't she? I see you two know each other."

"Yeah, she's cool. I told her about how great of a service y'all have here and that she should come."

"I appreciate that, Winston. As you know, I always have welcoming and open arms for anyone trying to join the congregation. A good shepherd can never have too many sheep."

"Amen."

Someone calls the Pastor's name. "I must go. Duty calls."

"I understand. It was good seeing you."

"Likewise son." I shake his hand and begin to walk away. "Hey Winston…"

I stop and turn around. "Yes sir?"

"A word from the wise. She's a keeper. From talking to her for that brief moment, I can tell she has a good head on her shoulders. If I was you, I'd make sure to keep her around for the long haul." They call his name again, this time louder. "Good seeing you. Be blessed Winston."

I sigh, "You too Pastor Lee."

I stand there for a few seconds as I process everything that just happened. When I come to, I go outside to my car and drive home.

My car is silent. I'm listening to nothing but my thoughts, all about Natalie. Our final moments together keep replaying over, and over, and over again in my mind. I get about halfway home before I just break down in tears. The fact that Natalie just walked out of my life had finally hit me. All of the emotions I felt, pain, anger, sadness, just spewed out of my body. As a man, especially a black man, you're taught to never show your emotions. To never have your heart on your sleeve. To be a brute, emotionless, masculine force that protects and provides for his family no matter what.

For the next couple of minutes, all that stuff went out of the window.

I had never felt for a woman the way I felt for Natalie. She was perfect in my eyes. The way she thought, acted, looked. She had no flaws from my perspective.

I just couldn't hold it in anymore. I could no longer continue to ignore what I was feeling. I lost her. All of the penned up emotions I had, I let go. Tears began to fill my eyes, taking my vision away and hindering my awareness. I went from driving a smooth 75 mph on the highway to a speedy 93 mph.

I'm about five minutes from my exit when a pickup truck erratically swerves over into my lane. My vision is blurry from crying, so I'm not able to see it or react in time to completely avoid the collision. I try to steer out of the way at the last second, but I'm too late. I graze the back of the truck and begin to spin off the road. I pass out as soon as the nose of my car viciously smashes into a tree, the only thing stopping my car from spinning into a ditch. I thought I was gone. I just knew my time on Earth had come to an end.

When I wake up, it's Sunday night. I'm laying in a hospital bed surrounded by my mother and aunt.

"Doctor, doctor! He's waking up!", my mother yells as she's standing over me. She then caresses my head and says, "You'll be okay, Winnie. We've been here the past couple of hours praying for you. God will never fail you."

My aunt stands up and taps my leg as the doctor walks in and examines me. "He'll be just fine. He has a minor concussion and a few bruises and scratches, but there's nothing serious. We'll run some more tests throughout the night, but he should be able to check out and return home in the morning.", the doctor says.

My mom grabs my aunt's hand, "It's a miracle! Thank you Jesus! Thank you Doc."

"No problem Ms. Williams. I'll let you all be. Just ring if you need anything."

"Yes sir, we will. Thank you.", my aunt says to the doctor as he walks away.

"I appreciate y'all driving down here, but I'll be fine."

"Boy hush, we rushed here as soon as we got the call from the hospital. I see we're still listed as your emergency contacts. But anyway, don't think cause we're here we just gon' wait on you hand and foot. As soon as you're back okay in your house, we're leaving. Me and ya momma have plans tomorrow night.", my aunt says.

"What y'all doing on a Monday?!", I question.

"When you're up in age like us, you have to get it when you can honey.", my aunt sassily says as me and my mom laugh.

"Betty, let's go drive around the city and let Winston get some rest."

"We can't just leave him by himself, Lo.", my mom exclaims .

"Girl, he'll be fine. He has nurses ready to tend to him hand and foot. I'm trying to find me one of these Ricoville sugar daddies and retire a few years early.", my aunt responds.

I grab my moms hand, "I'll be fine mom. Y'all go have some fun. There's plenty to do on a Sunday night. It's early, too."

My aunt grabs her purse, "You heard your son. Lets go."

"You'll be okay Winnie?"

"Yeah mom. Go have fun."

"You heard him. Let's take the night!"

My mom kisses me on the forehead, grabs her purse, then leaves out of the room. "We'll see you in the morning Winnie. Love you."

My aunt waves goodbye, "Love you."

"I love y'all, too.", I exclaim.

About twenty minutes after they leave, a nurse walks in to bring me my dinner. She's a beauty. She has dark melanin skin, an illuminated smile, and has a beautiful, short afro. The blue scrubs she's wearing don't look too bad on her either. If I wasn't still distraught over Natalie, I'd definitely talk to her. It was the perfect opportunity, but I had a terrible headache, and a heartache just as bad.

She knocks on the door, "Hey Mr. Williams, I'm nurse Bri and I'll be serving you your dinner."

"Hey Bri, what's on the menu?"

She smiles then says, "Here you go handsome. I hope you enjoy it. It's Salisbury steak, mashed potatoes, and green beans. Mmmm."

I smirk and ignore her compliment. I then sarcastically say, "Mmmm indeed."

"Trust me, it's not as bad as it looks."

"Eeeh, we'll see. I hope you don't let me down."

She stares at me for a while then says, "I won't. You'll enjoy it. Just let me know if you need anything."

"I got you, Bri. Thanks."

She smiles at me then walks out of the room. When she leaves, I just sit there and eat my food while I watch TV. I doze off a few minutes after I finish my, surprisingly good, hospital food.

Later that night, I hear footsteps in my room and begin to wake up. I assume it's my mom and aunt returning to check on me, but as I begin to open my eyes into the dark room, I notice it's not. It's MP.

LXIV

I SIT UP IN MY BED, STARTLED.

He moves closer, "Shh, shh. I come in peace. Relax Winston. An officer informed me of your accident, and I wanted to personally stop by and check on your well-being. Robert would have been here too, but he's handling some business for me." He smirks. "He also said that you haven't been answering his calls. He said he was calling and texting you all yesterday, but nothing."

"Tell Mr. Langston I'm sorry for that. I misplaced my phone. And I appreciate your concern, but I'm fine. You can be on your way."

"I'll be out of your hair soon. I see you're well taken care of. That pretty little nurse is outside ready to wait on you hand and foot." He pauses for a moment. He looks out of the window at Bri, then back at me. "I'm glad you're okay, Winston. If you're feeling better, please stop by my place Friday morning."

"I would, but I'm busy Friday. I have meetings to attend and work to do all day. Sorry."

He laughs, "I see that concussion made you forget that you don't have a job."

Sarcastically, "Oh yeah, that's right. YOU got me fired."

He rubs his chin as he starts to grin, "I simply offered you a promotion, but that's neither here nor there. That's the past. I want to make good. I've taken the liberty of blessing your accounts until you're back on your feet. Take all the time you need."

"I'm fine. I don't need your money. I have…"

"You HAD $790.43 in your account before I put $15,000 in there. After your rent, car note, and insurance alone, your account would likely be in the negatives. You'll be evicted and probably carless within the next month. And those *investments* you brag about? That measly $50 they all collectively accumulate won't help that much either. You may appear like you're big money, but we both know the truth. You work your ass off, but Mr. Jacobs continues to undercut you and take more than he should. And since you were terminated, all of your pending transactions have been terminated and handed over to Jacobs. Winston, you're better than that. But I must say, your humility and humbleness is what I admire about you most."

"What do you want from me?"

"Nothing at all. I'm sorry for everything before, I just want to make sure that you're good. I want us to have a fresh start. Please think about coming over Friday morning. You get your rest. Hopefully, I'll see you Friday at eleven." He taps my knee then walks out of my room.

As he leaves, nurse Bri walks in and stands by my bed. "You okay? Anything I can do for you?"

"I thought visiting hours were over?"

"I'm sorry, the mayor said he knew you and that he had to see you. When a man that powerful requests something, you do it."

"I guess."

"Anything I can do for you though, before I clock out?"

"I don't think so. I should be fine."

She rips out a piece of paper from her notepad. She writes her phone number on it then hands it to me. "If you ever change your mind, please don't hesitate to call, or text me." She then rubs her hand across my chest before she walks out.

There I was, I had a beautiful woman ready to eat out of the palm of my hand. Her burning desire for me penetrates through her dark brown eyes every time she looks at me. Bri had looks, smarts, and personality, but she didn't compare to Natalie. I don't think anyone ever will.

I spend the rest of the night reminiscing of my short lived time with Natalie before I drift away into slumber.

Softly, "Mr. Winston, wake up. It's time to go home. Winston, I'm here for you. Wake up, the car is outside waiting for you." I slowly open my eyes and see that the gentle sweet voice waking me up is Natalie. Seeing her here by my side in a white sundress brought a smile to my face. *My angel is here.*

"C'mon sleepy head, it's time to go home."

"I thought I'd never see you again, Natalie."

"I was upset then. Now, I see one mistake doesn't negate all of the love you have for me." She kisses me on my lips. "Let's go home babe. Grab my hand." I grab her hand as she helps me get out of bed. "Easy now Mr. Winston. Your body's probably so sore. I'll make sure to massage it when we get home." We smile at each other as she helps me get into a wheelchair that a nurse brought into my room.

"You're all set Mr. Williams. Y'all have a good day.", the nurse says as we exit the room.

We walk out of the hospital and into the bright sunny weather outside. The car is already in front waiting for us. As Natalie is about to help me into her car, I hear someone yell my name in the distance.

"Winston! Winston!", Natalie and I simultaneously turn to see who it is. "Winston! No, come with me!" It's Sharon dashing towards us out of the hospital with her black sundress blowing in the wind. "Winston! Stop, I'm here for you."

"This bitch.", Natalie murmurs. "Winston, please put your groupie in her place."

"Hoe please, you're the groupie." Sharon runs over to us and begins pulling on the wheelchair, trying to pry me away from Natalie. Natalie pulls back.

"He's coming with me!", Sharon yells.

"Hey, stop! My gown is blowing, y'all know I don't have any draws on. Chill, hey!", l try to stop them, but my efforts are futile.

They pull, and pull, and pull. Eventually, they both pull a little too hard and I flip out of the wheelchair. I bang my head on the pavement and black out.

"Winnie. Winnie, wake up." My mom says as she gently shakes my arm.

"Pour some water in his face, Betty. That'll wake him.", my aunt jokingly suggests.

"I will not." She continues to shake my arm. "Wake up. We have to go, Winnie." I begin to open my eyes and sit up in my bed. "Easy now, easy."

"Where's Natalie?! Where's Natalie?", I urgently ask.

"Boy, who's Natalie? Ain't nobody been up in here but us."

LXV

———

I SIGH AND HANG MY HEAD AS I COME TO THE realization that everything that I *thought* happened, was merely a dream. That moment made me accept it. Natalie was never coming back.

"Natalie must be the girl he had all them rose petals, balloons, and candles for Betty. Bet you had yourself a good ole Valentine's Day, huh?"

Confused, "Y'all was at my apartment?"

"I know you ain't expect us to spend no money at a hotel when you have space at your place. Is that a problem sir?"

"No mam, I was just asking. What happened to y'all sugar daddies?"

"Ask ya momma."

We both look at my mother as she blushes and looks away. "It was nothing."

"What happened ma?"

"Yeah, tell him what happened, Betty.", my aunt jokingly adds.

My mother clears her throat. "It was nothing. Anyway, who's this Natalie woman you were asking for Winnie?"

My mood instantly shifts from joyous and playful to gloomy and dismal. Just hearing someone say her name is too much for me right now.

"You okay Winnie? You look pale." My mother says as she puts the back of her hand against my forehead.

I snatch my head away then rudely say, "I'm fine, I'm fine. Am I good to go now? I'm ready to get home and lay in my bed."

My mother looks at me for a second, stunned, then walks out of the room to find a doctor.

"You better watch it boy. I know you ain't bump your head hard enough to make you forget you can't be talking to your momma like that.", my aunt sassily says.

Apologetically, "Yes mam, I'm sorry. I just have a lot to deal with right now. I lost my job, my car, AND my girl in less than a week."

She walks over and places her hand on my shoulder, "Don't stress yourself to death. It'll work out, honey. It always does. You're known for making something out of nothing and seeing the best in the worst. Been a little bundle of optimism since you were a baby. You know, your momma wasn't supposed to have you."

"I know, I know. I'm the little miracle baby that nobody expected to be born."

"Exactly, you've been overcoming obstacles even before you were born. What's a few more? And you know if you need anything, me and your momma are right here for you...Don't ever let anyone or anything take your joy, Winston."

"I hear you, but I'm lost, auntie Lo. Not so much about my job and car, those are easily replaceable. But that woman, that woman was everything to me. Natalie was perfect. I don't think I'll ever get over her honestly. I planned on..."

"Boy, if you don't go somewhere with that foolishness! You almost got slapped. I'll be damned if I just sit here and let my nephew sulk over a woman, especially one I ain't ever met. If she was the right one, we would've met her. If she can't survive a week or however long y'all was together, then she ain't the one, simple. And besides Jesus, a perfect man, woman, or relationship doesn't exist. Y'all kids nowadays are confused on what love or even a real relationship is. Y'all just wanna hump everything and have fun. Then as soon as the smallest bump in the road hits, y'all leave. Me and your uncle were married 35 years before he passed. Things weren't always great, but we had love, real love. I'm not gonna sit here and preach to you because you should know better. But, the moral of the story is that a good relationship is like a roller coaster. It's gonna be a lot of scary loops, drops, spins, and bumps, but there will also be a lot of smooth coasting and joy. A great roller coaster has the perfect balance. You understand me, Winston?"

"Yes mam, I got you."

"The right one will make herself known to you. You're a great man. Any woman would be blessed and lucky to have you."

We smile at each other. "Thank you, auntie Lo. I appreciate that."

"Hell, I helped raise you. I'd know." Me and my aunt laugh as we hug each other.

My mother walks in. "The doctor said you're clear to go, just don't do any strenuous physical activity for the next few days. Did I miss something?"

"Get in here ma. I owe you one." I exclaim with my arm out.

We all embrace each other for a moment then separate.

"I put your clothes on the table over there, Winnie. Go on and get dressed. We'll be outside in the front waiting for you. We're going to bring the car around. Don't take too long, I want to be on the road before it gets dark."

"Yes mam, I won't be long."

After I put on the sweat pants and t-shirt they brought me, I go meet them in front of the hospital. I get in the car and we drive to my apartment.

Minutes later we arrive. "You'll be okay, Winnie?"

"We still have a couple hours to burn if you need us.", my aunt adds.

I get out of the car. "I'll be fine. You two need to go get on the road, y'all have a big night ahead of y'all."

They laugh then get out of the car to exchange hugs. "I love you, Winnie. Take care of yourself."

"I love you, Winston, and remember what I said."

"I will. I love y'all too."

They get back in the car then wave goodbye as they drive away.

I walk up to my door and notice an envelope taped to it as I put my key in. It's labeled, *Dear Winston.*

LXVI

———

I TAKE THE NOTE DOWN FROM MY DOOR AND THROW it on my counter as I walk in.

To my surprise, my apartment is spotless. *Mom and aunt Lo must've been tipsy and bored when they came in last night. I see that led to them doing me the honors of cleaning my apartment.* All of the rose petals I had romantically scattered through the floor had been swept up and thrown in the trash, the dishes in the sink were washed, and the balloons were popped and thrown away as well.

I grab a bottle of water out of the fridge and sit down on the couch to watch TV. I had intentions of relaxing and celebrating being unharmed from my accident yesterday. To spend the rest of my day in peace and solidarity, but all of that quickly disappeared seconds after the thought of Natalie consumed my mind. I still smell her sweet vanilla scent on my couch. I see strands of her black, luscious, curly hair left behind from the moment we got passionate. I still even feel her presence.

I let out a long sigh as I submerge myself deep down into my couch. The pain, the anguish, the heartbreak I felt was unbearable.

It felt like my heart was being belligerently squeezed. The longer I sat there, the more aggressive the squeezing got. I get up and move to my room. I was expecting and hoping the pain would go away, but it got worse. Her smell is even stronger in my bed. She has hairs on my pillows, and there are memories of our sexcapde all through my sheets and bathroom.

After a bad break up, people will usually say there's plenty of fish in the sea. My question to that is, what if you just had the best and biggest catch escape your line? What happens then?

I walk into the bathroom to wash my face. I scrub and scrub, but I still feel the same.

"Get yourself together, Winston.", I say as I slap myself while I look in the mirror in disgust.

I then turn my shower on and begin to undress. I throw my clothes in a corner in my room, then step into the hot, steaming, running water.

The shower is my sanctuary. The place that comforts me the most. A place where I can think calmly and quietly. I expected that getting in the shower would destress me and help me relax. With that being said, the exact opposite happened. I tried to ignore and forget the events that took place a couple of days ago in the shower, but I couldn't. I quickly hopped out and stood in front of the mirror as I stared at myself.

I realized what I had to do. First, I dried off and threw on a pair of gym shorts. Next, I started de-Natalitizing my apartment. I go on a cleaning spree. My mom and aunt tidied up, but my apartment needed a full out detox. I stripped my sheets and put them in the washer. I sprayed my couch with disinfectants and air fresheners, scrubbed my bathroom, and picked up and threw away anything and everything that makes me think of her. Her toothbrush, chocolate she forgot to take, and the hair and makeup products she left all went in the trash. That note she left on my door got thrown away as well. I didn't even bother opening it.

Upon cleaning, I found my phone, dead, in the sheets of my bed. I grab it and sit it next to me as I sit on the couch. Normally, I'd charge it, but the way I'm feeling, I just leave it next to me and let it be.

Even though I thoroughly sprayed and cleaned the couch, flipped the seats and everything, I still smelled her scent. Her heavenly vanilla fragrance. I tried to get up, but I couldn't move. I just sat there and suffered. Once again, I was troubled by the pain that every man hates to endure, the pain of losing a good woman. Knowing I had everything I wanted, everything I needed, right in the grasp of my hands, and lost it because I was an ignorant ass was intolerable. Replaying the situation over and over again in my head made me numb.

Eventually, I got up from my couch, but it was only to get the food that was being delivered to my door. The only use of my cell phone for the next couple of days was to order food. I was ignoring all calls, texts, everything. Sharon tried, my mom and aunt tried, Mr. Langston tried, hell, some of my clients tried, and even Chino tried to get a hold of me. Monday, Tuesday, and Wednesday, I didn't talk to anyone or leave my apartment. All I did was eat the pizza and Chinese food I got delivered, and melancholically sit on my couch binge watching reruns of my favorite shows. Thursday, I planned on doing the same thing. That is, until I got a knock on the door.

KNOCK, KNOCK, KNOCK.

LXVII

———

I IGNORE IT AND JUST HOPE WHOEVER IT IS GOES AWAY. KNOCK, KNOCK, KNOCK.

"I know you're in there Winston, open up!", says a muffled voice through the door.

"Go away!", I yell as I lay on my couch.

KNOCK, KNOCK.

"You can't hide in there forever!"

I laugh. *Watch me.*

They knock one more time, KNOCK, KNOCK, KNOCK, then there's about a ten second pause. I assume they gave up and left, but my doorknob starts to rattle. It jiggles a bit and the unknown knocker begins to enter my apartment. It's Mr. Langston, entering the room wearing a grey suit, white shirt, and a black tie.

"You must've forgotten who cosigned on this nice place of yours.", he says as he walks into my dim and gloomy apartment. "I know you didn't think you were just going to keep ignoring me forever. I heard about your accident. Thank God it was nothing serious, you look great. Well, going based on the condition of your car you do. But as far as everything else goes, you look a mess. Keisha told me what happened. You alright?" He flips a light switch.

Snappy, "Don't I look alright?! And turn that off."

"You look how it smells in here, terrible. Get up man. We have plans tonight."

"I'm actually booked solid for the next few weeks, Mr. Langston, I'm sorry. Me and my couch have breakfast, lunch, and dinner reservations. It'd be rude of me to cancel with so late of a notice."

He walks over to my couch, "Come on, Winston. There's a big game tonight and I want you to come check out my new suite. You need to get out of the house and get some fresh air. I'm worried about you, son."

"I'm fine, I promise you. I'm just taking some ME time to get my mind together. That's all. I'm okay, really."

"Winston, it smells like a dumpster in here. You have a pile of food containers and pizza boxes surrounding your couch, it was just pitch dark in here before I hit the lights, and you have at least seven different stains on your shirt that I can see." He scooches me over and sits next to me on the couch. "Look, I know breakups are rough, but they're not the end of the world. They usually end up being the beginning of something new, something better. You just have to have faith. I know you've heard the saying, 'When one door closes, another one opens.' Well, that's a fact. Just trust it, and trust me. From experience."

"I loved, no, I love her though. Natalie is the perfect woman, Mr. Langston. She's gorgeous, smart, and fun to be around. Her eyes, lips, and her smile is just perfect. And the sex! It was…"

"Winston, listen to yourself! You sound like a horny high school kid. Natalie is a very attractive woman, I understand that, but how many times was she concerned about your well-being, or y'all had a serious conversation about life? Honestly, what do you know about her besides the fact that she's a beautiful young woman?"

I pause for a second, "We talked about how her father quit being a professional basketball player to help raise her and her siblings. I know where she's from, what sport she played, her favorite colors, candies, animals..."

He laughs, "Winston, Winston. What makes her happy? What makes her sad? What are her long term goals? Where does she see herself in five years? How many kids does she want? Does she even want kids, Winston? What about marriage?"

"I made her happy and she made me happy. All that other stuff, we would've discovered eventually."

"Winston, I love you like a son. If you truly made her happy and fulfilled her spirit the way she does yours, she wouldn't have left so easily. She'd be over here trying to work it out instead of me being here trying to..."

I wasn't trying to hear anything he was saying. Even though he was right, it wasn't what I wanted to hear. "You don't understand! We're in love. She'll be back."

He puts his arm on my shoulder and pats me on the back. "No, Winston, you were in lust. There's a difference." He pauses, then says, "And I admire your optimism, but she's not coming back." He removes his hand and then rubs his knees nervously, as if he was hiding something.

I sit up and become more engaged in the conversation. "Mr. Langston, why isn't she coming back?"

He sighs then says, "Look, Winston, I'm only telling you this because I love you."

I take a gulp and brace myself for what he was about to say. Any time someone says, "I'm only telling you this because I love you", the news is never good.

"Keisha told me not to say anything, but I feel like you must know. Tuesday, she got back together with her ex." My heart drops into my stomach and I put my hands over my face. Mr. Langston pats me on the back. "Being in love means working out your issues with one another, no matter how big or small they may be. Being in lust is simply moving on to another individual during the slightest trials and tribulations. Like I said Winston, when one door closes, another one opens. You made a mistake and invited a female friend over while Natalie was still here. It's not like she was your sidepiece or anything. She was a friend. If she left you for something as minor as that, she's just too blind to see how great of a man you are. Now, forget about Natalie! You're about to get ready and have the night of your life."

"I appreciate it, Mr. Langston, but I'm good, honestly. And even if I did want to go, I don't even have a car, remember?"

"Oh yes, about that. I'll have a rental dropped off for you tomorrow morning. You should like it, BUT, that's only if you come. And as for your transportation for tonight, I'll have a car pick you up at six. That gives you about two hours to get yourself together. I'll tell him to knock on your door when he's here, and to bust it down and grab you if you don't answer."

I don't want to go, but maybe it's what I need. A night full of excitement to take my mind off of Natalie. And hearing Mr. Langston say he'll fix my car situation doesn't leave me with much of a choice either. I have to go now. I release a long sigh then say, "I'll be ready."

Mr. Langston smiles, taps me on my knee, and stands up. "Splendid! I have to be there early so I must get going. Remember, Carlos will be here at six to pick you up." I walk him to the door and shake his hand as he leaves. He looks me in my eyes and says, "I love you, Winston. You'll be okay. Trust me."

I nod my head. "Love you too, Mr. Langston, and thanks."

I close the door and he walks away. When I turn around, I look at the terrible mess I've made over the past couple of days.

Winston, you're better than this. She's not worth all this pain, trouble, and disarray. She basically left you to be with her ex. Forget that woman!

At that moment, I realized it was indeed lust, and not love. Everything Mr. Langston and my aunt told me finally started to sink in. I felt as if new life had been breathed into me.

I then begin to clean up and get ready for the great night that was ahead of me.

Now, it's about five forty-five and I'm almost ready. As I'm finishing buttoning up my purple shirt, I get a knock on my door.

KNOCK, KNOCK.

Carlos is early.

They knock again. "I'm coming bro. One second!"

I finish buttoning my shirt and open the door.

To my surprise, it's Sharon. She's standing at my door wearing her usual work fit, a pink sweater and black skirt.

With a surprised voice, "Sharon, what's up? What brings you here?"

She springs on me and gives me a hug. "I thought something bad had happened to you. I had came by and left a note on your door Monday morning, and you never got back to me about it. I waited and waited to hear from you, but you never returned any of my calls or texts. I came by yesterday, too. I didn't see your car, so I just turned around and went home. You were on my mind all day at work today, so I had no choice but to stop by when I got off. I didn't see your car, but I noticed the trash outside of your door. I figured somebody had to be home. So, yeah. Here I am. I'm glad to see you're alive and okay." She peeks inside "I'm not interrupting anything am I? I don't want a replay of last time."

We laugh then I say, "Nah, you're good. Come in." She walks in and I close the door behind her. "I appreciate you coming, really. And I'm sorry I ain't get back to you. I just haven't been in a talking or social mood the past couple of days. Life's been crazy."

With a gentle voice, "It's okay. I completely understand." She puts her head down and starts rubbing her arm as a depressed expression consumes her face.

"You okay, Sharon? Why you looking like that?"

"I see you weren't in the reading state either."

"What you mean?"

"I take it you didn't read the note I left you."

"I'm sorry, Sharon. To be honest, I thought it was from Natalie and threw it away. What did it say?"

She takes a deep breath, "It's fine, no biggie." She starts biting her lip, fidgeting with her hand, and looking away from me.

I grab her hand, "Sharon, what's up with you? Why you acting funny? Are you okay?"

She looks up at me. Then with so much emotion, passion, and intensity, she says, "I love you, Winston!" I stand there breathless and stunned. I had nothing to say. "I. Love. You. As a matter of fact, Winston, I'm in love with you, and I have been for a while now."

"Sharon, what are..."

"Listen, Winston, we broke up because we both didn't know exactly what we wanted. With the time I've spent thinking and discovering myself lately, I've come to the conclusion that I want you, Winston. I need you in my life. I'm done trying to hide my feelings for you. You're the one for me and I'm the one for you."

I look into her dark brown eyes and say the first thing that comes to mind, "What about James? Are y'all not together anymore?"

"We broke up Saturday. That's what he wanted to talk about at lunch. At least he had the decency to do it in person. I respect that. And to be honest, he's a great guy, but he's not you. The money and lifestyle that came with it was nice, but we never had the type of connection that me and you had. That we have. When he broke up with me, I was sad at first, but the first thing, first person that came to my mind was you. Was us. Whether your girl was here or not, I just had to let you know how I felt. That's what was in the note."

I grab her hand and we walk over to the couch and sit down. "Look Sharon..."

"Wait Winston, before you express how you feel, I want you to know that I understand if you're still hurting and need time to heal. We both have fresh wounds, and I don't want you to rush into saying anything that you don't mean because you're caught in the moment. We've been friends for a while now, and I completely understand if you want to remain that way. I'll wait for you, I promise."

A hundred different thoughts are racing through my mind. *Should I say this, or should I say that? She's staring at you, Winston. She's anticipating that you say something. You just can't sit here in silence forever. Say something!*

I lick my lips and decide to just speak from the heart, "Sharon, I..."

KNOCK, KNOCK.

"Mr. Williams, it's Carlos! I'm sorry I'm a couple minutes late. Traffic is crazy. We gotta go.", Carlos yells through the door.

KNOCK, KNOCK, KNOCK, KNOCK.

"Yooooo Mr. Williams, you there?!"

"One second, Sharon." I get up and go open the door. Carlos is a short and chubby fellow that, to his credit, doesn't look too bad in the black suit he's wearing. "I'm coming, Carlos. I'll be down in a minute.", I tell him.

He peeks inside and notices Sharon sitting on the couch, "Ooohhh, my bad playa. Do ya thang big dog, do ya thang. I ain't mean to interrupt you. Just know traffic is terrible right now and they're expecting you at seven thirty."

"I'll be down in a second Carlos, I got you."

He nudges my arm then whispers, "You need some rubbers man? Safe sex is the best sex, my brotha."

"I appreciate you Carlos, but it's not that type of party."

"Oh, you need that blue pill? I got those too pimp."

"I'll be out in five man.", I say as I close the door. I let out a deep breath and redirect my attention to Sharon.

"You gotta go?", she sadly says.

"Yeah, Mr. Langston's invited me to the game tonight. You want to be my plus one?"

"Ummmm, I really don't want to see him. I know you understand."

"Oooh right. I'm sorry. I totally forgot."

"Yeah, I'll just go and we can continue tomorrow." She gets up and walks towards the door. I stop her as she tries to open it.

"How about you just make yourself comfortable here and we can just continue when I get back. I'm only going because Mr. Langston came by earlier and demanded I finally get out of the house. I shouldn't be out no longer than eleven."

"Yeah, okay. Just remember some people actually have work in the morning.", she jokingly says.

I grab her head and kiss her forehead, "I'll be back." She smiles, then gives me a hug before I walk out the door.

I scurry down the steps and make my way to the black SUV Carlos has parked in front.

"You a quick pumper, huh?" He says as I get in. "I had pills for that too."

LXVIII

―――

I LAUGH AND LOOK OUT THE WINDOW.
    We drive smoothly for about forty minutes before traffic brings us to a halt. We stand still for about thirty seconds before Carlos says, "Hey, Mr. Winston!"

"What's up, Carlos?", I dreadfully ask.

"You wanna hear a joke?"

I sigh, "Sure, what you got?"

Carlos starts grinning, "Okay, so there's this woman right. A guy pays $5 to have sex with her..."

"Woah, woah, woah. I don't know what Mr. Langston told you, but I don't get down like that Carlos."

"Relax Mr. Winston, it's just a joke. A funny one."

"Go ahead man."

He clears his throat, "As I was saying, a guy pays $5 for a night with a lady. They do their thing and go their separate ways. When my guy wakes up in the morning, he has crabs. You know, that itchy itch scratch scratch. Well anyway, he's mad as hell. He goes to find the lady and confronts her. He finds her and he's all like,

'What the hell shawty?! You gave me crabs!' When the dude gets done talking, the lady looks at him and says, 'For five dollars what did you expect? Lobster?"

I couldn't help but laugh at the foolishness he just said. "That was funny bro, I gotta give you your credit. I hope that wasn't based on an actual experience of yours."

He pauses for a second, then says, "Nah man, a TV show I watch said it on there."

"Mhhmm, okay. Whatever you say. Just make sure you're taking your own advice with your condoms."

"Yeah, I learned my lesson", he says under his breath.

"What was that?"

"Uh, I said we should be there in about an hour. Hold tight."

He turns up the music and starts to speed through traffic.

An hour and forty-five minutes and a speeding ticket later, we finally arrive at the arena.

I open my door. "Appreciate the ride Carlos, and sorry about that ticket."

"It's all good. They always go away. Uncle Robbie usually handles these things. But anyway, you enjoy your night, Mr. Winston."

"You too. Be safe.", I get out of the car and begin my search for Mr. Langston's suite.

After twenty minutes of asking about ten people for directions, I find it.

"You're a little late Winston, it's almost halftime.", Mr. Langston says as he walks up to me as I enter the room.

"Man, blame Carlos. He got us pulled over and got a ticket."

He sighs, "If he wasn't my sister's son, I would've been fired him. That kid is quite the character. Why didn't you call?"

"He's definitely that. And because I left it at home. By the time I realized it, we were already forty minutes away stuck in traffic."

I begin to look around the packed room. A chill runs through my veins when I see her. In a dark brown chocolate dress and tan heels, Natalie was sitting at a corner table with Keisha and Celeste. "W-what are they doing here, Mr. Langston?"

He puts his arm around my shoulders and turns me away. "I'm

so sorry about that, Winston. I invited Keisha up here, and they popped up midway through the first quarter. It was too late to do anything about it."

I had been betrayed by the very person that invited me here. The sole purpose of me coming was to get my mind off of Natalie. Ironic, isn't it? Even though Sharon's heartfelt rant got me thinking, Natalie was still very fresh on my mind, and my heart.

"Mr. Langston, come on man. I thought this was supposed to be a boys night out? How you gonna turn it into a date night?" I shake my head then begin to walk out of the suite. "Call Carlos so I can go back home."

Mr. Langston follows me out and stops me, "Winston, you can't run from that woman forever. Seeing her is going to be inevitable. Keisha's not going anywhere anytime soon, and that means Natalie's not either." He laughs then says, "You were right. Keisha definitely isn't like other women I've been with."

We both chuckle, "I told you so."

"Now Winston, let me make up for the mixup. Don't leave, stay. I promise you'll have the time of your life, trust me. Now there's plenty of people here. You'll barely notice the name that shall not be said."

I smile then turn around. We re-enter the suite.

Keisha rushes over, wearing a black dress and heels, and hugs Mr. Langston, "Is everything okay baby?"

"Yeah, just had to talk to Winston about a couple of things. That's all."

"Hey Keisha.", I say with a slight wave.

Keisha looks at me. "Hmph! Okay baby, long as you good.", she kisses Mr. Langston on the cheek and walks back to their table.

He looks at me and I just shake my head.

We walk over to a table full of drinks that's in front of us. Mr. Langston hands me a glass of wine. "You need it.", he says. "It'll help you relax a little."

I take it then we sit down and watch the end of the first half. We're at a corner table on the opposite side of the one room that Natalie's sitting at. Halftime comes. I try my hardest to resist, but it's killing me not to look. Mr. Langston is busy on his phone, and I can't help but to stare at Natalie and think of a million what if situations. There's about a hundred people in this room, but I only see her.

She catches me staring and just blushes.

As soon as I get the courage to get up and go talk to her, Mr. Langston says, "Now, your night will officially begin. It's time."

"What do you mean?"

"I've invited a few of our dancers and cheerleaders to come party with us, well with you." I make a whipping sound. "Make all the jokes you want, but I'm making a business decision. If I even look at one of those girls too long, Keisha will turn this whole place upside down and get us all kicked out and banned for life. And besides, this night is for YOU. Let Natalie see what she's missing out on."

A few moments later, the girls come up and the suite turns into a huge party.

"You enjoy yourself, Winston. I'll be over there with the girls.", Mr. Langston taps me on the back and walks away.

From that moment on, I paid zero attention to the game or anything relating to it. I was dedicated to having a great time while Natalie watched. A revenge party you could call it. Full of dancing, drinking, and fun. With this being a big game, possibly the biggest of the season, there was no open space for Natalie to go.

I wonder what her ex is doing now? I know she's probably over there wishing she didn't end things with us. She has to be miserable pretending to watch the game, trying to avoid seeing me have the time of my life.

The girls tried to join in on the party, but I could tell it wasn't the same experience for her.

I'd frequently give a glance her way and notice her staring at me. She'd look away as soon as I turned my head in her direction. It was as if we were petty high schoolers playing a game of eye tag.

Eventually, the game ended, but the party didn't stop until about an hour later.

The music stops playing and everyone groans.

"Thanks again for coming ladies and gents, but it's time to go. It's past my bedtime.", Mr. Langston announces.

"Yeah, it's time to go!", Keisha loudly adds.

I try to get a few numbers as the suite clears out, but I strike out with every woman I talk to. I wasn't drunk, but I was buzzed enough to slur my words and act like an ass. Every time I get rejected, I see Natalie giggle out the side of my eye. I was so embarrassed.

When the suite is finally empty, we circle up outside of its entrance. "Let's go Winston. I'll drive you home and they'll ride with one another."

"That's cool with me." I say with a big smile. "And you ladies look absolutely dazzling tonight. Especially you, Natalie." I wink at her and she rolls her eyes.

Mr. Langston laughs, "But first we must congratulate Mr. Love on a historic night. He broke the franchise's scoring record with seventy-three points. Definitely worthy of a face to face congratulations."

In amazement, "Most definitely. That's craaaaazy."

"Winston, are you okay?" Celeste asks, wearing a red dress and black heels. "It looks like you had a little too much to drink."

"Look who's talking...", I say with a slurred voice.

Mr. Langston grabs me. "You ladies go ahead, we'll catch up."

"Yeah, control him. Don't get ya mans messed up.", Keisha sassily mumbles at Mr. Langston as she walks by.

"Winston, relax. I think you had a little too much. Are you going to be able to control yourself for a few more minutes?"

I smile then say, "Yeshh."

He then takes me back into the suite and makes me eat pretzels, wings, and mini sandwiches to sober up. He hands me a bottle of water and a sports drink, then we leave to catch up to the girls.

About ten minutes later, we meet them in the players area.

No longer than two seconds passes before I see James Love walk out of a sea of reporters and get attacked with a hug from Natalie. "Great game babe!"

LXIX

———

T HEY KISS THEN BEGIN TO POSE FOR THE PAPARAZZI.
If the food I just ate didn't sober me up, that sure did. Keisha
and Celeste follow after Natalie and shower James with
congratulations and praise. They smirk and look at me out of the
corner of their eyes to see my reaction to all of this. I smirk.

Mr. Langston walks closer to me, "I'm sorry, Winston. I
honestly had no clue."

Sarcastically I say, "You're on a roll today Mr. Langston. You
need to go play the lotto before this hot streak you're on wears off."

"If you need to go I understand, Winston."

"Honey, come here! It wouldn't be right if the new owner
didn't join in for a picture." Keisha yells. "Winston, you can come
too. Aren't you like a huge fan?"

"You don't have to, Winston. I know how hard it must be for
you. I can give you the keys and you can wait in the car. I'll tell
them you aren't feeling well." All of the pain, agony, heartache,
torment, and anguish one would assume I was experiencing at
that moment, seeing James and Natalie together, weirdly didn't

exist. Seeing her snuggled up with James Love and trading kisses with him only made me realize that what we had wasn't real. I realized I was just a rebound, not even a rebound, but a hurdle in THEIR relationship. I was simply an entanglement in their brief separation. As was Sharon, we were both just carnal pawns in their game of life. I was more disgusted and angry than anything. Our emotions and feelings meant nothing to them. That helped me realize the difference between lust and love.

"Winston, you coming? I'm trying to get this over with.", Mr. Langston asks.

I clear my throat. "Yeah, let's take these pics."

"Can we get a pic with just the fellas please?", one photographer asks.

We walk over and partake in their mini photoshoot. "Congrats man, great game! You were en fuego. And it's good seeing you again." I say as I shake his hand.

"Yes, you played a hell of a game, son. You keep playing like that and we'll get that championship sooner than later. What got into you tonight?", Mr. Langston adds as we huddle up to take a few pictures. James in the middle, me and Mr. Langston on his sides.

"Thanks, I appreciate the both of you. And to answer your question Mr. L, I had my good luck charm tonight. I always play good when she's in the stands.", James says as he looks at Natalie.

She smiles back at him then blows him a kiss. As much as I wanted to ask him where Sharon was to make Natalie feel bad, I knew it would only backfire and make Sharon look like another one of James's groupies, a disposable and replaceable female when she's far from that.

After a while, I had enough of watching Natalie and James exchange googly eyes and smiles. I ask Mr. Langston, "Can I get the keys? I'll go start the car up. This modeling thing isn't me."

"C'mon, just a few more, Winston. Enjoy the moment.", James pleads.

"Let's take some couples pics now! Me and my honey and then Natalie and James. Such a beautiful couple.", Keisha exclaims.

"Mr. Langston, keys?", I murmur.

"A34", Mr. Langston says as he hands me his keys. "I won't be long."

I shake James's hand, "Good game again bro, congrats. I'll see you around."

"Thanks fam. Be safe. It's some real ruthless people out here."

"Tell me about it.", I sarcastically say as I begin to walk away. I then look towards Keisha, Natalie, and Celeste. "Y'all lovely ladies have a good night, too!"

I get to the car and immediately pass out.

"Winston, wake up. Winston, Winston you're home. Wake up.", Mr. Langston says as he shakes me.

I groan. "Five more minutes."

Mr. Langston shakes me harder, "Your unemployed ass can sleep all you want when you get in your apartment." I don't move. "You really trying to have Keisha on my case, huh?" He pours a water bottle he had laying around in his car on me. I wake up gasping for air. "Wake up son, you're home."

"We're here already?"

"Winston I love ya, but you gotta go. It's already one thirty."

I rub my eyes. "Sharon! Thanks, Mr. Langston. I'll call you tomorrow." I get out of the car and rush upstairs.

"Sharon! Sharon!", I yell as I open the door. I look around the apartment, but she's not here. I look to my right and notice a note on my kitchen counter.

It reads:

> *I see you left your phone so I figured a note was the next best thing. Hopefully you read this one. Anyway, I tried waiting for you, but I got sleepy around one and headed home. Maybe tonight was just a sign we should remain friends. There are no hard feelings, Winston. You'll always have a place in my heart. I'll see you around.*
>
> *With love,*
> *Sharon.*
> *PS: I hope you enjoyed your night out.*

I grab the note and take it with me as I walk over to the couch.

PS, I hope you enjoyed your night out? What the hell does she mean by that? She's probably just mad I didn't come back at eleven. I'll just talk to her tomorrow.

I put the note down and pick up my phone off of the table.

I'm flabbergasted to see I have a text from Natalie.

"It was good seeing you tonight."

LXX

———

W*ELL, I GUESS THAT EXPLAINS THE PS. SHE PROBABLY thinks I lied and left her to go see Natalie.* I suck my teeth. *I can't believe she even had the audacity to send that. To text me at all really. She's a mess.*

My phone dings. It's another text from Natalie, "I hope you made it home safe. Also, I think I left some hair stuff at your apartment. Can I swing by and get them tomorrow when I get off of work?"

Even though I was annoyed with her, I couldn't help but to crack a smile. My plan had worked. Seeing how happy I was without her must've driven her crazy. I had her eating out of the palm of my hand again. The ball was back in my court. I became ecstatic. I put my phone down and look up at my ceiling as I enjoy the moment.

As I reach for the remote to turn the TV on, I notice Sharon's note.

Sharon! I couldn't do that to her. I can't run back to the woman that's probably the reason her relationship abruptly ended. The woman who was probably still talking to James even though she told me she wasn't...The woman that was the love of my life. Well, the woman I thought was the love of my life. Natalie or Sharon? Both were sublime beings of admiration. Both were very intelligent women, and both of them were pounding on the door of my heart. I had an immense amount of love for the both of them. It's hard to choose just one...but then again, why choose at all? I'm young, handsome, and I'm about to enter the prime of my life. Maaaan, I'm a free spirit. I tried the settling down thing, and it hasn't worked out yet.

My mind knew what I wanted, but my heart knew what I needed. My decision had been made. I wasn't listening to either of them. I decided to tell both Natalie and Sharon that it's best that we just be friends.

As I'm about to text them, my phone dies.

Ugh, I'll just do it in the morning. I'm tired.

I go to my room, shower, change into some gym shorts, plug my phone up, then go to sleep.

I wake up from the weirdest dream around eight. It was a play by play of the first time I saw her. It was as vivid as it could be. It left me yearning for her. It was like God had made my decision for me. She was literally the woman of my dreams. After I woke up, there was nothing I could do to stop that moment, that memory from replaying over and over again in my head. It was as if I had fallen for her all over again. I had came to the realization that she was the one for me, and there was no denying that.

I wipe my eyes then begin to get ready for my day. I take a shower, brush my teeth, then pace around my closet as I try to decide what shirt to wear with my black jeans.

I'll wear this one. Her favorite color.

I put on a purple button up and a black bomber jacket. I then head to The Spot in the blue convertible Mr. Langston dropped off for me.

It's around eight forty when I get there. *I hope I'm not too late.*

I walk in and see Natalie sitting at a booth by herself. The sunlight from the window was reflecting off of her orange blouse, giving her a delightful, angelic glow. Her hair was slicked back, allowing everyone to see her gorgeous face. I momentarily get side tracked as I stare and admire her for a couple seconds. I snap back to reality and realize I haven't heard any wisecracking from Chino. I look around for him, but he's nowhere to be found. I ask one of his employees where he's at, and she says he called in sick. *It's unlike Chino to ever call in, let alone be sick.*

"Mr. Winston! Did you get my messages? I was worried about you."

I sigh and smile. I walk over to her and say, "What's up Natalie? Good morning to you too."

She smirks, "Good morning. Are you mad at me, Winston? I was truly concerned for your well-being last night. You got a little tipsy on us. And I meant it when I said it was good seeing you."

"I got home just fine. Why aren't you out having breakfast with James? I'm sure you can afford to be somewhere better than this."

"You're not where he is, Winston. And he's busy with his trainer and what not anyway."

I get testy, "Look Natalie, I'm not about to play with you."

"What do you mean Wi…"

"Just answer this, was any of it real? Did you really have feelings for me, or was I just a convenient confidence booster for you when y'all broke up? Did y'all really even break up in the first place?" I wait for her to respond, but she just looks down at her plate. "I'm waiting. I'm kind of on a tight schedule right now, so if you could hurry up, that'd be nice."

"It wasn't supposed to happen like this, Winston, honestly. The morning you first saw me here, we had just finished an intense belligerent argument. A few days later, we decided to take a break. We planned on spending some time apart, then having a heart to heart conversation after that. Saturday when we met, he told me how he'd changed and all of this stuff. I missed him, so I fell for it. He was my first real love, so I couldn't help it. And after that stuff with Sharon happened at your place, I was hurt and even more vulnerable…"

"So instead of talking it out, you ran straight to him. You've said more than enough Natalie…"

"Wait. Winston, just hear me out. I really like you Winston. I…"

"I'll see you around. I have to get going." I look into her depressed eyes on her dejected face. "No hard feelings, right?"

I walk out of The Spot and make my way to my next destination.

LXXI

———

I PULL INTO THE PARKING GARAGE AROUND NINE thirty. I park my car and begin to make a phone call.

The phone rings about three times before there's an answer, "Good morning! This is Sharon with Jacobs and Co Consulting. How may I help you?" I don't say anything at first. I just sit there and smile at the sound of her voice. "Hello, is anyone there?"

I chuckle, "I'm sorry. It's just funny being on the other end hearing that."

"Winston?! What you want? I have to keep this line free for our clients."

"Come outside."

"I'm working, and I'm sure Natalie's somewhere waiting for you. Bye Winston."

"Wait!" She hangs up the phone. I immediately call back and she instantly hangs up. I call again.

Aggressively, "Winston, stop calling before I have to block you. You're about to make me act an ass in here."

"I love you too, Sharon!"

Stunned, "W-what did you say?"

"You heard me. Now say you left something in your car and bring your ass down here." She doesn't say anything. "Sharon?"

"I'm coming. I'll be down in about five minutes."

"Okay." She hangs up the phone and I sit in my car waiting for her.

Ten minutes later, she's walking out. *Pink sweater, black skirt, and black heels, she makes the basic look extraordinary.*

"I'm sorry I took longer than expected. I had to do a couple things first. Now, what was that you were saying, Winston?"

"It's fine. I'm just happy you came." I reach out and grab her hand.

"Winston, what are you…"

"Sharon, just listen. The first time I saw you was in this parking lot, right over there. It was my first day here. You caught my eye when I drove in, and I just knew I had to have you. I remember it like it was yesterday. It was a cold, brisk, yet sunny morning. You were just standing there. Your beautiful, chocolate, melanin skin glowing from the rays of the sun, your hair blowing in the wind, your black skirt showing off your glazed enticing legs. I parked next to you after I saw you get back in your car to do your makeup. I was so nervous to talk to you. My hands started sweating at the thought of approaching you. I tried to wait it out, but I folded. I choked and decided just to go to work. But as soon as I got out of my car, you got out of yours. I took it as a sign. I looked your way and saw you were having trouble zipping up your sweater. I think you had just bought the pink one that you're wearing now the night before. You struggled and struggled. After watching you for a couple seconds, I just went for it. I had mustered up enough courage to ask you, 'You need help with that?' Of course, the oh so stubborn and independent Sharon declined. You said you got it and that I should probably get going. I was going to walk away, but I looked into your eyes. I could tell that your words were saying one thing, but deep inside, you really wanted the other to happen. I walked over and introduced myself. I told you my name, and I told you how blown away I was from your beauty. You started to smile and blush. You told me your name was Sharon because your mom is a big Sharon Serengeti fan. You thought it was lame, but I thought it was unique and cute. We smiled at each other, then you let me help you with your sweater. After I zipped it up, our hands touched. I got anxious and walked away. I told you I was running late for work and had to go. Moments later, we end up stepping into the same elevator, getting off on the same floor, and working in the same office. You've been a big part of my life ever since. Besides my mom and aunt, no woman has ever looked out for me or cared for me the way you have."

"You took us down memory lane to say what? To give yourself props for fixing a sweater? Because you'd remembered how corny you were? Or is this all just a really terrible apology?"

"I said all of that because THAT, that was the moment I fell in love with you, Sharon. It was love at first sight. Fate brought us together. I'm sorry for being an insensitive jerk sometimes. I'm sorry for being a terrible friend. And most importantly, I'm sorry it took me so long to realize that you were the one for me. We didn't break up because we didn't know what we wanted, we broke up because I was scared to admit that you were the person I needed." She begins to tear up and my phone starts to ring. I just ignore it. "I love you Sharon Renae Jones. Be mine again, please? You really make me a better person, and a better man. I can't do this thing called life without you."

My phone rings again. She wipes her eyes. "You want to get that?"

"I'll worry about it later. This moment has been long overdue." I pull her into my chest, gaze into her eyes, and kiss her. She wraps her arms around my neck and we embrace in the kiss of a lifetime. It was as if it was a love scene in a movie. The wind starts to gently blow, leaves circle around us in a whirlwind, and Sharon lifts her right leg up. The passion and intensity that I felt was unlike anything I'd ever experienced before. It felt, right.

My phone rings again. Sharon pulls away. "Just answer the damn thing, Winston. It has to be important if they're blowing you up like this. It might even be a job", she jokes.

I sigh, "I'd much rather be kissing you though."

"Boy, just answer it." She then rubs her index finger seductively down my chest. "We'll have plenty of time to continue this whenever I get off." I grin and she gives me a quick peck on my lips. She then says, "But for now, I have to get going. You know how crazy Friday's are. They're so unpredictable and chaotic. I'll call you when I get off."

"Okay, enjoy your day."

"You too, and I'm glad you finally came to your senses." She smiles and walks away.

I finally answer my phone. "It's ten o'eight, Winston. I hope you're on the way over. I know you didn't forget about our meeting."

Hesitantly, "H-hey MP. I had to make a quick stop, but I'll be there soon."

"You know how I feel about waiting. I don't need to send someone for you, do I?"

"No sir. You're about forty-five minutes from my current location. Be there in a jiffy."

"I hope so. I'm a very busy man, Winston, and I promise it'll be worthwhile. I've been waiting for this moment for quite some time now."

"Mr. Langston knows about this?"

"Actually, Robert is the one that suggested the idea."

"You just can't tell me over the phone? I'm sure it'll save us both some time."

"No, no. It must be done in person. I'll be in my office waiting for you. I'll leave the front door open. I'll see you in an hour, Winston. Drive safe."

He hangs up the phone and I just stand there, confused.

What the hell does he want now?

Still off of the high I got from kissing Sharon, I just let it slide and head to MP's place.

Because of a traffic jam, I arrive at his house twenty minutes later than expected.

I hope he doesn't trip.

I park out front and get out.

KNOCK, KNOCK, KNOCK, KNOCK.

I stand at the door and wait there a minute or two before I remembered that he said it was open.

Winston, you're a goofy.

As I walk through the living room to go to his office, I notice that his back door is wide open. *I guess he's enjoying the fresh air from the beautiful day.*

I knock on his office door and open it. *Agh!* I nearly faint from the gruesome sight of what I see. MP had been shot. He's surrounded by blood and I can't tell if he's still alive or not. I grab my phone to call 911. As I'm about to dial, I see his hand move. I rush over and try to sit him up so he doesn't drown in his own blood. I prop him up and he's barely breathing.

I continue to call 911, "The mayor's been shot! The mayor's been shot! Send help to his house, please!" MP starts to cough. I drop my phone and use the other hand to help prop him up. "We'll have help coming for you soon, don't worry. You're going to be okay."

With the little strength he has, he takes his right hand and uses it to bring my ear close to his mouth. I became terrified and despondent when I realized that he was about to possibly say his last words. I've seen this situation millions of times in TV shows and movies, but nothing could've compared to or even prepared me for this.

I anxiously lean in to hear what he was about to say.

In a low, agonizing whisper, he says, "I'm your father, Winston."

Acknowledgements

FIRST AND FOREMOST, WITHOUT GOD, THIS WOULDN'T be possible. Secondly, I'd like to thank my support system for being there for me. Thank you for all of the encouragement and criticism. I wouldn't have gotten this far without it. My parents, friends, family, brothers, sisters, thank you. And to EVERYONE that played a role in this novel, thank you. From the edits, reading, and support, it's all greatly appreciated. Lastly, I'd like to take a moment to thank Elijah Floyd for the impact he had on my life. I wouldn't be the man I am without him. I know he's in heaven watching over me. I hope I'm making him proud. Rest easy.